GRAVE
SECRETS

GRAVE SECRETS

A NOVEL

MARLENE AUSTIN

Covenant Communications, Inc.

Cover images: © Jupiter Images, www.jupiterimages.com and © Getty Images, www.gettyimages.com.

Cover design copyrighted 2007 by Covenant Communications, Inc.

Published by Covenant Communications, Inc.
American Fork, Utah

Printed in Canada
First Printing: July 2007

14 13 12 11 10 09 08 07   10 9 8 7 6 5 4 3 2 1

ISBN 978-1-59811-234-4

DEDICATION

I will never forget the night I sat studying a book on local history. As I read the story of a woman who buried two husbands and raised twenty children, it slowly dawned on me that the author was talking about my own Susanna Shattuck—dear Susanna Shattuck Morse Fay Brigham, 1643–1716, who lived in Groton, Massachusetts, just over the hills from where I live in Westford. Few families of the Marlboro, Massachusetts, area were not affected by this courageous woman who bore nine children of her own and who was also mother to eleven others. I dedicate this book to her.

This book is also dedicated to the Beals, the Perrys and Freemans, Brewsters, Wilsons, Whittens, Cummins, and Morses. And it is dedicated to Susanna Follett Sibley, 1659–?, whose husband was impressed into the British navy after the Revolutionary War; to Elizabeth French Loker, 1578–1648, who raised her four children alone in a new land; to Tamesin Treloar Ayer, 1649–1700, mother of at least eleven, whose descendants during the following century were said to have made up over a third of the population of Haverhill, Massachusetts.

I cannot leave out Rebecca Maxom Coltrin, 1742–?, whose sons followed Joseph Smith and established a family strong in the gospel and in the restored priesthood with sealing powers that allow us all to be united eternally as a family.

I'd also like to dedicate this book to Caroline Hopkins Clark, whose diary of her family's trek from England to Upton, Utah, recounts a trail of five small graves across two continents. The testimony borne on every page of that book serves me well when I visit my own son's grave.

Most of all, I dedicate this book to all those who suffer hardship, loneliness, and fear, but who nevertheless exercise the courage necessary to survive.

ACKNOWLEDGEMENTS

I am grateful to the many, many people—especially Angela Eschler and the Covenant staff—who helped me move Bethany's story from a narrative into a book. They have had great patience with me.

I especially want to thank my daughters, Mary and Jen, for their patience during the fifteen years I spent on this book. They were forever waiting for me to get off the computer and to take them to music and gymnastics lessons, to take them shopping, to make meals. The phrase they must have heard most often during that time was, "Wait until I finish this sentence . . ."

Of course, I am most grateful to my dear husband Tony, who has put up with it all, never mentioning well-done food or frozen dinners on those days when I couldn't make myself leave the computer. He is the epitome of patience and never complains that I am forever writing or doing family history. He cheerfully ignores the "temporary" office I've established in the family room and only mentions laundry when he is out of clean socks. What more could I ask? Thank you.

PROLOGUE

November 3, 1640

She held the burning twig against the candlewood, impatiently waiting for it to flare before she brushed the chunks of bark from her long, russet skirt. She glanced at Thomas, then turned to the room feeling a deep satisfaction as the smoky flame spread a glow across the plank wall. The mixture of moss and mud Thomas had filled into the chinks had dried, and she had lined the wall with barrels of dried and pickled food. Finally they were living in a house, not a bark wigwam. They had a home.

The room was quiet except for an occasional cough from the baby and the sputtering samp that simmered over the hot coals. Her expression turned to a slight frown as she studied Thomas, then stirred the cornmeal porridge.

She normally felt peaceful in the evenings when Thomas, having finished his outdoor work, removed his knife from its leather casing and hung the holder near the door. He would sit on his stool by the Indian-fashioned, birchbark cradle Nasset had made for Samuel, swaying it gently with his knee while he whittled on a spoon or cup until supper was ready. The evening routine, the three together settled securely in their home, was the most contented time of the day for her, but tonight she felt an inexplicable uneasiness.

Perhaps it was Thomas's unusual behavior that was niggling at her. Thomas had lingered outside gazing into the forest before coming in for supper. He had not spoken to her, just quickly washed his hands then sat rigid on the stool, his knee tapping the cradle in determined pulses, which, rather than soothing the child, seemed to lull him into only a restless sleep. Thomas still had his knife case fastened around his waist while he gripped the weapon, obviously forgetting the rounded, partially hollowed cup in the other.

She carried a trencher of samp to the table and watched as he slipped his knife back in its case and moved silently to the table.

His worry was clearly evident. His tan forehead was wrinkled and damp; his eyes squinted in concentration. What was the matter?

Maybe he was thinking of the winter and the child. She, too, was concerned about Samuel, who was young and vulnerable to the winter air. Even with the chinks filled, the cold weather could bring back his choking cough and the feverish nights. Since Chief Shabanah and his people moved inland for the winter, the three of them were now isolated with no one to help them in a crisis. There was always the possibility of a devastating storm, an accident, or dwindling winter supplies. She took a deep breath, forcing herself to calm. Perhaps Thomas was merely troubled because he had lost another day of hunting before the storms set in.

She lifted the spoon but could force herself to do little more than nibble at the golden paste as she considered their visitors of the afternoon. Their arrival had been unexpected, and Thomas had wasted his afternoon—and a slab of venison—feeding them. Perhaps it had been their peculiar mannerisms that had made her uncomfortable. Their voices had been loud and boisterous, their gestures bold.

Suddenly her mind stilled and panic welled up in her throat. *That is why Thomas wants silence!* She drew in a quick breath of fear, feeling her own brow suddenly bead with moisture as she fought to swallow the thick samp. *He is listening for the Indians.*

Looking down at the trencher she closed her eyes in silent prayer.

The baby coughed. She jumped, her nerves set off by the sudden sound.

Thomas's reaction was even more intense. His eyes jerked open as he reached for the knife at his side. Realizing the noise had come from the baby, he took a deep breath before scooping his spoon next to hers in the trencher. She knew it was as impossible for him to swallow the food as it was for her, but it seemed important that they pretend. Their spoons touched as they lifted them, full of the thick mixture.

It was then that they heard the birdcall. Their spoons clattered to the table, and she felt the skin on her arms erupt into goose bumps and the hair on the back of her neck bristle.

Thomas's head rose, cocked like a trapped animal judging the nearness of his predator, as he heard an echoed response. His expression told her more than his brief explanation. "They are back, and it won't be for food this time. We've got to go. Now." She turned from the fireplace to catch up the baby in his blanket as Thomas stepped to the door. He simply said, "I'll draw their attention. You hide in the woods while they follow me."

She glanced at the musket leaning against the corner of the doorframe. The slight shake of his head confirmed the thought she was already considering. For him to load and carry the musket would only slow him down, enough so that he'd never be able to outrun the six Indians creeping about, ready to bawl out their war whoops.

Or even three Indians. Or less, if she could distract more of them.

There was no time for indecision. She knew what must be done. "No, Thomas, I'll draw their attention. You take him. You have a better chance of outrunning them than I." She thrust the baby into his arms, not allowing herself to think of the face covered by the blanket or the burbling sounds of his limited vocabulary.

Thomas raised his head to protest but did not speak. The look on his face showed the torturous conclusion they shared. His lips barely grazed her forehead as she swung past him, their eyes clinging for the instant before she pushed on the door. She felt the cold air slip past her, heard the fire roar as the air from the opened door fanned it. Then all the comforting elements of her existence were replaced by the chill—and a shrill, irregular birdcall.

The calls of the savages alerted her to their proximity as they raced toward her through the woods. She darted into the forest, terrorized as the screeching, but invisible, huntsmen seemed to circle around her. She made her way up and down the steep hillside indirectly moving toward the path which led to the ocean, listening for the occasional birdcall, judging the movements of the savages.

She knew immediately when Thomas left the house—the night awakened to more calls of the Indians, the rustling of tangled leaves, the cracking of branches. The forest was punctuated with movement, and she knew Thomas was in danger.

She could hear the baby's frightened cry fading into the distance.

Several Indians' birdcalls hovered near her, but the other sounds were distancing themselves, moving back into the forest where Thomas must have gone. She hid in a thicket listening to the sounds still audible above the thundering of her heart. The nearest calls slowed and moved back and forth around her until finally she could see the movement of the brush and a dark figure. She stood silently shaking, shadowed by the evergreens, praying that the hunter would not see her. She caught another glimpse of his movement in the basin below her. She held her breath, hoping her quivering legs would not rustle the branches around her. The dark shadow moved on.

She relaxed and lifted her long skirt to step over the brush and out of the concealment of the trees. In terror she froze when she heard a twig snap on the hill above her. She closed her eyes and waited, praying the Indian had not seen her movement. She stood perfectly still, her muscles aching from the restraint. She must wait.

Would they never give up? What was Thomas doing?

The birdcalls near her had ceased, but she could hear uncomplicated trills moving away from her into the forest.

They were all following Thomas and the baby. Her heart clutched with dread.

She quickly moved toward the clearing, ignoring the noise she made as she broke twigs and branches, dislodging a stone from the hillside, which then rolled into another, making a dull thud. She heard repeated warbles moving toward her again. She slowed and gulped before stepping into the opening she had before avoided, knowing she would be fully visible to the Indians. Surely her appearance would divert their attention from Thomas—and from Samuel. She ran, pulling her skirt high above her ankles, trying not to stumble over the uneven ground as she scanned the edge of the clearing for the boulder that marked the top of the trail.

Had they followed her? Were they watching her? She pulled herself behind the rock, her throat dry, her breath coming in gasps. She crumpled at the base of the stone, gulping in crisp air as she listened. She knew what she must do and she pulled herself to her knees.

Please, help Thomas. Let them come after me. Please.

She tried to slow her breathing so she could hear beyond her gasps. There was only silence.

Please, she prayed again.

Stillness surrounded her. The thin clouds of the earlier evening had thickened. The darkness seemed impenetrable. She was unaware of the occasional snowflake that melted in the dark strands of her hair, unaware of the brittle twigs that tore at her skirt and scratched her arms. She listened, willing herself to hear something, anything so she could know they were safe, but the forest was noiseless, hushed except for the quiet murmur of waves on the beach below her.

She looked at the path again. *Not yet.* She knew the trail; she would need her strength and every bit of wit she possessed to traverse it in the dark with the savages chasing her.

The silence was complete. She waited, her breath still too ragged. She looked at the path again. *Soon. I will go soon.*

The birdcall shot into the darkness around her, nearby but not close. The answering echoes were scattered in the forest. Four of them.

She would not allow herself to answer the question that she could not block from her mind as she stood unsteadily, then looked toward the cove.

It was time.

She looked with dread at the path she had to follow and its steep descent to the water's edge below. *Direct my steps. Please guide me.*

The darkened night spread around her. The soft pellets of scattered snow had thickened. She stepped from the boulder onto the steep slope, grabbing at a tree trunk as the pine needles under her feet began to slip. She pulled herself to the center of the path where the needles had blown clear and started down the incline, hunched forward to catch at the branches as she carefully descended the path.

She heard the Indians calling back and forth again, this time much closer. She had to go faster even at the risk of stumbling. She pulled herself erect and started down the hill, only catching at the branches around her on the steepest stretches. She stumbled once, catching herself on her hands and a knee. The abrasive rock scratched her knee, but she ignored the sting as she pushed herself up and struggled down the trail.

She knew her pursuers were getting closer. She could hear the breaking twigs and, occasionally, sliding rocks. Soon they would be able to see her on the lengths of straight path between the curves. Were they carrying bows?

She tried to steal a quick glance behind her as she came to a bend, but she caught her foot on a tree root and nearly tripped. It took her only a moment to regain her balance, but in that instant an arrow flew past her.

She would not get away unless she gained ground on them.

She thought about the path in front of her. After a few turns it leveled for several rods before it twisted tightly through a section of trees and brush. Then it went down a steep slope before leaving the woods to meander between large boulders until it reached the sandy beach.

She was tiring. Again it was hard to catch her breath, and her legs ached. *How can I ever outrun the savages? And why try? Why are so many chasing me if they caught Thomas with Samuel?* And Thomas would not allow them to capture Samuel while either of them was alive. Why not simply allow herself to be taken too?

Weariness overtook her. Her pace slowed.

Then she heard the sound. The soft wail could have been made by a tree moaning in the wind or a distant coyote, even by an Indian, but it could have been the distant cry of a child—and if there were any chance that Samuel was alive, she had to survive. She would not let them capture her.

But she was tired. She needed to rest if she were to try to outdistance the Indians.

If she could just get to the twists in the path. She paced herself with deep breaths until she turned the first curve, then increased her speed and lengthened her stride, though her lungs felt as if they would burst, and her legs felt weak and unsteady. By the second turn she could tell from the noise that she had gained distance on the unsuspecting pursuers. By the time she reached the twists she was certain they could not see her.

She silently eased herself behind a bush still covered with browning leaves, then lowered herself to the ground until she could only see the path through the bottom twigs.

The Indians followed the path, striding confidently as they came out of the turn. They did not seem alarmed when they did not see her; they did not change their gait nor look out into the brush. Perhaps at this point capturing her was needless. Maybe they already had their prize. Would they just leave?

She lay on the ground breathlessly waiting. The snow had quit and the clouds seem to be clearing, opening the sky to cloud-dulled moonlight.

She had begun to believe that she was safe until she heard the birdcalls spreading out from the sand below her, starting to move rapidly back toward the mountainside. She was immediately up, fighting her way through the tangled limbs that hid her from her trackers, skirting the path and the boulders. She knew where the boulders would shield her from their view and offer a safe course to the beach. And she knew where she would go for safety.

She slid down behind a boulder, ignoring the stiff twigs that jutted into her skin as they tangled at her skirt and pinned her against the hard rocks. She wedged her way slowly through the boulders, around the base of the cove, listening with satisfaction as the calls moved past her back up the mountainside.

Thomas had to be alive. The cry had sounded so much like the baby, and she knew her baby's cry. Thomas would have outwitted them. He knew the area. He knew the trails. They had given up trying to find him and had come to capture her, thinking that would draw him out.

It had to be that way. Her family had to be alive.

She would trick the Indians too, and tomorrow night their family would cuddle securely together in their house.

She was more confident now. She could see the path that wound between the boulders to the beach. She would be there soon, and her family would all be safe.

The birdcalls were spreading back down through the forest now. They were getting closer and she must hurry.

She brushed against the boulders, skinning her arms, bruising her legs, but it didn't matter. Thomas had to be alive.

She was nearly to the beach now. There were still risks, of course. There was a space where the boulders were nearly submerged in the hardened soil and she would be visible. Then, once she got to the sand it would be difficult to run, and if the Indians spied her, there was nowhere to hide until she got to the cave and the ocean water. Surprise would be her only weapon.

Surprise and their fear.

Nasset had shown her the tidal cave worn on the outer rim of the cove and told her the Indian legend about the jealous sea god who destroyed any who entered its opening. No native would dare go into it for any reason, Nasset had assured her.

She slipped past the boulder into the open. *Please, let the tide be weak and ebbing.*

She ran from the split between the boulders, through the short brush that grew between the rocks. The uneven surface twisted at her feet and she felt her ankles weaken. Straggling stocks and tall grass caught at her skirt and nearly sent her sprawling until she lifted the fabric so high she could hardly see where she was running. She did not listen for the calls; Thomas and the baby were alive, and she had to survive to be with them.

She was running on the loose sand, nearly to the cave entrance when the moon's light broke through the clouds.

He appeared as a specter only yards down the beach, coming out at the edge of the boulders just as she had. His darkened face was highlighted with slashes of white, which seemed to distort his features even more than the feral look in his eyes. His whoops were no longer disguised by bird songs as he screeched to his companions.

She reached the wet, hard-packed sand just as he did. He was closing in, but she could get to the cave before he did—she had to. He reached to his back for an arrow. The shot went wide, and he dropped his bow, scooping his knife from its casing.

She dashed into the water in front of the cave opening, her skirt swirling in the undertow like broadcloth drying in a snowstorm. She turned to look at the savage to avoid his grasp.

She saw his face then and his expression, which was filled with utter depravity and savagery. She realized that Thomas could not have survived this brutality. Thomas could never overpower this fury and ferocity, the barbaric nature of this man and the others with him. But had Thomas somehow saved Samuel?

She saw him raise his weapon, saw the look of elation on his face as he sliced it toward her. She also saw the surge coming behind him and felt the wave sweep her into the dark confines of the rock, away from the sharp blade.

She was submerged in the water that nearly filled the cave and sent her bubbling to its surface. She clung to a ledge inside the cave as the wave washed back out, leaving her shoulder-deep in the water. She wiped at the liquid that flowed down her face so she could breathe, then watched for the Indian's silhouette to cross the cave entrance. The sounds of lapping water covered any noise from outside the cave. Another wave washed over her.

She stood silently waiting, holding firmly to the ledge as she shuddered. She bowed her head. "Please, let the Indians be afraid," she begged desperately. Then with faith momentarily overcoming her fear, she remembered to whom she addressed her plea. "O Father, let the sea crest and the tide ebb. Let me see the dawn and have strength to follow its light. Let my child live and raise his own children. Father, please, let me be with my family again."

Even as she spoke a wave filled the cavern and crashed against her as she clung to the slippery rocks.

"Please—"

1

"Have you been able to get your graduation cap to stay on?" Kim asked as she walked into Bethany's bedroom. "Mine falls off every time I turn my head."

Bethany laughed as her roommate's graduation cap immediately slipped over her eyes, substantiating her complaint. She held out a handful of hairpins to Kim. "Try some. The woman who measured me for my gown said they're supposed to help. I haven't decided whether to wear my hair up or down yet, so I haven't tried them."

"Are these really supposed to hold it on?" Kim asked, her short dark hair and dark eyes barely showing beneath the cap. She determinedly pushed bobby pins through her hair and over the bulky fabric, even though they slipped off nearly as fast as she could put them in.

Dee walked into the room just as several of the pins slipped out and dangled from the end of Kim's hair.

"Oh, that looks good. Headline: A new hairstyle created just for graduation from Brandeis. Great." They all laughed as Kim's cap slipped down over her eyes once again. "Those caps look so strange. Your hair's got to be just right or they make you look weird. How're you wearing your hair, Bethany?" Dee sat on the floor and pulled her legs into a yoga position as she tipped her face to consider Bethany's appearance.

Bethany scooped her hair away from her face. In sunlight it gleamed with deep auburn tones and lay smoothly down her back, but today it was darker and the humidity relaxed the ends into loose curls. "I don't know. Shall I pull it up or back or wear it down?"

"Down! Definitely down," Dee insisted.

"No, back." Kim looked at Bethany. "You always wear your hair pulled back. It's going to be hot, so why change for graduation?"

"Oh, let me see." Dee moved to Bethany's back and quickly twirled her hair into a French twist. "There!" she said as they snickered. "Or how about this?" She pulled the hair into a ponytail at the top of Bethany's head as they continued to laugh. "Or," she said as she reached for a brush, "How about some ratting?" She loosely back-combed Bethany's hair so it spread out around her like a spiky ball. "Now," Dee commanded. "Now, for the graduation cap!"

"Oh, yes." Kim laughed and her cap slid off her head again.

"I think I'll go for a more conventional look," Bethany chuckled as she began combing through her hair. "Which should I do, down on my shoulders or back?" She always found it hard to make decisions on hairstyles.

"Do something comfortable," Kim suggested. "Why be fancy?"

"Well, maybe so her hair will look its best in case Peter comes. Boyfriends do come to their girlfriend's graduation sometimes . . . If they're not too busy talking to other girls," Dee said with a touch of sarcasm.

"Just because you saw him talking—" Kim looked frustrated as she stopped midsentence. "I know. You told us all about what you saw, but Peter isn't like that." She turned to Bethany who, tilting her head toward the floor, was obviously trying to avoid the discussion. "Anyway, why don't you wear your hair so that you're comfortable?"

"Well," Dee interrupted, "maybe there's someone else to impress. Maybe Joseph, your grandma's attorney, will show up. You know, as your Grandma Amelia's attorney, Joseph might be the one bringing Amelia or arranging her trip, and that's why she didn't get back to you about her plans—although her silence doesn't surprise me."

Bethany tried to ignore Dee's cynical remark about her grandmother. She knew from their semester as roommates that Dee—though usually correct—was overly blunt, even caustic. Several times her comments had driven Bethany to her bedroom crying.

"Joseph won't be coming," Bethany responded, avoiding any mention of Amelia. "Not everyone is courteous enough to let you know their plans in advance, but he does." Bethany scrutinized her appearance in the mirror, brushing her hair around her shoulders before pulling the sides of the graduation cap down over it.

"Oh, did you hear that?" Dee chuckled then mimicked Bethany's words. "'Not everyone.' Hmm. I wonder who you'd be referring to by that statement?" she said with a grin. "Sweet Grandma Amelia or your sweetheart Peter?"

Kim looked at Dee with a glance of incredulity. "Enough, Dee," she said as she turned to look at Bethany. Dee stood up with a slight shrug and walked from the room.

Bethany stood in front of the mirror, hoping her expression was unreadable, although she was sure that Kim, having been her roommate for a bit longer than Dee, could tell her feelings by the way her eyes darkened. *Why did Dee have to bring up Amelia now?* she wondered. Dee knew Bethany was sensitive about the way her only living relative ignored her, and that she had been lonely most of her life because of this. And yet Bethany felt particularly edgy today, since she'd been expecting some definite information about her grandmother's arrival and her plans for the summer vacation Amelia had suggested they share.

"Haven't you heard anything from Amelia?" Kim asked with a quizzical look. "Isn't she at least going to call?"

Dee's harsh, "Yeah, right," came from the back of the apartment. "Since when does your grandmother bother to call? Seriously— you'd think the woman would realize how much you do for her approval."

Bethany saw Kim roll her eyes at Dee's usual skepticism. Although Bethany and Kim were not overly close—mainly due to Bethany's private nature—Kim was always making efforts to shield Bethany's fragile feelings. Hoping either Amelia or Peter had emailed, Bethany pulled her laptop out of its case. Although Kim knew of Bethany's pain regarding her relationship with her grandmother, she didn't know the latest about Peter—how Bethany hadn't heard from him for two days. Bethany felt too confused and worried to tell anyone. Confused because Dee had seen him with a strange girl just last night, but more worried because of Peter's strange phone calls after their date three days ago.

"D'you two know what time it is? If I'm dropping you off at graduation before I go to work, we'd better get moving," Dee called as she hurried down the hall. "I don't know how the traffic'll be and how close to the hall I'll be able to drive you. I'm not going to be late for work to get you there for the processional."

Bethany looked at her watch and then at Kim's cap. "She's right. Why don't you try some of those clippies on your cap and I'll check my email in case something has come in at the last minute." She clicked on her laptop. "Nothing from Amelia, but a message from Joseph's office," Bethany announced.

"What does he want?" Dee asked as she stopped at the doorway and twirled her long, bleached-blond hair into a bun against her head and then twisted an elastic around it. Dee was always interested in Joseph—or any other good-looking guy. "If he invites you to dinner, I want to go too."

Bethany didn't respond, trying to comprehend the brief message before her. *Amelia died three days ago. It was her request that you attend your graduation and enjoy it as planned.*

Bethany sat shocked. Amelia gone? Amelia dead?

She reread the missive in disbelief. It left her numb.

"Come on. I'm gonna get caught in traffic and be late for work as it is," Dee urged, stepping back in the room. "Kim, your cap is fine." Dee turned to Bethany at the computer and hit the CLOSE button hastily without inquiring further about the message. "Come on, lover girl, you can read Joseph's congratulations when you get back." She handed Bethany her cap and gown to carry to the car. "You can put those on when you get there."

Bethany took the items and, in a daze, started to follow Kim to the car. "Are you all right?" Kim asked, then added, "Do you have your graduation pass?" Bethany went back to the apartment for the pass, nearly forgetting why she'd returned once she was in her room.

The landlord was waiting at the door when she opened it to walk out. "I know you're in a hurry," he said, "but I need to know how many graduates need guest parking tonight. I just caught Kim and she said to ask you."

Guest parking. Guests. Amelia had died. Amelia wouldn't be a guest, and knowing that changed everything. It didn't matter if other guests came because Amelia had died.

"There won't be anyone here for me," the words came out ragged as she struggled with her emotions. "I just found out that my grandmother died," she added through the breaks in her voice.

"Oh, Bethany. I'm sorry," he exclaimed. "Can I do anything to help?"

"No," she responded, her hand over her mouth so he couldn't see her cry. She was supposed to go and enjoy herself, the email said. Amelia wanted her to enjoy herself at graduation! The thought was preposterous; she needed to sit, to comprehend, but Amelia's wish was for her to go to graduation. "I'm going to be late," she added and turned to the car, which Dee already had in gear.

Traffic was heavy, and double-parked cars sporadically blocked the streets as students moved their belongings out while others waited to exchange parking spaces to move their things in. Bethany didn't notice. She saw an elderly woman with hair like Amelia's. She saw a cluster of columbine that reminded her of Amelia. A car drove by and the passenger looked like Amelia.

"Are you okay?" Kim asked Bethany as Dee waited for a car ahead, which was dropping off other graduates.

"That must've been quite a note from Joseph. You haven't said a word since you read it," Dee commented as the car in front of her pulled out. "Looks like you have something to think about that'll keep you awake during the speeches. At least you'll enjoy graduation," she teased with a grin

Enjoy graduation? *Enjoy graduation as planned,* the note had said. The email's timing couldn't have been worse. In the first place, any chance of really celebrating graduation or enjoying her summer had somewhat dissolved with Peter's mysterious disappearance—a worry she could not even begin to deal with right now because of Amelia's death. But now her one remaining hope—the hope for a closer relationship with Amelia, a loving grandmother-granddaughter relationship rather than the distant one that had been theirs—was also lost to her.

The words gnawed at her. How could she enjoy anything when everything reminded her that Amelia was gone?

Bethany went through the ceremony as if in a trance. During the first speaker she dabbed at her eyes until the graduate beside her whispered, "Allergies?" and handed her a new package of tissues. She didn't hear a word of the speeches and had to be tapped on the shoulder when it was time to stand. She felt nearly claustrophobic as the celebrating graduates finally threw their caps in the air.

She had quickly walked down the auditorium steps and left the line of marching graduates who searched through the crowds of guests for their families. She paused, not sure if she should take the bus or walk home. She waited at the bus stop until a cluster of laughing students stopped next to her. Anxious to be alone and afraid she'd embarrass herself by crying, she began to walk.

She had walked only half a block, her eyes directed at the sidewalk, when a chickadee flew past her. She inadvertently looked up, her eyes meeting those of a stranger whose expression changed to pity as he glanced at her teary eyes. She purposefully turned her head away, afraid he would speak, and fled toward her apartment where she immediately lay on her bed beneath a warm comforter and went to sleep.

It wasn't until that night that she finally told her roommates. Kim tried to console Bethany, and so did Dee—in her straightforward and candid, though tactless way. Bethany knew that Dee had her moods, and her response to Bethany's grief was typical of what Bethany should have expected, but the comments seemed cruel—even if they were also true.

"Really, Bethany, why is Amelia's death bothering you so much?" she asked from the floor where she sat polishing her toenails. "Amelia's never visited you here, never called you or sent a gift. I can't ever remember you getting a letter from her. What change will her death make anyway?"

Bethany knew her face had gone pale. She knew she couldn't explain how startling, nearly shocking, it was each time she remembered that Amelia was gone. Dee wouldn't understand the desperate feelings of loss, the unexplainable yet constant emptiness she felt after reading the email. Bethany also knew she could not explain that the very things Dee mentioned were the things about Amelia's death that pained her most. She and Amelia would never share delightful, homey experiences—or understanding and love.

Kim tried to support Bethany by defending Amelia. "Amelia was a busy woman with a lot of important things to do. You can't measure love by gifts and visits. You can't judge unless you know someone's heart, and I don't think you know Amelia that well, Dee."

Kim's words sounded wise and comforting, but later that night, alone in her bedroom, Bethany admitted to herself that Dee was right. Amelia had acted more like an appointed guardian than a grandmother. But that hadn't stopped Bethany from wanting her love. And it had never kept Bethany from loving Amelia.

The next morning, the morning after graduation, Bethany found a vase with white snapdragons spreading into lavender daisies, then mixing into magenta roses and deep purple gerbera daisies. After spying a touch of ivy clustered in them, she knew that the letter lying beside the vase would be from Amelia.

"The landlord brought those over last night," Kim told Bethany as she'd picked up the letter. "Someone tried to deliver them yesterday during graduation but left them at his place when no one was home here."

The flowers were beautiful, but they puzzled Bethany. They were arranged in Amelia's signature style, a style she had created that few were aware of. But Amelia couldn't have arranged them because she had died four days earlier. The flowers would have wilted by the time they arrived. Who had delivered them and how had they learned to arrange the flowers? But the most perplexing question also held the most emotion. Had Amelia actually cared about Bethany enough to have made preparation for her to receive the flowers? Amelia had never taken time for her before. Why would she in her last days?

Bethany thought back on her relationship with the woman who had raised her after her parents' death. Most of her memories were with her nannies and at the private school, and they were all tinged with loneliness. Had there ever been a time when she hadn't hoped to make Amelia proud of her, or felt a surge of excitement at the thought that Amelia might praise her or say that she loved her? But Amelia had never responded as Bethany dreamed she would. Amelia never called her. When Bethany called Amelia, her secretary took messages.

During those childhood years, Bethany spent all her time trying to earn the only thing she thought would get Amelia's attention—a dazzling scholastic record. She ignored invitations to roller-skating parties, pizza parties, and pajama parties; and much later she avoided sororities, all so that she could study. Academics became her world.

But academic achievement hadn't stopped her from longing for a family or from wanting Amelia's love and acceptance. They both loved gardening, and on the very rare occasions when there was a school break during the gardening season, Bethany was sometimes able to help tend the plants and cut flowers, then watch Amelia arrange them. Amelia always placed a few tall stems of white or pale blossoms in the center of a vase, then gradually added darkening hues around them until the bottom layers of blossoms were rich and deeply toned. Bethany would wait in anticipation for Amelia to reveal her signature touch—an unexpected sprig of greenery or shower of delicate flowers in a contrasting color. Amelia loved working in her spring perennial beds. It was there as a college student that Bethany sensed an emotional depth in the older woman that she had never suspected. "Spring is beautiful. It's the beginning, the dawn. Each shoot, each bud holds such promise!" It was not because the words were poetic or the thought original that Bethany remembered Amelia saying them, but because they seemed so uncharacteristic of the stern, insensitive woman who never spoke of the husband or the daughter she had lost.

Bethany drew in a breath as she touched a rose petal. Kim had since left the room but Bethany didn't notice. She picked up the envelope left beside the flowers and hesitantly turned it over from the handwritten name to open the back. Would Amelia's letter explain her silence and help Bethany feel more peaceful—or would it be a meaningless, emotionless collection of words?

Bethany opened the letter with a sigh.

My Dear, Dear Bethany,

Since you first applied to the university, a member of the university faculty has kept me apprised of your superb work and your many achievements. Though I have neglected to ask you personally about your accomplishments or compliment you on your achievements during

*those infrequent visits we have shared, you have always
made me proud.*

Bethany stood stunned as she read the words—words that hurt
more than the loneliness she had felt the day before during the
graduation ceremony. The remote, seemingly uninterested woman
Bethany had continually tried to please decided to call her "my
dear" *now,* in a letter, after she'd died? Bethany felt outraged. If
Amelia could write the words in a letter, why hadn't she spoken
them to her?

Bethany ignored the tears running down her cheeks as she angrily
slammed the partially read letter on the table and, nearly stomping,
paced the floor.

"Why, Amelia?" she cried out furiously. "Why couldn't you say
something nice to me before, when it mattered? Why couldn't you
praise me, or congratulate me, or even just telephone me once in a
while? When you knew about my grades and awards, you must have
realized how hard I was working to get them. Why didn't you
encourage me? Why didn't you ever make me feel wanted—or let me
feel loved while you were alive?" She was outraged, but she picked up
the letter to read more.

Perhaps the remainder of the letter was meant to explain the
contradiction, but instead it left her even more confused and angry.
She threw it down on the table when she heard her cell phone ringing
in her bedroom.

Joseph Panninon, Amelia's attorney, wanted to see her the next
morning.

* * *

Bethany raised her eyes from the letter slowly. She looked at the
beach where seagulls called their discontent above the rustle of
cattails. Warm, moist air left a haze above the bay. Bethany gazed
past it to the ocean.

Wind wafted through the windows of Joseph's BMW and tousled
her hair. A stray strand tickled her cheek, and she brushed it away
impatiently. What was taking Joseph so long? She looked toward the

beach and the snack bar, wishing he'd hurry. Even though she was not looking forward to their upcoming talk, she needed a distraction from all her troubling thoughts.

Although she'd wanted to do more recreational activities after grad school—Brandeis was a tough university, and medieval literature was an exhausting degree—Joseph's proposal that they take a drive up north for the day to discuss the graduation gift Amelia had left for her had not seemed like a break. In truth, she felt no enthusiasm for this trip to Maine—or anything else. Peter's disappearance and Amelia's death had stolen any hope she'd had for her life after graduation. Now, it felt as if her main objective would be to survive.

Nevertheless, she knew Joseph Panninon could help her feel better. He'd always been staid and constant. He was emotionally dependable and solid. There hadn't been a lot that felt solid in her life, and she'd relied upon that strength through the years whenever their lives would intersect as he took care of Amelia's affairs. He'd take her out to dinner occasionally during her senior year—that first year he'd begun working for Amelia—and from time to time throughout her years in college. They'd always laugh together like siblings as they discussed whatever legal items needed to be addressed.

Their modest friendship had become important to Bethany for various reasons, and her confidence around Joseph was certainly one of them. As a teenager she'd been reluctant to talk with boys her own age, but she'd always been able to confide in her grandmother's attorney, despite his six-foot-plus blocky frame and an eight-year age difference. Back then she never felt shy looking into the deep brown eyes of the precise, even-tempered counselor. But the few times she'd spoken to him during her graduate studies at Brandeis, she'd felt awkward—and today was no exception. It felt strange talking as an equal to someone she'd always viewed as . . . more mature.

She looked again toward the snack bar, trying to pick out the attorney. Besides his steadiness, she needed a little of his wry humor to cheer her now. Waiting in the car left her too much time to think. Had it really only been just a week since she'd heard from Peter—and just days since getting that earth-shattering email? It now seemed years ago that she and Kim stood in their apartment laughing, trying to fit their graduation caps on their heads.

A sudden tap on the car window startled her and she jumped, tipping her purse to the floor. No one was near. Perhaps it was just a pebble dropped by one of the gulls overhead, or a twig blown off a tree. Bethany kept glancing through the windows as she reached down for her purse and the contents. She felt nervous on top of everything else—probably due to all the ways her life had recently changed. But this feeling of trepidation bothered her. As she gathered her things, her fingers ran over the edge of the letter. Her stomach clenched. Things were so different now . . . Only weeks before she had been sure this was the summer when her life would change—maybe she'd get more serious with Peter, maybe she'd get closer to Amelia.

Bethany glanced out the car window looking for Joseph, then again at the fragile paper and the words she had nearly memorized.

My Dear, Dear Bethany,

She skipped the opening paragraph, which still angered her.

I want you to know that I loved your mother dearly. I gave her much of my time and every conceivable thing she wanted. She was lovely and naturally charming. She was also willful. Her governess warned me that she needed a firmer hand, but I wouldn't listen, and your mother became persistently defiant. When she insisted on an unescorted trip to Europe as part of her graduation gift when she received her master's degree, I refused. So she went to New York with friends, and then, without my knowledge, flew to Paris and eventually ended up in Genoa where, after nearly three years, she married. Three years after that, you were born. She invited me to visit, and though she was maturing into a loving woman willing to sacrifice for her family, I would not go. You were nearly four when she and her husband, whose name I had not yet learned, were killed.

I resolved I would not raise you as I had her. I remembered her governess's cautions. Certainly, I would see to your needs—but there would be no coddling, no doting, no gratuitous praise. I would hire a full-time nanny to be with you nearly twenty-four hours a day and carry the full brunt of your upbringing. I also decided that once you were of age I would send you off to boarding schools so that your time under my roof would be limited. And even when under my roof, I planned to be absent as much as possible with other affairs so as to reduce our contact.

When I first saw you, I wanted to ignore my resolve. You reminded me so much of your mother that I often left the room in tears. I was afraid to be with you for fear I would soften and pamper you, and then you too would become self-indulgent and leave me.

I wish I could tell you who you are. I am afraid that my absence from your life has challenged your confidence and that you are unaware of the talents and beauty that are innately yours.

The letter continued, but Bethany stopped reading. Even though it had been a day since she'd received it, and she had read and reread it several times, the words still confused her. There were times when she found the letter touching and she was grateful for the glimpse it gave of her mother and even of Amelia, but most of the time she felt bitter and angry. According to the letter, Amelia had avoided Bethany not because of her hectic business schedule or even her priorities; Amelia had knowingly and purposely made the decision to stay out of Bethany's life, basing her decision on her experience with Glennis, Bethany's mother, a completely different person with a completely different personality.

How could Amelia rationalize denying them both the relationship they could have shared? How could she be so insensitive when she, herself, had suffered such loneliness? How could she ignore the despair she was causing the child she supposedly loved?

The thought suddenly filled Bethany with guilt. Her grandmother had not died to purposefully abandon her! She hadn't planned for Bethany to learn about her death in an impersonal electronic communication minutes before she was to leave for graduation. Bethany felt completely torn by her feelings. She felt adrift without Amelia as a safety net of stability, distant as she might have been. She felt lost without the hope of Amelia's approval to motivate her, without the dream of building a better relationship with Amelia to give her hope. But she also felt betrayed and angry, and when she tried to make sense of it all she felt guilty. She could not feel peaceful about the relationship she had had with the woman who'd raised her and whom she loved. She needed answers—now.

Bethany looked out the car window for Joseph. She hadn't really talked to anyone about how painful Amelia's loss was to her—how devastating it was knowing she could never tell her good-bye, never hug her. How could she explain how unfinished their relationship seemed, how empty she felt, acting as though nothing had changed when she wanted—no, needed—to tell Amelia so many things? Bethany had barely acknowledged her disillusionment and her fear of the future to herself, let alone anyone else. When Joseph picked her up he had expressed his condolences, but then he immediately began discussing her inheritance and the estate. So, taking her cues from him, she hadn't brought up Amelia's death. But she needed to know more, and Joseph was the person with the answers she needed. She couldn't stand waiting any longer.

Pushing the car door open with more force than necessary, Bethany nearly ran toward the beachfront. Joseph was still in line at the snack bar as she approached him.

"Bethany, what's wrong? You look—"

She interrupted immediately. "I need to know more, Joseph. I was told Amelia was in remission."

A look of sympathy filled his eyes as he stepped from the line, gently drawing her to him. "She *had* been in remission. Unfortunately, earlier this year the cancer metastasized to her bones. The oncologist found it in her back, but he still thought she might be able to have the summer with you. Amelia made all her doctors—and me and my staff—promise not to tell you about the change in her illness before graduation. She wanted to tell you herself when she was with you after the celebration. I waited until today to come because I was pretty sure all the graduation festivities would be over, and that was important to her."

"I should have been at her funeral—not at graduation! Why didn't anyone tell me?"

"There was no funeral. I—"

"Of course not. Why would there be a funeral? I suppose she wanted to be cremated and have her ashes dispersed over some field of flowers in the Himalayas or something," Bethany guessed sarcastically. Suddenly, the fact that her grandmother had chosen a lawyer, not her, to be her confidante, broke down her defenses. The pain suddenly seemed sharper—stinging, clinching her throat and stomach. She stood, determined not to cry in front of Joseph.

Joseph smiled gently at the assumption. "Well, something like that, maybe. I already told you as much as I can—legally." He paused awkwardly, volunteering no further information. "Why don't we step a little farther away from the crowd?" he suggested quietly.

Suddenly embarrassed and now uncertain if Joseph were free to answer her anyway, she didn't ask what had been done with the body. She wasn't going to beg to be told the location of the grave. If Amelia didn't care whether Bethany knew, then why should she?

"Joseph," she said, humiliated but also desperate, "why didn't you tell me personally? Why didn't you at least call me—prepare me for the shock? Why an email just as I was leaving for graduation? It was so . . . horrible. And then getting Amelia's letter, and still no word from you . . ."

Joseph frowned. "Bethany, listen to me. I don't know what you're talking about, I promise. I did try to tell you personally—when I showed up today—but surprisingly you already knew. You were visibly upset—which is understandable—so I didn't think I should pry about your source of information until we were on the road talking—"

"Then you didn't send the letter or the flowers?" she interrupted.

"No. I should have ordered flowers, but I've had three busy days taking care of the arrangements for your grandmother's body—" He shook his head with a slight frown before he finished. "I don't know anything about the letter or the email. I haven't told anyone in the office about Amelia's death. Do you have copies with you? Can I see them?"

"I have the letter." Bethany pulled the papers from her purse and handed them to him, then stood with her hands clasped tightly as he skimmed the pages.

He went through the letter quickly, then, still frowning, read through it more slowly. "This is definitely Amelia's handwriting and phrasing. I'm sure she wrote it, but I have no idea how it or the flowers got to you. And the email—you say you got it just before the ceremony?" He shook his head. "The timing was simply cruel. I can't begin to imagine anyone who would be that callous."

"You have no idea who sent them?"

"None. Did the flowers and letter come at the same time?"

His cell phone began a quiet buzz, and he took it out of his pocket and glanced at it. "I have to take this call, but I'll definitely have someone look into it." He walked a few steps toward the ocean before he put the telephone to his ear.

Bethany began rereading the letter as he talked, her irritation building. He had hardly hung up when she startled him by blurting out more questions.

"Why did Amelia write this letter? Did she think she could ignore me all my life and then, after her death, heal any hurt she might have caused me with one sugar-coated explanation? It's not working! Was she trying to explain why she acted the way she did, or was she rationalizing it away? What was she trying to do?"

Joseph had no answers. "I don't know about the letter, but . . . Bethany, there's so much to explain. In truth, we're not just going on a drive today—we're going to see your graduation gift. Your grandmother bought you a house in Maine, as well as transportation. Neither of them is in great condition. I have to tell you, Bethany, the house is small, and some people would consider it old and worn out. But she really was hoping it'd be a new start for you, to make up for what she'd done.

"Amelia really wanted the best for you. She recently decided she had failed you—she had placed you where you would have what she wanted for you but you weren't offered many opportunities to explore your own preferences and really express yourself. So, knowing your dream of writing a novel, she found a place where you could be on your own. She wanted you away from distractions, someplace where no one would associate you with her and her assets. She thought the house would put you in a position where you could find out who you really are and gain more self-confidence. That's what's in Maine—a chance for a new beginning and time to think . . ."

Bethany glanced away momentarily—angry with her grand-mother's choices and finding it difficult to believe Joseph's explanations. The "gift," she angrily concluded, would finally show how little Amelia really cared about her. Amelia had the time and money to give Bethany nearly anything, and she had bought some old cottage miles away from anything and anyone. That was it? What about some kind of relationship with the woman she'd always seen as a mother, or an idea of who Bethany's parents were, or guidance about what an heiress of an estate was supposed to do? What about the companionship she'd sought for her whole life? She'd spent over twenty years trying to impress or please Amelia so the woman would notice her and get to know her! Bethany wanted to be loved; Amelia had responded with real estate.

Bethany tuned Joseph out while he continued to talk about the house as though it were some magical cure for Amelia's detachment— for shutting Bethany out of her life and now her death. Bethany cared much less about the value of her inheritance than she cared about the relationship with Amelia that it symbolized. She *did* hope to find some evidence of Amelia's love in Amelia's choice of an endowment for Bethany's future. But Bethany began to wonder if Joseph were inten-tionally avoiding a discussion of Amelia's will—after all, he was her lawyer. *Maybe this really is all she left me and he doesn't want to admit it.*

The irony of the situation wasn't lost on Bethany. In spite of Amelia's alleged intention to help her granddaughter develop a sense of self and explore her own interests and preferences, the woman was still dictating where Bethany would live and what she would do.

It wasn't the will, the house, or even the insinuations, though that hurt so badly that she felt like bending over and clutching her waist. Amelia's letter seemed to say one thing while her actions said the opposite. Had Amelia loved Bethany all this time but never told her? Why hadn't Amelia given her a chance to show she loved her, too? Bethany suddenly knew that Joseph couldn't fix what she was feeling. "I think I'll go back to the car," she interrupted him quietly. "Could you get me a sandwich along with the drink?" Before he could answer, she turned and was gone.

Back at Joseph's car, she gazed past the boulders and grass toward the small pines, twisted and spindly from their continual struggle against the salty wind. Amelia had planned for her to live and write in a house somewhere on the coast of Maine. The only thing Bethany wanted less than to see it was to live in it.

2

Bethany was relieved to see Joseph walking across the sandy parking lot toward the BMW, carrying a couple of food bags. "Okay," he said as he opened the door, "I know losing Amelia and finding out about her death the way you did has been devastating, but this seems like much more. You're not only angry but you seem almost . . . what, nervous?" He slid into the driver's seat and handed her a bag with a sandwich in it. "Ham and cheese?" He sat back in the seat, pulled out his food, and began to eat, though he looked at her steadily.

She *was* nervous—and so many other things. It seemed impossible to sort out everything she was feeling about Amelia and about her suddenly uncertain future . . . and she was by now convinced that Peter had to be in serious trouble. She wanted to tell Joseph, but ever since Peter had warned her about telling anyone, she was worried about Peter's safety as well as her own. What was more, her relationship with Joseph had been changing as she became more of an adult, and she wasn't sure what to tell him anymore. She didn't know if she should still confide in him as an older brother, or if she should distance herself more and act like an independent, mature business acquaintance. The problem was that Bethany didn't really have anyone to confide in because she'd always kept people at a distance. She didn't really know anyone well except Joseph and now Peter—as well as you could know anyone after a couple of months. And now that she felt this awkwardness with Joseph, she wondered how well she even knew him.

Bethany knew she would have to do something about Peter's disappearance soon. But what? He had warned her not to say a word, but how could she remain silent?

"Joseph, I . . . I guess I'm just stressed. I'm sorry about the way I questioned you."

"You've got a lot going on. Graduation, moving—not to mention the fact that you're grieving over your grandmother. Of course you're stressed and tired, and, under the circumstances, you should have a lot of questions."

"I should have waited until we were in the car or at least not in public to ask you. I wasn't very composed."

"As though anyone who has gone through what you have this week would be composed. Do you have any more questions, or would you like to forget about it for now? You could probably use a more cheery topic."

Bethany knew that Joseph's answers about Amelia's death, no matter how accurate or comforting, could only satisfy her curiosity—not bring Amelia back or change their relationship and alleviate her sorrow. She instead gave a quick shrug and said, "I'm okay for now, I guess."

"Then, how about if I start with a compliment? I was noticing earlier, that, despite the stress, you look good. I like your hair."

"Thanks." Bethany was suddenly quiet. The compliment would not have felt strange in the past when she saw Joseph more as a brother, but now that she was in her mid-twenties it felt awkward—and she had no idea how to respond.

Joseph didn't seem to notice. "It makes you look more relaxed." He looked from the road toward her in apparent appraisal. "And more mature."

Bethany could feel her cheeks warm in an embarrassed blush. Glad that the traffic was diverting his attention, she tried to think of something "mature" to say, but her mind seemed as numb and muddled as a medieval mummy.

Finally, realizing she could ask about his job, she began to speak—just as he turned toward her and also spoke.

They both stopped, waited expectantly for the other to begin, then grinned and chuckled when they again started at the same time.

"You first," Joseph insisted with a smile.

"I was just going to ask how things are going at the office. I didn't recognize the voice of the secretary who answered the last time I called."

"Oh, Stephanie moved out to Oregon with her husband so I tried a new girl—and I mean *girl*. I've kept her—Holly is her name—for the past couple of months hoping she would learn to be responsible, but I'm training someone else and I'll let Holly go next week. Kids these days. She rarely gets back from lunch on time. When I need her she's invariably gone. She's always running off without letting the other secretaries know where she's going or when to expect her back. Just gone. You know the type?"

"Oh, yes. Been around lots of them." *Just gone. Amelia was always "just gone." Peter is now "just gone."* Bethany sighed, suddenly tired.

Joseph looked over at her questioningly. "Are you sure you're okay?"

She drew in a deep breath. "Sure. I guess the week is catching up with me. What were you going to say?"

"Oh, that can wait. There are still a couple more hours of driving before we get to Faunce Cove. Why don't you take a nap?"

Bethany didn't protest as she relaxed into the seat and leaned her head back. She could feel Joseph shift the car up and down as they traversed the curve-filled coastal highway after turning off of Route 95, the interstate that stretched across the state. She was relieved to have an excuse to close her eyes. She needed to work through some of her feelings.

Since receiving the email, Bethany had continually felt an uneasy gnawing in her mind—especially now that Joseph told her he did not write it. She was relieved that Joseph had promised to investigate. She couldn't imagine who would have the motive, the interest, or the knowledge to announce Amelia's death to her before Joseph did. But it wasn't just the mysterious email that was troubling her. There was more. At first she attributed her feelings to Amelia's death, but during those short intervals when she was able to put that aside, the feeling continued. Now, knowing there was no service to attend, no grave to visit, the panicked thought kept surfacing: Where was Peter?

She let her mind go back to several months ago when they first met. Her memories of Peter, especially the early ones, were warm and inviting. She remembered studying in the university library, flipping through an article on medieval literature. She hadn't noticed the wiry but attractive man studying the numbers on the stacks next to her until he turned and spoke. His mischievous expression might have made her suspicious if his smile had not seemed so genuine. "I can't find this book!" he half whispered. "Could you help me?" His little-boy grin was appealing, but the book he was looking for didn't seem to exist. She would have given up except for the flashing humor in his eyes and his glib comments as they skimmed over a dozen shelves.

"Are you sure this is actually a book?" Bethany finally questioned in a low tone, smiling at him.

"Well, the only way I know to find out for sure," he responded quietly, a gleam in his eyes, "is to search the whole library. You game?"

After learning each other's names, they ended up at the student center eating hamburgers rather than looking for the book. Peter knocked on her apartment door the next morning. To her startled question, "How did you know where I live?" he simply answered, "Hey, you can't live around a university without learning a few things." He grinned and, for once, she did not feel self-conscious when she smiled back; neither did she that evening when she sat beside him at a movie, trying not to giggle as he stealthily fed her popcorn during the promotions.

Dating Peter meant new adventures—sailing, canoeing, and hiking. Bethany had never laughed so much nor felt so alive. Often she would find her mind wandering as she read through her research notes, and she hummed as she walked across campus. She found herself smiling more than usual.

Peter was very complimentary and even more attentive, finding a reason to see Bethany almost every night, sometimes coming over just to relax. She learned to relax during those months too. Peter's humor turned her intense nature and serious comments into jokes that left them both laughing. Kim noticed the difference. "He's so good for you!" Kim exclaimed after Peter left one night. "You look so happy—you're almost glowing!"

That last night together—it had been only three days before graduation, the same day that Amelia died—they'd enjoyed a marvelous Italian dinner with witty conversation that left him with laughing eyes, and her with a dreamy mind. There had been one cell phone call which interrupted their evening, but it hadn't been until they were leaving the restaurant, so it didn't seem like a big deal at the time. But on the way home, Peter acted strange and sullen. When Bethany asked him what was wrong, he'd answered crossly, "I'm just stressed about work."

They drove the rest of the way home in silence, but Bethany noticed Peter glancing in his rearview mirror anxiously. He took an early exit, driving blocks out of their way to get to Bethany's apartment. Then he circled the block an extra time.

Stopping in the parking lot outside her apartment, Peter walked her to her door, his eyes flitting into the shadows. She tried to persuade him to come in, but he refused. He gave her a quick, inattentive kiss and said, "I'll call you later. I need to take care of some things." Then he turned abruptly toward his car.

Bethany couldn't stop the fears twisting around in her mind that night. What was bugging him? Who had called between dinner and the drive home—and what did they say? Bethany went to bed early, wondering how she could persuade Peter to confide in her, to tell her what was happening with his job.

When the phone rang two hours later, Bethany was still tossing and turning in bed. She picked up the phone before it could ring a second time. Hearing Peter's voice she said, "Peter, what's wrong? What's happening?" Peter hushed her questions. "I'm not supposed to talk to anyone, so I can't talk long. Just listen," he pleaded quietly.

In guarded references—never using identifying names or explicit facts—he explained that his boss had told him he was in danger, and that it might not be safe for him to stay in the area. Suddenly, Peter said, "I've got to go. I'm sorry, Bethany." Then he hung up. Feeling desperate, Bethany tried to call him back several times during the night. She agonized when no one answered the phone. She finally drifted into a restless sleep as the sky was beginning to lighten.

The next morning while she was in the shower, Peter called again, leaving a long, garbled voice mail. Bethany couldn't understand most of it—he'd obviously called on his cell phone, and his voice kept cutting in and out. She thought she recognized the words "trouble" and "the organization," even the phrase "situation was taxing." But it all made no sense, and she wasn't certain whether he actually said "they're after me" or if she imagined it. There had been something more about "evading" and "fraud" before the connection improved.

Then she clearly heard him plead, "Don't tell anyone what I've told you about the organization. And don't tell anyone about me until I contact you again." The static increased, and she could barely understand his voice until he spoke emphatically. "Try to leave, Bethany. Go somewhere secluded." The static intensified until it sounded like an activated Geiger counter, but his voice was loud. "Don't confide in anyone, especially those you think you can trust, Bethan—" The message abruptly ended but the machine kept humming. Nervously, Bethany pushed at the buttons trying to stop it. She heard it click and quickly pushed the REPEAT button. When there was no response she pushed again only to find she had pushed DELETE.

"No, no, no!" she'd cried, trying the buttons again in a panic.

Her shrieks brought Kim running. "What's wrong?" she'd asked.

"Oh, I deleted a message from Peter," she said frantically, still studying the buttons. She barely stopped herself from explaining more, remembering Peter's charge not to tell anyone about the situation.

"Something important?"

Bethany searched for the right words and forced herself to act calmly. "Just Peter. You know, his voice and everything."

"Oh," Kim said, her smile widening. "I'm sure he'll be calling back soon."

Unable to listen to Peter's words again—and unable to reach his cell phone—she'd gone over and over the words she thought she'd heard in her mind, memorizing them.

Bethany had not heard from Peter since then. The first day she tried calling his cell over and over, leaving voice messages until his number was suddenly disconnected. Then the night before graduation, Dee reported that she had seen him in Cambridge talking with a pretty blond. Bethany hadn't known how to feel—she was sure he hadn't been conning her with his "absence," but how Dee could have seen him locally was confusing to her. Then came graduation and Amelia's death. Intense grief had pushed worry over Peter aside until last night.

She'd woken the previous night from a nightmare with Peter running away from an unseen pursuer, his life in danger. Now, driving along with Joseph, Bethany began to also worry if the fact that she told her roommates last night about Peter's disappearance could endanger them as well—although she didn't tell them the real reason. It had been late the night before when Kim had brought up his absence. She was surprised that he hadn't been by to see Bethany since Amelia's death, and so she had asked about him. Remembering his warning, as confusing as it was, Bethany knew she could not use his job as an excuse. Instead she told them that Peter had called that afternoon to tell her he wanted to break up. As usual, Kim had been solicitous, but Dee had called him a jerk and said to forget him. "He's gone, just gone, and you're lucky." Dee repeated the phrase several times during their conversation.

Unable to confide in anyone, Bethany felt even more alone than she had before meeting Peter.

* * *

Bethany climbed stiffly from the silver BMW, while Joseph jumped out and walked quickly to the passenger side. The drive from Boston had taken longer than she'd expected. The afternoon haze had cleared to a brilliant dusk, the ocean a series of quiet aqua ripples, dotted with lobster boats and buoys bobbing like balloons in the wind. Bethany drew in a deep breath as she listened to the rhythmic murmur before turning to look at the forest. Sun-drenched, apple-green deciduous trees contrasted with tall, stately evergreens that tiered up the steep mountainside in a surreal yet beautiful panorama. Nearer the driveway where Joseph had stopped there was a small house surrounded by tall grass that gently waved in front of an imposing rock wall.

"That forest is so thick you can imagine almost anything could be hidden in it. And that rock wall . . ." Bethany pulled her jacket around her as she glanced at the place she was supposed to call home.

Joseph, pushing his dark hair from his forehead, gently propelled Bethany toward the walkway. "We're losing daylight."

He struggled with the key and the knob until, after several attempts, the door to the house finally opened.

"Is there electricity?" Bethany asked as he felt inside the door for a light switch.

"Do you mean has the electricity been turned on, or is it wired?" Joseph looked at her with a teasing grin as she hesitantly stepped through the door.

The stark interior of the house, a single, dimly lit room, seemed dreary in the dusky light. Bethany looked around curiously, questioning why her grandmother had chosen such a place. It was nearly square, about twenty feet by twenty-two, with an ostentatious staircase minus a few spindles splitting the back section of the room nearly in half. It led up to a barely noticeable loft. One side of the room's back wall was covered by a large, blackened fireplace, except for a doorway that opened into a hall where the bathroom and a back door were located.

The apparently unventilated room smelled of age and humidity, and Bethany was reluctant to go in any farther. She wanted to believe that Amelia had planned this gift out of love. Yet if that were true, then why such a gloomy place?

Joseph moved toward the fireplace. "Look! This must date back at least to the 1700s. This flooring," he pointed to the planks, which were each nearly fourteen inches wide, "shows that the original house was built when the area was first settled. Bethany, can you imagine . . . ?"

"Joseph," she began, "can we go?"

Joseph shifted his dark eyes to Bethany as she spoke.

"This is just an isolated, dilapidated, dank room. Is this really supposed to make up for all the other things? All I wanted was Amelia's love. Does this look like love?" Her voice was barely audible as she fought back tears while she looked out at the view—the azure ocean, the jagged line of boulders with evergreens framing it all. Then, unexpectedly, Joseph's friendly arms were around her, comforting her. She leaned toward him, grateful for the solace.

* * *

The next morning Bethany heard voices and footsteps on the porch as she stood at the door of the bed-and-breakfast and watched Joseph carry the bags down the stairs.

After herding her redheaded twins out to the bus, Alice McClere, who ran the inn, walked back into the house while chatting with an elderly man. She wore blue Levi's and a large sweatshirt, her blond hair loosely braided and bouncing on her back as she moved.

"This is my dad, Ethan Savage," she stated, a smile crinkling her blue eyes. "Meet my guests," she continued, introducing Bethany and Joseph. "Bethany here is thinking of moving into the old house up by Faunce Cove."

"I hadn't heard about that," her father replied cordially, his thumbs in the pockets of his overalls.

"Dad makes the rounds every morning." Alice looked at him teasingly. "And what news he doesn't get from the café, he gets at my sister Judith's house—her husband is the chief of police. Then he comes on down here to collect some more breakfast and tells me everything, adding his own editorials, of course. He keeps a special vigil out on the mornings I have guests. Otherwise, I serve oatmeal." She grinned.

"So, you're interested in the old Faunce place." The elderly Mr. Savage stood on the porch in the warming sunshine. "Used to be a lot of old houses up in these parts, even some pretty big ones. I imagine most of them have been gone for over a century now. But you're not interested in all that."

"Actually, I was surprised to see that the house at Faunce Cove seems to be from colonial times. When were the first settlements made in this area?" Joseph asked, putting the bags down on the porch.

Bethany still had questions about the Faunce Cove home that Joseph seemed to ignore. Amelia had apparently bought it, but it seemed as though everyone thought Bethany was considering it as a rental opportunity. Still, Bethany figured Joseph was silent on this point for privacy issues. After all, Amelia had said she wanted Bethany's stay there to be low profile. Why was this whole affair treated with such secrecy? Not having the answers, Bethany suppressed her impatience and tuned back into the conversation at hand.

"A lot of the first inhabitants were sent up from Plymouth in the 1600s. Most all of them got killed off by Indians or starvation, but a few survived—and every once in a while in the woods, you'll come across an old chimney or rock foundation remaining from one of those houses," Ethan Savage was saying. "Of course, the forest is so thick you can't see them until you nearly trip over them. There are deserted villages up there and a huge place hidden somewhere off the North

Island Road. You wouldn't have passed it because you take the upper bridge onto the island rather than the Seacrest Bridge to get to it."

"Do you know any of the history about the Faunce Cove house?" Joseph leaned back on the porch railing.

"That house up there by Faunce Cove?" Ethan paused to think. "I'm supposing it dates back to about the same time period as the one on North Island Road. It's been kept up pretty well. Can't remember anybody ever living there, though."

"Didn't Ally say the social studies teacher told them there was a story about Faunce Cove and the first woman who lived there?" Alice queried. Then she turned to Bethany and added, "Ally's my fourteen-year-old niece, Judith and Tom's daughter. She's looking for a topic for a high school research paper next fall. I think she has her mind set on finding out about the Faunce Cove woman."

"She'll probably have to go to Augusta to the state library and look at some of their handwritten collections," Ethan inserted, then turned his attention back to Bethany. "You pretty much set on moving in at Faunce Cove? Sure couldn't find a prettier spot."

"Are there many people around?" Joseph asked, ignoring the question.

"There aren't a lot of year-round people," Alice answered, "although we do have some who vacation here. But there are so many winding roads and remote homes and cabins on these islands that it's impossible to know how many people there really are in the area. Oh, speaking of the remote areas, there is one possible drawback if you're really interested in the Faunce Cove place. I don't think there's cell phone service out on the coastal side of the mountain. I don't know if that's a plus or a minus. Some days I sure could be happy without mine."

"Well, thanks." Joseph looked encouragingly at Bethany's uncertain expression as he picked up the bags and they walked down the front steps toward the car.

"I have a question." Bethany hadn't felt much like talking that morning, but she suddenly remembered something she wanted to know. "Is there a Latter-day Saint church nearby?"

Alice didn't have to think. "Why, yes. In fact, our family doctor, Dr. Noel, is a member of that church. I'll have to ask him where they meet the next time I see him, and then I'll make sure I pass that on to you."

"Thank you," Bethany said and smiled as she walked out.

As they got in the car, Joseph commented, "I didn't know you were a churchgoer."

Bethany just smiled and looked away. She'd tell him about her baptism and her new faith sometime soon . . . But for now she had too much on her mind—and a big decision to make—to think about much else.

Joseph changed the subject. "They seem like nice people, and the bed-and-breakfast is really quite homey. That's something to keep in mind."

"Nice people and homey places?"

"Yes."

The car was silent as Joseph drove down the scenic road.

Peter was nice. Our relationship felt homey. Lot of good that was. She sighed and shifted in her seat to look at Joseph. It had been nice of him to comfort her the evening before. The gesture had broken down some of the barriers she'd felt before, but now she felt a different strangeness between them.

Joseph pulled up in front of the entrance to the little house, drawing her from her thoughts, and they both got out of the car.

"Look! The door opens without excessive violence!" she commented dryly as Joseph pulled at the knob. "And doesn't the whole place look inviting?" she added sarcastically as she reluctantly stepped into the doorway.

"Come here." Ignoring Bethany's remarks, Joseph motioned her farther into the room.

Bright with slanting sunshine, the room looked quite different than it had the previous night.

Joseph brushed at the stones on the fireplace. "You know, with a little sandblasting I bet this could really look nice." He turned to Bethany. "And Amelia did provide a budget for limited remodeling with my approval, simply to ensure that we keep the home's historical integrity. You can make changes except to the fireplace and the original foundation." He waited while she looked around the room. "D'you want to see your transportation?"

Bethany followed Joseph out the door. He helped her into the car, then drove through Seacrest toward Walachias. A few miles past the town, he pulled into an auto repair shop that advertised used cars. Then he stopped between a new car with a dented bumper and an old Jeep. Bethany hesitantly climbed from Joseph's BMW and looked at the dented car.

"I hate to tell you this," Joseph said as he closed his car door, "but yours is the Jeep."

As they examined the Jeep Amelia had chosen, Bethany could tell it was at least ten years old, but it looked more like twenty.

Nonchalantly, Joseph warned her, "You may want to do some fixing-up on the Jeep, just like the house. It will need some repairs and a little upkeep—the brakes squeak when they're wet, but they're fine. And the door handle sticks unless you oil it when it's been humid. A good machine, though." He patted the rusting metal with a grin, turned to her, and added, "Oh, and one more request Amelia had concerning your living here. You must not mention to anyone your grandmother or any of these things she's provided for you. I think this goes back again to her desire for you to have a low profile and private place in order to find yourself. I think you'll find in small towns like these that the locals can be a little curious about newcomers and will try and poke around in their lives to see what they can find."

Joseph paused for a moment, allowing Bethany to process all he was saying, then finished his explanation. "And the best news is that you won't need to find work outside your novel writing. You'll have a weekly stipend for your expenses. And you won't need to use checks or credit cards. In fact, Amelia requested that you use only the designated funds from her."

Bethany stood in utter silence. What was there to say?

* * *

As they drove over the bridge that connected the town of Seacrest and the island chain that linked it to the mainland, Bethany thought about the house at Faunce Cove. The view was spectacular, and some furniture could cheer up the blocky room. She supposed Amelia *had* given her the ocean and the sunset and a retreat, and not just a broken-down hut. But why in such a strange place, and with such mysterious rules?

As Joseph adjusted the cruise control on the BMW, Bethany wondered what it would be like living in a remote house provided by a woman whose motives and love both seemed questionable. One consolation was that if Peter were able to contact her again safely, perhaps she could persuade him to come to Maine. It certainly was an isolated area. He would know to contact Joseph if he wanted to find her—she'd mentioned Joseph's practice and their resultant relationship a number of times. What could be safer than Seacrest?

That night Bethany prayed about moving to Faunce Cove. Her answer came as positive, warm feelings that nearly overwhelmed her.

She realized that her future truly was wide open. She'd kept the summer free since she thought she'd be spending it with Amelia, and as for after that . . . she had not yet made any definite plans about what she would do with her advanced degree. She figured she could always teach, but it was writing that remained her secret passion. And Faunce Cove seemed like it would provide the perfect haven for that to occur—especially with Amelia offering to cover her living expenses for the next year, which would allow her to strictly focus on her writing.

Bethany also realized that the underlying reason she hesitated to accept Amelia's offering was that Amelia had, once again, made decisions about Bethany's life without consulting her. And yet she also felt impressed that she should not let her pride get in the way of what was perhaps a providential opportunity.

Although she'd received the answer that moving to Maine was a good decision, she still had many unanswered questions. Tired and unsure of what her future would hold, Bethany decided to push the ambiguity aside and try to fall asleep. She'd been told that Faunce Cove was a good place for her right now—and she supposed that for the moment, that was enough.

3

Sitting on the dusty steps of the Faunce Cove hut, as she had dubbed it, Bethany stretched and looked around. As much as it irritated her to live in a place chosen by Amelia, she had to admit that the feeling of antiquity in the simple structure created a sense of serenity in her, and she wanted to learn more about the little house's history. Besides, she did need to get over her feelings about Amelia. And maybe she *could* actually write a book—something she had dreamed of for as long as she could remember.

Bethany wadded the waxed paper from the doughnut she'd snatched from Alice's serving plate and stuffed it into a garbage can. Lovely as the view was, Bethany was ready for action. The sooner she cleaned the house, moved in a minimal amount of furniture, and set up her computer, the sooner she could write her novel. Then she could move out and move on. And if she put enough work into it, she might be able to make a fair amount on the resale.

As she walked around the room, much to her surprise, Bethany found herself intrigued with the idea of spending time at the hut, perhaps even time enough to become accustomed to living there. And rather than thinking about a plot for her novel, she spent the afternoon pacing back and forth, considering possibilities for the hut, for the home she would make it into.

The focal point of the small house was the fireplace, a grand mass of smooth, rounded stones surrounded by the honey-gray, softly worn timbers of what Bethany assumed was the original flooring or, at the very least, an early floor. The effect of the two together was strangely comforting. She liked the idea that others had lit fires there and worn the floorboards until the grain was slightly ridged. And if she removed the walls from the small closet hidden under the slant of the staircase, there would be a space for appliances. And the whole area— the back quarter of the house stretching from the wall past the fireplace to the under-the-stairs area—would make a perfect kitchen and break- fast nook.

She could picture Peter warming his hands before the huge fireplace on the evenings when he'd come to visit her. She just had to keep believing that he was safely hiding somewhere, away from the danger. And that as soon as it was possible to get in touch with her, he would call her and she could convince him to move to this remote corner of Maine.

More ideas tumbled about in Bethany's mind as she drove to her room at McCleres' Bed-and-Breakfast. She decided to leave the laptop she'd use to write her novel at McCleres' while she remodeled, and she would extend the rent on her room for an indefinite amount of time, until the renovations were completed.

On the phone that night with Joseph, who had driven back to Boston once the weekend had ended, Bethany listed all of her remod- eling ideas. Although Joseph expressed concern about how such changes might affect the home's original layout, as well as the time her plans would take, Bethany persisted. Finally, Joseph reluctantly agreed that the closet could be taken out if the supporting studs were undisturbed. Despite his lack of enthusiasm, Bethany penciled KITCHEN NOOK in heavy, determined letters on her diagram of the hut. Then, in a moment of joyful enthusiasm, she wrote WINDOWS boldly across the walls of the main room and even added skylights.

In bed that night she reviewed her conversation with Joseph. There was something about the hut—or her resentment toward Amelia— that had given her the determination to actually behave obstinately with Joseph. In all her years with her grandmother, and with her own roommates, she had never demanded her way in anything. She felt elated about her newfound courage, before succumbing to the idea that perhaps she should feel a little bit guilty.

Why had Joseph reacted so skeptically anyway? Did he still see her as a quiet, shy child or adolescent? Whatever his reason, she decided to be more pleasant with him. After all, she wasn't going to impress him with her mature, gracious nature or her amiable personality by quarreling with him; besides, he held the purse strings to the hut. Possibly more. Had Amelia also given Joseph authority over her inheritance?

* * *

When Bethany mentioned her ideas for renovation to Alice McClere the next morning, Alice suggested that Bethany contact her nephew Scott Marshalle and his friend Andy, who always wanted odd jobs during the summer. The next day the two young men took out the hut's closet walls.

While they tore down the lath, with chunks of plaster spraying the area, Scott, whose blond hair was sun-bleached to a shade nearly as white as the chalky dust, tried vaulting over the railing at the bottom of the stairs. Suddenly he found himself on the floor in a heap of splintered spindles.

"Some of these probably need to be replaced or reinforced," he sheepishly advised Bethany after he apologized for the broken spindles and assured her he was unharmed.

"I'm glad we discovered those now." Bethany twisted a wobbling spindle. "Although Joseph is going to have a fit."

"We can at least put in temporary replacements for the worst ones and those missing at the top," Andy suggested as he pointed to a pile of two-by-fours left over from the closet demolition. "This could be dangerous if left as is."

It didn't take long to replace the weak spindles, but the once-pretentious staircase looked rather bereft.

Amid their laughter as they looked up at the strange mixture of spindles and supports, it occurred to Bethany that a different style railing could make the complete room seem cozier. And if she replaced the unevenly worn and stained flooring in the main room with a raised floor, she could create an illusion of two separate rooms, the kitchen area being several steps below the living room. The boys agreed and then decided to grab lunch together, satisfied with their day's work.

* * *

Joseph's attitude about remodeling the hut hadn't changed by the time he arrived the next Saturday. He frowned when he took Bethany's clipboard, glancing skeptically at her carefully drawn plans.

"You have a lot of changes here, Bethany."

Bethany's heart pounded and her hands were damp, but she spoke firmly. "You said I could change anything but the foundation and the fireplace."

"There's too much glass, not enough support for the roof," Joseph responded without looking up at her. "Could be dangerous."

"I want to see the ocean and the trees," Bethany explained. She wondered why Joseph was so against her making changes. After all, the money was hers to use at her disposal. *Does that bother him—that the money he used to control and make decisions about will soon be passed over to me?* she wondered briefly. She pushed the thought out of her head as silly. Joseph wasn't tied to Amelia's assets; he was her professional advisor and that was all. She tipped her face toward him with a hopeful smile and added, "I'd at least like to talk to a carpenter."

He looked at her thoughtfully. "I suppose an architectural firm could tell if this is feasible—if you really think you need to have it." He looked back at the clipboard. "Is there somewhere we can discuss it over lunch?"

The small Seacrest Café was pleasantly intimate, and by the time they had finished looking at the renovation plans, they were laughing and enjoying themselves.

After lunch and a stroll through the sand at the cove, Joseph accompanied Bethany through the hut, listening attentively to an enthusiastic review of her ideas. He finally agreed to have blueprints drawn up, with the stipulation that he be the one to consult with an architectural firm and deal with the contractors. On the weekends he would come up to check their progress.

Bethany protested.

"I don't mind," he stated firmly and then added a smile that made her feel like a blushing teenager. "That way I can check on you, too. You know, the hut isn't my only interest around here." He looked at her before hastily adding, "You *are* still my client."

Bethany wasn't thinking about the hut that night as she tried to sleep, and—she realized with a touch of guilt—she hadn't thought much about Peter that day either.

* * *

Bethany found it difficult to get up in time for church the next morning, especially since she had to drive up to the mainland early to meet with a counselor in the Relief Society presidency. But ever since her baptism nearly a year before, she had held to her resolve that she would attend her church meetings.

She hesitated to accept the call this sister extended her to be a visiting teacher, secretly dreading the social interactions that it would require. But she had agreed when the counselor mentioned that many of the sisters in the short-staffed ward had only one visiting teacher rather than the usual pair. Bethany knew she tended to be a recluse and that it would do her good to socialize more. While it was much easier to keep to herself, the ward seemed to need her, and she determined she would try to be a good visiting teacher.

Monday afternoon Bethany came back to the bed-and-breakfast exhausted. Getting ideas for fixing up the hut had been easy; gathering measurements and choosing colors was not. But there was more to it than that. She was beginning to consider how Peter would think of the changes she was planning for the hut, and thoughts of Peter always resulted in a nagging worry that tugged at her mind.

In the quiet of her room, Bethany envisioned Peter the last night she'd seen him, talking briefly about the travel his job required. Before that, he hadn't talked about his work unless she had queried him—except for one time after they'd been dating for several weeks, when he'd canceled plans for a dinner cruise because his work hours had changed.

"I'm afraid this won't be the only time this happens," he had explained. "I'm being promoted, so I'll be on call with a lot of traveling and erratic hours."

"You've never really told me much about your work," Bethany had commented.

"When I'm with you, I want to think about us, not work. If you really want to know, I guess you could say I study human interactions during extreme crisis. That's not the title the government gives it, but that's basically it."

"Meaning?"

"Well, let's just say I'm working with law enforcement agencies as they identify criminals. I watch the suspects for when they make an error—I've uncovered huge fraud schemes this way. Since a lot of the cases have judicial implications, client privileges and court gag orders are in effect so I can't talk about them."

"And that's why you've never talked about your work?'

"Smart girl," he had replied with a grin, then promptly changed the subject.

Brought back to the present by her reflection in the mirror, she squinted as she slid a brush through her hair, trying to remember the weeks that followed that conversation, just a few short months before.

There had been adjustments during the next several weeks. Peter had called instead of coming over most evenings. When he did come over, he usually fell asleep in the middle of a movie or TV program. Bethany soon found herself dreading his work-related calls that required him to leave immediately. A few times he hadn't even called to cancel their plans, and she had anxiously waited several hours for him before finally giving up and going to bed. His cell phone rang more and more frequently when they were together, and his assignments took longer, sometimes several days or more. Bethany could tell Peter was tired.

Peter hadn't said much about his job after that, other than one Monday after a long weekend away when he'd returned dispirited and exhausted. "Bethany, I'm not working with criminals or the government, exactly, I'm in—" he had blurted out. Then he stopped abruptly. "Bethany, you have to forget I said that. Promise. You won't be safe if you don't. I'm too tired to know what I am saying."

Standing now in her room at McCleres', Bethany thought about Peter's outburst that day, when he had come so close to telling her what he really did for a living. For about the millionth time, she wondered what could be so dangerous that he couldn't tell her the truth about it.

Bethany felt relieved when Alice tapped on the door and told her it was dinnertime, although suddenly she didn't feel like eating.

4

Bethany hummed as she danced around her home and carefully covered the new furniture with sheets. It was mid-July, and work on the hut was going well. The living room now shimmered with natural light from floor-to-ceiling windows and large skylights, and new spindles for the staircase lay covered by plastic and awaiting installment.

That left the kitchen nook and the bedroom loft.

Bethany planned to knock out the center, non-supporting section of the front wall of the loft, which overlooked the living room. The solid wall of the loft would be replaced with louvered doors that she could open to let in the light from her new windows. Since she'd come up with the idea after the approval of the other plans, and knowing Joseph's cautious nature, she'd not included him in her project. With no major carpentry projects in progress, she didn't expect Joseph to come for the weekend. She wanted the hut to herself.

Perhaps Joseph still considered her unable to make major decisions on her own, but Bethany was feeling more secure each day. Remembering the day of Scott and Andy's attack on the downstairs closet wall, she decided to take matters into her own hands. One day while the contractor was at the hut, she questioned him about the advisability of removing the wall and inserting louvers.

"Well, let's take a look, should we?" he said. "Okay, the first thing we can rule out in this wall is plumbing. There's none up here in this loft. Now, then, we'd better check on the electricity."

They soon determined that the two outlets in the loft and the single light fixture were all running off the same circuit—and none of the wiring went through the wall in question. Reassured, Bethany continued planning.

Bethany took the hammer and wrecking bar out of a toolbox under the staircase. She carried the tools to the top of the staircase and gave the plaster a blow. The hammer head sank only halfway into the wall. After hesitating just a moment, she thought of Amelia, their confusing relationship, and all that her silence had put Bethany through—and she hit the wall again. Harder.

She was rewarded by a splintering squeak as a crack spread through the wall and chunks began falling. Bethany felt a surge of satisfaction as she pulled the nails from the two-by-fours, enjoying the screech as the metal resisted her strength. Then she pulled on narrow strips of lath, watching pieces of plaster flip through the air.

It was easy to pull the wall down, but it seemed impossible to bundle the baseboard and the narrow strips of lath without having ends stick out in all directions. She reshuffled the sticks, trying to fit them through the bedroom doorway, but instead found herself stuck between the doorframe and the wood she held. With an impatient shove, she forced her load through the door and out between the two railings that skirted the staircase.

It wasn't until Bethany felt the pile of rubble shifting underneath her feet that she realized the stairs were cluttered with wobbly chunks of plaster, and her weight was creating a slide. Entangled with the strips of wood, she recognized she was in danger of a treacherous ride down the staircase. She was tipping down, tilted toward the left banister, her load of debris knocking the rails on her sides as she moved. She saw the banister wobbling, and she tried desperately to regain her balance, but the banister snapped and fell to the floor. Now nothing separated her from a similar fall.

She frantically opened her hand beneath the scraps of wood so she could grab at the spindles and catch herself, but the load of sticks, freed from her grasp, fanned out even more, hitting the spindles and sending them flying.

Suddenly, Bethany felt a jolt as the sticks butted against solid wood. The pieces of lumber she held caught between a reinforced two-by-four on one side and a sturdy spindle on the other side of the staircase. Fearing they would also rip loose, she closed her eyes. But the spindles held firmly and she was safe.

Bethany gingerly stepped through the chunks of plaster on the stairs to solid footing. Her legs were shaky as she stood looking around her.

She slowly rearranged the boards, not caring when some slipped out of her grasp and clattered onto the kitchen floor. Then she cautiously carried the rest down the remaining stairs and placed them in a pile at the bottom of the steps. It seemed impossible that she had only slid down half a dozen steps and that, other than piles of plaster and lath covering the steps and the chalk particles floating through the air, the room seemed quiet and normal.

Glancing down at the floor beneath the staircase, she saw the bar and spindles from the broken left banister. It was then that she hunched forward with her hands crossed protectively over her chest. She could see that the bottom of each spindle was sawed almost all the way through.

Bethany sat down on the chalky sheet that covered her love seat, her arms hugging her stomach.

How could this have happened? Certainly, no one would purposefully create such a hazard, unless . . . Bethany forced the fear from her thoughts. Surely there was no connection between the dismantled spindles and the strange warning from Peter—the voice mail that made no sense. She didn't know anything about Peter's investigations, and, at his request, she hadn't told anyone that he'd contacted her since his disappearance. There was no reason for someone to harm her, and even if someone wanted to get at Peter through her, she didn't know where Peter was. Obviously, hurting her wouldn't help anyone find him.

Slowly Bethany relaxed, realizing that anyone seriously trying to injure her would have made certain it happened, and she would not have been able to sit there worrying. Undoubtedly, the carpenters were preparing to replace the spindles and ran out of time. It was just a simple oversight. Still, she should have been warned that the spindles were loose.

If she told Joseph, he would be upset and insist on getting a different crew, which, of course, would delay the work for weeks.

Bethany would take care of the problem with the contractor herself. She took a shaky breath and looked around the room.

Fragments of lath, plaster, and banister covered the floor of the dining area, and a film of fine, chalky white lay over everything. She started cleaning, the broom stirring up clouds of dust. Eventually, she found a dustpan and began scooping up the mess.

Bethany was completely covered with dust and holding a loaded dustpan when Joseph knocked on the door she'd left open for ventilation. She jumped, tipping the debris back onto the floor in a cascade of swirling particles that caught in her nose and throat, sending her into a fit of sneezing.

Joseph's expression turned from astonishment to amusement as he began laughing in a deep, satisfying rumble that was unfamiliar to Bethany.

"I wasn't expecting you this weekend!" she said indignantly, once she could speak. She grabbed at a rag and rubbed her white hands as she waited for him to chide her.

Joseph, looking strangely casual in dark blue Levi's and canvas shoes, grinned at her outburst. "What is all of this?" he asked as he gingerly stepped across the layer of white dust. He looked up the stairs toward the loft.

"I'm changing the bedroom," Bethany explained as she pointed to the opening that revealed the dusty room at the top of the stairs. With all the debris, Joseph didn't notice the missing section of banister.

"Why didn't you let the carpenters do it? That's why we pay them." He looked at her, shaking his head as he laughed.

"I wanted to do something by myself," she retorted defensively as she looked down at her dusty hands and clothes. Then she laughed. "I love it!"

Joseph looked around the room, then down at himself. His shirt was open at the collar, his tie missing, but he still had his cuffs buttoned securely at the wrists of the long sleeves. Despite his grin, he hesitated when he asked, "I don't suppose you could use some help?" He bent down and carefully picked up a piece of lath and put it in the garbage can.

The idea of Joseph covered with white grime seemed totally incongruent to Bethany, but then so was the laugh she'd just heard.

She couldn't resist. "Sure. Have a dustpan." To her amazement—and amusement—he proved quite adept at shoveling the debris and getting it all over himself.

Most of the dust was cleaned up when he put down the broom and glanced up the stairs where white powder still filtered through the sunlight. He looked over at Bethany, who held her breath, waiting for him to ask about the banister.

"Strangely enough, my plans for today didn't include an encounter with a white avalanche," he commented wryly as he rubbed his chalky hands on his pants. "I brought things for a picnic on the cove, and my swimming trunks for a swim. Maybe we could relax for a while, then drive up to get those doors. I assume you plan to replace the wall with something—louvers, I suppose. We've got plenty of time. I've got a room at McCleres' for the night."

Bethany was delighted, both with his attitude and with the prospect of spending more time together. There was something about the way he looked, a get-down-in-the-dirt-and-do-this-thing expression so unlike him she couldn't help smiling. She could tell he liked being a clandestine comrade in this Saturday forget-the-rules exercise.

Was Joseph romantically interested in her? Something about the way he looked at her lately made her wonder. Although the thought excited her, she also wanted to be true to Peter. But then again, it was not as if they were formally exclusive. Or were they? Silently mulling over what to do about her divided interest, she pushed the dilemma out of her mind with her usual indecisiveness, slipped on her flip-flops, and headed out the door behind Joseph.

* * *

It was late afternoon when Bethany and Joseph returned from the hardware store. As they put the doors by the fireplace, Joseph noticed the box that Bethany had set aside to stow the objects she had found as she cleared the old closet.

"I hoped there would be more," she remarked as she handed him a small, heavy iron from a box by the fireplace and watched him study it before he put it on the mantel and picked up a piece of pottery.

He looked up from the pottery and saw her expression.

"Something wrong?"

"No, no," she answered hastily. "I was just thinking how different you are today, you know, standing there in Levi's looking at antique irons." She shrugged. "You don't seem like Joseph."

"Is that good or bad?" he wondered, looking at her with a teasing grin as she handed him a very old, misshapen bowl, a piece with nearly the same coloring as the mortar of the fireplace.

"I don't know," she replied self-consciously. "I'm not sure what Amelia would say."

"Does that matter?" He took the bowl before looking her squarely in the eyes. "I don't think she would be surprised. You know, you're not the teenager I remember either." He put the bowl down on the mantel and turned to her. He seemed uncomfortable. "Uh . . ."

Bethany looked up at him expectantly.

"Oh, never mind."

He picked up the bowl again and examined it carefully. "Look at that." He pointed to an impression on the back of the bowl. "This was scratched into the clay before the piece was fired. It must've been somebody's mark." He held it out to her. "Can you make it out?" He wiped the bottom of the bowl with a handkerchief he retrieved from his pocket.

"I can't tell what it is," Bethany said, relieved by the change in the conversation but aware that he was close behind her as she moved toward the window. "It looks like two straight lines—or three." Bethany pointed between the deeper marks to a line that angled down from the top of the first line. "I've seen that mark somewhere . . . oh, I remember now . . . the fireplace when they cleaned it!"

Still aware of his closeness, she showed Joseph the faint indentations on the mortar by the hearthstone. It was obvious that the two symbols represented the same thing—though the impression in the fireplace included additional marks—but it was impossible to read the scratching.

"I wonder . . ." Bethany mused. "There's an old shed built against the rock wall in the back. I couldn't get the door open, but we might find more out there."

With Joseph following her, Bethany made her way through the grass toward the shed.

"I wonder why anyone would build a rock wall out here," he commented as he gazed at the stones. "With the pines so thick you can't even see more than a couple of feet into the trees, let alone get through them. By the way, watch out for all the poison ivy." He pointed to a small patch of the plant and turned to Bethany, adding, "Be careful. You can get a rash by touching the twigs, even in the winter."

After several minutes, Joseph scraped enough dirt off the gnarled roots blocking the shed's old door that they were able to swing it open. Finding that it merely contained old gardening equipment and supplies, Bethany was disappointed.

Joseph picked up a hoe worn thin by the rocky soil and observed, "Someone has used this a lot more than I used the one I had in my youth." He moved to her, and she felt the edge of his sleeve touch her arm.

"You mean you used to hoe?"

"Sure," he grinned. "I was raised on a farm in upstate New York." He laughed at her expression. "You're surprised!"

"I've never thought of you as anything but Amelia's attorney."

"That's how you've always known me, but I did have a childhood, you know. And Amelia needed an attorney long before I started practicing. When I was younger my Uncle Laramie was the Carlisle family attorney. He was with Amelia when she picked you up at the airport. By the way, Amelia was always saddened that this was when she finally learned your name." Joseph paused for a moment and gently held Bethany's gaze. Then he continued, "Uncle Laramie's also the one who filled out your adoption papers for Amelia. Laramie liked me even after my parents got tired of my shenanigans, and he convinced me to go to law school. He eventually took me on as a partner, and I replaced him when he retired."

Joseph returned the hoe with the other equipment and stepped to the back of the shed. Above a workbench on one side of the wall were container-filled shelves, and Joseph identified several of the faded labels as garden fertilizers.

Bethany reached into a box. "Why would anyone store candles here?"

"The same reason they left a key." Joseph pointed to a nail nearly hidden by the box, shaking his head at the random items left within the shed. "Obviously the previous owners were not too careful about clearing all their items out."

The sun was setting by the time Joseph opened the door of the Jeep for Bethany, grimacing as he pulled on the door handle. "Amelia sure knew how to keep a person humble, didn't she?"

Bethany climbed into the driver's seat and put the key in the ignition while she waited for him to close the door.

He stood beside the footboard looking in at her. "Bethany, before you go, I need to talk to you. As your attorney there are some legal matters I think we should discuss."

She waited for Joseph to speak, but he seemed hesitant, so she prodded lightly. "What do you, as my attorney, need to tell me?"

Joseph looked at her nervously. "Well, as your attorney there are certain regulations that restrict my, uh . . . my . . . well, let's say, the way I interact with you."

Bethany was puzzled.

"You know, like we said earlier, you are starting to see me in a way you never have before—and I guess I'm seeing you in a different light as well. Anyway, as your legal counselor, I have to tell you that I, uh . . . well . . . legally, I have to tell you that I'm not here . . . well, let me rephrase that . . . I would *like* to see you not as your attorney or even as a family friend—although I want to remain both—but on a more personal basis. If you wouldn't mind, or rather, if you'd like, I'd like to come up to see you, uh, to get to know you a little better. If that's all right with you?"

"You mean . . . ?"

"To take you places, to find out what we have in common. You're a beautiful woman, and you're interesting and intelligent. As your lawyer, I'm obligated to admit that I'm not seeing you as a client—or not *just* as a client. Is that all right?"

"Sure," Bethany answered, hoping that he couldn't see her blush. "I like that idea."

Joseph reluctantly looked down at his watched and sighed. "Time passes too quickly with you, Bethany. I'm afraid I've kept you out too late already." Realizing he had come in a separate car, he suggested, "Why don't I just follow behind you down to the bed-and-breakfast since I have a room there tonight myself."

After he shut her door, Bethany watched in her rearview mirror as the lights on his BMW flipped on. As she navigated the road's twists and turns and watched his headlights follow behind her, she felt a sweet happiness. Her gentle excitement increased as she took a deep breath and realized, *Joseph feels this too.*

* * *

That night as Bethany changed into her pajamas, she thought about Joseph—not Joseph the attorney as she'd known him ever since her senior year in high school when he began working for her grandmother, but Joseph the appealing man who seemed to have more than a passing interest in her. She remembered the first time she'd regarded him as anything other than Amelia's legal advisor—it was during her second year of undergraduate studies.

"Hello, Bethany. This is Joseph." The telephone call was certainly nothing out of the ordinary. He frequently called to check on her needs and relay information from Amelia. "Hey, I'll be in Boston two weeks from Thursday, and I'd like to take you to dinner while I'm there. I hope this gives you enough notice. What do you think?"

"Sure, I'd love to go," she said without hesitation, even though she felt torn. She enjoyed dining out with him and she didn't want to seem ungrateful, but she had a difficult final scheduled the next morning. She'd have to squeeze some extra studying in before he came.

"Oh, Joseph," Bethany said in amazement as they entered the candlelit restaurant and were met by the maître d'. The decor was a study in understated elegance, and Bethany was amazed with the beauty of the place.

Dinner had progressed through the first two courses when Joseph got an important business call, which he stepped outside to take care of. Because there had been no extra time to study earlier as she had hoped, before Bethany had left for dinner she'd stuffed her study notes in her purse. Joseph's absence gave her the perfect time to glance through them. The lights were dim so she slid the papers closer to the candles, not noticing when an edge caught fire.

"Bethany, what are you doing?" Joseph demanded as he ran back to their table, jerking the paper away from her and dousing its edge into her ice water. Her singed study notes emitted the faint odor of smoke, causing their waiter to rush over, ready to throw a full pitcher of ice water on the table. Already nervous about the test, she had been thoroughly shaken by the commotion and had momentarily gulped back tears before taking a breath and forcing herself to laugh. Then she couldn't stop herself from laughing. Joseph had looked at her questioningly, but then he too began a quiet chuckle that had mixed with her laughter and calmed her mood.

They ended up having a wonderful evening together, laughing as friends and enjoying one another, legal issues concerning Amelia never even coming up. As they walked from the restaurant later that evening, she took his arm. The gesture felt not only comfortable but natural. Although this was the first time she remembered seeing Joseph as a true friend rather than merely a professional acquaintance, she never imagined that her grandmother's mature attorney would take a romantic interest in her—even if there was only about an eight-year difference between them.

After Joseph took her home, however, as Bethany replayed the evening's events, she realized that developing any notions of a relationship between them would only be a waste of time and make their professional relationship awkward.

And yet here she was nearly five years later, finding herself wondering about Joseph all over again.

* * *

The next morning after slipping on a lightweight, pale blue sweater and a patterned skirt, Bethany brushed her hair in long strokes, her mind topsy-turvy. She took a deep breath as she turned from the mirror and nervously walked down the stairs to the inn's living room.

Joseph sat in the front room reading *Curious George* to Joshua, the McClere toddler, who rested contentedly in his lap, forgetting to suck the thumb he held in his mouth. Joseph looked up as Bethany approached.

"Breakfast is being served, but we've already eaten. Is it all right if I go to church with you?"

"Sure," Bethany agreed. "I didn't know you were a churchgoer, especially not to Latter-day Saint meetings." She suddenly realized that she hadn't explained to Joseph about joining the Church in the past year.

"I'm generally not, but I knew you'd inquired about church meetings, so I came prepared with a suit."

Bethany tried not to show her surprise; Joseph had not come just to inspect the hut or to relax on the beach. He had planned to be with her and to go to church. That was very different from her experience with Peter.

She had known Peter only a few days before she mentioned the Church to him. He had looked puzzled at the designation "LDS" until she had substituted the term "Mormon" for it. She asked if he would like to go to meetings the next Sunday, and for several weeks he had put it off, but then one Sunday morning he had picked her up looking almost like an elder ready to enter the Missionary Training Center. After that, he attended meetings with her most Sundays, and he said he wanted to take the missionary lessons. Still, Bethany had wondered how serious he was. He always seemed to have something else scheduled when the missionaries mentioned a time to get together, but his wittily phrased declines generally left the missionaries chuckling, and she had been afraid he would lose interest if she pushed him.

* * *

Sunday-morning tourist traffic in a village near Walachias slowed Joseph and Bethany's drive from the island to the mainland chapel. As they finally entered the building, the organist was playing the prelude as Dr. Noel, his graying hair parted neatly above his rounding face, greeted them at the chapel doors with a vigorous handshake. Although Bethany had moved to the area only the month before, Dr. Noel was already assigned as her home teacher. Alice's children had appeared uncommonly shy a few days back when their family doctor came home teaching at the bed-and-breakfast.

Bethany wondered what Joseph's response would be to the down-to-earth atmosphere and a couple of children squirming through the last fifteen minutes of sacrament meeting. She also worried that the three-hour block would be a problem.

On the drive back to Seacrest, Joseph said the meetings were quite enlightening and that sacrament meeting had been interesting despite, or maybe because of, the excess commotion.

"You know, it takes a lot of patience to try to manage kids like that. My parents didn't take us to church, but when we'd go to Grandma's all the grandkids went. Of course, we entertained ourselves any way we could think of except by listening to the sermon, so Grandma came up with a strategy. Afterward at dinner, the best-behaved grandchild got dessert first and got to choose the dessert for the next Sunday. The last thing she'd do before shepherding us out of the house to church was to march us past the pie or cake she was cooling to give us a good whiff." He chuckled. "She was quite the lady."

"It sounds like it," Bethany responded, thinking of her own religious upbringing—sitting stiffly beside Amelia at church.

"You know, Amelia was a lot like her," Joseph continued. "When there was a problem, she didn't sit around and wait for it to solve itself. She dug in and came up with a solution. Usually it was a pretty good one."

Joseph's comment stoked Bethany's curiosity—he seemed to be talking about a woman very different from the one she remembered.

"What was Amelia like when you first met her?"

"The first impression I had of Amelia was that, though she was not necessarily beautiful, she was gracious and lovely. Laramie told me that she sometimes came off as cold and unfeeling because she simply didn't allow her emotions to surface, but that didn't bother me. She was an excellent organizer, and her brusque personality gave her an advantage when it came to collecting funds or favors—it was very, very difficult to tell her no."

"Was she hard to work for?"

"At first she was intimidating and seemed inflexible, but when she decided to do something, she did it wholeheartedly. She saw things in black or white with no variations. Later, when she started discussing more of her personal problems with me, I began to feel like family. I had gotten out of contact with my folks, but there was always Amelia. I felt like I was part of her family."

Bethany sat quietly. It seemed ironic that Joseph would feel he was part of Amelia's family, while she, Amelia's true family, felt so alone.

5

The Jeep was not fast or pretty, but it did get Bethany where she needed to go, and she was determined to keep it running, even though Steve—Alice's tall, blond husband—and Scott teased her about it regularly. She had it thoroughly checked, so she was baffled one night to find that one of the headlights was flickering. Remembering the curve-filled road to Seacrest, she pulled into the service station she frequented. It didn't take the mechanic long to pop out the light fixture and reconnect a loose wire. But as he began to walk toward the station, he stopped at the front passenger tire and looked at Bethany quizzically.

"Who's the last one to change that tire for you? It better not've been one of my guys or he's looking for a new job!"

Bethany looked at the tire, which looked fine to her until the mechanic pointed to the lug nuts. He gently tapped one. The metal cylinder slowly rolled toward the end of the screw and, with a few more taps, fell off. The mechanic picked up a lug wrench.

"A couple of miles with lug nuts that loose and you'd have been watching that tire roll down the road in front of you! Not one of them nuts on that tire was on solid!"

As he checked the rest of the tires, Bethany assured him that the tire had not been changed at his station. She slowly pulled back onto the road, her hands trembling. As soon as she was out of sight of the service station, she pulled onto a side street and locked the doors, too upset to drive. The teenage apprentice at the service station hadn't changed her tires, but he had checked them the week before, and she'd watched him as he fit the wrench on each lug nut and tightened it. His face red with exertion, he'd barely been able to move any of the lug nuts. No one had touched the tires since, at least as far as Bethany knew. And why would all the lug nuts on one tire be loose and the nuts on the rest of the tires be tight?

Had someone tampered with her tire? And if so, who and why?

She had no reason to suspect anyone would want to frighten or harm her. Very few people in Seacrest knew her and everyone there seemed friendly. It had undoubtedly been a teenage prank, a random act brought on by too much time with too little to do. And she would soon be able to move into Faunce Cove anyway, away from bored kids who lived closer to town.

Suddenly an image of the broken spindles came into Bethany's mind and the last-minute warning Peter gave her during his cryptic voice mail, "Try to leave, Bethany. Go somewhere secluded." She hadn't remembered those exact words until now, and for a moment she wondered if the banister incident and the loose lug nuts had anything in common. But she came back to the same question—why would Peter's job put her in danger?

Bethany sighed in frustration. She was sure that it was just her overactive "writer's imagination" trying to connect dots that weren't even there. She was just overanxious about Peter's absence—that was all it was. Besides, if Peter really felt it best that she go somewhere secluded, there were few places more isolated than the hut.

* * *

Even though Bethany had persuaded herself the tire incident was a prank, it still dampened her mood, and she felt out-of-sorts when Joseph came up for the weekend. He found her on edge and irritable. She didn't mind when he checked the Jeep's brake fluid, but when he insisted on checking the oil too, she nearly asked if he didn't trust her to take care of the Jeep herself. She resisted the defiant comment, reminding herself that he had always taken care of her like a brother, and he was not used to her new independence.

Joseph suggested that they take a drive in his BMW, and they ended up at a shop filled with unique tourist curios. While Bethany stopped to look at the kitchen gadgets, Joseph wandered to the camping gear section. She felt relieved to have a moment alone.

It had been fun to learn to cook with Alice. Bethany's first attempt at kneading bread covered her with flour and kept Alice's twins laughing, but later no one suspected that Bethany had made the Sunday dinner rolls. During her temporary stay at the inn, she had learned to fry chicken and brown a pot roast, then make gravy so savory no one noticed the occasional lump. She had hulled strawberries, podded peas, snapped beans, and sorted blueberries. She was looking forward to cooking at the hut.

Bethany spent several minutes looking at the assortment of unique cooking utensils the store offered. Then she chose a potato peeler with a delicately flowered ceramic handle and took it to the register.

The clerk had already scanned the bar code when Joseph picked up the peeler and began examining it.

"This blade isn't fastened into the handle very well. Do you really want this?" he asked before he walked back to the kitchen section and retrieved a different style of peeler, while the line of customers behind them began to grow.

The clerk eyed Bethany questioningly. Bethany watched, embarrassed, as Joseph placed the second peeler on the counter.

"No reason a woman can't have two potato peelers," he explained, smiling at the clerk as he paid for them. Guiding Bethany toward the doorway with his hand on her back, he said proudly, "Now you've got a good peeler."

"I already have one." She could not keep a hint of annoyance out of her voice. "I want this for decoration."

"Why didn't you tell me?"

Bethany was silent, biting back the question she wanted to ask. *Can't I buy a potato peeler without having to explain it to you?*

"If I'd known I would have bought the whole rack. You'd have a peeler for apples and a peeler for carrots, turnips, rutabagas . . ."

"What?"

"Rutabagas, like turnips. A peeler for rutabagas and rhubarb and beets . . ."

"You can't peel beets with a peeler. You have to boil them until their skins slide off. Then you slice them into vinegar and spices."

"And since when did you become such an expert?" he quizzed with a grin.

"And since when shouldn't I be?" she countered with more emotion than she had planned. "Actually, Alice is a great teacher," she added with a hint of a smile.

"Did she teach you that peelers aren't worth quarreling about?" he asked.

"It isn't the peeler as much as . . . I felt embarrassed. I don't know. You seem to be an expert about everything, even rhubarb peelers."

There was a pause. "And I treat you as though you aren't? I'm sorry, Bethany. I didn't mean to belittle you. I really think you're doing a great job with the hut, and you've learned a lot from Alice. But," his tone changed, "you really don't need to peel rhubarb!"

"Oh!" she cried, trying to playfully free her hand from his. She relaxed against the seat as they drove toward Seacrest, trying to make sense of her thoughts. *Why was I so annoyed? He was only trying to help,* she thought as she looked up at his profile. *After all, he didn't have to go shopping with me. It's just . . . sometimes I feel like he hovers over me, like I can't—or he won't let me—make choices on my own.* Bethany realized for the first time how much this move was changing her. She was making her own decisions, voicing her own opinion, and standing on her own two feet. She briefly wondered if this was what Amelia had in mind when she bought the hut, then tucked these new thoughts away to be pondered later as they pulled up to the McCleres' inn.

Joshua was standing on the porch bouncing a small rubber ball. He tossed it to Joseph with a giggle. Joseph caught the ball as Joshua shyly slid down the steps and ran toward the sandpile. Alice watched with a smile.

"Joshua doesn't generally take to non-family. You two are the only ones he'll stay with in the same room. I don't know what you do, Joseph, but he considers you right up there!"

"It's just that we have similar taste in literature!" Joseph laughed and then turned to Bethany. "I'm going to get the things out of the car."

Bethany was not aware that Alice was looking at her as she watched Joseph go.

"I think someone else considers him right up there, too."

* * *

As Bethany and Joseph drove back from an auction in Walachiasport the next weekend, Joseph commented on her silence.

"Bethany," Joseph encouraged, "there is something bothering you, and that bothers me."

"It's nothing," she hurriedly assured him.

"Tell me." He feigned shock as he looked at her. "Or Bethany, is there another man?" He grinned.

"Oh, Joseph!" she exclaimed in exasperation, emphasizing that really wasn't it. Although she still worried about Peter and felt a twinge of guilt about her budding relationship with Joseph in his absence, spending time with Joseph had given her a chance to compare the two and to realize that she and Peter had never really communicated about anything important. She had decided that while she would remain Peter's friend once he returned, it was Joseph who she really cared about. Still, Joseph sometimes pried more than she liked, and this was one of those times.

"If it's not another man, why won't you tell me?" he teased, apparently trying to cheer her.

"It might be dangerous for you."

"Dangerous?" Joseph's response was nearly cavalier. "Not too many people threaten a guy as big as I am. Where is this danger going to come from anyway?" He sobered at her expression and demanded impatiently, "Bethany, tell me what's going on."

She told him about the recent problems with the Jeep—the detached wire on the headlight and the loose lug nuts on one tire. Then she sat silently, wondering if Joseph thought she was overreacting.

"Has there been anything else? Have you felt like someone was watching you or stalking you?"

"No, not really. I've actually felt very safe—and when I'm running errands around town, I haven't had any problems with anyone."

Joseph listened attentively, his eyes unreadable in a pensive squint as they drove through Walachias, then down the familiar road to Seacrest.

"Anything else that has made you wonder?" he queried.

Bethany thought about the spindles on the staircase. The contractor couldn't remember assigning the job to anyone, but there had been a lot of men around. Undoubtedly, the spindles had been loosened as a result of miscommunication, not anything sinister. If she told Joseph and he took her seriously, he would be upset that she hadn't told him earlier, and he would probably blame the contractor.

"No." It was more a nod than a word.

"You know, I think the stuff with the Jeep is just par for the course with an old vehicle like that. I don't think there's anything to worry about."

His reply made sense and Bethany relaxed as she watched the road wind toward Seacrest. It was nice to cuddle against Joseph's shoulder and to feel so protected.

* * *

Bethany got a surprise phone call from Kim that evening and was excited to hear from her old roommate. They had not communicated since graduation when Bethany had moved to Faunce Cove, and Kim to San Francisco with a job offer. Although Bethany didn't feel really close to Kim—she was too much of a loner for that—she was still grateful to have even a distant girlfriend to keep up with from time to time. Kim asked about Joseph, and as Bethany gushed about how much she enjoyed spending time with him, she forgot all about the lug nuts and the headlight.

"I always thought he was nice when he took you to dinner," Kim replied happily. "I guess Dee wasn't the only one in our apartment who wanted to get to know him better! I think you sound happier with him than you did with Peter, and he seems better for you, too. Peter made you laugh, but Joseph just seems more mature and stable."

Joseph was maybe more mature, Bethany thought after she'd hung up, but the problem was that she still couldn't consider marriage outside of the temple, and Joseph wasn't showing any real interest in the Church. He seemed to enjoy the meetings and the people, and he talked about taking the missionary lessons. But, like Peter, he kept putting them off. Joseph didn't drink coffee in front of her, but she had noticed discarded coffee cups in his car's trash container. Even more telling, however, was that he had not moved the bookmark in his Book of Mormon since she had given it to him that first Sunday they'd attended church together. There would be no baptism, much less temple marriage, unless he progressed—and Bethany would not consider getting truly serious until that happened.

Bethany felt frustrated. She loved the concept of eternal families and longed to be a part of one with a good priesthood holder— possibly Joseph if he joined the Church. Even without a family here and now, she'd wanted to at least be sealed to someone; she thought back to her previous dreams of being sealed to her parents and Amelia, but her efforts and prayers to feel at peace about Amelia seemed futile. She wondered if she were losing her hope for ever being a part of an eternal family, and hated to lose the enthusiasm she had felt when she'd first joined the Church.

After her baptism a year ago, Bethany had begun praying for opportunities to tell Amelia about the Church, and Amelia, in turn, had suddenly seemed more aware of Bethany. That's when Amelia invited her to share the summer with her, and Bethany planned to share the religion she had joined. Many times Bethany had pictured them together, pausing over a partially filled vase of flowers, Amelia asking her about her conversion or the two intently discussing some gospel principle.

It had been over two years since she had dialed the number on the television screen for a copy of the Bible and had met with the missionaries. She loved the restored gospel—especially the concept of eternal families. As a member of The Church of Jesus Christ of Latter-day Saints, she could have the opportunity to be a part of her family forever.

Of course, her roommates—not members of the LDS Church— didn't understand. Bethany remembered the day after the missionaries had taught her about eternal families, when she'd brought up the new concept with her roommates. Stretched out on the floor working over her interior design assignments, Kim barely looked up long enough to say that families sealed together forever sounded strange. Dee had made a face as she pulled her long, blond hair into a braid. Yet in her typical fashion she then said she would like to hear more about it, but from the two good-looking missionaries rather than from Bethany.

A month later when Bethany announced that she was going to be baptized, Dee had been equally blunt. "Don't Mormons have all sorts of rules about drinking and smoking and what you can do on dates?

Isn't that going to turn guys off? You'll never go out unless someone is looking for a second wife!"

"I'm not sure that a girl should choose her religion by the number of dates she thinks it will get her," Kim said in defense of Bethany.

Later, when Dee left for a movie, Kim brought up the subject again. "Have you really thought through this baptism thing? We've talked about how we're both pretty much loners and how you tend to cater to people." Kim paused gently for a moment, then continued, "I remember a conversation once when you told me that you've always been too busy trying to please your grandmother to do anything you really wanted for yourself. And that whenever you get mad about something, you avoid dealing with it by getting involved in some new project. Are you sure you're not doing this just to be a part of a group or to have something to do—some new project—after you graduate, or to have something to tell Amelia?"

Bethany had talked enough with Kim during their time as roommates to respect her opinion and perceptions. Kim, five years older than Bethany, had learned a lot about people in the various jobs she'd held between graduating from college and returning to graduate school. Bethany considered Kim's comment and her own feelings about the Church before replying.

"I know I've never been really confident, and a lot of the time I seem wishy-washy, but I'm sure I want to be a member of the Church. It's not about being in a group or being bored."

Kim had frowned thoughtfully. "I know you like the members, but I'd hate to see you join expecting to get something you might not get. You keep talking about an eternal family. Can anyone actually give you a family or guarantee that you'll have one after you die?"

"Well, the missionaries said it depends on my righteousness and whether my family chooses to accept the gospel and want to be together as a family."

"That's what I mean. If Amelia ignores you and never talked about your parents all your life, why would she suddenly want to be with you and them after you're all dead?"

Kim's frank observation had stung Bethany. From the time she'd been old enough to recognize Amelia's neglect, she had rationalized it away by telling herself that Amelia had been too busy with her corporations to think about a child. She had never considered that Amelia might have purposely chosen to ignore her.

Now, as Bethany thought about Amelia since her death, she wanted to believe in that promise of an eternal family. And yet, after remembering what Kim had observed about Amelia's actions while she was alive, it was hard to even consider it a possibility.

* * *

During Bethany's temporary stay at the inn, she tried to at least begin to write. She pulled her computer from its case and set it up on a card table Alice had lent her, anticipating a good start to her novel before she moved into the hut.

It didn't happen. On her hard drive, Bethany had six folders for novels—outlines of mystery plots, and even a couple of titles for historical novels—but when it came down to actually writing, she couldn't seem to concentrate. Hot, humid August afternoons became sparkling blue September mornings, but still her daily routine rarely involved her computer.

Perhaps, she thought, *I am still too preoccupied.* In addition to her relationship with Joseph and her concerns about Peter, she was also spending a lot of time thinking about Amelia.

One evening after a casual dinner with the McCleres, Bethany escaped to the backyard orchard and the swing, hoping the soft breeze floating toward the ocean would inspire her to write. She always seemed to feel edgy these days unless she was at the hut. She couldn't concentrate to write or read; all she wanted was to be alone or to sleep.

"Mind if I join you?" Bethany turned toward Alice's cheerful voice. "The kids are ready for bed so I decided to take a walk."

"I came for inspiration. I can't seem to get motivated to write these days."

"I noticed you haven't been eating a lot. Are you feeling okay?" Alice sat down on the grass as she looked up at Bethany.

"Oh, I'm fine. Just been doing a lot of thinking lately. Maybe too much."

"Thinking about a certain handsome attorney?" Alice asked with raised eyebrows and a grin.

"Maybe," Bethany answered with a slight smile before the frown returned to her eyes. "But more about my grandmother and her death. It's strange . . . in some ways I feel so much stronger since I moved here—making my own decisions and really being me, yet in other ways, as I think about my grandmother and my relationship with her, I feel so mixed up and unable to cope."

Bethany was suddenly interrupted by Judith's voice, which came from near the house. "Hey, Alice. Are you out there?"

"Come on out," Alice called to her sister. "We're by the swing." She looked at Bethany. "I hope you don't mind if Judith joins us."

"No, of course not," Bethany replied as Judith walked across the yard, her sandals swinging from her hand. She sat down on the grass beside Alice.

"Hope I'm not interrupting."

"I was just complaining," Bethany confessed.

"Not complaining. You're grieving," Alice assured her. "We lost our mother in a car accident when we were teenagers and we know about grieving. You're mourning."

The thought that she might be mourning for Amelia struck Bethany with surprise. She considered it briefly. "Actually, I don't think it is grieving. I'm just cranky and moody. Sometimes it's hard to concentrate. I'm angry about some of the things my grandmother did. I'm not really thinking about her death or that she is gone."

"You're grieving," Judith said with conviction and a nod.

"Do you remember when we were like that?" Alice asked Judith.

"Do I remember? How could I forget you lying on the bed, crying day after day? Sometimes you said you were crying about Mom, other times school, doing dishes . . ."

"And all of a sudden *you* started running around with the school rowdies." Alice looked at Bethany with a twisted grin. "And I really didn't cry that much," she defended herself.

"Well, talk about not being able to concentrate, you forgot to bring your homework from school, then you forgot to do it, then you forgot to take it back." Judith chuckled as she leaned back on her arms on the lawn. "And boy, when I reminded you, would you get mad!"

"Well, you deserved it. You and all those kids you ran around with trying to make trouble." Alice made a face at Judith as they laughed.

"That's grieving?" Bethany questioned. "I mean, crying, sure. But forgetting and getting mad?"

"And don't forget, doing crazy, unpredictable things," Alice added, looking at Judith.

"Oh, Bethany, you should have seen our aunts," Judith responded. "One of them acted like nothing had happened. She went to a dance after the wake. One of them went to the cemetery every day and wrote letters to Mom besides. Grandma, a devout Christian until the end, went to church to pray for Mom all the time. And Dad would stop in the middle of work and just stand there thinking."

"Were they ever able get over it and heal?" Bethany sat still on the swing.

"Sure, but no less than about five years or so later. Grieving is a slow process—and I wonder if it's ever completely done, although later on, there is less pain," Alice answered. "Oh, none of us are the same as if we hadn't lost Mom. We had some real challenges and some hard times emotionally, but we learned a lot of important things and we survived. We're all healthy, functioning adults."

Judith jumped in to explain further. "Everyone reacted differently—denial, sadness, pain, anger, guilt, depression—and everyone healed differently. It took some of us longer than others to get over her death, depending on our relationship and our personalities and a whole lot of other things. But basically, it was an individual experience with everyone going through it in their own time and in their own unique way." Judith then added, "Of course, when the police caught me with my friends trying to open a locked car so we could go joyriding . . ."

"You did that?" Alice's eyes were wide with surprise.

"We tried. Everyone at home was always crying or upset, and I was tired of feeling sad all the time. The stuff the other kids in the group did wasn't all that exciting, so I came up with a plan, and the police caught us."

"You never told me."

"Never told Dad either. The policeman knew Dad and knew about Mom and made me promise to talk to Dad about missing Mom. Then he got me a volunteer job at a couple of police charity functions where I met this cute guy interested in becoming a policeman . . ."

"You mean that's how you met Tom?"

"Grieving can have its good points. Speaking of Tom, I better get back to the house and see that his shirt is pressed for tomorrow."

"And I've got to get Joshua into bed."

The two sisters stood up and, after telling Bethany good night, walked back toward the house, laughing.

Bethany thought about the conversation long after the sisters had gone. That night she felt she understood herself much better, and as she prayed she pleaded for help. She yearned for her earlier desire to share the gospel with Amelia and to be a part of Amelia's family, but she still didn't feel an urgency about having Amelia's temple work done. The small, framed picture of the Boston Massachusetts Temple she kept on her nightstand seemed to mock more than comfort her—and she longed for the days when it would beckon her. She could only pray that the Lord would help her feel that way again.

6

As the forest arrayed itself for its showiest time of the year, the renovations to the hut were finally finished.

It was early October when Scott and Andy helped Bethany rearrange the heaviest furniture and hang the drapes. Before they left they carried her mattress and chest of drawers up the stairs. Then she was finally alone in her hut.

Her hut! It had a nice ring to it—a pleasant, happy sound. She had planned to spend the night at the bed-and-breakfast and pack up her computer and the other things she had left, but she was exhausted. Deciding instead to pick them up the next morning, she thrilled at the thought that this would be her first evening alone in the hut.

By the time she put the sheets on the bed and found the bedspread, the sunlight had disappeared and the hut was dark. Evening shadows fell over the home as a stiff wind blew, shifting the branches on the maple beside the hut. The mountains seemed to echo with quiet noises—noises too loud to ignore but too soft to identify. The moon was a gleaming, bright beacon. But scattered, wind-blown clouds scurried across it, occasionally obscuring its light, darkening the trees and then brightening them again, leaving the night full of ambiguities.

Sitting on the couch, too tired to switch on the lights, Bethany was caught in the mood of the night around her; her life was equally full of ambiguity. She had spent over three months renovating the hut, but for what? She had let herself get so caught up in that process that she hadn't stopped to consider her future in the long term for quite some time. What would life in the hut bring her? And where would that ultimately lead her?

Would living in the hut, as a gift from Amelia, serve as a persistent reminder of the unhappiness their relationship had caused Bethany? Would she be able to put aside her bitter feelings and have Amelia's temple ordinances done, then seal herself, her parents, and her grand-parents together?

What would happen to Bethany's relationship with Joseph now that work on the hut was finished? Would Joseph still make time to see her, or without the renovations to supervise would he get bored with her and the cove? Seacrest was a long drive from Boston. And would Bethany be living in the hut when Peter returned? Although she'd come to terms with what their relationship truly was—and what it wasn't—that still didn't keep her from worrying about him or wanting to help him.

Bethany also wondered if the hut would fulfill Amelia's hope, as a haven where Bethany could write. After all her years of analyzing the work of well-known authors, she wondered if she would be able to come up with something worth writing and, then, worth reading.

Staring at the night sky, Bethany found herself feeling a bit of melancholy at the sight of the moon with the clouds drifting past it. Then the clouds surrendered the full moon to her view, a brilliant white without any competing artificial lights. If Amelia's memory dimmed the hut's appeal to her, perhaps thoughts of Joseph would restore its attractiveness. She sighed, wishing Joseph could see the moon from this vantage point. She was grateful that he was as pleased with the renovated hut as she was, and he credited her with its renewed charm.

A cloud drifted past the moon. *Did something just move near the Jeep?* Bethany studied the yard carefully, feeling a return of the brooding fear she hadn't felt since the last strange "near accident" occurred months ago.

She then saw a shadow move on the driveway—two quick move-ments in a row. Terror exploded in her heart. Who would be out there at this time of night? For that matter, who would visit the hut at all without first calling her? Few knew Bethany had moved in today—only the McCleres and the Marshalles—and, of course, Scott Marshalle's friend Andy. Staring out the window, she watched for any stealthy movement, her hands clammy and her heart pounding.

Almost frantic, she picked up the phone and poked at the brightly lit numbers. Alice's line was busy. Redialing several times, she paced the floor. The line remained busy.

Looking out fearfully into the blackness that surrounded the hut, she wondered how she would escape if someone broke in. She could make a dash for the Jeep now, hoping no one would emerge from the trees to pursue her, or she could dart to the maple, then the pines behind it and hide in the woods. But then, she considered, she knew nothing of the surrounding area. Being independent was one thing, but being foolhardy was entirely different.

As she continued to look fearfully out the window, Bethany saw more shadows scurry across the yard. But this time she could tell the shadows came from several twigs with dead leaves, blown by the wind through the tall grass in the flickering moonlight. She breathed a big sigh, her fear subsiding. Then she laughed, although weakly, at her own paranoia.

Suddenly, Bethany felt a melancholic longing for Peter. She'd had a couple of dreams about him lately, sometimes reliving their tender moments, sometimes his temper flare-ups when he had been stressed by work the few weeks before her graduation, but in her dreams he always apologized. Where was he? Then she sighed, realizing once again that it wouldn't do her any good to think about him.

She moved across the room to study the forest more closely, this time with interest rather than fear. There was something . . . something about the hut and the area, too. She felt a pull, an attraction to the place that she couldn't identify or deny. Perhaps it was the feeling of taking up where others had left off—others who had lived in this remote, antiquated house.

Vaguely Bethany remembered back to the day she and Joseph had arrived at Seacrest and met the McCleres. Alice had mentioned something about the first woman who lived at Faunce Cove. Now, as she thought about the long-ago inhabitant, she wondered, *Did that woman live somewhere in the forest in a house now decayed, now nourishment for one of the trees that shadowed the mountainside? Did the woman carry stones like those of the hut's fireplace to put around her own fire hole? Why did she come to this desolate spot? And what eventually happened to her on this mountain?*

Bethany climbed the staircase in the darkness and used only a small lamp as she prepared for bed. Excited about her new, albeit temporary home, she eventually drifted off to sleep.

* * *

Bethany hung up the phone. Alice was going shopping for Halloween decorations, so Bethany needed to get to the bed-and-breakfast as soon as she could to pick up the computer and the rest of her things that she had not retrieved the night before.

It was a clear morning and the ocean was vibrant as Bethany put the Jeep in first gear. Surprisingly, she had slept relatively well her first night at the hut, and she was anxious to get her computer set up. As she gently eased off the clutch, the vehicle barely jerked as it moved forward slowly. Gradually accelerating, Bethany shifted up to second, then third gear. Driving the Jeep, wind in her hair, sun shining on her bare arms, was down-to-earth joy.

The road curved from the tree-lined inlet to the side of the steep, rocky mountain, with the scarred facing of the rock on one side and an open embankment dropping down to the ocean on the other. Only a guardrail, browned with rust, obscured her view of the cove. She glanced out at the ocean spread before her.

Turning her attention once again to her driving, she looked back at the road with a start to see that it was covered with a large puddle of black liquid. She hit it without a chance to brake, gliding into an uncontrollable skid.

Pushing down on the clutch and thrusting the gearshift down to second, Bethany pumped the brakes lightly, hoping to slow the Jeep. But no matter how she turned the wheel or pushed on the pedals, she had no control of the Jeep as it planed across the center line of the two-way road. Aware that she was headed for the open embankment, she visualized the long drop and the landing that would await any vehicle that plunged through the guardrail.

She sat rigid, every muscle preparing for the collision with the band of metal. Would the guardrail hold, or would she plummet into the ocean?

The Jeep started to lose speed, but it was still skidding. Finally the tires began to grip the road. Bethany pushed in the clutch and grabbed the gearshift, praying she could get it into first gear and could slow it before it hit the railing. The Jeep caught in the gear, the engine grinding down and slowing the vehicle's movement. Then, as she urgently pumped the brakes, the Jeep came to a halt against the rusted railing.

Sitting in the Jeep, Bethany continued to grip the steering wheel, determined to stop her shaking. When she felt steadier, she tried to open the door, but it was pressed against the guardrail. Instead, she stretched out the window to look. She was terrified by the open expanse she gazed upon, seeing only boulders jutting from the water far below her at the bottom of the mountain. If the Jeep had been going faster, if the bolts holding the railing had rusted through and had given way . . .

Bethany dodged the gearshift as she slid across to the passenger side, opened the door, and climbed out. Immediately a strong scent assaulted her as she examined the roadway. No wonder she had slid! A large section of the road was covered with black oil, and it looked and smelled like the type used for road construction.

She tiptoed through the oil around the Jeep to check for damage to the vehicle, ignoring the slippery fluid as it splattered over her shoes and onto her Levi's. Because the left side of the Jeep was pressed so tightly against the railing, she couldn't see well enough to know if there was any real damage to it. Unable to glance back down at the water below, she hurriedly returned to the other side of the Jeep and climbed in.

Could this have been caused by . . . ? Bethany tried to force the thought out of her mind, but it rankled at her. Loosening lug nuts on someone's private vehicle was one thing—but oil on a public road? It had to be a coincidence. Anyone who drove this route would have hit the oil puddle, and anyone could have been seriously hurt—or worse.

She was relieved when the engine caught, and even in reverse, she was able to back up without killing the motor. Slowly, she drove back to the hut.

When she inspected the Jeep in front of the hut, she realized it was in better shape than she was. There were scrapes on the paint and a dent in the side of the vehicle, but they were no more noticeable than the marks that had been there when she'd gotten it. Bethany knew she was in no condition to go anywhere; she had nearly quit shaking, but she couldn't stop pacing the floor while she dialed Alice's number to explain.

"I appreciate the town taking good care of the road," she quipped, hoping she sounded like she was kidding as she tried to hide her anxiety from Alice. "But I think they put a little more oil on it than was necessary. And I got all the extra on me!" She looked down at her hands and shoes, wondering how she was going to clean up the mess.

That afternoon she took the Jeep to the nearest car wash and then stopped by the McCleres' to pick up her belongings.

"I went over to see Judith before Tom left for the police department and I told them about the oil on your road. He was surprised," Alice informed Bethany as she stepped up into the Jeep. "The road maintenance department always contacts him about any highway repairs, and he hasn't heard anything from them. He doesn't know how the oil got there. Someone must have spilled it."

* * *

Bethany gazed past her computer out the window at the changing colors of the leaves, then back to her writing. She glanced at the clock, remembering she had promised Alice she would pick up some end-of-the-season vegetables from her while Joshua was down for his nap and before the twins got off the bus. Alice and her husband Steve had planned a long weekend at Bar Harbor, and they didn't want the produce to spoil.

When Alice met Bethany at the door, there was a look of disappointment on her face. "Judith can't watch the kids, so we won't be going to Bar Harbor. Ally broke her leg and is in the hospital!"

"Ally! What happened?" Bethany asked, picturing Alice's redheaded niece who closely resembled her mother, Judith.

"She fell on her bike, trying to avoid being hit by a car. The driver— a tourist, of course—wasn't watching where he was going."

"How bad is her leg? How long will she be in the hospital?"

"Well, Dr. Noel wants to get another X-ray on Monday. Then— hopefully—she can come home. She'll have to be off her leg and out of school for a couple of weeks and in the cast for at least another month.

I guess she is more worried about missing school than about her broken leg!"

"It shouldn't be hard for her to keep up with her schoolwork, should it? She seems like a pretty smart kid."

"That's the problem. She had her heart set on writing a spectacular term paper about the woman that lived at Faunce Cove."

"I've thought about that woman, too. I wonder what it was like with the rain pelting down." Bethany paused and looked at Alice. "You know, I wouldn't mind doing some preliminary research. I'm not getting anything done on my book—I might as well do something constructive." She didn't add that it would help her keep from thinking about Amelia, and Joseph, and Peter, and every other worry swirling around in her head. "Meanwhile, what about your weekend? There must be some way you can go to Bar Harbor."

"I can't leave three kids with Grandpa, and it's too late to make other arrangements. We'll just plan another time."

"I could watch them." Bethany wondered at her own suggestion.

"They'd be a lot of work, and Joseph is coming up, isn't he?"

"He'll be here Friday night. We could babysit together!"

"There's a thought." Alice grinned as she gathered some tomatoes into a bag. "You'll make major points with Joseph when he sees you with kids."

"I wasn't thinking of that."

"Well, truthfully, we *are* talking about Joshua, Jessica, and James. They might scare any thoughts of home and family right out of Joseph's head! I'm not sure he would appreciate you volunteering him. Anyway, he probably has plans for the two of you."

Joseph did have plans, but he assured Bethany when she called that it was nothing that couldn't wait. He would have to leave early on Sunday since he had to be in his office on Monday morning, but he insisted he wouldn't mind spending the time with the kids. He began listing off ideas on how to entertain them faster than Bethany could relay them to Alice.

Finally, Joseph asked to speak to Alice, who was laughing when she hung up. "They're never going to want to see us again after all the things he's planning!" She looked around the room. "What am I doing, just standing here? I've got some packing to do!"

She looked at Bethany with a grin. "And let me warn you, sometime during this weekend while the kids are being . . . well, kids . . . you're going to ask yourself what you're doing here, too."

7

Bethany thought it would be easier to stay at McCleres' than move everyone up to the hut and get the twins to the school bus, so she slept at the bed-and-breakfast Thursday night. By midmorning Friday she wondered how Alice entertained Joshua and still got anything done.

The twins, off their bus at three thirty, were anxious to tell Bethany about their day and to show her all the school papers they had accumulated that week. They insisted that she see their newest bike tricks, which meant a trip to the old barn where they kept a voluminous accumulation of seashells and their collection of sea glass—broken pieces of colored glass worn smooth by the sand and surf. Arranged in a circle, the sea glass reminded Bethany of a stained-glass window.

When she commented on the pretty pieces, the twins clamored for her to take them to the sand flats to look for more. It was only when Joshua asked for a cookie that she realized it was getting late and Joseph would be arriving within the hour.

The phone was ringing when they reached the McCleres' porch, and Bethany hurried, Joshua on her hip, to pick it up. It was Joseph calling from his car.

"What've you been up to? I've been trying to get you for nearly an hour!"

"Just you wait. I've put in my time this afternoon! Tomorrow you get to entertain!"

"It's a deal, although you don't sound like you've suffered a lot." He chuckled. "Is there anything you want me to get on the way up? I can pick up hamburgers or pizza."

Glancing at the table still covered with papers and littered with the remains of their lunch pails, Bethany gladly agreed. When Joseph arrived, she was delighted to find that he had also picked up a movie.

The evening went smoothly. Joshua fell asleep in Joseph's lap, leaving Bethany to quietly open the door to the toddler's room and watch as the large, robust man gently laid the small child in his crib and softly tucked the blanket around him. When Joseph and Bethany returned to the living room, he couldn't resist a tussle. The twins jointly struggled to pin him to the floor. Bethany couldn't stop laughing as he effortlessly escaped their attempts while pretending to be overpowered. He rewarded their "win" by reading them their favorite book while they, in their pajamas, sat on the arms of his chair.

When the children finally quit giggling and settled down in their beds, Joseph found Bethany in the kitchen finishing the dishes.

"Feels like I just exited the eye of a hurricane!" Joseph chuckled. "They really are active kids, but they're great. I have a feeling we are going to need a good night's sleep. I'll spread my sleeping bag out on your couch at the hut, if that's all right with you."

She looked up, surprised.

"Attorneys know to avoid any risk of gossip." Joseph leaned over and kissed her as gently as he had covered Josh with the blanket. "I'll be back before you wake up."

He wasn't. Josh woke early, and Bethany rocked him back to sleep as he murmured for his mother. Then Jessica wanted water. Although Bethany had barely slept, she had been up and dressed for quite some time before she heard Joseph's sharp rap on the door.

It rained all day Saturday. Bethany watched in amazement as Joseph entertained the children. By lunch they were tired of games, and Bethany suggested they make cookies. James protested, claiming that cooking was only for girls. But when Joseph joined in, who had suddenly become an expert on rocket and dinosaur profiles, they ended up mixing a second batch of dough. They had barely cleaned the kitchen before it was time for Bethany to boil the spaghetti, feed and bathe the children, and get them to bed.

For the first time during the weekend, Bethany and Joseph had some tranquil moments relaxing in front of the fireplace. Joseph turned on the TV to catch the weather, then left it on for the rest of the news. Before long, both Jessica and James got out of bed and persuaded Joseph to read them another book. Bethany had fallen asleep herself before she heard Joseph come back downstairs and leave the house for the night.

Although she thoroughly enjoyed her weekend with Joseph and the kids, Bethany was also looking forward to resuming normal life. Driving back to the hut on Sunday evening, she thought how satisfying it felt to have her own place . . . her own retreat! She'd lived there less than a month but it already felt like home.

* * *

"Look!" Ally beckoned Bethany over to her seat in the library. She was nearly finished with the armload of books Bethany had gathered for her from the library's computer listing. Ally had set aside several books with pages to be copied and was carefully examining a particularly old volume.

"Most of this is about the peninsula and its chain of islands, but some tell about Seacrest, and two even give stuff on Faunce Cove. This one was in storage, but the librarian got it for me." Ally held up the thick volume. "And it has the story!"

"Really?" Bethany asked, revived from the weariness she had felt after her fruitless jaunt to the courthouse where she had looked through hundreds of land records, all on faded pages with crumbling edges, trying to identify the original owners of the hut. She slid the book over and scanned the map showing details of Faunce Cove.

"See!" Ally pointed to a paragraph on the opposite page. "I haven't had a chance to read it, and I don't think it's the whole diary, but it gives a bibliography listing the original pages as part of a collection of early settlement papers."

Bethany felt a surge of elation. The intrigue she felt for the Faunce Cove woman had grown as she helped Ally research her life. She had even talked to Sister Winton, the family history consultant in her ward, to find out how she could trace the posterity of the original property owner, *if* she could identify whoever that was, to a modern-day descendant who might have more information. "Why don't you finish looking through the books while I do the photocopying. Then you can read this to me on the way home."

The photocopied journal entry was brief but gratifying. The "Faunce woman" came from Plymouth Colony and married at the age of eighteen. Her unnamed husband was originally attached to a fort, but when it was abandoned due to sickness and dangerous Indian raids, he took her to an isolated cove to build their home.

For over three years their life was simple but good, until Indians came upon them one winter night. She escaped by hiding in a cave hollowed by centuries of ocean tides, outwaiting the Indians as they watched from the shore, the waves washing higher and higher into the mouth of the cave. She supposed they were waiting for the tides to surrender her to their savagery. But she had clung to the rock, gulping for air as the high tide covered her. When she was finally able to emerge, the Indians were gone—but not without leaving a reminder of their brutality. They had left her husband dead.

Through the continuing winter months, she lived in fear. Though the Indians had virtually destroyed the small clapboard house her husband had built, she managed to pull enough remaining boards together to make a shelter around the one feature that did remain, the fireplace. Though she dared build only small fires, unwilling to risk detection by roving bands of marauding Indians, she was able to survive the coldest nights huddled against the warmth of the rock.

Ally's eyes were full of emotion as she read Bethany the last paragraph of the selection.

> *The cold that comes within the night be not the worst of my fears, but the dreams that bead water on my brow. For they come nearly nightly and again I feel the hardness of the rock against my back, the fierce strength of the brackish water on my skin and in my mouth. And I wake calling the words I echoed through my mind to keep me up that evil night, "Let the sea crest, let me see the dawn and follow the light." I watch each night for the light to announce the coming of day and kneel in gratitude each day when finally the night is spent.*

Ally stopped and took a breath. It was several seconds before Bethany spoke, almost reverently.

"'Let the sea crest.' What finally happened to her?"

"That is all there is except for a copy of some faded lettering that is supposed to be her name. I can't read it."

"What do the letters look like?"

"Well, the first letter looks like an *R*, though it is hard to tell which lines are from the signature and which are from the copier. I don't know if there is a line coming down from the loop or not."

"An *R*? What colonial names begin with an *R*? Maybe Rachel or Rebecca? What does the second letter look like?"

"Like an *e* or *i*, though it could be an *a* with some of the loop missing. The bottom parts of the letters are really faded. I can't tell if there are really lines there or just marks. Maybe the first letter is a *P*, not an *R*."

"Priscilla? Patience? Prudence?"

"The third letter has a tall line, like an *l* or *h*, but then it's hard to tell about the rest. Each letter could be an *i*, or an *e*, or an *a*, or something like an *m*—anything that has spikes or humps. I don't know," Ally replied. "There are one or two more tall letters—the second one may be a short letter with a scratch on top or a tall letter with a part of it missing, then some more spiky things!"

"That definitely spells it out!" Bethany said with a laugh. "No wonder no one knows her name!"

"I wish my paper didn't have to be factual. Wouldn't it be great to write a story about her?"

The thought had not been far from Bethany's mind since she had begun her research. She looked at Ally before asking hesitantly, "Would you mind if I did? I don't want to take anything away from your paper, but all this information just seems to call to me. Do you know what I mean?"

"I think so," the teenager answered. "She seems so real." She laughed. "No, I *know* she was real, but I can imagine her doing things. You could write a historical novel about her! It would be fun with both of us writing about the same thing but in different ways."

"And you wouldn't mind a trip to Augusta? Wouldn't it be great if we could find out what her name really was?"

* * *

Although the local population offered a number of adamant opin-
ions—after all, the story of the woman at Faunce Cove was local
legend—Bethany and Ally were unable to verify her name. Their
excursion to Augusta proved as satisfactory as expected; they found
the book from which their material had been taken, but they found very
little new information. The photocopy of the name was identical. The
book stated that the original document was in the custody of family
descendants, but, unfortunately, it did not list any of their names.
Searching for marriage and birth records was impractical since
Bethany and Ally had no names and could only guess at the dates in
incomplete records. Therefore, the mystery remained unsolved—
although Bethany, after carefully studying the photocopy, considered
Patience to be the most probable interpretation of the name.

"At least we know her last name was Faunce, don't we?" Bethany
asked as she sat in the Marshalles' den, looking through papers as
Judith knitted and Scott pretended to do homework.

Ally looked up from the papers she was working on. "One of the
historians in Augusta said that the Faunce Cove region went uninhab-
ited for a number of years, and that no one knows if Faunce is the
name of the home's original owner or the one who moved in later. He
said that," her voice deepened and took on the quality of an authority
as she quoted her notes, "'undoubtedly, the cove was named after the
later owner rather than the very much aggrandized woman who
supposedly inhabited the area for a short period of time in the seven-
teenth century, although no proof of her existence can be found other
than a rather questionable diary written in a most dramatic manner.'
Personally, I prefer the diary to that old stuck-up fuddy-duddy!"

"Well, you must admit," Judith commented to her daughter,
"there isn't a cave around here like the one she described. That would
have to be a pretty noticeable hole."

Ally was undaunted. "Well, there's Thunder Hole by Bar Harbor.
The waves washed out a cave there."

"Yes, but we don't have a Thunder Hole," Scott stated with a touch
of brotherly contempt.

"Maybe there was one then," Ally retorted defensively.

"Then where did it go? The rock would have to be out far enough
to be within reach of the tide. And it would have had to have been

covered at some point between the lifetime of your Rachel—or Patience or whatever her name was—and now. Not to mention the fact that it would take something pretty big to block it. Unless it fell in."

"Maybe something got rolled in from the ocean," Ally guessed.

"Maybe the professor's right." Scott smirked.

"Maybe a boulder rolled down and blocked it," Judith offered in a conciliatory tone. "Now, Scott, go finish your homework!"

Unperturbed by the lack of evidence and the historian's doubts, Ally finished a paper that Bethany considered exceptionally well written. Feeling inspired, Bethany was finally able to write. In fact, the writing came so naturally that she often had to remind herself to stop and eat or sleep. She generally spent her mornings writing. Then she took a break for lunch and a stroll along the shoreline.

At first Bethany had hoped to find the cave described by Patience, but, as Scott had predicted, it didn't seem to exist. Perhaps Patience had referred to a gorge or even a channel worn and altered by three hundred years of water. Perhaps it was not on the cove itself.

Bethany considered climbing the mountain behind her hut. It tempted her even more when she realized that any remains of Patience's home were almost certainly concealed by the thick forest, but the tall stone wall blocked any access from her own property. Besides, she was nursing a red, itchy welt on her ankle that Alice had said was from poison ivy. Bethany could now identify the three-leafed stems, and she had found the foliage to be as plentiful along the edge of her grassy border as were the towering pines on the other side of the wall.

In spite of the poison ivy, she planned daily hikes through the autumn leaves as restful breaks from her writing, but Bethany could not put Patience out of her mind. She often came back from her walks with new ideas or possible solutions to puzzling aspects of her emerging plot. Frequently, she awoke in the morning thinking of Patience, not Peter or Amelia or even Joseph. And she considered that to be a good thing. Perhaps her stay here really would provide her a chance to heal.

Bethany wished she had access to the records held by Patience's descendants. When the librarian at the stake Family History Center showed Bethany how to access Salt Lake City's Family History

8

Bethany realized that it was nearly Halloween as the leaves crunched under her shoes when she walked to her mailbox. She smiled as she pictured the McClere twins in costumes, knocking at her front door and calling, "Trick or treat!" with little Joshua chiming in.

Pulling the stack of mail from the box, Bethany quickly flipped through the envelopes and advertisements. In addition to the ever-present junk mail, most of the mail consisted of utility bills. She also noticed a Halloween card with Kim's return address. She smiled, remembering that Kim never forgot a holiday.

Next Bethany noticed a small envelope made of ivory parchment. She quickly tore it open, then gaped open-mouthed at the words inside.

> *Hey, pretty girl. How do you like being alone? Are your friends disappearing?*

Bethany suddenly felt sick to her stomach. Who would write something like that and why would anyone want to frighten her? She pushed the earlier incidents out of her mind and read on.

Near the bottom of the page in smaller letters, Bethany read: *Anyone you tell about this will be in danger. We'll be watching.* Bethany sighed raggedly and turned over the envelope. Of course, there was no return address; and, like the message inside, the address had been created using rubber stamps. Noticing that the envelope contained no postmark or postage, Bethany realized the threat had been hand delivered. Whoever was threatening her had been at her mailbox!

A tremor ran through her body. Bethany reread the words several times. Why would mentioning the message to someone endanger them? Then she remembered the phone message from Peter with his warning not to talk to anyone. That was the only concrete thing she could think of that connected Peter to this current threat. Suddenly Bethany knew that she could not deny that the *missing friend* mentioned in the threat had to refer to Peter. It did no good to rationalize that she didn't even know where he was. Peter's life was in danger—and now her own was being threatened.

Bethany drew in a deep breath as she admitted to herself what she'd been denying all along. Was Peter hurt, or even alive? Would she always wonder if he were safe and if he would return? And if he never did—would she ever be able to think of him without a feeling of foreboding?

Shaking, Bethany dialed Alice's number. When Alice heard Bethany's tremulous voice she immediately asked, "What's wrong, Bethany?"

"I just got a threatening letter in the mail, and I don't know what to do! Should I call the police? I'm so—"

Alice cut Bethany off. "It's okay. Judith said Ally received a weird note in the mail too. Judith had her take it over to the police station to show her father, and Tom said that a half dozen other girls had received similar messages. The police are still investigating, but rumor has it that a couple of teenage boys sent the notes as a Halloween prank. They apparently thought it was funny, but as soon as someone gives up the pranksters' names, the district attorney intends to press charges. And—"

"So you're sure it's nothing?" Bethany interrupted. "What did Ally's note say?"

"Let's see . . . something about her being watched. It was rather vague."

"That sounds just like the note I got! What else did it say?"

"To be honest, I don't remember the exact words, but you could call Tom and give him your note as added evidence against the boys. I'm sure Tom would appreciate that."

"I'll just give it to Tom the next time I see him." Bethany sighed in relief.

The topic turned to the twins and their Halloween costumes and Alice's recipe for the peanut butter–filled chocolate cupcakes that Bethany planned to take when she went visiting teaching, but Bethany still felt uncomfortable about the letter. What kind of creep would write something like that and why? Would the person ever actually harm any of the girls in town? And why was the warning in the note so similar to Peter's?

* * *

By the middle of November, Bethany had completed a preliminary outline and two chapters about Patience. Then Joseph called and suggested she spend Thanksgiving week with him in Boston. While she did not want to leave her writing, she was delighted with the prospect of being with him. She drove down to Boston on the Monday before Thanksgiving Day.

Although her Jeep was serviceable, the idea of a new, clean, undamaged car was irresistible. Yet as she parked her rental car in the parking garage and took the elevator up to Joseph's condominium, she suddenly felt out of place. Joseph was not a struggling, new-at-the-job graduate, but a successful, affluent attorney. Bethany was glad she'd stopped at the hotel and changed from her wrinkled blouse, jeans, and running shoes—clothes she had chosen for comfort on the trip, but not to ride up the elevator in a fashionable tower condominium. Even in a nice pantsuit she still wasn't sure she was dressed appropriately. It seemed like a long time since she'd dressed to go out. She would have been almost relieved if Joseph had not answered her timid knock, but he opened the door immediately. His kiss washed away her insecurity.

Dinner was delicious, the Boston Symphony concert beautiful, but being with Joseph was delightful. She nestled against him as he drove her back to her hotel.

"You look absolutely stunning tonight," he told her as he opened her door.

Bethany felt as captivated by his compliment as he seemed to be with her.

Although she had considered telling Joseph about the strange message she had received before Halloween, after hearing his compliment, she decided not to break the spell. Then again, why should she mention it? Alice had assured her it was a prank.

Unfortunately, Joseph spent most of the daylight hours in his office, except on Thanksgiving Day. The first morning, Bethany walked through a few stores, but shopping was not appealing, and she found herself thinking about Patience. She caught the T's red line, part of the Boston transit system, to Harvard Square and spent the afternoon studying library catalogs. She looked through several books on colonial America, resolving to return and delve further, and then headed back to her laptop to type up her ideas. She was nearly finished when Joseph knocked on the door. Bethany opened it to see him standing there with a puzzled look on his face.

"Have you spent the whole day writing? I thought you'd be out shopping or at a museum, maybe taking in a matinee. That's what I've been told women do when they have time on their hands. You're not even dressed for dinner! "

"I did go shopping, but when I kept thinking about Patience, I decided to see what I could find at the library."

"I think you are becoming obsessed with her," Joseph teased. "I'm wondering if you came here to be with me or to do more research! Who is it, Patience or me?" he joked as he picked her purse up from the chair and sat down.

"Who do you think?" Bethany responded coyly.

"Well, if it's the one I'm hoping you'll choose, you'll stop writing and get ready for dinner so I can eat and look at those sparkling eyes again!"

After her stay, on her way home to Faunce Cove, she stopped at the McCleres' and told Alice about Joseph's reply. Alice laughed. "Was it still hard after that to think about Joseph instead of Patience?"

"It got a bit easier," Bethany confided. "But it would have been nearly impossible if the films I'd ordered from the Family History Library had arrived!"

* * *

Bethany's week-long absence had left the hut feeling chilled and lonely. After placing a bag of groceries on the small counter, she started a fire in the fireplace. While she began to put the groceries away, she listened to her answering machine, hoping for a message from Joseph.

Suddenly her head jerked up. She recognized Peter's voice immediately.

"Bethany." His voice sounded casual, as though he were calling from a local grocery store around the corner to check whether she needed milk before he came over for the evening.

The bag of apples Bethany held fell to the floor.

"Sorry you're not there. This is the first time I've been able to call without endangering us both. I am safe—so far. Some pretty rough guys are still trying to find out what information I have about them, so I'm being hidden in something like a Witness Protection Program."

Bethany's heart pounded. As much as she tried to tell herself that her relationship with Peter was over, she was still thrilled to hear his voice—he was okay, he was alive—but fear quickly filled her thoughts as she recognized the peril of his situation.

His tone remained matter-of-fact, but then, she remembered, that was part of Peter's personality. "I can't tell you any more about that. I just want you to know that I'm all right."

"Bethany." His voice softened. "I wish I could see you. I want to hear your voice."

The sudden gentleness in Peter's voice took Bethany by surprise. He sounded exactly as he had the first time he admitted his feelings for her. There was a slight pause before Peter spoke again on the phone, his tone sure and nonchalant. "I can't get caught calling you, so I'll make this short.

"Bethany, my agency is currently running an investigation on Amelia's lawyer's firm. I can't be specific now, but I want to emphasize to you that it's not certain you can trust him. Do not make any decisions about your inheritance from Amelia or sign anything until I contact you again." As Peter said this, Bethany got a sick feeling in her stomach. *Not Joseph!* Her mind reeling and knees weakening, she steadied herself against the fireplace. *And yet why hasn't Joseph discussed the inheritance more with me? And why did he react so negatively when I mentioned spending money on remodeling?* More questions swirled through Bethany's thoughts, but she forced herself to focus on Peter's phone call.

"Remember, Bethany, the agency is doing everything that can be done to protect me and settle the problem. This investigation has some significant consequences, and getting anyone else involved would put the whole thing in jeopardy. Don't tell anyone that I have been in contact, and make sure that you erase this as soon as you've heard it. Bethany . . ."

The message suddenly ended. Breathless, Bethany sat down. Peter was in some kind of danger, but he was alive, and he had called her! She listened to the message over and over again, careful not to erase it as she had his last message a few months back. She'd let herself savor it throughout the day before deleting it later that night.

She finished putting the groceries away and unpacked her luggage, then sat on the love seat, looking at the fire. Suddenly, emotion filled her, and without warning she was crying, sobbing until her body shook the cushion she leaned against. Peter had called. His news about Joseph was frightening, and she'd have to be on guard now with him. But Bethany felt a huge weight lifted from her shoulders concerning Peter's welfare. He had called!

It wasn't until Bethany finished crying that she realized Peter had not explained how he'd gotten her phone number.

Later, after several hours of sleeplessness, the answer struck her. Peter was working on the case with other investigators who would undoubtedly have continued to probe into Joseph's practice and would have gotten access to Joseph's files and Bethany's address. Knowing this, Peter would have insisted that they forward her phone number to him. The thought that he could help her even from this distance was comforting. She was smiling when she finally fell asleep.

9

Bethany had some decisions to make after Peter's phone call. And frankly, she didn't know whom she should trust. Should she believe the man she'd been in love with those past few months—and doubt the one she was dating now? Should she put her trust in the one who'd been like a brother to her since high school, and simply tuck Peter's warning away in her mind as a probable mistake until his company confirmed any allegations? She finally decided that although she would not stifle her budding romance with Joseph or start to suspect him of anything dire, she would be more cautious about the information she shared until Peter got back to her. She was sure that that nothing would come of it.

Joseph wanted Bethany to come to Boston for Christmas to enjoy the shopping and see the *The Nutcracker,* but Bethany wanted to celebrate at the hut. If Joseph really wanted to be in Boston for the holidays, they could spend New Year's there.

They compromised by agreeing to spend Christmas at the hut, then some time in New York City for New Year's. That arrangement solidified after Kim called later that night, thoroughly disillusioned by a disastrous quarrel that had ended a promising relationship. After checking with Joseph, Bethany invited Kim to join them at the hut. Because she and Kim did not have an extremely close relationship, she was surprised that Kim would turn to her when she needed support rather than anyone else. Bethany was glad that Kim saw her as a dependable friend, even if they didn't keep regular contact.

And now if things were going according to schedule, Joseph would be meeting Kim at the airport within the hour, and they'd be

on their way. They planned to arrive at the hut in time to help decorate the tree as part of their Christmas Eve.

Bethany had put up a few simple Christmas decorations to
brighten the dreary gray of early winter, then set up the Christmas
tree ready to be decorated. Her preparations for Christmas dinner
were finished; all she was waiting for now was her guests.

She looked anxiously out the window for snowflakes. The weath-
erman had predicted a Christmas Eve storm—a howling nor'easter
with a savage wind, sizeable accumulations of snow, and possible
whiteouts and drifts. Hopefully, the storm would blow out quickly. If
Kim's flight arrived in time, she and Joseph would get to the hut
before the inclement weather hit.

Bethany had hoped to get one other thing done. She turned on
her computer, wondering how much of her hesitation to leave for the
holidays had been due to the thought of putting Patience aside.

Joseph had sensed her hesitation about leaving the hut and
wondered how she could refuse his offer. "Don't you want to get away
from Seacrest and meet new people, go to some cultural events?" he
had queried.

Joseph had been perplexed at Bethany's admittance that she really
didn't need entertainment or more friends. She spent time with the
McCleres, and Dr. Noel was a reliable and helpful home teacher.
Together with Sister Clark, her very conscientious visiting teacher, and
the sisters she went to teach, she had all the social circle she currently
wanted. She had been invited to join a family home evening group
with several other single members, but she had used the travel
distance as an excuse to miss several times.

"But don't you ever want to do something beyond writing?"

Obviously, Bethany had not convinced Joseph that she truly
enjoyed her simple lifestyle. Whenever she mentioned Patience, he
had changed the subject. He simply could not understand Bethany's
fascination with the woman.

Alice had listened attentively when Bethany told her of the conversation. "Have you ever thought that Joseph would like you to show
more interest in his life? Have you two talked about your relationship?"

Bethany had not thought about their relationship for some time
now. Although she'd decided to all but disregard Peter's suspicions

about Joseph, she was generally too busy thinking about Patience to put much thought or time into her relationship with him. But she still looked forward to Joseph's phone calls and their weekends together. She enjoyed the warmth of his hands on hers, the security of his broad chest as he held her, the smell of his aftershave when she cuddled against him. But she was hesitant to consider that she might be in love with him. Although he continued to attend church with her, he hadn't yet found time for the missionary discussions. But she remained as adamant about the Church with him as she had been with Peter; she would not marry outside the temple.

It seemed strange to Bethany that she couldn't imagine being married to Joseph; on the other hand, she couldn't imagine not having him around. He was the most constant person in her life, the closest thing she had ever had to family except Amelia.

Bethany had thought a lot about Amelia as she prepared for Christmas. She had read Amelia's last letter over and over, her anger at times rebuilding to near defiance, at other times dwindling into nostalgic sadness and longing. Ultimately, she had been able to concentrate on the last sentences of the letter, to have more of an understanding for Amelia's final decisions. Amelia wanted Bethany to learn who Bethany truly was and to learn what would make her happy.

She had always felt uneasy around other people, but equally distressed at being alone. As a child, then a teenager, Bethany had gradually found comfort in solitude and studies, accepting Amelia's lack of attention. She had forced herself to be more social when, after her baptism, she attended the singles ward. Still, she had felt out of place a good deal of the time until Peter had started attending with her. Even as an investigator, Peter had been more at ease than she. He was disarmingly casual and when she was with him she felt accepted. But writing about Patience made her feel more than accepted; it made her feel satisfied. It filled an emptiness inside her.

She was not escaping from reality into a fanciful delusion when she thought about the woman who had written so passionately and courageously about that perilous night. Instead, Bethany identified with and wanted to cling to the strength of the woman who had also felt intense loneliness and yet had survived. She could not explain, even to herself, the connection she felt with Patience, and she wondered why Patience's prayer about the cresting sea and the light of dawn remained in her thoughts.

If Bethany didn't understand, how could she expect Joseph to understand? All she knew was that the inner strength she was gaining from writing made it almost impossible to quit—even for the holidays.

The telephone rang, and Bethany glanced out the window as she picked up the receiver. Large snowflakes as airy as delicate lace filled the sky.

"Kim just called me from Chicago. The plane is grounded there because of the storm." Joseph's voice was warm, and her feeling of disappointment made her wonder about her earlier thought. "Are you all right?" he asked.

"Yes," she replied, although the snow seemed to have lost its beauty and, instead, lent a cold gleam to the beginning shades of dusk. "I have everything ready. I wish you were here. Do you have any idea when Kim will get to Boston?"

"They said the earliest Logan Airport could open would be late tonight. We might be able to get there tomorrow morning, but it could be later in the day, too. Is it snowing up there yet?"

"It just started. The waves are getting bigger."

"Well, we'll get there as soon as we can. Anything you want me to bring?"

"Just yourselves. I'll miss having you here for Christmas Eve."

"I'll miss being there, too, but we'll be there soon. You be careful."

"I will."

As Bethany was about to lower the phone from her ear, Joseph's words came nearly as an afterthought. "You have things in case the electricity goes out?"

"I've got a flashlight and extra batteries. Besides, I don't really need anything with the fireplace."

"That's true," he said, sounding relieved.

"And I've got enough goodies here to last a week in preparation for your arrival. If the power goes out, we'll simply throw the turkey on the spit and start turning." She forced a cheerfulness into her voice that she did not feel.

"I've been lifting weights just in case we need to do that." He chuckled. "We'll come as soon as Kim's flight gets in and the roads are passable. I'll call from the car."

Bethany put the phone down with a sigh and glanced around the room. She had planned to decorate the tree as part of the Christmas Eve festivities with Joseph and Kim, but she would now do that herself since they wouldn't arrive in time to help her.

She was pulling out her Christmas CDs when she heard stomping on the front steps. Bethany opened the door to a cheery chorus of "We Wish You a Merry Christmas" from the McClere–Marshalle gang. She invited them in, but the sisters sent their children toward the car.

"We were planning to come tonight but decided we'd better get out here before the storm really sets in," Alice explained, handing her a plate of homemade doughnuts. "When will Joseph and Kim get here?"

"The airport is closed so they're not going to get here until tomorrow."

"Then grab your coat and scarf," Alice replied enthusiastically. "You can stay at our place and celebrate Christmas Eve with us!"

"Oh, do! Please," begged Ally, who had circled back with Jessica to the hut to avoid the snowballs the boys were throwing.

"You don't want to be here alone during a storm, especially on Christmas Eve, and we really would love to have you come," Alice added.

"I appreciate the offer, but Joseph and Kim might get here early in the morning. Besides . . ." she said as she tweaked Jessica's upturned nose, "how would Santa Claus know where to deliver my presents—or don't you think I've been good enough to get any?" She winked at the child.

"You're sure?" Alice persisted.

"Yes. I'd better stay."

"Then at least let me leave you some rations in case the storm gets really ugly," Judith said before she called to the boys. "Scott and Andy, will you two please bring the things from the trunk?"

Andy, who seemed more like a member of the family than a friend, pulled a red container of kerosene and a lantern from the car.

Before Bethany could protest, Judith explained. "Tom sent these out especially for you. He said to tell you to keep them handy in case of an emergency."

"But I have the fireplace for warmth if the electric heat goes off."

"If the wind takes down the power lines you lose your fireplace fans, and it can be hard to keep a fire going without that circulation," Judith continued as Alice pulled her coat closer. "It can get very cold very fast without any heat. It's hard to get a wood fire started by hand in the dark, and with a storm like the one they are predicting, you can be without power for a week or so up here in the wilds."

"Are you sure you won't stay with us?" Alice repeated with apprehension.

"No. I'll be fine. I don't think I'll need the lantern, but you can leave it just in case."

"Show Bethany how to light the lantern, Scott," she instructed him, then turned to Bethany. "By the way, how is your woodpile?"

By the time the McCleres and Marshalles left, the snow was thick and sticking to the road, but they had stacked wood from the woodpile near the door, and the red kerosene container and the lamp were stored inside.

"I'm sure you're not going to need any of this," Alice reassured her as they prepared to leave, "but this is your first storm, so it won't hurt to learn about it anyway for the future."

"One thing you might want to remember, though," Judith advised, "is to be careful with the kerosene. I never light a match until I've cleaned up any spills after I've filled the lanterns."

Bethany nodded.

"Look." Scott pointed toward the snow-filled sky, which was beginning to gust into whiteouts. "I think we better get going."

Alice looked at Bethany and turned to give her a hug. "Hey, there's really nothing to worry about. Most storms end up being a few gusts, not real blizzards. We just want to make sure you're okay. The invitation to come is still open."

"Thanks, but I'll stay at the hut."

"Merry Christmas!" they called as they climbed into the car.

Going back into the hut, Bethany shut the door against the freezing air. As she snuggled into the love seat, she realized that in order to reach the top of the tree she'd need to retrieve the stepladder from the tool shed behind her house. After getting it, she filled the hut with Christmas music and went to work. As she placed the final ornaments on the tree, she glanced out the window, deciding that the falling snowflakes made an excellent background for the scene.

It was nearly seven when Bethany took the stepladder to the back door, leaning it against the wall. She was grateful now that she had bought it instead of the taller, heavy-duty ladder. Generally, she didn't need the extra height, and the extra weight would have made it much more cumbersome to use. Eventually, she would put it in the shed, but not during the storm. She didn't feel like putting on her tall, cold boots and the rest of the winter gear she had stored in the chilly back hall.

She looked at the clock, remembering the plans she'd made for Christmas Eve with Joseph and Kim. She picked up her CD of the *Messiah* and put it in her player. The music soared around her as she reached for her Bible where she had already marked Luke's account of the Nativity to read as part of the celebration. She had piled her Christmas cards together next to her leather-bound scriptures, waiting to arrange them until all the greetings had arrived. Without Joseph and Kim to entertain, she decided she had plenty of time to reread the messages from some of the Walachias ward members, as well as cards from members of the singles ward she'd attended at the university. Then she would spread them on the mantel.

She nestled into the love seat, warmed by the fire, as she pulled the brightly colored cards from their envelopes, saving the ones she'd collected from the mailbox that afternoon for last. She would read about the Nativity in her scriptures later, as a climax to her Christmas Eve.

She looked at the cheerful façade of the last card, an envelope with a clever black-and-gray border, trying to decipher the postmark that was nearly unreadable, camouflaged by the design. She frowned as her gaze wandered to the stamp, then she gasped.

It pictured a 1920s car. The whitewalled back tire featured an orange hubcap that matched the rest of the car, but the front hubcap was silver and had been marked with small dots arranged like lug nuts. Someone had altered the stamp.

Bethany held her breath for several seconds. Obviously, the card had been sent by the same person who had loosened the lug nuts on her Jeep! She carefully opened it, trying not to damage the stamp.

The writing could have come from any computer or printer. It said: *Your friend is still in danger. Tell us what he told you, or he and his investigations will die. We will tell you where to deliver the secrets. In the meantime, keep your mouth shut. This is his last chance and yours as well.*

Bethany paced the floor, forcing herself to breathe normally. It took several minutes before she could calm down enough to sit and think about the implications of the message. Whoever had sent the first threat—and this one—had also loosened the lug nuts, or knew about the incident. And then there was the oil spill to consider, and the sawed spindles here in the hut. Were all these events connected, as she'd feared all along? Bethany shuddered.

Shaking her head in disbelief, Bethany wondered, *Who lives near enough to get at the Jeep or into the hut? And why would they want to?* A panicky feeling started in her stomach.

The note might give her more information. She reread it hastily.

There was no doubt that the "friend" the note referred to was Peter—the note specified "he," and Peter had been involved in investigating some kind of fraud. The "secret" must be referring to something he'd discovered. But what?

What had he said about his job? What information had he given her in his calls?

Bethany picked up a pencil and a Christmas card envelope and hastily jotted down the words she recalled from the first garbled call. He had mentioned an "organization," some "trouble," something about "taxes" and "evading them," and that they were after him. And then there was the day he had let it slip that he was not working for the government, *exactly.*

She saw it almost immediately: *tax* and *evade.* Peter hadn't worked for the government; he must have worked undercover for an "organization" *affiliated* with a government agency to investigate a *tax evasion* scheme. That must have been what put him in danger, forcing his boss to put him into a witness protection program.

That had to be it.

She took a deep breath. She might understand now, but what good did it do? She didn't know the company he worked for, or the corporation, and she certainly didn't know what secrets he had discovered. But she did know that the person sending the card was someone who was close enough to Faunce Cove to leave a threat, or sabotage her Jeep and maybe cut the spindles in the hut. The confirmation that someone threatening had been in the hut turned her cold.

Bethany stood and paced the floor again.

The note said not to tell anyone. What if she had told the police about the loosened lug nuts and the first threat, which she'd incidentally not brought up yet to Tom? Would she have received a personal visit rather than a written threat? Should she now report the threats to the police?

The thought that struck her was sickening. *Could* Joseph have anything to do with these threats? The letter seemed to be written by someone that Peter was investigating—and Peter *had* mentioned Joseph in this regard. But that thought seemed preposterous! Joseph threatening and trying to scare Bethany into sharing what she knew? The idea seemed surreal, and yet so was her very life at this moment.

Bethany quickly slipped to the floor beside the couch. "Please help me know what to do," she prayed earnestly. "Help me make good decisions."

The darkness seeping in from the open drapes seemed to fill the room with frightening shadows. She closed the front drapes, sensing the violence of the storm in the roar of the ocean waves. She left the side drapes open where, behind the barren maple tree, several large pines served as a windbreak, allowing the snowflakes to dance peacefully downward, illuminated by the outdoor lights.

Still, she felt completely vulnerable, alone in the hut. Alone and scared. She picked up the phone to call the police station. There was no dial tone. If the storm had knocked out the phone, wouldn't it also snap the electric wires? How did she still have power?

She could tell the storm was intensifying—she could hear the eerie whistling of wind around the chimney and through the old window frames up in her bedroom. The sounds also intensified her fright. She could not help thinking of that lonely woman who, somewhere near the cove, had spent her nights huddled against this same cold, hearing the same wind, fearing the return of savage Indians. Bethany, too, would be comforted to see daylight and, with it, the relief of an abated storm and the security of Joseph's presence. Patience's words drifted through her mind in a singsong melody: *Let the storm cease. Let me see the dawn and follow the light.*

The howling wind swept up and down the scale like fingers on a harp. Bethany glanced out the side window in the living room. In the swaying trees, she could see the wind's fury. The pines, usually tall and stately, danced in a grotesque, whipping motion, pausing during the lulls only to bow and tip again when the wind renewed its strength. Planning to block the gloomy reminders of the weather, she pulled on the drapery cords.

At that moment the almost deafening sound of splintering wood and shattering glass filled the hut as the pine nearest the house crashed past the maple and into the hut. Bethany felt a rain of glass and the lashing of limbs as the force of the falling tree mercilessly threw her to the floor. The hut was instantly thrust into darkness except for the flickering light of the fire. Within moments, the sudden onslaught of wind and branches ripped through the hut, throwing wet evergreen boughs at the fireplace. After sending up a cloud of steam, the boughs smothered the fire.

10

Bethany lay on the floor, terrified by the rush of cold and the fury of the wailing wind, its melancholic tune no longer hushed by the protective walls of the hut. She had no idea how long she had lain there.

Her forehead throbbed, and as she fingered the spot, she felt torn skin under a moist film that must have been blood. Stabbing pain traveled up and down her left arm, but the pain in her right leg concerned her most. She was sure it was broken, and with the sudden cold and the wind, she was chilling and would go into shock if she did not keep warm.

Trying to ignore the pain, she pulled on her leg, causing spasms that took her breath away. Finally, she succeeded in freeing her leg from beneath the tree, but she remained on the floor, too shaken to move.

As Bethany fought panic, the piteous cries of the storm resounded through the room. She lay there waiting for a lull in the wind, willing a few moments of silence so she could think clearly. But when the wind did subside, she heard another sound: the soft, almost soothing gurgle of liquid.

Kerosene! She could smell its acrid odor. A branch must have hit the kerosene can and knocked it over, and now it was spilling from the container. Without the flashlight, she couldn't see how much fluid had spilled or where it had spread—she couldn't even find the container to place it upright. She had set the can on the top of the steps that led down into the kitchen. Had it fallen down the steps or seeped toward the fireplace?

Bethany remembered Judith's warning about kerosene, and a feeling of desolation came over her. She knew it would have been difficult to start a fire in the dark when she had unrestricted movement. Now it seemed futile as well as hazardous to try. But she had to get warm.

She thought of the quilts on her bed and the additional bedding in the wardrobe. Slowly, she crawled toward the staircase, but the tree branches blocked her way and she couldn't even reach the base of the stairs.

Soon the temperature in the hut would dip to the arctic low of the blustery outdoors—except for the back hallway, which was protected from the rest of the hut by the door in the kitchen. Bethany dragged herself across the opening by the stairs in a slow, careful motion, trying not to knock her throbbing leg against the debris, and checking the floor and steps for moisture as she moved forward. The smell of kerosene saturated the air, but luckily she had not come into contact with any yet.

She used the countertop to support her weight as she pulled herself into a standing position on her good leg. Then leaning against the cupboards and supporting herself on the countertop, she moved from the kitchen into the back hall where she groped her way along with her fingers. She tugged at the kitchen door to shut it, grateful that Joseph had insisted on a door with a seal to help keep in the heat. Anxious to get as far away as she could from the invasive odor, she moved down the hallway.

Once she reached the back door, Bethany relaxed against the wall. The windowed door, one she had not replaced, let in enough air that she felt safe.

"Please, help me!" she prayed repeatedly. Then, as though the words were not Patience's mantra but her own, she added, "Let the storm cease. Let me see the dawn and follow the light."

When Bethany made herself open her eyes again, she had no idea of the time. It could have been ten minutes or three hours since the tree had struck the house. Knowing that the temperature and exhaustion would work against her, she was desperate to find heat.

She played the situation back through her mind. She could not start a fire because of the kerosene. She was afraid to light even a match or burn a candle in the hut. She could not get to the blankets. In the hallway where she stood, the air was bitterly cold, and the currents that cut across her face from the old window chilled her even further. Even if she could find a more protected place, the fumes would still reach her.

Trying to reassure herself and think her way through the fear, she could only repeat the words that came to her mind. "The storm will cease. I will see the dawn and follow the light." She repeated the chant over and over.

In her mind, fuzzy with exhaustion, a picture appeared, a picture of a tiny flame at the top of a candle. The box of candles in the shed! She could light a candle in the shed!

She felt the matches in her pocket, thankful that she had left them there after starting the fire in the fireplace earlier that afternoon. Then she stared blankly at the back door, trying to decide what else she might need. She would need a coat and a hat, and she must put on her boots.

Reaching past her lace-up leather work boots, which sat near the back door, Bethany retrieved an old pair of Scott's rubber boots he'd left one day after hiking in the rain. As she pulled the tall, rubber casing over her right foot and around the calf of her leg, Bethany nearly passed out. Pain arched through her muscles before receding into near numbness. Once the blackness that nearly engulfed her vision had cleared, she put on the left boot and rested. Next, she put her right arm into the sleeve of her long woolen coat, but was unable to move her left arm back far enough to slide it into the armhole. She gingerly slipped the left side of the coat over her shoulder, then wound the belt around her with her right arm.

The storm would cease, she told herself. She would find the light, the light in the shed. As she slowly opened the door, the wind whipped at her coat, sending blustering drafts of snow at her face. The shock momentarily sharpened her thinking as she stood at the doorway, and she realized she could not walk to the shed. In the fringes of her thinking, she recalled the feeling—it seemed almost like a confirmation—that her leg was broken. She needed something to lean on. Reaching into the hallway to steady herself, she touched the stepladder. With a sigh of relief, she grabbed it, spreading its legs to form a stable base. It would work.

The journey to the shed seemed endless. Leaning against the ladder with the right side of her body, her right arm lying across one of the steps and her hand gripping the back of the ladder, Bethany lifted it enough to push it forward slightly on the uneven, snow-covered ground—only an inch or two at a time. With her weight supported against the ladder, she could then hop forward on her good leg before dragging the other even with it. The freezing wind blew as if to purposely unbalance her and the ladder, but she kept moving forward. At times wishing the ladder were a little sturdier, she was at the same time grateful it was not heavier. She knew she could not have moved it with one arm.

Almost unbearably cold and in excruciating pain, Bethany began to doubt that she could reach the shed. She tried to pray, but Patience's mantra was all she could think of. As she repeated it over and over, the doubt left her mind. She did not know when, but the verses changed: *The storm will cease. I will feel the warmth and see the light.*

It was not until the ladder hit the structure that Bethany knew she had reached the shed. She wondered if the door would open, but the gusting wind had swept most of the snow from the door's path, and it opened easily.

Dragging herself into the shed, she pulled the door tight into the heavy rock casing, cutting out the moaning wind. Hazily, she remembered the candles and groped her way past the nearly darkened window to the back of the shed.

She pulled out a candle from the box and set it on the shelf, then reached into her pocket for the matches. With little feeling in her fingers, she had difficulty lighting a match, but the candlewick caught immediately. Bethany looked down at the flame. She had light and she could feel its warmth on her fingers. But she was tired, and she needed someplace to rest.

Moving into the corner, she leaned against a wall. But before she could relax, the flame of the candle wavered and died. She dragged herself back to the shelf for support as she tried to light another match. It took several tries before she could light the candle again. The words of the chant circled endlessly through her mind, making less sense as exhaustion crept over her. She forced herself to try to think through the confusion. She waited until the flame burned high, but again, as she moved toward the wall it flickered and went out.

Bethany tried again and again. She needed heat and light, but she would run out of matches soon. She felt too weak to stand without support, and the candle kept dying. She wondered why the flame would waver, why it kept going out. The answer came in her own faint voice, "It was blown out."

She held another match to the candle, carefully holding her breath as she moved it toward her. The flame sputtered, then disappeared. Bethany slowly drew her hand across the space where the candle had been. There was a draft in the corner—the corner of a solid rock building!

Bethany drew her hand across the wall to intersect the air movement, finding a hole concealed in the mortar between the rocks in the wall. The small hole was surrounded by a metallic rectangle. Even in the slowness of her thoughts she realized it must be a keyhole.

Joseph had found a key near the candle box. Fumbling around in the dark, she found the key. It took several tries to slide the key into the hole, but she finally slipped it in despite the blackness that was gaining control of her vision.

It took all of Bethany's remaining concentration to grasp the small, metallic circle at the end of the key and hold it tightly enough to turn it. By the time she felt the key click, blackness had completely surrounded her, and she leaned against the cold, dark surface.

* * *

Bethany was in a long, dark tunnel, or so she thought. She heard noises—low groans, high wails, moans that came in rhythmic patterns, singing, crying. Or were they voices?

Had she been sleeping?

Her clamped hand was numb and she pushed it into her pocket to warm it. *Something is wrong!* she remembered. *I'm supposed to do something, but what is it?* All she knew was that she was in a dark, cold space with echoes all around her. She lay back and tried to relax, but the small voice in her mind became louder, and she remembered. *I must find the light! Yes, that is it. The storm will crest, the dawn will come, and I must follow the light.*

But now there was no light and she was tired. "Please help me!" she called out desperately.

She would sleep . . .

And yet sleep eluded her—for, far away, ever so far away, there was a light. Dim, barely discernible, but at the end of the long, narrow enclosure that trapped her, she saw a faint flush of white.

The side of the wall was embedded with rock, and she pulled herself to stand wearily on her good leg. She groped her way slowly along its length, using the rocks as handholds as she hopped and dragged, hopped and dragged. The light seemed so far away, and her movements toward it so ineffectual at reducing the distance. She doubted that she would ever reach it, but she must try.

After a brief rest she began again, and yet this time she did not try to stand but dragged herself over the surface of the smooth stones that formed the floor. The light was brighter now. It was still far away, but not unreachable. The pain in her leg and arm had numbed, as had the throbbing in her head, and she was beginning to feel a comfortable warmth. She had an overwhelming desire to sleep, but Patience's mantra pulled at her until she obeyed.

Continuing toward the light, she noticed that it seemed to grow brighter.

Bethany looked around at the rock wall, suddenly realizing that she could now see the rocks clearly. She could distinguish their shapes, their differing hues. Looking above her head, she saw an opening in the ceiling, but it looked strange, like an opaque window. She pulled herself to stand, then twisted against the rock wall to get a better view of the light. Studying the rock wall again, she discovered that it cornered with a smooth surface. She was at the end of a tunnel and had found the light. But . . .

She felt the smooth wall in agony, groping at it, searching for a way to get past it. She had found the light, but now, now . . . What was she to do now? Her mind slid into hopelessness, and once again the blackness closed in on her. Her limp weight rested against the smooth surface. Suddenly it shifted.

"What in the . . . ?"

A man came toward her from across a warm, brightly lit room.

She fought at a sinking feeling, unable to understand or comprehend reality. She tried to explain. "A tree broke my window!" But she wasn't sure if she had spoken the words or just thought them.

He came toward her anyway, and she felt his hand gently lift the hair that had matted over the cut on her forehead.

"That's a bad cut you've got there," he said matter-of-factly.

She wanted to reply, but she couldn't speak as the warmth of the room caught at her breath. As she slumped toward the doorframe, she tried to lower her head, afraid that she would faint.

His hand slipped down her back and he lifted her. "Did that tree do anything else to you?" he asked in an even, controlled voice as he carried her across the room.

She gasped as the movement drew a pain across her arm. He glanced at her face, his dark eyes revealing concern.

"Let's see what we've got here," he said. She closed her eyes as he gently laid her down and slid the coat off her shoulder. "Anything more?" he asked as he picked up a pair of scissors and began cutting at the arm of her sweatshirt. Then she saw his eyes go down to her leg, and she heard him exhale. He looked up quickly into her eyes.

His hands were gentle but steady as he cut off her left boot. "This may take a little pull," he explained kindly. "Are you ready?" he asked, then waited, his eyes meeting hers with a look of compassion. Vaguely she remembered she had seen the expression before.

She looked around the room for something to concentrate on. She searched for a light but instead saw an arrangement of flowers. She stared at it, immediately identifying the sprays of white delphiniums and snapdragons surrounded by pink lilies, then a mixture of deep maroon lilies and deep red roses. The arrangement was strikingly simplistic and breathtaking, but a single curve of green holly convinced her that her first conclusion had been correct.

"Ready?" he asked again. He spoke gently as he carefully began to remove the other boot, each movement reawakening the pain she'd felt earlier.

Bethany was not ready, and she called out, "Amelia!" as blackness closed in and quieted her question.

11

Everything seemed muddled when Bethany opened her eyes.

The last thing she remembered clearly was the sound of jangling glass as a blast of cold air hit her in the darkness. After that there were flashes of remembrance, glimpses here and there, but nothing seemed in sequence. There were changing faces, unfamiliar, moving rapidly, pacing slowly, in dimly lit rooms. As far as she could tell she was in a hospital in Boston. There were needles and IVs, trays thrust at her with food she did not want to eat. Her leg was set in a cast so heavy she could barely move, while her arm stung with pain under the bandages. She felt burning hot, then clammy and chilled.

But the physical sensations she could deal with. It was the memories—in bits and pieces, unconnected and confusing—that were more disturbing. Bethany had a faint recollection that something had deeply disturbed her before the tree had fallen, the stress of which seemed to clench her stomach in a constant vice, and yet there were no memories in her mind that she could draw from to explain. She ended up surrendering to the fog that clouded her mind, allowing her body to give into the constant sleep it required.

Bethany remembered seeing Joseph and Kim, and being surprised that Kim was still in Boston. Sometimes she and Joseph walked into the room separately, sometimes together. Sometimes one was telling her good-bye while the other fussed with her flowers. Sometimes they sat in the corner talking quietly, quickly coming to her bedside to tip a straw into her mouth or fluff her pillow if she was awake. Sometimes a doctor or nurse spoke of a coma or pneumonia, of X-rays and MRIs, of seizures caused by a concussion. But it all flowed together like clips on an unedited video, with no order or logic.

The thing Bethany remembered most vividly was the bouquet. She had first noticed the arrangement of yellow tulips and daffodils when the nurse roused her to take her temperature. The sunny arrangement seemed incongruous when juxtaposed against her memories of the Christmas storm. The bright spring flowers spread from a base of large, butter-gold tulips to a crest of dainty, pale cream narcissus. Small, delicate blue iris spread through the arrangement in a graceful curve. The card was not signed. It said only, "You are not alone." When she was coherent, Bethany had spent most of her time gazing at the flowers.

When she first read the card, it—or perhaps the sedative the nurse had given her—had soothed Bethany into a peaceful sleep, but she had awakened feeling panicky. She pictured the words not on a colorful card like the one she'd just held, but on a blank piece of white paper. Yes, it seemed, there was something about a warning she should remember. Or was the uneasiness she felt simply part of her present situation and her pain? She forced herself to breathe slowly and think, realizing that the cheery card was not a warning or a threat. Chiding herself for even considering the note to have some kind of malicious intent, she wondered why she would even consider that. And yet the underlying stress she carried in her stomach persisted—although she still could not identify its cause.

Throughout that day Bethany continued to wonder who had sent the flowers. Suddenly memories of Peter came trickling back—his absence, his garbled phone calls, the danger he was in. Had Peter found out about the accident and sent flowers? Bethany's excitement dissipated as she realized Peter knew nothing of Amelia's flower arrangements. Could Joseph or Kim have signed the card? Bethany fell asleep still puzzled.

Pain medication kept her groggy and asleep most of the time, but that night she had a dream so vivid that it woke her. Amelia, smiling radiantly in her flower garden, held out a basket of brilliant blossoms to Bethany. Bethany reached toward her but before she could grasp the handle firmly, Amelia's grip loosened and she dropped the basket and faded. The flowers in the basket, too, wilted and then shriveled as she searched through them frantically. Shaking with sobs, she pulled each dead blossom from the basket until she saw one delicate, fresh bud resting on the bottom. Her sobbing increased as the tiny, luminous petals opened to show the delicate white and gold of its center.

Then she awoke before dawn, the feelings of loss so intense that she could not stop the tears, and her body shook with sobs. She turned toward the vase of spring flowers and saw a man sitting behind them. In the strip of light that spread from the slightly opened door, she could not distinguish who he was, but she felt comforted by his presence. Though the darkness of the room hid the rest of his features, she knew she would never forget the soft, caring reassurance of his eyes. He seemed to understand her anguish, to care deeply.

She had seen that look before, those eyes—the eyes of the man who had helped her when she reached the end of the tunnel.

He sat silently behind the flowers, and her eyes locked with his until the calmness she found there soothed her thoughts, allowing her to fall asleep once again.

When she awoke the next morning, she felt peaceful, then relieved when the nurse sent Joseph and Kim out for a break. "She's doing much better now. Fever's down. Her doctor even thinks we can cut back a little on her pain reliever. You two need to go out and get some fresh air. Take a break. She's just going to sleep."

As Bethany heard their voices fade as they walked down the hall, she felt relieved not to have them worrying around her. "Nurse?" she called to her attendant, who was just stepping out.

"Yes?" she replied, apparently surprised that Bethany had not yet drifted off.

Bethany tried to shake the fog of sleep from her mind as she asked, "Last night . . . I woke up just before dawn and there was a dark-haired gentleman sitting here in my room. Do you know who that might have been?"

"Hmm . . . my shift started at six thirty this morning, so I wasn't here that early. But visiting hours end at ten o'clock, so it seems sort of strange that you'd have a visitor then. A dark-haired man? Your nurse last night was Sheila—and she definitely doesn't fit that description." Bethany's nurse smiled with a giggle. "Could it have been a dream perhaps? That's my guess."

Bethany looked down at her crisp white sheets, slightly embarrassed. "Well, I guess it really could have been. The dream I awoke from was so intense and realistic—but maybe I didn't really wake up like I'd thought . . . and that man was just in a later part of my dream."

"That doesn't surprise me at all, honey. Some of those meds we have you on for comfort can do that to you," her nurse explained gently, then tucked Bethany's top cover slightly under her feet in a nurturing gesture. "Just lie back now and let yourself get more rest."

For several nights, Bethany woke from the same dream. Several times when she awoke crying, those eyes with the sad, gentle expression comforted her, and she was able to rest again. And each morning that followed, Bethany was never quite sure if the eyes were a part of her dream or reality.

Then the dream changed one night. As she studied the glowing smile on Amelia's face, it turned into an expression of remorse and sorrow when the basket tumbled from her grasp. Bethany had never seen that look on her grandmother's face and never thought that Amelia could feel emotions that intensely. She could not stop her own tears, sobbing as the feelings of loneliness and regret flowed over her. Why had Amelia chosen to bear her grief alone? Why had she left her granddaughter to do the same? Bethany covered her face with her hands as she cried.

Then a voice came quiet and firm, as tender as the eyes, and she knew immediately who it was. "You are not alone, Bethany. Remember, you are not alone." He reached over and very lightly wiped at the tears that had gathered on her cheek. He slid the long strands of hair away from her face and repeated, "You are not alone."

She felt the pain drain away, and her loneliness was replaced with an inner warmth as she hovered on the edge of sleep. And yet before giving in to slumber, she fought for clarity—wondering if she really were awake or if his healing touch were still part of her dream. Unable to discern and too tired to fight, she gave into the peace that enveloped her. The sadness melted as easily as a snowflake on a sun-drenched bud, and she fell into a deep, peaceful sleep.

* * *

Bustling with cheerfulness the next morning, the nurse tucked the clean sheet on Bethany's bed and made the announcement.

"The doctor said you can be released and transferred to a rehabilitation center in Brighton this afternoon! Aren't you the lucky one? They'll have physical therapists to help get your arm working again and occupational therapists to help you learn how to take care of yourself while you're healing. We want you to regain complete use of that arm and those fingers."

Bethany was less enthusiastic. Now that her brain felt normal again, she had not thought of where she would go when she left the hospital. It had been a place of security for her the past ten days. Her leg still sported a hefty cast, and her arm was bandaged and in a sling. She supposed there was little else she could do until she could take care of herself. She couldn't manage crutches, and needed help even to get into a wheelchair. But all she really wanted to do was go home to the hut and write.

"I'll be back to help you pack. The ambulance will probably come around eleven."

Bethany looked around the room to see several vases of wilting flowers. The cleaning woman had volunteered to discard them—including the daffodils, which had become paper thin in the warm hospital air—but Bethany had declined, trying not to show the emotion she felt at the thought of losing them. They would question her if she took them to the rehab center, but she could at least take the card, which promised her, "You are not alone." Was it a coincidence that the man who had helped her the night of the accident had said those same words—who also had flowers arranged like Amelia's?

Bethany warily slid over to the edge of the bed and pulled the small stack of cards toward her. She looked through them, searching for the one she remembered so clearly. It was not there, even though she knew she had seen the nurse place it with the rest. She went through the pile several times but could not find it.

* * *

For a rehab center, the room was probably nice, but with the light green-striped wallpaper, the geometric designs on the drapes, and the uninteresting prints on the walls, it made Bethany miss the hut even more.

Before heading back to San Francisco, Kim had taken an extra day off to help Bethany settle into the center. With only a couple of paper bags to unpack, everything was settled before the cafeteria called with the lunch menu. Bethany was grateful that Kim had planned to visit other college classmates during her trip back East; she'd only planned to spend a day or two with Bethany and the rest with other friends. At least that way her vacation days weren't wasted sitting in the hospital with her.

Bethany's exhaustion from the move discouraged her, and she didn't feel like eating. Joseph stopped in during his lunch hour. Seeing Bethany's expression, he insisted that she rest. "Bethany, it's been a big day for you. How about we get out of your hair for a while and let you sleep. I'll just take Kim out for a quick lunch and then bring her back right after so that you can have the late afternoon and evening to visit and say good-bye. I'll even drive her to the airport to save the time it would take to get a taxi so you and Kim can have more time."

"Oh, you've both been so patient and considerate. Thank you so much!" She gave them both a tired smile, then flattened her pillow behind her as she prepared for a nap. Suddenly she sat up slightly and asked, "Oh, Joseph . . . I've been meaning to ask you more details about my accident. What exactly happened? I know I asked you this before, but that was just days after it all happened and I must admit I don't remember much during that time."

"Well, we got a phone call from the hospital early the next morning saying that you had been admitted several hours before, and we didn't know much about your rescue until we got here. As I understand it, someone from Seacrest—I imagine one of the Marshalles or McCleres—came by to check on you, and after finding you immediately called 911. Emergency responders then dispatched LifeFlight to bring you here to Boston."

Bethany continued her questioning. "Joseph, I know I brought this up to you last time, but I can't forget about a dark-haired man who also cared for me and was definitely part of the rescue—you know, the man in that tunnel. Have you found out any more about him?"

Joseph looked down at Bethany gently, then gave her forehead a kiss, softly easing her back into her pillow. "Bethany, you've been through a lot—and have plenty of time ahead of you to work through all of your questions about that night. For now just rest, sweetheart. We'll talk more about this later."

Bethany slept much of the afternoon, but had awoken and finished her dinner by the time the two returned to the rehab center. As they walked into the room, Kim was flushed and laughing. Joseph carried several shopping bags. "I'm sorry it's so late! We stopped at a few shops on the way to the restaurant. Then we just got talking and before we knew it, it was dark, and we were still there nibbling." She took off her coat and put it over the back of the chair. "But we came up with the best idea! After you get out of here and are up and around, why don't you come out to San Francisco for a couple of weeks? I have an extra room in my apartment, and it would be the perfect place for you to recuperate."

Bethany looked at Joseph, expecting an outright refusal or an indecisive response, but he was as enthusiastic as Kim.

"I can come out for a weekend and fly back to San Francisco with you, or Joseph can fly out with you and stay to do some sightseeing with us!" Kim looked at Joseph questioningly.

"It does sound like a good idea," Joseph said, looking at Bethany. "We could get you away from all your memories and fears, back to normal life with normal thinking. I've been to San Francisco a couple of times, but it's always been on business trips. It would be great to have a vacation."

Kim interrupted him. "I'll show you around. Bethany, I know you will love it, especially after being cut off from everything up there in Maine. And you don't want to be here in New England during the rest of the winter."

They didn't seem to notice her lack of excitement about the trip.

* * *

"You just aren't acting like yourself," Joseph insisted. "You seem moody. You say you wake up every night crying. It's been over two weeks now." He reached over and took her hand. "Bethany, talking to a therapist will help you feel better."

"But Joseph, how do you expect me to feel? I'm cooped up in here when I want to be at the hut writing." She looked at his expression to see if he was convinced. Apparently he was not. "Besides, sometimes I am in pain. Is it so unreasonable to get a little discouraged?"

"No, but you had a tough night Christmas Eve. Don't you think it would help you to talk about it?"

"Why do I need to talk about it? There was a storm, and a tree broke the window and parts of me along with it! I did what I needed to do to get to some shelter, that's all." She was too tired to try to explain again.

"But Bethany." Joseph's voice sounded strained as he hesitated.

She didn't wait for him to continue. "I don't want to talk about the tunnel anymore." She knew where he was leading. From the beginning when she'd recounted to him the events of her rescue, he listened with great empathy, although he never addressed the tunnel or "mysterious man" directly. But now that she was stronger, Joseph had confronted her with his doubts. It turned out that he hadn't believed the details about the tunnel the entire time, convinced all along that she'd been incoherent due to the trauma—and that maybe she'd imagined most of her rescue.

"Had you ever seen the tunnel before? Do you think it really exists?" Joseph pried.

"Joseph!" Couldn't he see how this repeated questioning disturbed her? "If we were in Walachias, not Boston, I could just send you to the shed to find the door yourself, but under the circumstances that's impossible!"

"That's actually not a bad idea. I'll ask one of the guys on the work crew over there repairing your roof to go inside the shed and take a look around. Sound good?" Joseph sighed deeply, then took her hand. "Bethany, I'm not trying to upset you. I just think you went through a lot more physical trauma that night than you realize.

And then all those meds in the hospital . . . I think it would do you a lot of good to talk through all this with a professional. I mean, honestly, I was even concerned about you before this whole accident even happened. You know, how caught up and almost obsessed you were with your book, and Patience and all that."

Bethany turned her face away and closed her eyes, trying to block out his words.

12

Dr. Pam Jackman's long black hair was pulled back from her narrow face, her glasses anchored on top of her head. She held a pad and pencil in her lap. Joseph had gotten his wish, and Bethany found the therapist cordial and soothing, not at all intimidating as she had expected. And unlike her conversations with Joseph lately, Bethany had looked forward to her second session with Dr. Jackman, but she had not told that to Joseph.

"You told me about your lovely home and that you are writing a book. Where did you get your idea for the story?"

Bethany smiled as she thought about Ally and the time they had spent together researching. She spoke enthusiastically about Patience, telling Dr. Jackman much of what she'd learned about the Faunce Cove woman.

"And this woman spent the night in a tidal cave, waiting for the dawn?" Dr. Jackman asked.

"Yes. I wish you could read the quotes from her diary. It's very touching. She kept repeating a chant, kind of a prayer, while she was alone."

"And you related to her loneliness."

"I don't know if it was her loneliness. I wish I had her courage and determination."

"I think you do. You didn't stay on the floor pinned down by a branch. You didn't let a broken leg keep you from escaping the kerosene fumes." Dr. Jackman smiled. "Maybe you two are more alike than you think."

"Well, I wouldn't want to have been in her shoes."

Dr. Jackman looked at Bethany's toes sticking out from the cast. "And I'm sure that she wouldn't want to be in your shoes now either! You showed a lot of inner strength."

Bethany was silent. It hadn't been her strength that had saved her, but her pleading prayers. Each time she had prayed, her mind had been filled with Patience's mantra. It had kept her searching for light and warmth, had led her to the tunnel and safety. She felt it had guided her throughout the ordeal. But the experience felt too sacred to talk about with a therapist who was still a stranger. Especially when Joseph shrugged the incident off as dementia.

"You walked from your home—you call it the hut?—to a shed on a badly broken leg?"

"I used a stepladder, moving it like they use the walkers here. By leaning against it, I could move without putting weight on my leg."

"You are a fighter, aren't you?" Dr. Jackman asked, then waited as Bethany remained silent.

"You've lost other lovely, important things before, haven't you? Your parents? Your grandmother?"

There was a long pause as Bethany watched the angle of the January sun across the ledge on the window.

"You miss your relationship with Amelia. But more than that, you miss the relationship you wish you had with Amelia and your parents, and now you are trying to work through it. You said you are a Mormon. I went to the open house at the temple here before it was dedicated. They talked a lot about eternal families—does the concept of families being united forever help you?"

Bethany didn't respond immediately. How could she explain the dilemma she felt? "It gives me some hope, but I don't know if Amelia really wants me in her eternal family. And I'm not sure if I'm good enough to be a part of any eternal family."

"It sounds as though your relationship with Amelia was pretty complicated and that you have a lot of questions about yourself. That kind of thing can interrupt anyone's sleep. Are you getting more sleep now? Have the dreams changed?"

"Not really. Amelia leaves, and I cry," Bethany spoke nonchalantly, but then she paused uncertainly. "And I still dream about the man with the kind eyes who took care of me not only in the tunnel but later on at the hospital, although one nurse I had dismissed his presence there as still part of my dream," she said quietly. Why did she long to see the eyes of a man who had existed for only moments in her life before disappearing—and maybe not even at all? At first she had expected him to visit her at the rehabilitation center. She had turned each time the door opened, hoping to see him. She had found herself looking toward the door even while Joseph sat with her during the evenings.

"What do you think about the man and the tunnel?" Dr. Jackman asked.

"Joseph thinks . . ." Bethany hesitated.

"I'm not nearly as interested in what Joseph thinks as I am about what you think."

"I really think that I found a tunnel and there was a man with the flowers—but it does seem rather unbelievable." With Joseph's continued skepticism, she had begun wondering if finding the tunnel had been an answer to her prayers or just her imagination.

"That isn't something a person would typically find in the middle of a storm when wandering around with a broken leg and a stepladder."

Bethany had to smile at the image the therapist had created.

"But I don't suppose that eliminates it from the realm of possibility," Dr. Jackman added. "Is there anything that could give you proof that either the tunnel or the room exists?"

"Yes, Joseph asked someone on the cleanup crew to check it out this week. So I'm sure that will solve it," Bethany stated with a hint of uncertainty.

"Let's hope. And you did some research on the area before you started the book, didn't you? Did you look at any maps showing buildings or lots?"

Bethany thought for a moment. "Yes, there was a topographical map, and one that showed property lines in other parts of the area, but there was nothing near the hut. So that means either the map was incomplete or the same person owns all the property around the cove, which wouldn't make sense now that I own the home."

"Is there any chance that there would be another house in the area that has a tunnel connected to your shed?"

Deep in thought, Bethany looked out the window before turning to Dr. Jackman. "I know what you're trying to show me. Joseph said it was all just a part of a dream world I have created around Patience. He thinks I was in the back hall of the hut the whole time." She looked up at the therapist.

"The hospital records show that you were picked up by the emergency helicopter at—let's see, I have the address here somewhere." She shuffled through some papers. "At Faunce Cove #1."

"That's the hut. So you agree with Joseph—it was my imagination."

Dr. Jackman did not turn her eyes from Bethany's. "What I think, or what Joseph thinks, is not important. In fact, I'd bet that what happened or didn't happen isn't as important to you as *why you want it to have happened.* You seem to desperately want there to be a tunnel with a gentle man. You dream about it frequently, and you think about it during the day." Her voice was soft but firm. "Bethany, do you know why you want—really want—there to be a tunnel with a room at the end?"

Bethany hesitated, silently praying for guidance to recognize the truth. Her voice was barely audible. "I really believe that they are there and that it happened." The words felt right and true as she said them. Her voice gained strength and was nearly defiant. "I saw the man in the hospital, too, and there were flowers."

"I looked at your charts from the hospital. Besides the injuries themselves, you had a high fever which could have created delirium and memory loss, and at least one of your pain medications could have caused hallucinations. Your memories—actual or distorted—could have been caused by a number of things." She looked at Bethany, who looked pale. "I was hoping that information would relieve you, but you seem upset."

Bethany did not respond, feeling completely exhausted.

Dr. Jackman's voice was very soft. "What do those symbols represent to you? What are you willing to do to yourself or give of yourself to try to keep those hopes alive? Is it worth it?"

A hesitant tap on the door interrupted them, and Dr. Jackman stood, pushing her black-rimmed glasses back into her hair. "It also sounds like you have company, and I think you've got plenty to think about."

Bethany nodded as Dr. Jackman opened the door to the new arrivals. "Is this Bethany Carlisle's room?" a familiar voice asked.

"Bethany!" Sister Clark pulled a scarf from her carefully coifed silver hair and stepped through the door. "Is that you?"

Bethany recognized her visiting teacher and Sister Winton, the ward family history consultant, who entered the room with her. Droplets of melted snow covered their winter coats, but they nonetheless smiled irrepressibly. "We came down to the temple for a couple of days, and we just had to see you!" Sister Clark exclaimed. "I've never driven in Boston before, but Grace helped me by being the map reader, and we even found a parking garage close by, so here we are!" She took a big breath after her one-sentence explanation, leaned down, and hugged Bethany warmly. "Tell me how you are doing. We've been so worried about you."

Bethany pulled herself up in the bed. She had not expected to be so happy to see members of her Walachias ward. Sister Clark, comfortably round in her polyester pantsuit, pulled a box of cookies from her bag, while Sister Winton retrieved a chair out of the corner of the room. Bethany felt surrounded by a whirlwind as she listened to Sister Clark's cheery chatter. While Sister Clark filled Bethany in on the ward's news and urged her to snack on the cookies, Sister Winton sat quietly, nodding at the appropriate times.

Finally, after several minutes, Bethany could hold it in no longer. "So, Sister Clark, I have to know. Do you know who found me after the storm?"

Sister Clark looked confused. "Why no, dear. I understood it was your friends Joseph and Kim who found you."

"That's strange," Bethany said slowly. "How could that be? Because I know for sure that it wasn't them. Joseph was the one that told *me* that it was some of my friends from around there."

"Well!" Sister Clark said, puzzled. "Well, perhaps then it was Dr. Noel or someone from Seacrest. Although I'm sure I would have heard something about that at church by now if it was one of us," she said, still frowning.

Bethany was surprised at the miscommunication surrounding the rescue. "Well, I'll talk to Joseph about this when he comes back today. I'd like to know what really happened."

"I'll say," the two older women said in union—causing all three to laugh at the coincidence.

Nearly an hour later Sister Clark pulled up the sleeve of her vividly patterned jacket to check her watch. She stood, saying brightly, "We've got to get going!" She turned to Sister Winton and added, "We'll be late for our appointment with the doctor!"

Bethany looked up at the two, alarm showing on her face. Sister Winton quickly reassured her. "It's nothing bad, just a lunch appointment with a doctor who lived in our ward before you moved in. He's a very nice man."

"Good looking, fun to be around," Sister Clark added. "I don't think I ever laughed as hard as I did the time he told about—"

Sister Winton looked at her watch and interrupted Sister Clark. "That will have to wait for another time unless you want to be late, Blanche." She took Bethany's hand. "By the way, your questions about your Patience from Faunce Cove have got my curiosity up, and I have some ideas we can work on if you'd like."

Bethany nodded, then smiled as the two left the room. Sister Clark and a doctor who had lived in Walachias—probably retired, wife died so he moved to Boston. Good for Sister Clark!

* * *

Alone in her room later that day, Bethany pushed her dinner around her plate with her fork absentmindedly. She couldn't concentrate on eating or anything else until she had some answers about the day of the accident.

Suddenly she heard a soft knock on her door, "Bethany? Can I come in?" Joseph asked behind the door.

"Of course, Joseph. I'm just eating dinner," she answered as he came through the door and over to her bedside to kiss her forehead. As he looked down skeptically at her full dinner plate she hedged, "Well, not exactly eating yet."

Joseph had a look of worry on his face. "Difficult session with Dr. Jackman today?"

"No, it's not that at all. Joseph, Sister Clark and Sister Winton came by earlier today to visit. I asked them if they knew any more details about who rescued me, and they said that it wasn't anyone from the ward. In fact, Sister Clark had been told that it was you and Kim who had found me Christmas Day. Joseph, what's going on? How come everyone has a different story? You say that my Seacrest friends found me, but Alice didn't know any details about my rescue. And the memory I have of my rescuer as a dark-haired stranger doesn't fit any of those accounts."

Joseph's face registered bewilderment equal to Bethany's. "Sister Clark thought that I found you? How could that be? The first time I saw you was after I arrived at the hospital. You're right, Bethany. It is strange that there are so many different accounts." Joseph's eyes narrowed into a puzzled grimace as he picked up his planner and cell phone. "I'm going to make some calls."

Twenty minutes later Joseph came back into the room. "Okay, Bethany, I think I've got some answers."

Bethany sighed with relief, hoping his news explained details about the dark-haired rescuer she could not shake from her mind.

"It seems that as of right now the Seacrest Police Department isn't sure of the exact rescue details. But after calling around to Alice and different people I've met in the community, apparently the rumor is that a group of college kids came up from Boston for Christmas break and were out enjoying the new snow on their snowmobiles. When they saw the damaged hut, they stepped in to investigate, and that's when they found you. Since they're all back at their various universities, the police are having a hard time tracking down the exact story."

"So it really wasn't anyone I knew. I'm pretty lucky they came by the hut," she said, though she considered her rescue an answer to prayer, not simply a lucky coincidence. She wondered to herself if one of the college boys was the dark-haired stranger.

"There's a lot we don't know right now, Bethany. And until the police find out more, we're just going to have to be patient and wait. In the meantime, I'd think about something else."

"Maybe you're right, Joseph. But I do have one more question about that night. Did you ever hear back from the cleanup workers about the shed and the tunnel door?"

Joseph sighed deeply as a dark cloud passed over his countenance. "Bethany, I'm sorry to tell you this . . . but I suppose now is as good a time as any. The contractors said that they couldn't get in because the door to the shed is blocked by frost heaves and drifted snow frozen too stiff to break with an ax. They said no one could have gotten into the shed."

* * *

"So, you are finally going to get out of here!" Dr. Jackman exclaimed. "Congratulations! Your doctors said you don't need all this anymore. You must be excited. Where will you go first, now that you're getting your freedom back?"

Bethany tried to make her response appropriately cheerful. "I haven't decided yet."

"After all these days of waiting, you haven't decided? Too many alternatives to choose from?"

"I guess, or maybe . . ." she started hesitatingly, then continued, "maybe the choice isn't exactly mine. Joseph wants me to stay in a hotel down here in Boston. He's worried I'm not strong enough to be on my own at the hut. He and a friend have planned a trip to San Francisco as soon as I'm able to travel, but meanwhile he made reservations for me here where it will be more convenient to get to physical therapy and doctor appointments."

"Does that seem like a good idea to you?" Dr. Jackman asked.

"Maybe, but I don't think he wants me to go back to writing at the hut—at least not about Patience."

"Does he try to control a lot of what you do? We haven't talked a lot about that. Are you planning a long-term relationship?"

Bethany had not expected the direct question and did not respond immediately. "Sometimes when I'm with him I feel kind of smothered. Still, I can't imagine my life without him. But he seems opposed to my writing, and I don't want to quit that either." She had spent a lot of time thinking and praying about Joseph's aversion to her writing the book. But she didn't feel it was the wrong thing to do and didn't want to stop.

"Do you know why it is so important to you to write about Patience?" the therapist queried. "Do you think you could be using that as a reason to avoid other things?" Then, after a long pause, Dr.

Jackman continued, "Are you using your book to avoid thinking about your relationships with Amelia and Joseph? And is Joseph opposed to your research, or to the fact that it keeps you physically and emotionally separated from him?"

Bethany drew in her breath. Was she ignoring other issues in her life—Amelia, Joseph, even her future career and marriage? And was her obsession with the gentle eyes of an unknown man another symptom of her avoidance?

She remained silent, looking out the window.

"Are you all right?" prompted Dr. Jackman.

"Well," Bethany replied wearily, "I am *going* to be."

13

February had come by the time Bethany was released from rehab. Winter had firmly entrenched itself. It was bitterly cold, and remnants of old snowstorms were still piled in parking places in the streets. It was evident that some of the snow piles concealed vehicles whose owners had stubbornly refused to relinquish their hard-won parking spots.

The bellhop assisted Joseph as he helped Bethany through the door of the Eliot Hotel. She had agreed with Joseph to a temporary stay in Boston, and he had chosen a lovely suite—which she felt she didn't need. Why should she be located in the middle of Back Bay when she could barely get from the bed to the bathroom? The French doors into the bedroom were nice and the Italian marbled bathroom luxurious, but she missed the hut and longed to shower in her own drafty bathroom.

The days passed quickly—getting ready for physical therapy, calling a cab, slowly maneuvering on crutches out to Commonwealth Avenue, struggling in and out of the cab, and in and out of the therapy center. In and out so many times that once she was back facing the French doors she was always much too exhausted and frazzled to enjoy her lavish surroundings or the French cuisine. She longed to walk into her own little kitchen at the hut and make a peanut-butter-and-jelly sandwich, to reach into her own refrigerator for a glass of milk. Most of all, she wanted to sit quietly at her computer and write about the woman who had survived the isolation of Faunce Cove.

When he had a free evening, Joseph would try to eat with Bethany, but by the time he arrived after work, she had usually eaten and felt more comfortable resting in bed. Joseph didn't seem to understand her fatigue, continually encouraging her to get out more.

"I thought this would be an ideal location for you. Why don't you stop at a museum on the way back from therapy? They have handicapped facilities, and I'm sure someone would help you. I think you need to do something to get your mind off your cast and your other aches and pains."

Too tired to respond, Bethany realized Joseph had no concept of how hard it was to drag her body across a car seat, then twist and stand and balance with only one arm and one leg to support her. He seemed quite disturbed by her lack of activity, much more so than she was. He wanted her to be cheerful. His demands that she pretend to be happy just added to her frustration. Did he think she *wanted* to be tired and irritable?

Bethany wondered about Peter, her throat tightening on those weary nights after Joseph left, when she was weakened with fatigue and her emotions were close to the surface. Would Peter have been more patient with her condition? She would never know.

One night a family home evening group from the singles ward she had been attending in Boston visited her. Bethany had not been able to attend the ward consistently during her rehabilitation and therapy—sometimes she was just too tired. Consequently, she didn't know the members well. They stayed only a few minutes, but the cluster of golden, grocery-store chrysanthemums stuck in an empty salad dressing jar had cheered her. After they left she realized the flowers reminded her of the daffodils in the hospital arranged in Amelia's style—and the kind eyes. The night after the FHE group visited, Bethany woke up and saw the flowers. She glanced around quickly, half expecting to see the man. He was not there. What would he think of her, irritated and depressed with her healing process? What would Amelia think of her granddaughter lying around in an opulent hotel complaining? And what of Patience?

Suddenly Bethany felt contented. Patience would have understood. Having faced the reality of tragic losses and survived, Patience would not have judged Bethany for being discouraged and distressed by the situation.

It took several weeks for enough strength to return to her hand and arm that she could use crutches efficiently, then several more weeks before the therapist mentioned a walking cast. Kim immediately reintroduced her idea of Bethany spending a week in San Francisco. Joseph encouraged Bethany to consider the trip. "I think it would do wonders for you."

It surprised her when Joseph announced he would accompany her. He said he could schedule some client meetings in San Francisco so he wouldn't have to take vacation time. He would spend a week there, then leave the women to enjoy a few days alone before Bethany flew back to Boston. He was not discouraged by her hesitancy. "You just need to get away and do something fun! By the time you get back, you'll be a changed person."

Bethany shrugged her shoulders. Did she need to change? If Joseph really cared about her, wouldn't he be more tolerant of her despondency? Besides, all she needed to improve her disposition was a computer, but Joseph had made excuses each time she mentioned it. Then, when she continued to plead, he had said that she needed to get away from her writing for a while. Though he did not say it specifically, she knew he meant she needed to quit thinking about Patience. Once again, he intimated that her obsession with Patience and the history of the cove had been the reason for her hallucinations the night of the accident.

* * *

Kim met them at the front door of her apartment in San Francisco.

"You're finally here and walking," Kim stated brightly as she hugged Bethany and then Joseph.

"With a cast," Bethany replied. Even with Joseph's attention and help, the flight had exhausted her. Now all she wanted was a glass of milk and a bed. But one sniff of the apartment told her that Kim had prepared a gourmet meal.

Joseph mentioned the inviting aromas coming from the kitchen, but he seemed uneasy intruding on their reunion. "Well, I don't want to get in the way, so I'll catch a taxi and get settled in the hotel."

"No, no," Kim answered, walking with them into the small dining area where candles and three place settings shimmered on the table. "This is a welcome to you both."

The wonderful food revived Bethany briefly, but she was still grateful when Joseph kissed her good night, Kim showed her the guest room, and she lifted her mending leg onto the bed. Joseph had started to leave, but Bethany suggested he stay and visit with Kim; just because she was tired didn't mean the whole world needed to come to a halt. She went to sleep with the reassuring thought that the two people who cared about her the most—and that she cared about the most—were in the next room.

The next day was beautiful, a perfect day to ride the trolley or go shopping—if you didn't have a cast. Or to go to the Golden Gate Bridge or any of the marvelous historical districts and museums—if you weren't too tired from jet lag and had a headache. By the time Joseph arrived from his hotel and they'd devoured the pancakes and eggs Kim cooked, a nap seemed more attractive that any of the tourist spots.

Joseph looked at her questioningly while Kim slid her arm around her shoulder.

"Well, what do you expect? You spent all day traveling."

"But Joseph only has a week to see everything." Bethany turned to Joseph. "You don't want to sit around here while I nap. Can you two sightsee without me?"

"I don't like leaving you. This is supposed to be your vacation," Kim said. "But, on the other hand, I'm not sure you could really rest with us here disturbing you. Are you sure you'd be all right alone?"

"I'm sure, and if I rest today, by tomorrow I'll be ready to go with you."

But she wasn't. She was still exhausted, and dragging a cast around didn't help. Kim suggested they rent a wheelchair, but Bethany turned down the offer. That would just seem like she was giving up, and the truth was she just didn't have the desire to sightsee.

On the fourth night of their visit, Bethany sent Joseph out to eat with Kim, once again too tired to face a menu and then karaoke in a crowded restaurant. She poured a bowl of cereal for herself, lay down on the couch, and sighed in frustration. She wanted to spend time with Joseph and Kim, but she was tired. Joseph was more understanding the first few days when she declined to leave the house, but by the end of the week it was obvious that he was frustrated. Bethany could tell by the way Kim grimaced that she was uncomfortable with the situation.

Bethany fell asleep on the couch almost wishing she'd stayed in Massachusetts. It was after 1:00 A.M. when she woke. Still half asleep, she tried to slip quietly into her room, surprised that Kim had been able to enter the apartment and go to her room without waking her. In her bed, Bethany was pulling the blanket over her cast when she heard Kim's laugh outside the apartment door, and then the sound of the lock release.

She heard Joseph and Kim enter the living room, then quiet footsteps by her door as she relaxed into her pillow. She saw a sliver of light as Kim pushed the door slightly open and then pulled it shut with a soft click. As the footsteps retreated to the living area, Bethany could hear Joseph and Kim's conversation.

"She's sound asleep."

"I thought she would be. I'm worried about her, Kim. She is always tired and depressed. She talked to a counselor a couple of times, but I'm not sure it helped. Bethany didn't tell me much about it and the counselor couldn't, but sometimes she just doesn't make sense."

"About that night?"

"She really thinks she found a tunnel going from the back of the shed and that she escaped through it."

"Are you sure there couldn't be something there?"

"I was in the shed with her last summer and I didn't see anything. The contractors fixing the hut checked the shed for me. They were able to pry the door far enough open to shine a flashlight in, but they couldn't see any door or tunnel. And, the area in front of the shed was the only logical place to put the debris from the fallen tree and the hut, so the shed door is completely blocked now. But besides the tunnel, Bethany thinks she made it through the snow with a ladder and a broken leg and opened a door blocked by frost heaves and drifts."

"But why . . . ?"

"She got too obsessed researching that woman who'd lived at Faunce Cove. Did she tell you about her—Patience? I think with Amelia's death and her grief, then being isolated at the hut, she's let her imagination run away with her. I thought getting her out here away from all of that would help, but it hasn't."

Bethany heard the voices fade as Joseph and Kim moved farther from her door.

She had been blaming Joseph for his attitude when it was all her fault—and her imagination. She turned over and sobbed into her pillow.

The next morning, even though she was still fatigued, Bethany pulled herself from the bed and carefully applied her makeup. She was fully dressed and pulling breakfast items from the refrigerator when Kim, still in her robe, joined her. Joseph's knock sent Kim scurrying to dress, while Bethany made an omelet. Her arm ached afterward, but she slid it into her jacket and laughed as she briskly swung her leg with its cast when they walked to the car. By the time they stopped for lunch at Fisherman's Wharf, Bethany was grateful when Kim suggested that Bethany take a break while she drove Joseph past the Presidio. Kim knew Bethany wouldn't be interested in golfing anyway, and it would give her time to rest and dress before they drove up to Nob Hill for dinner.

Alone in Kim's apartment, Bethany could not stop thinking about the conversation she had overheard the night before. The words had kept her moving all morning. It might be hard to find the desire to go out with them, but she would enjoy the rest of their time in San Francisco together—or at least she would make Joseph think so.

Bethany was nearly asleep when she thought of Joseph's description of the Faunce Cove shed, inaccessible because of the snow and frost heaves. Her memories of her journey during the blizzard were not vivid, but neither did they seem imaginary. It had been several months since the incident, and there had obviously been many more storms—but Bethany had to be realistic. As real as it had all seemed—the feel of the smooth stones on the tunnel floor, and the sharper edges of rocks along the wall—it was questionable at least and improbable at best. Joseph was probably right. There had been no tunnel, no floral arrangement. The man with kind eyes had only existed in her hallucinations that night and in her dreams in the hospital. Again she fell asleep crying.

When Kim and Joseph returned, they were discussing their favorite brand of irons and kidding about their individual forms.

Seeing the golf course, Kim reported, had inspired them to try a few swings at a local driving range and they had lost track of time. Bethany looked at her friend gratefully. Kim undoubtedly realized the toll that Bethany's increased effort to "enjoy herself" was taking on her and how much she needed the break. Kim had connived to keep Joseph out golfing so Bethany could rest.

Apologizing for being late, the two placed the takeout food they carried in on the table and suggested they go to dinner at Nob Hill another evening—another one of Kim's plans to rescue her, Bethany concluded. If they didn't make it this trip, then during the next one, Joseph quipped. There was no reason this had to be their only visit to San Francisco. Had he gained more empathy for her situation too, and joined in with Kim to make Bethany's vacation more enjoyable?

* * *

After Joseph returned to Boston, the pace of Bethany's "vacation" slowed considerably. Bethany enjoyed visiting with Kim in the evenings, and her daytime activities while Kim was at work were just as enjoyable. In fact, she'd set a goal that by the time she got back to Faunce Cove she would have a new topic to write about. Each morning Kim, with her portfolio full of fabric swatches and paint chips, dropped Bethany off at a library. When Bethany tired of her research, she caught a taxi and lumbered back down the hallway to the apartment.

She spent most of her time researching the heroines of the West, determined to find a new main character for her book. She had ideas for several novels—a pioneer saga or perhaps a romance spanning the Saints' westward trek—and she was ready to get back to the hut to write. *But not about Patience,* she reminded herself. Joseph had been right about her experience the night of the accident, so whether or not he was correct in blaming Patience for her distraction from reality, he deserved her trust. She would write about another subject. She nearly told him several times when he called. But she finally decided to wait and see his response when she told him in person.

14

Joseph met Bethany at the airport in Boston. He hugged and kissed her briefly, looking apprehensively at her face. "How was the flight? Are you tired?" Although drained, she denied it, content to have the long flight behind her and to be near him. The March evening was cold, and he walked her through the parking garage to the heated car. He helped her in and loaded her luggage into the car. Then he navigated the car between the cement pillars before reaching for her hand.

"I worried about you. It will be good to have you home tucked into your own suite where I can actually see how you are myself, rather than depending on Kim's analysis."

In retrospect, Bethany realized that she should have waited to mention her plans. Instead she blurted them out as he drove toward the airport exit. "Actually, I'm ready to move back to the hut. I think I can have everything packed by the weekend."

"I thought you might enjoy a few more weeks here. How about after we've vacationed in New York, we can sit down with the doctors and decide what you really want to do?"

"But that would mean I'd be here for at least another month! I'm ready to go back now." The protest came out before she thought about it. She knew it sounded like a whine.

"Bethany, you're still in a cast! How can you take care of yourself?"

"It will be easier at the hut than here with all these people. I won't have to contend with transportation or shopping. I actually have a lot of my food storage, and I'm sure Sister Clark or Dr. Noel and Alice will be glad to help. I'll be able to stay at home and just relax."

Bethany wondered how Joseph could have expected her to walk up and down the San Francisco hills, and yet now insist that her cast rendered her unfit to take care of herself. But she decided to remain silent on that point. She had a feeling that he doubted her emotional strength more than her physical strength.

"What will you do without anywhere to go? Remember how bored you were in the rehab center."

"I'll have time to write! Can you imagine being able to sit down and write for hours at a time without being interrupted?" She could tell by the look on Joseph's face that he was not pleased. "Please, Joseph. Once I get a book done I'll be able to leave it and settle down. I just need to get it out of my blood!"

Joseph turned to look out the window, his solid silhouette dark against the airport lights.

"I understand that's what you think, Bethany, and I know that's what Amelia wanted for you. And yet you've been through a lot since then. I'm really worried about you. You know . . ." Joseph let his sentence trail off when Bethany turned her face to look out at the lights.

As they approached the turnstile at the Callahan Tunnel, Joseph and Bethany remained silent. His wide frame was stiff as he concentrated on the traffic, while red brake lights blinked on and off in front of them. Bethany watched the tiles of the tunnel slowly slip by. She wanted to tell him that he needn't worry, that she'd decided to stop working on her book about Patience. She'd previously planned out how she would squeeze his hand or maybe kiss his cheek when she told him she was doing it to please him. However, she couldn't say the words, and they drove through Back Bay in silence.

When they reached the hotel and the bellboy lifted the suitcases from the trunk, Joseph turned to her, his expression conciliatory. "We're both tired and tense. We can talk about your plans later." He kissed her on the forehead. The strength of his arm around her shoulder felt good as she leaned against him, waiting for the bellboy to open the door.

Joseph insisted on attending her next appointment with the physical therapist. To Bethany's delight, the therapist was not concerned when she mentioned moving back to the hut. She said that initially

Bethany would need to limit her exercise, but that if Joseph were really worried, a home healthcare provider or a live-in nurse could ease the transition.

Joseph called Dr. Noel, who suggested that Bethany contact Sister Winton. Besides being a genealogist, she was a very capable widow who had nursed her husband through the long years of a heart ailment until his death. She might be interested in a job. *If*—Joseph repeated the word with emphasis—*if* everything was arranged with Sister Winton, he would take her to the hut the weekend after her final therapy session. Bethany had a feeling that he'd agreed to have Sister Winton temporarily keep an eye out for and care for Bethany because of her emotions more than for physical reasons. But at this point, freedom was freedom, and life at the hut was so close she could almost taste it!

* * *

The mid-March transition to the hut was not easy. The drive to the hut seemed interminably long and uncomfortable. The tension began when Joseph and Bethany got a late start after packing her things in the car. Bethany wondered, though, if that was the real reason for the strained atmosphere between them. Neither spoke other than about the traffic and the dismal weather.

When at last they rounded the curve into Seacrest in the late afternoon, the ocean seemed dark and silent. The only things that looked cheerfully homey against the bleak scenery were the windows at the McCleres' Bed-and-Breakfast, but Bethany was much too tired to stop.

As Bethany opened the door to the hut, the room looked as if it were waiting expectantly. A card from Alice assured her that the welcoming was not by accident. A fire smoldered in the fireplace, and the room smelled of homemade bread and mulled apple cider. Bethany did not know whether her tears came because of Alice's thoughtfulness or from the emptiness she felt despite the welcome. Perhaps the tears were just part of the exhaustion that seemed to have taken over her body as she had traveled with Joseph.

Trying to ignore her cast, she hobbled into the living room and looked around. The damage had been repaired, but, even though the room looked exactly as she thought it should, there was a chill that the warmth of the fire could not dispel.

Moving slowly to the kitchen love seat, Bethany pulled an afghan around her. She could not escape the agitation that had engulfed her during the drive. Joseph adjusted the fire, brought in several boxes, and carried her luggage upstairs. She could hear him wrestling with the closet door as she stood. Knowing what she must do before she would be able to feel secure, she limped into the dining area.

Bethany took a deep breath as she stopped by the window where she had stood that night. The snow had nearly melted from the side of the hut, and she was sure there were indentations in the ground where the pine had dug into the soil. She sighed deeply, relieved to have faced a moment she had dreaded for weeks.

She looked up at the mountain. She had not expected the opening left by the large pine tree that had previously curtained the sky, which now lay in innocent-looking pieces stacked by the patio.

No breeze swayed the remaining pines, but they seemed to dance a demonic ballet around her. Now, though she saw the huge panes of glass stretched shiny and bright between the window frames, her mind heard glass crack, splinter, and split, and her body felt the brilliant shards explode toward her. She trembled as she clasped her shaking hand over her mouth to keep from screaming. But there was no pain, and soon the trees no longer swayed behind the sparkling glass. She felt limp, nearly faint, frightened by the moisture that dripped from her cheek until she realized it was only tears.

After reliving the incident there in that moment, Bethany couldn't shake the feeling again that there was more to the incident than she was remembering—more danger she'd experienced than she now recalled. But the memory eluded her like the outline of a ragged cliff in heavy morning fog. She knew there was something there, but it seemed nearly impossible to focus the hazy scene into a solid memory and bring it back into her consciousness.

At that moment Joseph came silently to her side. "Is this where you were when it happened?" When she nodded, he pulled her into his arms, holding her as if she were a frightened child. He helped her to the couch. Then he sat with her as she cried. When her sobs subsided, he looked down at her tenderly. "When I made arrangements to stay at McCleres', I also asked Alice to have a room ready for you. I don't want you here alone."

Bethany didn't protest. After reliving that frightful experience and now reveling in Joseph's nearness, she knew that if at that moment he had asked her to move from Faunce Cove to Boston, she would have agreed.

Instead, he got up and opened the refrigerator.

"Someone left chicken soup. Would you like me to heat it?" he asked quietly. "You could listen to your voice mail while I get the soup ready."

Bethany agreed to have some soup but ignored Joseph's prompting to check her voice mail. If Peter had left another message and Joseph heard it, she would not only have to explain who he was, but then address the fact that he was missing and still hadn't returned. She wasn't ready to do that yet.

After eating the soup, she cuddled with Joseph under the afghan, watching TV. By the time Joseph suggested they head back to the bed-and-breakfast, she felt much better. Despite a rousing welcome by the twins and a quick chat with Alice about her new job as a cook at the school cafeteria, Bethany fell asleep immediately.

She woke late to a brilliant, sunlit morning. Because the McCleres had already left for their own church, Joseph relayed Alice's invitation to stop by for Sunday dinner or, if Bethany preferred, to pick up plates of food to heat at the hut.

By the end of sacrament meeting, Bethany's leg was aching terribly. She and Joseph left before Sunday School, but not before Sister Winton caught them in the foyer. She assured them that she would be at the hut so Joseph could leave for Boston before dark. Joseph stopped at McCleres' and picked up the plates Alice filled to be reheated at the hut. Bethany stepped into the back hallway to wash her hands and glanced out the back window. The door of the shed was blocked by a pile of rubbish. She pulled her sweater closer around her as she remembered Joseph telling Kim about it in San Francisco.

After they ate, he put on music as they relaxed together on the love seat.

"This feels so good," Bethany murmured as she rested her head against his shoulder. "I wish life were always like this."

"Maybe it could be," Joseph replied, playing with her fingers with his free hand. "You could come back to Boston with me. Get a nice apartment and do some more research on your medieval literature. You could write up your research and get it published."

Bethany straightened and turned to look at him, surprised. "Why write a research paper and not a novel?"

Joseph answered placidly, "I just think it would be better for you to stay away from that kind of thing until you are more stable."

"More stable? I'm not sure what you mean." She slid from his side to face him, her body stiffening.

"Come on, Bethany, I'm worried about you." He reached for her hand, but she pulled it away. "You know, the way you want to be up here away from everyone. You've been very despondent and tired since the accident. I just think it'd be good for you to relax here and get back to reality before you get caught up in Patience and your fictitious world."

She should tell him about her decision, she thought. She should tell him that she had realized that there had been no tunnel, no man, no flowers on a table. But if she told him now, it would seem like she was changing because of him, capitulating because he'd somehow straightened out her thinking. There was a time when she might have done that, but things were changing.

"I'm *not* caught up in a fictitious world! I found something I really enjoy, and I want to keep at it. Is that wrong? Isn't that what Amelia wanted for me?" She could hear her voice rising.

"I'm not saying that it is right or wrong." Joseph's calm voice was maddeningly placating. "I'm trying to tell you that I think it is unhealthy for you. Especially this Patience thing." He took the hand she had pulled from him and rubbed it softly. "Ever since the accident I've worried about you. Those first days of seizures, then the pneumonia and fever, I did some thinking. I realized how much I want to be with you. But it always feels like something is taking you away. You want to be up here, hours from Boston and me. Even when you were in Boston, you spent all your time thinking about Patience. I think it is unhealthy, and I think we should be involved in more things that we can do together."

He continued. "Today during church, I had an idea. Maybe we should compromise." He looked at Bethany, her head tilted as she studied his face. "I know that the Church means a lot to you and that you would like me to take the missionary lessons. I haven't had time, but I will make the time for you, if you will make more time for me—and for me, that means that you give up this thing about Patience."

Bethany sat stunned. If Joseph studied the Church sincerely, she knew he would gain a testimony. But what he had suggested felt like he was bargaining—blackmailing—her into a compromise he thought she could not resist. Perhaps she had misunderstood.

"You're saying that you'll investigate the Church if I quit investigating Patience?"

"Yes. I think that's a fair trade."

His words sounded brusque, thoughtless. Religion was not a commodity to barter, and neither were her feelings—including her passion for Patience. She couldn't believe Joseph thought so little of her—and the Church—that he would use the Church or her interest to buy the other.

Mistaking her silence for hesitation, Joseph said, "Bethany, I don't think I can go on like this. I'm always worrying about you, wondering if you will get so engrossed with your Patience and her world that you will do something dangerous. Have you ever considered what would have happened to you if you'd really gone out to the shed in that storm? What if you'd truly gone into some tunnel or wandered into a stranger's home? I'm afraid this Patience fantasy will lead you into that kind of thinking again."

The words hit Bethany like a stinging slap. She reminded herself that she, too, had concluded that she was delusional the day of the accident. But she was shocked that Joseph would throw it at her so bluntly. Did he really think she was on the verge of psychosis?

"That is unfair!" Bethany retorted angrily. She stood, unable to find the right words to defend herself or explain her reasoning. She tried to speak but could not think of the words that conveyed the disillusionment and disappointment she felt.

Joseph spoke precisely and deliberately as he rose and moved toward her. "But it is true. I don't know how much more of this I can take."

Bethany turned her face from him and looked out the window at the dusky view. "Then perhaps you shouldn't put yourself in that position anymore."

"I can't believe you won't give up Patience even though I'm willing to join your church."

"If you find the Church is true, then you should join. But that has nothing to do with Patience, or with me and our relationship. I don't want you joining the Church to please me." Fighting to keep her composure, Bethany hurried on. "And I'm sorry that I've worried you. You certainly don't have to be concerned any longer."

"Bethany, you're taking this the wrong way. I wouldn't be concerned if I didn't care about you. Can we just walk out to the shed and look for a door? I'm beginning to think that you seeing it's not there for yourself is the only thing that will make you realize how far into this imaginary thing you've plunged. We need to get it solved once and for all. You know, this isn't pleasant for me either." His voice was getting louder.

"Then you should—" She stopped herself before she said the word. She looked up at Joseph. "I'm sorry. I know you are just concerned . . ." For some reason she did not want to explain the changes she'd already made in her writing plans, but she would not let him worry about her so-called fantasy either. "We don't need to go to the shed. It wouldn't do us any good right now anyway. I looked out the back door and there's all sorts of junk—from repairing the hut I imagine—in front of it, and I'm pretty sure the frost heaves have pushed the ground up so much that we'd never get the door opened even if the area were cleared out and there wasn't any snow." She sighed and looked away. "I know that my memory was confused about a lot of things while I was so heavily medicated in the hospital. I know the part about the tunnel didn't happen. However, I do not live in a fantasy world. And I am not crazy. I promise I won't go to the shed unless I have a very good reason. I'm sorry for worrying you."

"What about Patience?"

She could not tell him that in her mind she had already given up Patience, and that she had done it for him. But she still felt indignant. She may have been delusional about Christmas Eve, she and the tunnel, but that had nothing to do with Patience. Silently, she sat down beside him. Joseph reached to her, his face drawn, his broad shoulders sagging. "Bethany, it's all right. It's been a busy weekend and you're tired. Maybe we just need a little time apart to figure out what we both want." His voice took on a hint of sarcasm. "And since you insist on being up here, we'll have plenty of that."

They heard a car door slam. "That will be Sister Winton," Bethany explained.

"And I need to get going." Joseph took a deep breath and checked his watch. "I'll call you tomorrow—it'll be too late to call when I get home tonight, and you need rest. Think about what I said, okay?" He pulled on his coat. His quick kiss on her cheek left her with no more feeling than had a stranger accidentally brushed against her.

15

After settling her things in the corner, Sister Winton bustled around the living room, making the couch into a bed. When Joseph had assured Bethany that Sister Winton would stay with her for several weeks, Bethany had been dismayed—especially when he said she would not have to be alone for even an hour. She longed for freedom and a chance to spend time alone. She wondered if Joseph had instructed Sister Winton to distract her from her writing. Bethany watched her fluffing a pillow into its case before the petite woman came down to the fireplace. Bethany nestled back into the love seat.

"You look like you could use some cheering," Sister Winton said as she slipped past Bethany to sit near the fire. "It must be hard to see Joseph leave. What you need is something to get him off your mind. Do you have a novel to read? Do you want me to get your journal or some paper to write letters?"

Bethany shook her head. "No, thank you. I'm fine." She sat staring at the fireplace.

"This may not be the best time to ask, but have you done any more research on Patience?"

Trying to contain her emotions, Bethany forced herself to speak in a calm voice. "I'm not upset because Joseph just left. We had a quarrel and it was about Patience." She sighed before she continued. "He thinks that I have gone totally overboard. I have to admit that I think about her a lot of the time. Is that strange, Sister Winton?"

"Call me Grace, why don't you?" the older woman said as she relaxed back on the end of the love seat. "That's how genealogists are—we have a habit of getting lost in our research. At first my husband complained that I spent too much time at it, but then he realized how much I enjoyed it and started encouraging me. Even before we joined the Church around thirty years ago, something about genealogy intrigued me. I couldn't find out enough about my ancestors."

"But Patience isn't my ancestor—she was the first woman who lived here at Faunce Cove. And unlike your husband, Joseph wants me to quit. He thinks that I need to get, as he puts it, 'back into reality.'"

Grace frowned. "Well, I've always found that when a person has strong feelings about someone they are researching, there's usually a good reason. Have you prayed about it?"

"I've been praying about it for months. I just don't seem to get an answer."

"What do you ask when you pray—if you don't mind me asking?"

Bethany shrugged. "I ask to know if I should be spending my time researching and writing about Patience, or if Joseph is correct."

"What do you think? What do you want the answer to be?"

"I want to find out about Patience. I feel good about that."

"Have you asked that way? Have you said, 'I feel good about doing this. Please confirm my decision if it is right'? Remember the brother of Jared, the prophet in the Book of Mormon? He had to come up with a suggestion and do some preparation before Heavenly Father helped him get lights for his ships. Maybe you need to come up with an answer yourself and then pray for conformation about it like he did. If learning about Patience is stressing you and your relationship with Joseph, maybe finding out about her can help you get finished with her so you and he can get on with your lives. Now," she said, rising from the love seat, "I think a little food and a good night's sleep would help a lot." She looked at the contents of the refrigerator. "I see some leftover chicken soup. Or I can grill some cheese sandwiches and open a can of tomato soup. Does that sound good?"

After dinner, when Grace had cleared up the dishes, she looked at Bethany questioningly. "I'm wondering," she said cautiously, "if you can be alone or if you need me here in the room with you. I'd like to put on a coat and watch the sunset from the steps."

"I'm sure I'll be fine alone. I have a few things in here to catch up on, so you go enjoy yourself," Bethany replied, thinking of her answering machine. She felt guilty at her impatience as she watched Grace pull on a coat, wrap a scarf around her neck, and slip her hands into leather gloves.

"If you're really sure you'll be okay, there is still enough light for a short walk on the road to watch the sunset."

"I'm fine. Joseph may not think so, but I'm ready to be pretty independent."

"Oh, good." Grace nodded and opened the door. "I've got a Walkman and some conference CDs I'll listen to unless you think I need to be able to hear if you call."

"No, really. In fact, I think I'll clear off the old messages on my answering machine. I'm sure I need to erase a bunch of them."

"Good idea. Then I'll take off and leave you to that." Grace smiled and put her earpieces in, then slid the door closed.

Now that Grace had left the hut, Bethany could listen to her messages in private in case Peter had called. If Grace were in the room and heard one of Peter's messages she would certainly have a number of questions that would be difficult or impossible to answer.

There had been no electricity in the hut for a few days, so the first messages were New Year's greetings from Dr. Noel and Sister Clark expressing their concern, not sure if she was still in the hospital or back at the hut.

Suddenly Bethany's heart caught in her throat when the next message played a familiar voice that was nearly swallowed up by background noise. "Bethany, I have . . ." It sounded like Peter! Then a clanging sound drowned out the voice. Bethany waited. Again the nearly unintelligible voice began, "Bethany . . ." Then the sounds ceased and the automated attendant declared, "End of message."

Bethany replayed the message. The voice had to be Peter's, but she couldn't be absolutely certain. She listened to the message several times but could glean nothing more from it. Then she sat down and listened to the rest of her messages, mostly sales pitches or requests for donations.

Suddenly, a new message began that made Bethany sit up straight. She could hear a slight thump over the low drone of a voice, but then the underlying tones vanished and the message ended. Bethany listened to it again, but she couldn't tell who was speaking.

Finally, the telemarketers were interrupted by ward members asking if she needed any help when she came home from rehab. There was one more voiceless call amid the varied callers.

Bethany again listened carefully to each of the strange calls. Finally determining that the saved messages weren't substantive enough to provide any useful clues, she reset the machine and deleted all the strange calls.

* * *

Grace went to bed early after persuading Bethany to let her make the love seat into a bed so Bethany wouldn't have to climb the stairs with her cast. It was difficult to find a comfortable position, but Bethany wasn't sure that was the reason she had trouble sleeping. Even after she quit thinking about the questionable phone calls, she couldn't get Joseph's words and her rebuttals out of her mind. She knew that she would not be able to write, really write, until she knew what she should do about Joseph and Patience. So, sitting in her makeshift bed, since it was impossible to kneel with her cast, she prayed as Grace had suggested. The answer was a feeling as warm and comforting as the heat from the fireplace beside her: she should continue to learn about Patience. She went to sleep watching the sparking coals send up blue flares and orange-bronze flames in the deeply shadowed fire hole.

Bethany slept late the next morning. She woke to find Grace dressed in corduroy slacks and a turtleneck covered by a cardigan. Gold-rimmed glasses framed her eyes as she flipped from one page to another in the collection of books she had spread over a couch and table in the upper room. She looked up with a cheery smile, then pulled the cords on the drapes and turned off the lamp she had been using. The morning was foggy, and even with the drapes open the hut felt enclosed like a peaceful retreat. Bethany glanced out at the mist as she sat eating the hot bowl of oatmeal Grace had sprinkled with raisins. She was thrilled to be home, eating breakfast in her pajamas!

"Did you have anything scheduled for the morning?" Grace asked cheerfully as she picked up the empty bowl. "Something I can help you with?"

Bethany turned from the window. She had longed for this moment for weeks. Now, though she wished Joseph could understand, she realized she could not change what she felt.

"I'm going to write about Patience," she declared quietly, smiling at Grace.

Bethany turned on the laptop and clicked on the shortcut to the file that contained the beginning of her book about Patience. Reviewing the scenario she had written months before, she found herself even more enveloped in the narrative about the woman who had struggled for her life as Bethany had—or thought she had.

As much as she had wanted to write, the task was still difficult. She spent the rest of the morning rereading what she'd written and studying her outline. By lunchtime she felt exhausted and discouraged. All the anticipation had brought her mind to a place she'd never been before with the story: she could not add a single paragraph to the manuscript. She continued to sit at the table after Grace had finished and her own plate was empty. Finally, she stood up restlessly.

Grace looked up from the stack of papers she had piled on the couch. She pulled her glasses down from her face, letting them dangle from the thin gold chain that looped around her neck.

"How's it going?" she asked as Bethany hobbled up the step from the fireplace to look out at the dim outline of the ocean, which was barely visible through the lifting mist.

"Not good," Bethany admitted. "All this time I thought I could just sit down and finish the book. Now I don't know what to do with it. Somehow I need to help Patience mature and make her into a woman in love. I'm lost! You said you had some research possibilities?"

"If you were researching your own family, I'd tell you to start by getting out all your family memorabilia—Bibles, diaries, pictures, everything. In this case, I don't suppose you have anything like that about Patience, do you?"

"All I have is a few pages photocopied from the library's historical collections."

Grace stood, reaching for a paper and pencil. "That's not a bad place to start. Let's have a look."

Grace briefly scanned the papers Bethany had collected.

"All right." Grace pulled out a clean sheet of paper. "Now, what do we know for sure? Let's start with her name."

"We don't know it for sure, but something like Patience, although it could start with an *R*, maybe Rachel or Rebecca—no record of her last name, maiden or married."

"Birth date and place? Marriage date and place? Death date and place?"

Bethany glanced through the papers. "Nothing," she sighed, then slid back in her chair, and with a touch of cynicism added, "At least that was quick."

Grace smiled. "Well, I think we can come up with more than that if we do some figuring."

"Really?"

"We know Patience lived here at Faunce Cove around . . ."

"I don't know if we really even know that. One historian doubted the account."

"But we know there was a woman. We have a photographed copy of a signature to prove that—the fact that we can't read it is irrelevant. People who never existed don't have photocopied signatures. Now, this may be way off, but there is always the possibility that since Patience was in this area, something from her—an item someone collected, old household articles that were still useful—was left in the hut."

"There is a bowl—and it has some markings on it!" Bethany struggled to stand and take the piece down from the mantel. "Why didn't I think of that before?"

"You weren't associating her with this house. The only real information you had about her indicated that her home had been burned by the Indians, destroyed except for the fireplace." Grace eagerly shuffled through Bethany's papers. "Now where is that photocopy of her signature?"

Grace held the paper by the bowl and compared the two signatures, then looked at Bethany with a triumphant grin. "The marks are almost exactly alike! The letters are illegible, but this is definite proof that Patience—or whatever her name was—was associated with this house or with someone who brought the bowl here later."

"There are some more marks there on the mortar." Bethany pointed to the joint between the fireplace and the hearthstone.

Grace knelt down and held the paper by the hearthstone, studying it intently. "And this shows her here in this house—your hut— kneeling just where I am, to put her name in the mortar."

"This hut? Here?" Bethany felt goose bumps rise on her arms. "This was her fireplace?" She pictured the woman in a long dress, a shawl around her shoulders. Her frame would be slight, almost Amelia's build, and she would be sunburned, her hands rough with wear. After pressing the marks into the mortar, she would look up, her eyes clear and bright.

"Oh, Grace!" She hugged the woman excitedly. "We found her! And Ally was right—she was in this area. She was here in this house! Whoever she was, she was here in this house! If her name is in the mortar, then did she help build the hut?"

"I can't imagine any other reason for her name to be here."

"This was her home. This was the first house at Faunce Cove? Can you make out the letters in her name?"

"It's too worn. I can see indentations, but not well enough to distinguish the letters." She looked up at Bethany's disappointed face. "But if I don't miss my bet," the older woman said, rubbing at the mortar near the impression, "if Patience wrote her name, so did her husband."

Bethany eased herself to the floor, her cast stretched out to her side, as she rubbed at the mortar near Grace. The indentations were barely discernible, but they were there.

"I can't tell what that one says either," she said impatiently.

"Let me try a damp cloth. A wet surface is sometimes darker." Grace gently rubbed at the spot to no avail.

"How about a flashlight? We can try to exaggerate the marks by creating shadows."

They worked on the area for nearly an hour. Even the rubbings they tried were illegible. No matter how steady they held the paper and rubbed the broad edge of the pencil tip across the ridges, no matter whether they used chalk, charcoal, pencil, or even one of Joshua's abandoned crayons on the paper, the marks could not be read.

Finally, Grace leaned back and stretched, then rubbed her back. "I'm not sure we're going to be able to get this. It's like Patience's name. You can tell there are downstrokes, but the connecting lines must not have been as deep, and without them, there's no way to tell what the name is."

Bethany sighed. Her leg ached and she had a twinge in her back from her unnatural position on the floor. If there were any other way of deciphering the name, she would have stayed longer, but there was nothing else they could think to do.

Grace glanced at her watch, then the window. "I didn't realize how long we've been at this. I've got to get some exercise. Do you want to join me for a walk? I'm up to a mile a day, but we can cut it short if that's too long. And don't worry about trying to keep up with me. I'm not exactly a speed walker."

It felt exhilarating to walk down the road. The cold air smelled fresh, and after a few minutes of matching Grace's brisk pace, Bethany unzipped her parka. Deciding that their first excursion together might not be the ideal time to try the steep path to the cove with its mud and its slippery, rain-soaked leaves, they walked along the road instead. After ten minutes of pacing herself with Grace, Bethany slowed. The fog had lifted, creating a shimmering tapestry of tiny dewdrops on each barren limb on the trees. The ocean seemed caught in the same humor, white caps frothing it to a glistening luster.

By the time they returned to the hut, the answering machine was blinking with several messages. Bethany's heart pounded as she pressed the button, suddenly aware of her desperate need to hear Peter's voice and to know what was happening to him after the unintelligible calls she'd played the day before. The messages were for Grace, but the reminder of Peter's situation put Bethany on edge.

It was too early to go to bed, and, though she knew she was too tired to write, Bethany turned on the computer, hoping that thinking about Patience would get her mind off Peter. At first she couldn't concentrate on Patience. But as she looked at the fireplace, she pictured the woman sitting next to it, warming her hands. What would Patience have thought about on a night like this when her husband didn't come home?

Bethany jumped when the phone rang. Grace answered, then turned to her and held out the receiver. "Joseph."

Bethany turned from the computer, took a deep breath, and spoke into the phone. "I'm glad you called."

His voice sounded casual. "How was your first day back at the hut? I suppose you spent half the day chatting with Sister Winton about ward members and the other half with Alice!"

Bethany closed her eyes, willing herself to think of something to say. The day had included so much—the discovery that the hut had been Patience's home, her fears for Peter—but she could not talk about any of that. "I got out for a walk with Grace," she said slowly.

"Great."

Bethany waited, hoping Joseph would continue, uncomfortably aware of the conspicuous silence, unable to find any way to break it.

"How was the ocean? Were the waves up after the rain?"

"It was lovely." She could tell him about the droplets of water trembling on each stem and branch, of the waves and their foaming rolls. But she couldn't tell him about Patience, and suddenly she didn't want to tell him about the rest.

"Are you all right? Is Grace still there with you in the room?" She could hear the alarm in his voice. "Bethany, are you all right?"

"Yes, Joseph, I'm fine, and Grace is right here." Bethany tried to think of something else to say, but there was nothing.

She could hear the strain come in Joseph's voice as he filled the silence. "Well, I imagine you're tired, so I'll let you go."

Though the flames no longer soothed her, she watched the fire burn. Long after she knew Grace had drifted off, she cried herself to sleep.

16

When Bethany awoke the next morning, Grace was humming as she scrambled eggs. The sun was shining gloriously in a teasing pre-spring way, and she could smell the buttered toast.

"Well," Grace said brightly, turning to Bethany, "ready to work on Patience again?"

"What can we do?" Bethany asked. "All we have is the signature, no dates or places."

"We do have a place—Faunce Cove—and there's more we can figure out." Grace placed a plate of food in front of Bethany and pulled out her own chair. "You know, we've got more to work with than just your documents. I think we can make a pretty decent time line."

"What do you mean?"

"The best tool a genealogist has in a situation like this is her ability to think—to reason."

Bethany looked puzzled.

"Writers create stories. Genealogists look for precise data. You're in between. You're trying to find the story that fits within the limits of your information—whether or not your data is totally correct." She sipped her orange juice. "So, let's see if we can fit Patience into a time line." She chuckled at the doubtful look on Bethany's face.

Once they had cleared away the breakfast dishes, Grace spread the table with family history forms and Bethany's papers. "Okay, let's start filling in blanks," Grace began, pulling up her glasses again. "Name . . . Patience. Date of birth . . ." She looked up at Bethany, who shook her head.

Grace picked up a pencil. "What do your photocopies say?"

"Nothing about her birth."

"Let's see." Grace picked up the papers and glanced through them. Then she pointed to a page of text and looked up at Bethany. "It says she came from Plymouth Colony to Maine, and at the age of eighteen she married a soldier. The fort where he worked was closed down and they moved to the cove where he was killed by Indians three years later." She looked up at Bethany. "Ready to start working?" she queried excitedly, handing Bethany a pencil.

"Do you remember when Plymouth was founded?"

Bethany shook her head. "Sixteen twenty?"

"Right. The Pilgrims arrived in 1620. Several thousand immigrants came in the next few years. They started expanding their commercial bases relatively soon. The colonists knew of the potential use of lumber from here in Maine, and Popham had already been founded to build ships. So, let's say Patience came to one of the forts that had been opened to protect lumber interests. That couldn't have been before 1625. Add a year or so to meet and marry and the earliest reasonable date she could have been married was around 1626." She pointed at the photocopy. "And she was eighteen years old."

"So the earliest year she could have been born was 1608?" Bethany asked.

"Right! And since the Pilgrims didn't land in Plymouth until 1620 . . ." Grace pointed to the line labeled "place."

"She was not born in Plymouth, but either in England or Holland."

"Exactly, unless she came to Maine much later. Remember, that was the earliest possible date."

"But how do we find out if she came to Maine later than that?"

"Well, according to the record, she was the first woman at Faunce Cove, right? When was the first town on the island established, do you know?"

"According to the histories I read, it was Seacrest." Bethany flipped through a pamphlet. "Around 1658."

"Now, look at the bowl," Grace directed her. "What style is the bowl? What culture does it come from? Colonial or Indian?"

Bethany squinted at the faint pattern that embellished the piece, trying to figure out where Grace was going with her analysis. "Indian, definitely Indian."

"Patience's story says that she was alone for the winter. But if there had been other colonists at Seacrest, surely she would have gone and stayed there. On the other hand, if there were no English, she would have had no choice but to stay on her own and even become friends with the Indians, maybe even learn some of their skills. My understanding is that the local Indians lived farther inland during the winter and came down to the islands for the warmer seasons. They were very friendly with the settlers."

"You are saying that Patience stayed with the Indians, even after they killed her husband?"

"Remember, there were marauding tribes with their own agendas who invaded the area off and on. I suspect Patience's husband was killed in a misadventure with intruders, not anyone from the local tribes."

"Then you think that Patience stayed with the Indians because there were no other colonists, and since Seacrest was established in 1658, her husband must have been killed before 1658?"

"Now you're thinking like a genealogist!"

"And since she was there long enough to learn Indian crafts, she was with them at least a year, but probably longer? That means— okay, 1657, minus . . ." Bethany paused, studying the copies. "The three years she and her husband were married—that would be 1654, minus her age, which was eighteen, gives her birth date no later than . . . 1636." She looked at Grace. "And if she were born after 1620, she could have been born in Plymouth or somewhere in the colony."

Grace looked up with a grin. "Right. You got it. Before, we were using facts that would give us the earliest possible birth year, but now we've got information that pertains to the latest possible birth date, and we have a birth year between 1608 and 1636."

"And she could have been born in England, Holland, or the colonies if she were born between 1620 and 1636," Bethany added. "And we also have a range for her marriage date, too, don't we?"

"Yes—1626 to 1654." Grace wrote the numbers on the chart as she spoke them.

"And the marriage was in Maine. Now, that really narrows it down!" Bethany commented with a laugh as she stretched back in her chair.

"Actually, at that time Maine was part of Massachusetts, not that it matters for what you are doing. Now, try to think like the colonists would have. What was the easiest way to travel? Would you hike over the mountains carrying all your belongings, or would you come by water?"

"Definitely by water."

"I think it would be safe to say that they were married at the closest coastal settlement, maybe even the fort where her husband had been a soldier, if there were still clergy there. And that does definitely narrow down the possibilities. Is there anything else in the documents that might help with the time line?"

"No dates or places, but there is something that makes me wonder. Patience repeated the phrase, 'Let the sea crest' in her prayer. Could there be a connection between that and the town's name? Ally, the girl I was researching with, focused her paper right on Faunce Cove, and since I was writing about Patience's childhood, I didn't really look into it. Could she also be connected to Seacrest?"

"I know of one good way to find out. I know Millie Beckom, the curator of the Seacrest Museum and Historical Society. What do you think? Are you well enough to take a field trip? Or do you need to rest?"

"I traveled to San Francisco. I can handle a trek to Seacrest. I only agreed to have help here because of Joseph." She laughed. "However, I'm not sure how pleased he would be that you are my accomplice in doing research on Patience."

When Grace called Millie, she said she'd love to have them come to the museum, but she couldn't have them until the next morning. Both Grace and Bethany were disappointed.

* * *

That night Bethany cuddled into the love seat and prepared to reread her manuscript yet again. Grace had gone to bed early, so Bethany used a small lamp to study the time line and then her manuscript. She picked up a pencil but found herself staring at the fireplace rather than her paper. Noticing that the fire was getting low, she carefully added a log, angling her leg in its cast so she could bend over.

Patience had done this same thing on a night like this, in this very place. Patience had lit the fire and had prepared a meal—venison, wild turkey, or fish, and cornmeal or bread—for her husband. Bethany reached over to the indentation in the mortar, fingering the illegible carvings, then those that suggested Patience's name. After writing her name, had Patience looked up and smiled at her husband? Had she fingered his initials over and over after he died?

Bethany slipped her finger back across the initial, then brushed at a spot of dust closer to the firebox. A jagged edge scratched the soft skin of her finger. Had Patience scraped her finger on that same spot? Bethany rubbed her finger. Had Patience rubbed her finger too?

An image came to Bethany's mind, but the woman she pictured rubbing her finger was Amelia bending over her seedlings, rubbing dirt from her hands. Bethany knew she should be working on Amelia's genealogy, not on that of a woman she pictured with Amelia's features and body! Still, Bethany's thoughts returned to Patience, and in the flickering light of the slow-burning log she could nearly see Patience, still moving like a young version of Amelia, working about the fireplace, her long skirt twisting shadows within its folds, curving in graceful turns illuminated by the flames.

What had given this woman the strength and courage to endure the wilderness after her husband was killed? Bethany drifted into sleep, unable to dismiss the questions from her mind.

She awoke sometime later from a dream so vivid that she sat up, the fire now reduced to glowing embers. *Where was the baby?* Patience's journal entry said that she had been married for three years. She could have had a baby, and in Bethany's mind, she *did* have a baby. The will to care for her baby would have sustained Patience through her husband's death and those terrible nights—here, within inches of where Bethany herself slept.

But where had the baby been the night Patience's husband was killed? It was doubtful that any child could have survived through the night in the sea cave. And the Indians had ravaged the house—the hut, Bethany realized with a surge of emotion—so the baby could not have been safely sheltered here. The baby, if indeed there had been one, should have died that night with his father. But Bethany didn't believe that. Where was the baby?

Bethany quietly turned on the lamp and read through the photocopies again and again. Nothing in the documents suggested a child, but Bethany couldn't dismiss the thought any more readily than she had been able to dismiss Patience. Was Joseph right? Was she getting too immersed in Patience's story? Bethany felt relieved when light began filtering through the drapes and she heard Grace step quietly across the floor.

Grace listened to her theory, her head to one side, eyes squinting in concentration. "You're right. There probably would have been a baby. But we have nothing to go on." Her eyes squinted even further as she thought. "The Indians of this area wouldn't kidnap a baby— they were friendly to the new settlers. But another tribe might have." She took a deep breath. "Since Patience's initials in the mortar are our only real proof that she lived here, I don't know how we can also prove the existence of a baby."

Bethany was absentmindedly rubbing the scratch on her finger when the thought occurred to her.

"Grace, look in the mortar. Farther back toward the firebox." The words came out staccato-like.

Grace found the raised edge immediately. "We may be able to decipher this one back here where it's less worn!" On her hands and knees in her chenille bathrobe, Grace traced the markings with her finger while Bethany hobbled to the cupboard to get a flashlight.

With the beam of light shining onto the marks, Bethany could easily make out the indentations, although it was a little harder to identify the letters. "*S* or *J*," she read off to Grace, "then *a*, I think an *n* or *m*, something, *el?*"

"Samuel." Grace nodded in agreement. "Well, Bethany, now you have your Patience with a husband, and a son named Samuel, building a fireplace here at the hut!"

Bethany leaned back against the stone. Patience had a son!

After they dressed, ate breakfast, and straightened the hut, the two women climbed in the car to visit Millie and her historical society.

17

The Seacrest Historical Society sat in Millie's backyard. According to Millie, it had been one of the earliest schoolhouses, though probably not the first. When the population of the town had outgrown the small building, it had been left standing in the middle of a field. Later, when the field became a cow pasture, the former schoolhouse served as a small barn. Still later, the structure had been a chicken coop. Millie's father had purchased the property along with the adjoining house. After researching its history, he placed his already existing collection of memorabilia where chickens had roosted for nearly a century. It hadn't taken him long to realize that smelly roosts and historical memorabilia couldn't coexist. So, after townspeople had donated old books and maps, even family Bibles and handwritten family records, he built new shelving to replace the chicken roosts.

Millie looked vigorous though fragile, with obviously colored hair curling tightly around the wrinkled skin of her long, narrow face. She pointed toward the books on the shelves, reciting their history as if the Mortons or Bakers had cleaned their attic or torn out their old bookshelves and brought the books the week before. Bethany followed Millie and Grace to the back of the small room, where Millie took a key from her sweater pocket and unlocked the glass doors of an old bookcase, obviously added later to the historic building.

"These are my prizes," she said in a loud, nearly shrill voice. "Can you hear me?" she asked, though she was the one who cupped her ear while they talked.

Bethany's eyes widened as she glanced at the documents Millie placed before her and Grace. Bethany looked at the yellowed papers with thinned creases that, it seemed, would crumble into dust at the least movement. Gently, she touched the plastic that covered them.

Millie looked at her with a pleased smile and turned to Grace. "She's one of us. Look at those eyes! I haven't seen anyone treat these papers with that much reverence since my father died."

Millie pulled out a thick binder. "Now, these are the photocopies of that same material. You can make copies of any of these you'd like." As she pulled out a copier on a sliding shelf, she pointed to the space beneath. "There's more paper down here, and I hope you'll need it, although right off I can't recall having anything specifically on Faunce Cove."

There was disappointingly little on the cove, and nothing that seemed relevant from the history of Seacrest—but only initially. As Bethany thumbed through the pages of the binder, she noticed a section entitled *Legends of the Abnaki Indians.* Not yet familiar with the history of the state of Maine, she glanced down at the subheadings on the pages. One caught her eye—The Legend of the Rock of the Sea God. *Could this have anything to do with Patience's cave?* she wondered. With her fingers crossed, she began reading:

> *Among the Abnaki Indians of northeastern coastal*
> *Maine was told the story of a young boy who disobeyed*
> *his parents and persuaded his friends to do the same.*
> *Their parents had told the youth many times not to enter*
> *into the cave of the Rock of the Sea God, which was*
> *along the shoreline not far from the cove, near the mouth*
> *of the brook. Could they not hear the Sea God's mighty*
> *voice moan and boom with anger when the ocean ran*
> *wild on stormy nights, as the ocean gathered into His*
> *cave? But the Indian boy did not wish to recall his*
> *parents' warnings. He had climbed into the cave to rest*
> *while his friends guarded the entrance.*
>
> *The ocean rose. At first the waves trickled into the cave,*
> *then washed the feet of the friends who waited outside.*
> *But then the winds began to blow, for the Sea God had*
> *found someone in His cave; the waves began to dance.*

*The boy's friends called into the cave, but the sounds of
the Sea God covered their voices and the waves lashed at
their backs. In terror they left him.*

*When the wind subsided and the sea left the rock, the boy
was gone. Several weeks later his friends found his broken
body on the shore where the Sea God had left him. No
Indian would enter the cave, for they had been reminded
that this, indeed, was the home of the Sea God, and the
Sea God was a jealous god.*

Bethany exhaled and stretched out her tightly clenched fists and crossed fingers. The story had a ring of truth to it, as if she knew it from somewhere else. As she read the legend again, her eye was drawn to a small asterisk that she hadn't noticed during her first reading. It referred the reader to further information later in the section. Bethany quickly riffled through the remaining pages until she found a section entitled "Notes."

The note by the asterisk read: "An early settler along the northeastern coast was said to have fled from hostile Indians by hiding in the tidal cave for perhaps as long as twelve hours, knowing that the natives would not enter it. This action, according to local legend, saved her life."

Certain that the early settler referred to was Patience, Bethany made copies of the pages. She could hardly wait to compare it with some of her other information. Then, out of curiosity more than need, Bethany copied the first five pages of the binder detailing the creation of the village of Seacrest. After Millie had shown Grace her newest acquisitions, Bethany promptly got Grace's attention.

"Grace, look at this. It has to be about Patience," she said as she waved the plastic covered pages in the air.

Grace was nearly as excited as Bethany and suggested they hurry back to the hut to see how the information might fit in with what they had already found.

Bethany looked longingly at McCleres' Bed-and-Breakfast as they drove back to the cove. She wanted to talk to Alice about Joseph, but Alice would still be at the school, and Bethany had the papers to study.

She hobbled into the hut and sat down in the love seat to read.

Once again she read the Indian legend, but there didn't seem to be anything new in it so she then turned to the history of Seacrest. It was very similar to the scenario Grace had suggested. Captain Richard Smythe, a young, enterprising ship captain, bartered with the Indian chief Shabanah for logging rights in his tribal territory. After several years of shipping raw lumber, Captain Smythe had brought in enough colonists to process the lumber before shipping it, creating one of the very early sawmills in Maine. And Seacrest was founded. Additionally, Smythe built a mansion along the North Road where he and his wife lived until they died sometime before 1689, when Richard's will was probated.

Bethany stopped reading after the first page, though the history continued. She moved her leg to a more comfortable position, then flipped through the pages and straightened them to go back into the folder. She stopped suddenly and skimmed for the words she was sure she had seen. They were on the third page. "Samuel Faunce, stepson of Captain Smythe, served as the territorial magistrate from 1680 to 1692." She reread the sentence.

"Grace?"

Grace read the words once, twice, and then studied them again a third time. "I think," she said, crossing her fingers, "I think you have found Patience's baby and her married name, as well as a second husband. It all fits. Faunce Cove—Samuel—Seacrest."

Bethany put the pieces together. "Patience married a Mr. Faunce somewhere on the coast of Maine. They moved to Faunce Cove, where Samuel was born—before they finished the hut, since his name is in the mortar. Then Indians killed her husband while Patience found shelter in the sea cave. The Indians must have kidnapped Samuel—that's the only way I can think that he would survive. But somehow he returned, and he and Patience lived with the local Indians until Captain Smythe came to buy the rights to the lumber, and he and Patience married."

"I think you're right," Grace commented thoughtfully.

"I wonder if Millie could help me more now that we've got this— all of this." She indicated the copies spread out around her.

"Let's see."

Back at the historical society later that day, Millie picked up the binder for a closer look. When they'd called and asked to see her again that same afternoon, she had not seemed surprised. She was nearly as pleased as they when they showed her what they'd found.

"What you really want now," she said, her voice uncomfortably loud, "are vital records. Of course, neither the captain nor his wife was born here, but both Samuel's marriage and death records might give the names of his parents and where he was born, along with the date. Back that far you can't be sure, but most gravestones gave the date of death and the age of the person at death." She pulled out a paper from the fly of the binder. "According to this, vital records for Seacrest don't start until 1695. Is that early enough?"

Grace glanced at her paper, although Bethany already knew. "No. They died before 1689."

Millie screwed up her face, her eyes nearly closed as she thought. "There still is a possibility," she said. "I think it was back in 1956 or so that one of the editors of the *New England Genealogical and Historical Journal* sent my father a manuscript on Captain Smythe to review. The information was deemed correct, but for some reason they didn't publish it. Let's see." She moved to a shelf and quickly searched the contents, stretching on her tiptoes as she inspected the top shelf, then moving down until she knelt to look through the folders. "Here it is!" she finally announced, pulling out a faded cardboard cover and reading from the bold print. "Captain Richard Smythe, founder of Seacrest, Maine."

"Now, you see what you can find in there." She handed it to Bethany triumphantly.

"As for the Faunces, I don't know of anything printed about the family. We haven't had any Faunces around for a long time."

Excited to peruse the information, Bethany and Grace left the old schoolhouse, thanking Millie profusely. As Grace drove, Bethany opened the folder and started skimming the article. "Here it is!" she called excitedly as Grace pulled into the driveway. "Captain Smythe's wife," she read, "was the daughter of Obadiah Pers, who died in Plymouth, Massachusetts, in 1627. Her first husband, Thomas Faunce, was killed by raiding Indians as he tried to escape with their baby in the winter of 1634. Samuel Faunce, their son, was taken by the plundering Indians, but was later recovered by friendly Indians of the area. A daughter was born to Captain Smythe while his family was temporarily living in England, but she died within hours of her birth."

Bethany sat back in the seat. She had suspected that Patience's baby had been taken, but now she pictured the woman differently. Patience, bent over with grief, huddled beside her husband's body. Had she known the Indians had taken the baby? Had she felt relief or near hysteria when she turned her husband's body over and their child was not with him? How long had she searched for the tiny body under piles of snow? Had she felt grateful or empty each time she brushed at a lump in the icy white to find a log, a pile of autumn leaves? And how had she felt when she once again held her son?

"You've got mail." Grace broke into her thoughts as she got out of the car and opened the mailbox. She held up an envelope with the return address of a nationwide photo-developing company. "Got any exciting pictures coming?"

"Kim must have sent me copies from the trip in San Francisco," Bethany said as she slid her cast out the door and held onto the frame of the car to raise herself. She reached back into the car for the folder. "But I can guarantee there is nothing in that envelope that I'm more interested in than what is in this folder!"

"Let me put them in the hut, Bethany. Then we can take our walk before it gets dark—unless you're too tired or can't wait to look at that. I'm worried that you're getting worn out."

Grace laughed as Bethany wrinkled her face and rolled her eyes. She was anxious to reread the new material but she knew she could do that later.

She started walking down the road, but it didn't take Grace long to catch up.

"It's nice to walk somewhere different," Grace said, her arms swinging back and forth with her body. "Have you explored many of the trails around here? Ever gone up the mountain?"

"Not really. There's the rock wall and too much poison ivy along my property line to get up into the forest, and the trees are so thick you'd have to dodge between the branches to get through. I think there could be a whole town hidden in these woods and you wouldn't be able to see it."

Grace nodded. "Up here it's like that. It can be surprising when you've driven through a place that looks like a forest in the summer, but find that with the leaves down and lights on in the winter, there's a whole community hiding just through the trees."

"With the woods so thick I've always preferred walking along the shoreline," Bethany said.

"I've noticed a couple of trails into the woods. Most of them look pretty steep, but there's one that looks quite well worn and much more moderate. Instead of going straight up the face of the mountain, it winds back and forth in switchbacks. I checked and I can't see anything that might be poison ivy. Do you want to try it? We'll take it slowly, and if you can't handle it with your cast and all, we'll come back. Agreed?"

It was a perfect afternoon. The weather was warm enough for them to meander without heavy coats but cool enough that the sunshine felt good. When Bethany's cast was on the downside of the hill, she could move relatively easily; when it was on the upside, after the trail turned back and was going the opposite direction, she moved clumsily.

After twisting back and forth across a small hill, the path evened off into a shaded hollow. Grace went slowly, although it was not too difficult for Bethany to move through the twigs and dried grass that covered the path. Then the path began a slightly steeper ascent, veering around several boulders.

Grace encouraged Bethany. "I don't want you getting hurt," she said as she leaned against the rocks, "but if you can get up here, there's a marvelous view and a dry place to sit and rest."

Bethany searched for finger holds on the sides of the boulders, impatiently thinking how easily she would have been able to climb the path without the cast. She gingerly put her weight on the cast, knowing that her plaster-encased ankle could not bend. Then she grasped Grace's elbow firmly, pulling herself, step by step, up the rise. It took several minutes before she was seated on the boulders.

It was worth the struggle, and though the exertion left Bethany breathing deeply, it was not the lack of oxygen that silenced her as Grace continued up the path. From the elevated position, Bethany looked at the ocean and the clear blue sky through the lacy branches on either side of the path. There were no leaves yet, only the swelling of tiny buds deepening with shades of gold and russet to announce the promised emergence of spring.

Bethany looked around her. Had Patience seen this? Had Patience climbed this hill, looking down to the ocean during that winter, longing to see a sail on the horizon, fearing to see a canoe? Had Amelia—?

Bethany stopped her thoughts short. Why had she thought of Amelia? Why did she always picture Patience with Amelia's features?

Tears formed in her eyes. Amelia had given her this. As much as Bethany could not understand or appreciate all her grandmother's actions, she could not deny that Amelia's gift of Faunce Cove—the only place where she could have learned about Patience—was one of the most extraordinary experiences of her life.

As she heard twigs crackling above her, Bethany looked up and Grace reappeared. She edged herself onto the boulders beside Bethany.

"Isn't it wonderful?" Grace asked, breathing deeply as she relaxed.

They sat silently, the dull roar of the ocean contrasting against the occasional flutter of dead leaves blown by the breeze.

Grace turned to Bethany. "I could look at this all day. How long have you been living up here?"

"I've been here a little more than nine months, and I love it more all the time."

"Were you raised around here? Where is your family from?"

"I'd never been here before I moved up last June. My grandmother raised me, and she died last year."

"I'm sorry. No other family?"

"My parents died in an accident when I was three, and my grandmother adopted me."

"Oh, Bethany! How sad!"

At other times and in other places, the same words had left Bethany emotionless. Coming from Grace, however, the words left her unable to respond. Grace understood. She had buried her husband. Patience had buried her husband. Bethany had not even been able to bury Amelia. She could not even visit her grave. And her parents . . . Bethany found herself sobbing.

Grace held her tightly, smoothing her hair. "Oh, Bethany," she soothed. "Oh, honey. It's all right. It's all right."

* * *

Grace turned off the lights in the loft just as Bethany pulled a glass from the cupboard and poured herself some milk. Even though she felt tired, she looked around the room for a magazine, something to get her mind to slow down. The information on Captain Smythe certainly wouldn't put her to sleep. Picking up the mail Grace had left on the counter, she yawned as she read the return addresses. There were the usual advertisements, a reminder of her doctor's appointment to have her cast removed, and Kim's photos. She used the blade of the scissors to slice open the top of the envelope.

The photos fell out onto the counter. Most of them featured Kim and Bethany, often with Bethany's cast as a prominent part of the photo. Bethany smiled as she realized how much fun it had been despite her handicap and the accompanying exhaustion. In several other photos Kim and Bethany had stood close together while Kim reached out in front and snapped a photo. Their expressions, usually with exaggerated smiles while they pulled funny faces, made Bethany laugh. Next were several photos of Joseph and Bethany from the days when she'd ventured out with him and Kim for one of Kim's famous tours of San Francisco.

Toward the bottom of the pile of photos, Bethany found two shots of Kim and Joseph holding golf clubs as they posed on a green slope. There was nothing particular in the picture that Bethany could pick out that bothered her—they seemed to be happy—but she suddenly felt weary and disgruntled. Was she jealous or was she imagining things? There was no one she could trust more than Joseph or Kim. She must be tired.

She flipped through the rest of the pictures—a shot of Joseph in a taxi, more pictures of the two women in Kim's apartment with Bethany's luggage conspicuously piled by the door, the loaded taxi with Bethany leaning out waving—but it was no longer fun or even interesting to view the pictures. She slipped them back in the envelope and climbed between the sheets Grace had spread on the love seat.

* * *

"Where do we go from here?" Bethany asked Grace as she put down the pencil she had used to fill in the blanks on the form. The family group record was beginning to look impressive.

"That depends on what you want to learn," Grace responded as she sat back in the chair. "We can go on the Internet and check Ancestral File or the International Genealogical Index to see if they list Samuel's descendants, or we can find out if Millie has more information on Samuel's life."

"I want more information about Patience's childhood. What did Obadiah Pers do for a living? What happened to Patience when he died, and how did she end up in Maine at a fort? I can't believe I'm saying this, but I wish I didn't have to get this cast off. I would really rather stay here and work on this than go to Boston. Joseph won't be thrilled to learn I've been doing research on Patience."

"Oh, I don't think it matters what he thinks, since *you* know you're doing the right thing," Grace responded with a chuckle. "Believe it or not, Boston would be a great place to find information on Plymouth. In 1850, Massachusetts passed a law requiring every town to collect all the birth, marriage, and death records from the time of the town's formation and submit them to the state. Of course, towns couldn't collect what wasn't there, so if the information had not been given to the clerk or recorded originally, or if the records had been destroyed, the records were incomplete. And remember, we're talking about a span of over two hundred years. The more conscientious clerks collected all the church and graveyard records, even went through family histories and Bibles.

"But then, you also have to remember that a lot of people came into Plymouth in a short period of time. Some were just moving through, not even buying property, so there was nothing to record about them. Some were buried without markers, or with wooden slabs that disintegrated. Gravestones crumbled, and the writing was worn down by the weather until it was illegible or covered by two centuries of debris. A lot of information was lost."

"Then I'm probably not going to find much information on Obadiah Pers," Bethany ventured, somewhat discouraged.

"To be honest, the chances aren't good. However, if there is any chance at all it would be in Boston at the New England Genealogical and Historical Society. They hold an extensive collection of diaries and family papers, some with accounts from early tradesmen—merchants, carpenters, and such. If Obadiah Pers bought on credit from one of the stores where the records have been kept, or had work done by one of these tradesmen, you might find something about him. Since you're going to Boston anyway, I'd love to come along and spend some time at the society with you."

When Bethany called Joseph, he was with a client, but his secretary assured her that she would have him call Bethany back. He called back a few minutes later, his voice relaxed and cheerful.

"So you're coming down to get the cast off. That's good news. I'll make reservations at Aujourd'hui. Would you like me to get tickets to the theater or the symphony?"

"Actually, Grace Winton is driving me down, and we're planning some pretty intense research at a genealogical library. I'm not sure I'll be up to much in the evening."

Bethany could visualize Joseph swiveling his chair to look out at the Charles River. "I imagine you're looking for more information about Patience?" he asked, his voice heavy.

"We've found the name of her husband and a son, a second husband, even her father. We're hoping to find out more about him and Patience's childhood."

"Bethany," he said wearily, "I'm glad you found what you were looking for, but listen to yourself. You've found all this information and yet you're still not satisfied. How long are you going to go on with this? Can't you see what's happened to you? When are you going to end this?"

"I'm getting what I need to write a credible book. That's what Amelia wanted. That's why you moved me up here."

"Right now, I can't imagine what it will take to get you back down to Boston. Well, can I take the two of you to dinner, or will you be too busy for that?"

18

Despite the early April hints of spring, patrons filled the research room at Boston's New England Genealogical and Historical Society, each deep in his or her own world of research. Some patrons sat with books carefully layered around a notebook or a laptop, others with books piled haphazardly as if they were in a race against time. Bethany had headed up the stairs after listening to the guided tour. Grace sat at the table writing busily.

"I think we have a long day ahead of us," Grace said quietly. "There are more books back there on Plymouth than Millie has files on Maine. Remember, you are looking for anyone who could be Obadiah Pers. Spelling was a very creative process for some of the clerks. I found one two-syllable surname spelled fourteen different ways. The phonetic approach seemed to carry the day in many cases. Back then they might have spelled Grace G-R-A-S-E or G-R-A-Y-S-E or even G-R-A-I-S. Who knows how many ways they would have spelled Bethany!" She picked up a book and sighed. "Well, here we go. I don't know of any shortcuts other than to check the indexes and stay within the time frame we know Obadiah was in Plymouth.

"I've checked the vital records, so this collection of epitaphs from burial grounds in Plymouth might be a good place to start. If there was a legible gravestone, you'll likely find it in here. Usually the names are listed alphabetically within each burial ground, and you'll want to look at all of them. There were a number of small burying grounds, so it will take awhile. In our case, though, it's probably the most direct way to get information." Grace picked up several more books. "And since we don't know whether the Plymouth in the article is the town or the colony, you may want to check the other burial grounds in the colony."

Bethany opened the book, wondering how long it would take to look through the volumes.

She was finishing up when Grace tapped her shoulder. "It's two thirty. Don't you think we should get some lunch?"

Bethany rubbed her forehead and stretched her shoulders. "I can't believe it's that late. I haven't seen anything at all about a Pers here, but there are some very interesting writings. 'Died suddenly under a wagonload of wood.' 'Mistakenly shot while hunting.' Then there are five children from the same family who all died within two months of each other."

Then, pointing to the book, she said, "Here's one where four wives of one man were buried in a row." Bethany paused as she glanced farther down on the page. "There is a notation underneath that says his first wife died in childbirth soon after they came to Massachusetts. She left him nine living children, the oldest being twelve. He married a second wife, age eighteen, eleven months later. They were married for three years. She had two more babies before she died in childbirth with the third. His third wife, Hannah, bore three children. Two were stillbirths. She also died during childbirth at the age of twenty-one. His final wife was eighteen when they married, but he died five years later. Their fourth child was born after his death." Bethany quoted from the book. "'Nehemiah Crayklor was known for his magnanimous generosity in taking in and caring for indigent and orphaned girls of the town. In fact, all but his first wife had lived in his household as servants before he married them.'"

Grace squinted her eyes. "Very interesting. Which cemetery is that in?"

"In—would you believe this?—Parting Ways Cemetery. It's on the border of Kingston and Carver. I've got two more cemeteries to look through, but they're pretty small. Are you ready to give up?"

"Only if you are. You're the one with the cast. What time is your appointment tomorrow?" Grace asked.

"At eleven. Too early to do much here before, and too late to come here afterwards, especially if you want to miss rush-hour traffic."

"I've got a couple of bags of nuts and crackers if you want to skip lunch." Grace rummaged in her tote to find the snacks and motioned toward the stairs. "No food in here with the books."

* * *

Finding no trace of Obadiah Pers in the remaining burial records, Bethany sat back in the chair, tired and despondent.

"Nothing?" Grace looked up from a stapled set of photocopied papers.

"Nothing."

"I've got a register from a store at Darby's Station and," she read the back of a binder, "the account of a carpenter that lived on Samoset Street. Which one do you want? They're both in Kingston."

"I'll take the store accounts." Bethany reached for the papers. "Oh, these aren't even indexed. They're going to take forever."

"The key is to skim for the name, but that's easier said than done. Some of these are quite interesting."

After skimming through several pages, Bethany settled back against the wooden slats of the chair. Surprised to see a familiar name, she exclaimed, "Oh, look. This is the same Crayklor as in the cemetery! Look at this list of fabric—all black."

Grace glanced over at the page. "And look, 22 yards of expensive 'searge' at the cost of 220 shillings, and silk lace—probably for the family clothing—and 16 yards of black cotton at the cost of 60 shillings—for the clothing for the indigent and orphaned girls, I imagine."

"So much for our good man's magnanimities," Bethany inserted dryly.

"Better than going threadbare, I suppose."

Grace turned back to the carpenter's account. "Oh look, Bethany!" She slid the book over to Bethany and pointed to a line. "What do you think?"

Bethany read the text and then looked at Grace. "'Paid to Ob Pierce to plane lumber on August 4, 1625.' Do you think . . . ?"

"I'm not sure." Grace skimmed the page in the carpenter's account of the wages he paid. "Ob's in this entry too." She turned the page.

"Here . . . here. We can compare the last date that Ob got paid here to Obadiah's death date in 1627. If Ob received money after our Obadiah Pers died, we know it's not him. If payments stopped then, we won't be sure, but it will look like a pretty good possibility."

It didn't take long to find that, indeed, Ob Pierce received wages regularly until July 1627, at which point his name disappeared from the records. Grace found that the earliest entry with the name Ob Pierce was 1623.

Bethany riffled through the store's registry, searching for entries. There were only a few mentions of a Pers or Pierse between 1623 and 1627, in purchases of nails and other carpentry supplies. Bethany felt defeated as she began to read the entries for July. She knew that Patience's father had planed logs for a carpenter, but that did little to identify what Patience's childhood must have been like. When Grace stood to copy the entries from the carpenter's journal, Bethany closed the registry. While she waited for Grace, she wearily opened it again.

The book reopened to the page where she had stopped searching: July 1627. Restlessly, she flipped the page. The item was listed under the date of August 23, 1627. It said simply, "One and one half yard black cotton for burial of O Pirs."

"Grace, look again in August of 1627!"

"You're right," Grace replied, so excited that several people at the next desk looked up. "I just looked for his wages!" She read from the receipts of the carpenter. "'August 22, coffin for Obadiah Pierce, no charge collected.' There it is! Obadiah spelled out! And look, Bethany. 'Coffin delivered to home of widow Randolf where O. P. resided, no charge.'"

"Do you think that's why he didn't buy any personal things from the store? He was boarding with a widow and probably paid her for everything?"

"He probably brought all his personal needs—clothing, a razor— with him, so all he needed was room and board."

"But where was Patience? Her mother must have died if her father boarded with a widow." She heard Grace's startled breath.

"Remember that man with four wives in the Parting Ways Cemetery?" Grace pointed at the book. "I have a Kraklor here— different spelling but same-sounding name. The carpenter that

Obadiah worked for built Kraklor some furniture."

"You think they knew each other?"

"Probably at least met, but there may be more. Look in your registry for purchases made by Kraklor around the time of Obadiah's death."

"Kraklor bought some of the cheap black cotton on August 23, 1627." She paused. "Oh, Grace! Listen. 'Three yards black cotton for orphan of O. P.'"

"And look at this," Grace added quietly as she studied a page from the book of epitaphs. "Kraklor's third wife died in 1631 at the age of 24. They had been married for four or five years—which means they were married close to the time that Patience was taken in. Patience married Thomas Faunce in 1631 at the age of 18. She was born in 1613 so she would have been around fourteen when her father died. I imagine she was 16 or 17 when she went to Maine. That would have been a year or so before Kraklor's third wife died. Maybe that wife was already sick; she had had two stillbirths. Patience was probably next in line—or thought she was."

"So," Bethany consulted the books around her, "Obadiah Pierce came to America in 1624." She paused and corrected herself. "*By* 1624, I mean, and worked for a carpenter near Plymouth and boarded with a widow with the surname of Randolf. He died on or shortly before August 23, 1627. Patience, around fourteen years old and evidently motherless, was taken in by some guy named Kraklor, who seemed to run his own version of an orphanage for female children."

"Patience found herself in the midst of, shall we say, a 'family in fluctuation'—lots of children with new mothers on a regular basis—and found that she was in the running to become the next wife and mother," Grace continued. She looked at Bethany.

"So around 1629 or 1630, she caught a ship for a fort in Maine, where she met and married Thomas Faunce and built my hut. But regrettably, they did not live happily ever after!"

It took over an hour to finish the photocopying and to get back to the hotel. Grace had an early dinner appointment with her doctor friend, a former member of her ward. Joseph was busy working, so Bethany looked over the research documents.

After about an hour of reading, Bethany felt restless. Searching for somewhere to spend a mind-numbing hour, she hobbled down to the gift shop in the hotel lobby. As she perused the postcards on a rotating display rack, she wondered if she could find one with a photo of the historical society. Grace would love to have a postcard of it as a memento. She bought a postcard, then walked over to a display of historical memorabilia. There were several prints showing antique car collections. After glancing at them, she started to walk away when one group caught her eyes. There was something familiar about them. The 1920s cars reminded her of something frightening . . .

She looked closely at the vehicles, which were mostly black with brightly colored doors and hubcaps, and white tires. She was looking at one with red hubcaps when the memory came to her—there had been an envelope with a stamp. The car's hubcap had been orange and the lug nuts had been changed . . . and the card had held a threat she now remembered—there had been an anonymous letter with a threat. She'd opened it Christmas Eve before the tree had crashed!

Bethany's doctors—especially the trauma specialist—had warned her that she could experience memory losses resulting from her head injury. But how could she have forgotten a threat? She remembered, now, how she'd tried to phone for help, how the phone had been out, and the fear she had felt. She remembered she had been frightened when she had received cards in the hospital—frightened that they were threats. Words from the note tried to resurface in her mind. Had it mentioned tax evasion and organization, or had those come from the earlier phone calls? Had the threat simply been in a dream?

Bethany found her way to a chair and sat, her thoughts jumbled and racing.

Think! she commanded herself. *Think.* It was hard to comprehend that she had actually received a warning, not just a card as a prank, like the one she'd received at Halloween—which she now reconsidered. What threat had that last letter contained? Would she be in danger at the hut? The bustle of strangers in the room distracted her as she repeated the question to herself. There had been a warning, she was sure. But what, exactly, had it said? She couldn't remember the words.

The first threat had come weeks, no months, before, and it had come to the hut, an isolated area far away from the Boston hotel.

Even during the time when she had been most vulnerable in the hospital, nothing had happened. And anyone who knew her at Faunce Cove, where the note had arrived, would not know where she was staying even if they knew she was in Boston. She realized nonetheless that Alice and her family knew where she was, as well as her visiting teachers, but none of them could be suspect. She took a deep breath of relief and stood slowly, ready to catch the elevator back to her room.

Then a thought struck her as she was midway between the elevator and her door.

If something as significant as a threat had been erased from her mind, what else had she forgotten? How would she know? She slid the plastic key card into the slot and quickly opened the door.

Another fear came to her mind as she walked into the room. If she had forgotten things so easily, had she also dreamed up other ideas? Had her mind created events to fill her memory's void? Had other memories been imaginings? Was Joseph right after all? Had she created her own fantasy, improvising memories to substitute for events she couldn't or didn't want to recall?

What had she done?

She limped to the closest chair and slumped into it, too tired to care that she was supposed to meet Joseph for dinner in an hour and a half. She was still there crying in hiccuping sobs when Grace opened the door.

"Bethany?" Grace asked as she saw Bethany in the chair. "Bethany, honey, what's the matter?" She dropped her purse beside the chair and knelt down beside Bethany. "Are you okay?"

It was difficult for Bethany to explain her apprehension to Grace, but by the time she had finished, they both agreed Bethany was far too exhausted to have dinner with Joseph that evening. Although she had originally declined Grace's offer to call Joseph, Bethany ended up letting her call him anyway. She was certain that Joseph would bring up her research and his concerns about it and the whole tunnel issue. She knew she wouldn't be able to control her emotions as she recalled her newly reestablished memory and its implications. She even thought of going in the bathroom where she wouldn't be able to hear Grace and Joseph's conversation.

On the phone, Grace quickly explained that she was in Boston with Bethany and that, regretfully, Bethany wasn't going to be able to make it to dinner that evening. After a slight pause she responded with a simple, "You're welcome. Have a good night."

Joseph hadn't even asked why Bethany would not be joining him for dinner.

* * *

The next morning Grace thought that Bethany should talk to someone about her episode the previous evening. Remembering Joseph's directive that Grace involve Bethany's therapist should Bethany have any emotional reactions to being back at the hut, Grace called Dr. Jackman's office and asked if she could fit Bethany in that day. Luckily, there had been a last-minute cancellation and Dr. Jackman had an available appointment early that afternoon after Bethany's appointment with the orthopedic surgeon.

"I was just hungry and tired. We were excited about the information we had found about Patience, and I was nervous about seeing Joseph. I overreacted," Bethany answered as Dr. Jackman talked with her in an empty treatment room. Still trying to make her way through the convoluted memories herself, Bethany wasn't ready to tell anyone else and cause the alarm that would follow until she was sure about it all.

"You're sure you are all right? You know it's important that you take care of yourself. You're still recovering, Bethany, even if your cast is off. Being too tired or stressed, or having low blood sugar significantly raises your risk of having another seizure or getting sick. Don't overdo. You want to research and write, but you need to balance that with rest and food and exercise. Are you sure there was nothing else going on?"

Bethany waited a moment before answering. Did she really want to bring up the threat?

"You look as though you have something you're afraid to say." Dr. Jackman waited for her to speak.

"I'm not sure about my memories. I don't know if I'm remembering things that really happened, or if they are hallucinations. Joseph thinks I'm crazy, or at least living in a fantasy world. But

Grace—who's been staying with me for the past couple of weeks and knows me pretty well—believes what I've told her. I remembered a threatening card that came to me in the mail, which I read right before the tree fell on my house. But I'm sure Joseph would just say it was my imagination. I don't know where I could find the note now to prove that I did get it, after all the damage in the hut. I can try to find it but I imagine it got thrown away."

"Basically, you are saying you were upset last night because you didn't know what was real and what you imagined Christmas Eve. Right?" Dr. Jackman asked.

"Well, that and whether researching and writing about Patience is taking me farther away from reality." Bethany looked at Dr. Jackman questioningly. "Do you think it is dangerous for me to continue writing a novel about Patience?"

"No, but you might want to balance out the rest of your life. You still sound a bit obsessed with her, but I certainly can't see where you are endangering yourself. You're not on the verge of a mental collapse like Joseph seems to think, not as far as I can see. You seem happier than the last time I saw you."

"Then what is Joseph so concerned about? Why is he acting this way?"

Dr. Jackman chose her words carefully. "I think Joseph is sounding like a protective big brother." She looked at Bethany intently and repeated, "A protective big brother."

19

Grace moved home the weekend after Bethany's cast was removed. With the decision made and confirmed, Bethany felt nearly giddy with freedom when she hugged Grace and watched her drive down the road. She would miss Grace, but they would keep in contact. And now she could write about Patience without interruptions.

At first Bethany had worried about being alone in the hut, not because of her health but because of the threats. She could not remember the precise wording of either card, but she knew both mentioned "her friend" and that talking to anyone else about it might be dangerous. With that in mind, she had locks put in, added a telephone to her loft, and had an expensive security system installed. Still, she questioned whether she should stay at the hut alone. But then, she reminded herself frequently, if they really wanted to hurt her, "they"—whoever they were—likely would already have done it. Undoubtedly the warnings had been about Peter and his secrets, but she would not let them control her life! Besides, Grace could not stay there forever, and Bethany would have to make the break at some point.

Above all, when she prayed about staying at the hut, it felt right.

She also thought back to her appointment with Pam Jackman and the doctor's last words to her. It had been a moment of discernment for her. Joseph wasn't trying to control her, but to protect her. And perhaps he didn't think her actions were crazy, just capricious. With a little sadness she realized that their relationship was not what she had thought. It was still that of a big brother and little sister—and, if she didn't make some changes, it probably always would be.

She remembered a slogan from Alice's refrigerator. "If you do as you've done, you'll get what you got. Change if you want something better."

Joseph had not dominated their relationship because he was overbearing but because she had allowed him to treat her that way. Would he be angry if she insisted on managing her own concerns and took more control of her life?

Bethany planned her wording for the phone call, making sure she wasn't defensive, and then practiced the call several times as she had for speeches in school.

"Hi," she said when Joseph answered his phone the following afternoon. "I just called to let you know I'm doing fine, even with Grace gone." She barely waited long enough for him to greet her before she hurried on. "By the way, there is still debris from the storm and repairs on the hut in the backyard. I'm planning to fix it up for the spring and I need to get started right away. Could you get someone over here this week to take care of it?" She drew in her breath as she finished.

"Well, Bethany," Joseph replied slowly, "the timing isn't good right now and I'm still worried that you'll overwork. Why don't you just wait until the summer when I can come up to oversee the cleanup?"

She blinked her eyes and grimaced before she started, holding her tone as steady as she could. "I'm sorry it's an inconvenient time, Joseph. I'll just get a contractor's name from Alice and have him send you the bill. I haven't accessed my monthly stipend for almost four months now so there should be plenty of money in that account for me to take care of the expenses if there is a problem."

"I'll give them a call, but I doubt that I can come up to check on them," Joseph said reluctantly. "Be careful, Bethany, and don't overwork," he added before he hung up.

* * *

The information she and Grace had obtained at the New England Genealogical and Historical Society had been invaluable. Bethany had found it effortless to rewrite sections on Patience's childhood. It was harder to write about the destitute teenager within the household of motherless children, with women not much older than herself losing baby after baby and then succumbing too. Had Patience watched fearfully, knowing she might share their fate? It was doubtful that she had been banished to Maine because she had refused to become another one of Mr. Kraklor's wives—Mr. Kraklor would not risk his reputation by exiling a near-child. She must have stealthily slipped from the house to stow away on a ship, more fearful of Mr. Kraklor than of her destiny at an unknown port.

Again Bethany found herself thinking about Amelia, not Patience. Patience had walked in these same places, but had Amelia? How much had Amelia known about the hut? Bethany could not imagine Amelia driving down a secluded road looking for a place to buy for Bethany, or describing the desire for a small, abandoned house in a secluded area to a real estate agent. Had Amelia vacationed near Seacrest? How had she ever discovered Faunce Cove?

Bethany did not understand many things about Amelia. Patience's emotions seemed transparent to her, but Amelia's were as opaque as the rock walls delineating the property line. Amelia had lost her husband and her daughter. Bethany had known her, had lived with her, recognized her shape and her features, but she had not understood her.

She often wondered about Amelia's will. Had Amelia left her enough money to be independently comfortable or—Bethany's mind went back to the battered Jeep and the old version of the hut—had Amelia for some reason basically cut her out of the will? Joseph would know, but she didn't want to call him again.

Alice had been upset when Bethany told her about Joseph's ultimatum when he'd left her at the hut. "Joseph said that? Oh, Bethany. Are you all right?" she'd asked. When Bethany told her of his response in Boston, Alice had been equally disturbed.

"How are you doing with all that?" she asked sympathetically.

"I miss him, but I don't miss him calling to either scold me or get silent and pout if I mention Patience," Bethany said as she smiled. "Have you ever heard someone pout over the phone? Anyway, I'm fine."

"And when you finish writing?"

"Then I guess we'll see what we have in common—if he wants to."

During the day she kept herself too busy to think about Joseph, but evenings were harder. The first night after Grace left and she was alone, she had longed to lean against his broad chest and hear his heart beat, to have him gently lift her face and look into her eyes. Then the thought came that Patience had shared those longings for her husband Thomas, and Bethany hurried to the computer.

Sometimes as she wrote, Bethany stopped in the middle of a sentence to wonder what Joseph was doing. She missed him in a way she couldn't explain, even to herself. But her book would be finished much sooner if she kept writing. Then they could see how they felt about each other.

She also found herself thinking of Peter. Peter had made her feel acceptable in a social realm she hadn't before dared to enter. In retrospect she could see that their relationship had not been balanced. Though they had spent a great deal of time together, she felt she didn't know any more about him than she had the day she met him. Maybe if his work had been different he could have communicated. He might have even joined the Church. Maybe with a different job he would still be with her and there would have been no messages, no fears.

At times the warnings about Peter haunted her, but after thinking about them for a while the thoughts mostly irked her. In fact, the more she thought about the warnings, the more vexed she became. Why should she be held hostage by threats that made no sense to her? Remembering how she had stood up to Joseph about the yard debris, Bethany decided it was time to take matters concerning Peter into her own hands.

Her emails the next day to Kim and Dee were filled with current news as well as nonchalantly asking if anyone had heard about what Peter was up to these days. She contacted other friends from graduate school as well, slipping in unobtrusive questions about him. Since she spent so many hours at her computer each day, she decided to use it as a resource also. Using various search engines and a number of key words, she searched the Internet to ferret out information about corporations recently investigated for tax fraud or tax evasion. The sheer volume of information was incredible. Maybe she would learn something, maybe not, but at least she was doing something. It felt liberating.

* * *

Bethany found herself hunched over the keyboard, her back aching and her eyes burning. After two weeks of almost constant writing, she needed a break. It was a sunny, cheerful morning and she couldn't resist. Spring was finally showing signs of a permanent appearance. She thought of walking by the cove, but realizing that blustery spurts of spring wind would blow the fine, cold spray into her face, she decided to pack a lunch and leisurely explore the path Grace had shown her.

Arriving at the boulder-seat viewing area she had shared with Grace, she decided to continue. The path cut through heavy pines, their roots forming steps up the steep hillside. It continued between the small, white trunks of a grove of aspens, where the sun burst through the open branches onto green moss. Bethany felt like she'd been transported to a strange land. While the ground eventually evened out, the well-defined path twisted as if in pursuit of some whimsical brook.

The path led to a footbridge that crossed a wide, flowing creek. The structure—if the formation of granite slabs could be called that—had been made from quarried stone placed on top of boulders that otherwise would have formed large stepping stones. It looked quite safe, though some blocks shifted slightly as Bethany moved carefully over them. She could see the current pulling at winter's dead leaves along the water's edge. Apparently, this same creek ran through a culvert under the road a few curves from the hut, and it was probably more formidable than it seemed, especially during spring runoff.

After winding up another gentle slope, the path led through a small copse of trees. To Bethany's surprise, a graying gazebo sat at the top of the path. As she walked down the front steps of the wooden frame, she found herself standing on a large, flawless lawn. A stream, the one she'd just crossed, ran through the lawn, rippling smoothly into large, shallow pools, before narrowing to swirl down miniature waterfalls. There were large beds of soft green plants along the bank. They resembled Amelia's perennial gardens, and Bethany looked at them longingly.

In this silent place Bethany saw neither people nor buildings. A thick mass of pines stood behind the budding branches scattered across the lawn. Drifts of gold and purple crocus enlivened the perennial flowerbeds under several of the trees. Bethany decided the early spring green grass was the perfect place to eat her lunch.

Looking around as she ate, Bethany wondered about the lovely place. Was it a park? A small botanical garden? A residence? It was isolated, certainly, but with no buildings nearby, it hardly seemed likely that it was someone's yard. Continuing her analysis, she convinced herself that even if it were private property, as friendly as the local residents seemed to be, they would hardly arrest her for trespassing. In fact, they would probably be pleased to know that their handiwork was being admired.

*　*　*

It was later than she expected when she returned to the hut, but she felt refreshed, stimulated.

Before going in to continue her writing, Bethany went to the mailbox. It held a single envelope. Finally, she had received a reply from the Family History Library in Salt Lake City.

As she went over the materials, Bethany was surprised at what she found. Not family histories—of course, she hadn't actually expected that—but locality histories for early settlements along the northeastern coastal waters of Maine.

Her eyes lit up and she held her breath as the word *tunnels* was mentioned and then repeated again and again. Tunnels were built during the French and Indian Wars for protection against the French and their Indian allies with an attack in 1758 on Louisburg on Cape Breton Island. Tunnels built before the English capture of Quebec and Montreal a year later. New tunnels were built and older ones used during the Revolutionary War by patriots for security. During the first naval battle of the Revolution in Machias Bay, northeastern Maine, June 1775 colonists captured the British gunboat *Margaretta;* when

British retaliation was expected, patriots were concealed in tunnels. "Spurs" of the Underground Railroad ran throughout New England and north into Maine during the 1800s. Small shiploads of slaves were transported from harbors, through tunnels, into homes of sympathizers, guided inland, and then north to Nova Scotia. Other groups hid in dense forests, were secreted in homes, guided through tunnels, and delivered to waiting ships for transport to Canada.

Bethany was overwhelmed. She raced out to the shed, determined to find her tunnel—the tunnel she knew existed. In frustration she clenched her fist and muttered, "Joseph! No." Debris much too heavy for her to lift on her own still blocked the shed's entrance.

* * *

Since she had enjoyed herself so much at the gardens, Bethany hiked the path again the next day. After arriving, she settled herself in the gazebo. She was pulling her lunch from her backpack when she heard someone whistling. She looked up to see a lanky man dressed in a plaid flannel shirt and Levi's walking toward the gazebo. His dark brown hair was covered by a baseball cap, its visor sticking out in back. Sunglasses and dark whiskers hid his expression.

Bethany hesitated as he walked toward her. "I hope I'm not intruding," she said cautiously.

"Intruding? No," he responded. "This land is in escrow, so the owners aren't around, and I'm handling some of the maintenance. I didn't think the flowers would be this far into bloom."

The man was younger than she had originally thought and his clothes were fresh and clean. Bethany was surprised that he spoke clearly, no accent, no up-home drawl. He sounded well educated as he clipped a shoot from an overgrown bush by the gazebo.

"The crocus are pretty," she commented somewhat lamely. "I've always enjoyed being around flowers."

"I usually do," the man replied, "although up here I'm finding a few exceptions. In case you feel like wandering around here—which you are welcome to do, by the way—I have to warn you. There are some man-grabbing rosebushes around here. I tried to prune one and got my sleeve stuck on the thorns and dropped the clippers in the process. It must have taken me fifteen minutes to get my shirt freed, and I thought I'd lose my arm when I tried to get in through the branches to get the clippers."

Bethany chuckled at the laid-back description. "Do tell me where these peculiar bushes are—if you're sure it's all right for me to trespass. I wouldn't want anything grabbing me."

It usually wasn't hard to identify some personality types, she thought, but he seemed different. At first she had thought he was an older man—not too many guys went around humming patriotic songs and wearing rubber boots to their kneecaps. Then he seemed to be one of those charismatic, good-looking guys with lots of brains that were usually very successful and not necessarily to be trusted. But that didn't fit him either. Why would someone like that be working as a part-time gardener? Maybe he was one of those happy-go-lucky types without enough motivation to stick with one thing. His demeanor was pleasant, and she felt surprisingly at ease around him, even safe.

"Willing to risk being seized by a bush to admire flowers? You must enjoy gardens," he offered.

"I guess it runs in my genes. And the hike up here is good exercise," she replied.

"You don't look like you need a lot of exercise," he replied, with a quick, approving look. "You live close around?"

"I'm renting a house down by the cove—wherever that is from here," she explained with a wry grin. "I lost my sense of direction in all the twists and turns on the trail."

"The road I use comes in from the back, and I'm always too busy to do much exploring, so I couldn't tell you exactly where your path goes." He looked at her. "By the way, my name is Rob."

"And I am Bethany."

"Well, Bethany," he said as he looked down at the lunch she had spread on the edge of the gazebo, "mind if I join you for lunch? I was going to get mine from the shed when I saw you."

"I didn't realize there was a shed."

"The tool shed. You'd be surprised at what you can find in these trees!"

Bethany thought of the garden she had discovered. "Yes, there are some very pleasant surprises out here."

"I'll say!" he replied.

She looked up at him. He was grinning.

* * *

When Bethany returned to the hut that afternoon, she was delighted—and satisfied—to see that the debris had been cleared from in front of the shed. She had been astonished earlier when she had actually checked out the mess—branches, chunks of tree trunk, pieces of glass, portions of the hut's wall and lath. They had all been heaped in a pile at least half as tall as the shed itself. Now there were only a few scraps and tire tracks left.

She quickly dropped her backpack inside the back doorway and ran out to the shed. The frost heaves and snow piled by the shed door had begun to thaw, although since they'd been covered by debris and shaded by the stone building, the process had been slowed considerably. Bethany grabbed the door handle and yanked. The door didn't budge. She put all her strength into another yank. The door opened a few inches. A third tug gave her a five-inch opening. But the door remained firmly entrenched in its final position, the opening too small for her to enter.

Bethany turned slowly away from the shed, disappointed. Apparently, today would not be the day to investigate the tunnel.

* * *

The next morning Bethany was pleased when she woke to find the sky bright and clear, another good day for lunch at the gazebo later. Since she couldn't get into the shed she decided to write instead. When she found she couldn't concentrate, she baked brownies and cut vegetable sticks. She thought of making fancy sandwiches, but decided against it, reminding herself that Rob probably wouldn't even be at the garden. She brushed her hair but left it hanging straight rather than braiding it.

As Bethany approached the estate, she saw Rob weeding along the stream near the largest of the waterfalls. He called, "Hey! Come over here!" When she obliged, he showed her the falls, surrounded by greening lawn with islands of new foliage tucked around huge granite boulders that appeared sporadically through the area. "Look. This is amazing. This streambed is the original bed—no one could have dug trenches into these granite outcroppings—and the lawn and flower beds have been planted around it. Can you imagine the hours of work it took?" He gazed around the lawn.

"I wanted to show you something else, though." He pointed at a bush on an incline above a large pond at the bottom of the waterfalls. "That," he said with a grin, "is the culprit—the official man-grabbing rosebush I told you about. Consider yourself warned."

He turned back to the lawn. "Look at this." He pointed toward a section of the flowerbeds erupting with pale green sprouts. "There'll be continual blossoms from now until late autumn. Delphiniums. Peonies. Columbines. Lilies. There must be acres of garden stretched out here!"

Bethany smiled at his enthusiasm. "Where did you learn to garden?"

"I worked with a wonderful teacher, and what she didn't teach me she inspired me to learn on my own. How about you?"

"Oh, my grandmother used to have the loveliest flower gardens you can imagine. I was too young to do much but watch her direct the gardeners. You must have been raised on a farm," she surmised, watching his precise movements as he clipped at the old growth, never injuring the new sprouts at ground level. She bent down and began clearing the dead stems from the young plants.

"Not really." He grinned. "I came from one of those inner-city areas in one of those not-too-large towns that aren't supposed to have inner cities. We had about enough lawn to turn a lawn mower around on. So we donated it to critters misplaced by civilization and let the weeds grow—or at least that's how my dad summarized the situation."

Bethany laughed. "Sounds like your dad was interesting," she said with a grin as she continued to pick off the brown stems.

"My dad raced cars until he was in a wheelchair after an accident. He got a repair shop. I never did much work there, but my dad traded some work for a motorcycle that was in pretty bad shape. He told me I could have it if I helped him fix it up. He thought that might get me interested in mechanics, but I didn't care a lot for little screws and bolts and unbending, inflexible pieces that had to fit in places where they had to be bent or flexed to fit. And I never liked dirty oil all over my hands."

"So what did you do?"

"Well, I fixed the motorcycle, then never entered the shop again except to repair it."

"And you rode your motorcycle happily ever after."

"Not exactly. My friends and I knew that if we took out a part of the muffler we could get a nice, throaty roar. When irate citizens called the police, thinking they were being invaded by Hells Angels, they looked us up—you could hear us most of the way across town—and checked our mufflers. Other kids had taken off the whole section from their mufflers and left them out, but I put all the pieces but the one that muted the sound back on so the police couldn't tell that it was missing.

"One night the cops stopped us right in front of our place. When my dad saw the police surrounding us like we were a bunch of hoodlums, he wheeled himself out. The police fined a couple of the kids but they just looked at my cycle and didn't say a thing. Then my dad told me to bring my bike down to the shop."

"What did he do?"

"Well, I got to work off triple the amount of the fines the other guys had paid before I could use my bike again. Then I still had to do dishes and laundry for three months before I could go riding at night!"

"But that taught you to be responsible, right?" Bethany asked, thinking about how Amelia had required strict adherence to the rules she'd set for Bethany.

"Well, it taught me not to get caught, or at least if I got caught to make sure I liked my punishment."

Bethany knelt down to clean the grass out of a bed of ground phlox.

"So what did you do next?"

"Oh, little odds and ends. Nothing very clever."

"Then your existence was pretty boring, or do you have more confessions?" She found it hard to believe that he had not found plenty of additional escapades to fill his time.

"Well, there is one more thing I could get off my chest, especially since it is to a charming young woman like you."

Bethany pretended not to notice the reference as she slid over to weed an iris bed.

"I didn't always choose to act in accordance with the established rules of deportment in class, and, hard as you may find it to believe, I was detained after school on a number of occasions."

"Oh, that is hard to believe," Bethany interjected, laughing.

"Well, I had biology from a lovely young thing named Miss Abbott, who was starting her second year of teaching and was quite idealistic as well as good looking. It wasn't difficult to get her to 'invite' me to stay after class, until she, with the enthusiasm of an inexperienced teacher, came up with a plan. We agreed that nothing was being accomplished by having me simply sitting in a desk during detention, so she challenged me to come up with a project. If I completed it, she would raise my grade one letter. It didn't take me long to realize that I could raise an F to a D, ensuring me of at least one passing grade during the term, so I started thinking.

"I decided to train the class hamster to follow the scent of Miss Abbott's perfume, thinking she wouldn't be crazy about that. But she liked the idea. She gave me some of her perfume and helped me teach the little creature, using a scoop of his food, to find a perfumed cotton ball.

"I was well on my way to a solid D when Miss Jerkins, a substitute, showed up. I dropped a perfume ball under her chair on the way to the pencil sharpener, then opened the latch to the hamster cage. Within five minutes, Miss Jerkins and half a dozen girls in the class were perched on top of their chairs. While they were jumping up and down, I realized one of them might land on the poor animal and I'd lose my grade. So, ever resourceful, I calmly picked him up, pretended he was trying to bite me—of course—and caged him. Miss Jerkins was impressed."

"What happened?"

"It ended up that Miss Abbott had to quit, and Miss Jerkins, who became the replacement teacher, kept on bragging about me, so I couldn't very well let on to her about the whole thing. I ended up doing homework and passing tests. Not your typical punishment.

Oh, and when I unintentionally raised my grades, I also got in with a good group of kids at school."

He looked up at her with a grin. "Enough of me. Did you know you've got mud on your knees?"

* * *

Bethany yawned as she sat in front of the TV that evening. She sat back and chuckled, thinking of the day and of Rob. She did not sleep much that night, tossing and turning in her bed. The sun's rays were beginning to brighten the tops of the pine trees she could see out the window when she finally fell asleep.

Bethany awoke several hours later and looked at the clock. She groaned in frustration.

After dressing quickly, she hurried to the garden, but as she had feared, it was empty. Bethany stared around the space halfheartedly. Then she walked to the tool shed, hoping Rob might be there. A note was attached to the door: *I'm not going to be able to spend much time here, but I will be around occasionally, and I hope we can share lunch again. Rob.*

Bethany looked at the note and smiled ruefully. She had hoped Rob would want to see her as much as she wanted to see him.

20

A rainstorm swept the area that weekend in the middle of April, keeping Bethany essentially housebound. She spent most of Saturday writing. On Sunday she took a nap after church, then puttered around the hut before settling down to email Kim.

Monday, with the trail still soaked and muddy, Bethany resolved to catch up on neglected odd jobs around the hut rather than hike to the garden for lunch. Rob probably wouldn't be there anyway, since he couldn't do much gardening in the mud. After receiving his note, she wondered if she'd ever see him at all.

Bethany was vacuuming when the phone rang. At first, she didn't recognize her former roommate's voice. Dee teased her through a fake survey before admitting her identity. For Bethany, it was strange to talk about graduate school days as if they had just happened, when so much of Bethany's life had changed. But with Dee, nothing seemed different. She mentioned name after name as if the women had been Bethany's close friends, even though Bethany remembered very few of them.

When it seemed as if Dee had recited most of what she knew about most of the people she knew, she stopped momentarily. "By the way, I got your message asking about Peter. Talk about a coincidence. I just saw him at a party a couple of days ago."

In great detail Dee described a party she'd attended over the weekend. She insisted that Bethany must remember Holly, a young woman from one of Bethany's medieval English lit seminars. Dee's description did bring back a memory, though not necessarily a pleasant one. Bethany recalled the heavily made-up girl who always stopped at her carrel when Peter was there, and who frequently stopped Bethany to talk, but only while Peter was walking her home.

Dee's next sentence jarred Bethany back from her brief reverie. "It was just like old times, you know, with Peter back and everything. We got talking about last year. Pete asked if I'd kept in touch with you and how you're doing. Right then I decided I'd have to call you, even though he said not to tell you I saw him since he wanted to surprise you sometime soon. But I decided it would be too fun to tell you anyway—and, wouldn't you know, I checked my email and saw that you had sent one a couple of weeks ago that I'd missed. Great minds, I guess."

So, Peter was back and safe. It had been a long time, but Bethany still felt the sudden excitement, the overwhelming longing, the racing heartbeat, the giddiness.

Then Dee, in a sudden burst of enthusiasm, interrupted her thoughts. "Guess what!" she said. "We all got talking about how much we missed you graduates and we want to get together! 'Course, we will be going to Florida for spring break, so we figured we'd take a little time off a couple of weeks after that and come up to see you for a long weekend!"

Bethany was stunned.

"Someone said you have a house on the beach and we could just cozy down in there with you. I don't suppose it's warm enough for much swimming in the ocean, but you probably have your own indoor swimming pool and a hot tub."

Bethany was confused by Dee's assumptions, and when she began to explain to her what her hut was like, she felt Dee's enthusiasm fade.

"But what happened to your inheritance? Amelia must have left you quite a chunk. Or is Joseph up to something, trying to keep it all?" Dee stopped for a moment to laugh obnoxiously at her joke, then continued, "Well, anyway, I just thought I'd get in touch with you, it's been so long and everything. Oh, I heard you broke your leg or something. You're all right, aren't you?"

Before Dee finally hung up, she returned to the subject of visiting Bethany long enough to acknowledge that the group's vacation plans were somewhat tentative. She would get back to Bethany in plenty of time for her to arrange the catering and entertainment if they were coming.

After she'd hung up the phone, Bethany sat on the couch and laughed. She wondered, *Was I ever really a part of that life?* But it took only a moment for her to remember that she hadn't been. Solemn, studious Bethany had never sought acceptance in Holly and Dee's society. She felt a stab at the thought that Peter had.

Peter! Why hadn't he contacted her lately? If it were safe for him to go to their party, why hadn't he come to Faunce Cove? Maybe he hadn't known her location, only her phone number. Or maybe he really did want to surprise her with the good news that he was back and the danger was passed. Still, why hadn't he called at least to relieve her worry?

Bethany's elation evaporated. What had Dee meant when she'd said it was "like old times with Peter back"? Peter had not been with them at their parties. He had been with Bethany. Perhaps Dee had meant Peter's being in the area rather than at their parties. Suddenly the hut seemed too confining for Bethany. She slipped into a warm jacket, even though she knew the trail would still be muddy—and the garden empty.

She climbed up the slippery trail, steadying herself by holding onto tree limbs, but still she kept thinking about Peter. The questions seemed even more confusing, then painful. And she felt angry. Why had he gone to see Dee first—even taken time to go to a party—when he knew she, Bethany, would be worrying?

By the roar of the creek, Bethany knew that it was brimming with runoff from the rainstorm. Impulsively, she followed it through the thick underbrush, rather than crossing the bridge. The swollen stream cascaded down the steep hill, spraying crystal droplets into the air as it hit the jagged rocks. She watched the turbulent water, feeling her own emotions quiet.

When she started back toward the hut, Bethany realized how far she had come and began looking for an easier way to get through the brush. She found the remnant of a small path skirting the hill and leading toward the road, but there was no way to cross the water except the bridge. She turned and followed the trail to the garden.

Bethany looked hopefully around the garden, past the swirls of dazzling yellow daffodils and deep blue hyacinth that had replaced the earlier crocus. Rob was not there, and Bethany had not seen him since the day before she'd found his note.

As she turned from the gazebo, the questions in the back of her mind surfaced with her disappointment. What was she really doing at Faunce Cove? Why hadn't Joseph told her precisely what was in the will? Was he really thinking about her best interests, or did he have other, perhaps less noble, intentions? Looking back after nearly a month without a word from him, she wished she had questioned him about her inheritance while they were dating. She realized now that letting her emotions keep her from asking about her future had been naive and foolish.

Peter was back, but he had not called her. Joseph had given her an ultimatum as if she were a school girl, notwithstanding the sizeable inheritance he might be handling for her.

Was she jeopardizing her own chances for a family by staying at Faunce Cove and obsessing about Patience?

She knew, as she scraped mud off her shoes at the door of the hut, that she would not be able to write that day.

* * *

Tuesday passed in a blur. She spent the day using the TV remote to flip from one channel to another, from one inane show to the next. After a totally unproductive day she went back to bed without a shower.

Wednesday's weather hadn't improved much, nor had Bethany's mood. But the rains over the past few days had been warm, and she halfway expected that the rains had thawed the ground enough that she could open the shed door and get in. She no longer had any doubt about what she would find inside—even though Joseph had told her that the contractor who had checked the shed had found no tunnel.

A huge mud puddle had replaced the large frost heaves in front of the shed. She looked at her shoes just long enough to decide that she didn't care if the mud ruined them. A swift turn of the door handle and an outward pull immediately opened the recalcitrant door.

Knowing where to look for the concealed door, she immediately saw the faint outline of it in the wall. Since the door opened into the tunnel, no wooden jambs were visible in the shed. Rocks had been skillfully secured to the thick door and some even extended from the wall above and on the sides of the door, appearing to be part of a solid wall, when actually they did a good job of hiding the opening itself. Instantly, Bethany's eyes sought the tiny hole in the mortar near the right side of the door—the keyhole. It too was almost indiscernible.

Once she had found it, her eyes surveyed the interior of the shed and the muddy puddle outside. *Where is the key? I know I had it Christmas Eve, but where is it now?* Neither careful scrutiny nor frantic scavenging unearthed it. Once again Bethany admitted defeat and returned reluctantly to the hut.

There is a door and there is a lock and somewhere there is a key, she told herself. She had felt all along that the tunnel was real. Now she knew that it existed. All she needed was the key.

* * *

By Thursday morning Bethany had decided she'd had enough slack days. The weather was still too wet to hike to the garden, but if she couldn't concentrate to write, she could at least finish the house cleaning she had started before Dee's call. She had searched the hut unsuccessfully, hoping to find the key to the tunnel door, but maybe it would turn up while she cleaned.

The computer was surrounded with clutter from those hurried mornings when she'd concentrated on writing, ignoring the odds and ends she had never found places for. Bethany pulled a box from the corner with a frown, realizing that the nurse at the rehabilitation center had packed it for her and that she'd forgotten to unpack it. Gathering the individual-sized bottles of lotion and powder the hospital had issued her, Bethany placed them in a grocery bag to give to Alice for Jessica. She wondered what else the hospital had sent.

Next there was a dry cleaner's bag covering an unfamiliar, hand-knit afghan that featured a cross-stitched rose motif. It was lovely, but it wasn't hers, so she set it aside to return to the rehab center.

Bethany recognized her coat—also in a dry cleaner's bag—at the bottom of the box and pulled it out. She had forgotten about the coat. Despite everything else, at least she'd had enough presence of mind to put on her coat that night.

Shaking out the coat, Bethany noticed a dry cleaning receipt and a small plastic bag pinned on its collar. She tore them off and opened

21

As she had remembered, the tunnel was amazingly long. However, it was not nearly as dark as it had seemed that stormy Christmas Eve. Rocks protruded from the walls and smoother stones formed the floor. As Bethany explored its construction, she wondered who had built the tunnel. And why. And when. During the early days when Indians had been the biggest problem? Perhaps during the French and Indian Wars?

The rock construction was dry wall—a process used before the invention of concrete. Tunnels were dug by hand and then rocks were carefully hand-placed to stay in position without reinforcement. It was not a haphazard construction, but one that required skill, determination, and old-fashioned hard work. Therefore, like the fireplace, it was several hundred years old but in nearly perfect condition. Obviously, someone had maintained the tunnel during that time, clearing out dust accumulations from the floor and spiderwebs from the walls and ceiling.

But who would have gone to the expense and work of excavating a tunnel in the middle of an isolated mountain through a forest? Bethany recognized that the rock shed was built differently, perhaps later. A mortar of some kind had been used to hold the rocks securely in place in all the walls and to disguise the door. But why would anyone do such a thing?

Bethany looked around her, more amazed at the reality of the tunnel than she had been when she had determinedly defended her memory of it. It was there, and it was as she had remembered it!

There was a light shining through a window near the ceiling at the far end of the tunnel—she could see it even as she opened the door—but it lacked the iridescence she had remembered. She rushed to look up at it and could see branches of forsythia in bright sunlight through the window now. Then again, it would have held a shimmering glow with snow thinly layered across its width.

She backed against the wall of the tunnel, excitement and relief overwhelming her. It had happened. It was real. She had been right and she was sane! Standing there she realized that the account Joseph had heard from the townspeople about the snowmobilers had been a rumor. After all, the police hadn't found any more evidence about that story—and standing before the tunnel's entrance, she realized that the memories of her mysterious rescuer might well have been accurate all along. But why hadn't he come forward and admitted he'd been the one to rescue her?

Emboldened by these realizations, Bethany knocked on the smooth surface that blocked the end of the tunnel and then pushed against it. A swinging door opened as if beckoning her.

Bethany surveyed the room opened to her. It was moderately large and warm, with rich wood paneling. In the corner sat a small, deeply grained, decorative table, a beam of sunshine from the ground-level window highlighting it and an ornate mirror behind it. The flowers Bethany vividly remembered seeing on the table were gone, but her eyes were drawn to the chair next to the table. She realized that the cushion was covered with the same rose motif as the one on the afghan that was in her box from the rehab center. The afghan must have been used as a blanket to warm her . . .

Bethany stood quietly, taking in a deep breath. If finding the key and the tunnel hadn't already exonerated her, identifying the matching motifs on the handwork proved that she had been in the room.

The room was lovely and inviting, but suddenly she realized she was an intruder in someone's home, and she had no idea whose home it was. Yes, the man who had been there Christmas Eve, *if* there had been a man there Christmas Eve, had been nice—he may have saved her life—but did he own the house or had he, like Rob, been a maintenance worker, a renter? And why had he disappeared so completely after accompanying or following her to Boston? What other explanation could there be for the way he had ended up in Boston in her hospital room—and her dreams? Would he reappear—

but what would he be like if he did? For months she had not considered the unexplained questions—questions she had ignored, halfway suspecting they and the reality they presented would never emerge. But they had, and now she stood in the doorway of that very room at the end of the tunnel!

With a growing sense of uneasiness, she backed against the door and stood there transfixed, wondering.

This room, on the same level as and attached to an underground tunnel, must be a basement, or at least the lowest floor of a larger building. What was the building and why was it there—evidently guarded by a purposefully placed rock wall and pines? What had the man she'd met there been doing? No one seemed to be living in the room now. Could there be any connection between this property and the property that Rob gardened? There did seem to be a good distance between the two, especially in comparison with the distance between the tunnel and the hut. Was it possible that the owner of this property had used that to his advantage? It wouldn't have taken any time at all to walk through the tunnel with a saw to cut into a pine or a spindle, to loosen lug nuts and spill oil, to check to see if she was home so he could make phone calls that would only be answered by an answering machine. Who would have an easier time harassing her? But what connection could this person have to Peter's investigations?

She felt fear rising within her, even though she realized her suppositions were groundless. There was no evidence that anyone had used the tunnel to disturb her. Still, she turned through the entrance to the tunnel and walked quickly down the passageway. It was hard to keep from running as she neared the shed, and she felt her heart beating rapidly as she pulled the heavy door closed, slipped the key back in the lock, and turned it firmly.

It was useless trying to concentrate on anything else the rest of the morning. Bethany paced the floor, thinking of the tunnel. It was a relief to know she had not been delusional, but the tunnel's nearness and the possibilities that it offered a foe for mischief replayed through her mind like a grating tune. It took her nearly an hour before she noticed the mud she'd gotten on her clothes. She hoped she hadn't tracked any of it into the beautiful room, leaving a mud trail through the tunnel as visible as Hansel and Gretel's crumbs. She grinned at the

22

Bethany pulled a towel around her wet hair as she stepped from the shower. Slipping on a comfortable pair of sweats, she felt tired but more at peace. There was a tunnel. She had not imagined it. She was justified.

As she unplugged the hair dryer, Bethany heard a car door close. She barely had time to run a comb through her hair before she heard a knock on the door.

She opened the door to find Peter standing there.

"Anybody home?" he asked.

Bethany stared at him. He was as handsome as she had remembered, his blond hair falling over his blue eyes, his short sleeves hugging his muscles. The only difference in his appearance from the year before was a pair of leather cowboy boots, decorated across the toes and legs with embedded turquoise stones.

All she could voice was a shallow, "Peter?"

"Yes, Peter," he replied with a throaty chuckle. "Aren't you going to ask me in?"

"Of course," Bethany said as she stepped back from the door. He caught her in his arms and pulled her to him. The kiss he firmly planted on her lips was unexpected.

Bethany was suddenly wide awake. She had slipped in and out of two different worlds during the last two days, and now Peter was kissing her.

"You're beautiful, as usual," he declared, stepping back to look at her. "Your hair has grown." He stopped and asked, "Are you okay?"

"I'm sorry," Bethany voiced, stepping weakly toward a couch. Peter held her hand and moved with her to sit down. "I . . . I'm just so surprised to see you."

Bethany sat silently, focusing on his presence. How many times had she thought of the gleam of his hair, the firm line of his jaw, the blue of his eyes? How often had she longed for him to hold her hand, to touch her hair? But now she felt only shock.

Peter looked at her with a wide grin. "I'm back," he said simply. "You don't know how many times I've thought about that quiet smile of yours and your laugh. I've missed you so much."

Peter was back, but she felt herself stiffen, and she pulled away from him.

He seemed to sense her questions before she began to ask.

"I heard you were back, Peter, but why didn't you call?"

His finger touched her lips, quieting her.

"You don't need to ask questions. Just let me tell you." His eyes looked deeply into hers. "It wasn't the way you thought, Bethany, sweetheart." The endearment sounded strange. He had never spoken to her that amorously while they were at the university. "I couldn't contact or see you yet. It was too dangerous." He gently pulled her closer to him and put his arm around her shoulder. "Honey, I wanted to see you with all my heart, but I was afraid of the consequences." His voice was soft and gentle as he sighed, then took her hand.

"I'm sure you figured out I was working for the government, but not really doing the job I described to you, right? That I was actually with the FBI or something similar? Well, when I met you I was working undercover, getting information on a major corporate scandal that looked like it might include tax evasion. I was assigned specifically to investigate the corporation's legal staff for the possibility of tax-related charges. Sometimes it's easier to get convictions for tax evasion than for other crimes. Things were going pretty well. I was getting a lot of information and my boss was really impressed with me. Then I had met you, and you liked me. I was on top of the world."

"Yes," Bethany interrupted, "but what does that have to do with your being in hiding, and the allegations against Joseph, and these threats I've been getting, and—?"

"Hold on, Bethany. That's why I need to tell you the rest," Peter reassured her. "Well, about then another agent said some things when he should have kept quiet, and the corporation management caught on about me. But not before I had found some pretty incriminating information that would not only close down their corporation—and a couple of others besides—but also put some of the executives in prison for a long time. They wanted to know exactly what I had and they were pretty nasty about it.

"Our agency had another guy with his toe in the door, and he kept me informed. After I left, he found out that the corporation had started putting out feelers to find me. They tried bribing some associates to tell them where I was. They contacted a couple of close friends and threatened them. They told a cousin they would pay me and him a good sum of money if I would contact them.

"When they realized that either I wasn't getting the messages or I wasn't going to buy, they got a lot uglier. As you know, the agency realized that I was in serious trouble."

"You mean that last quick phone call?"

"I didn't want to leave without telling you more than I did, but my boss absolutely refused to let me. It was too risky and the case was too critical. They slapped me with a new name, transferred me to the agency's version of the Witness Protection Program, and shipped me to a desolate town in northern Minnesota. I had to stay hidden until the case was solved. Being separated from you was the worst part—except knowing that if I contacted you, we might both be in a dangerous situation." He pressed her hand warmly. "Did they contact you?"

Bethany thought of the threatening notes and shuddered. "They sent some messages."

Peter swore, then grinned at her sheepishly. "Sorry. My associates have obviously had a bad influence on my vocabulary."

He became serious again. "I hoped they hadn't involved you in any of their threats."

Bethany shook her head without thinking, unwilling to let him change the subject. "But what happened to you? You called at Thanksgiving."

"On Thanksgiving, even Gary—the agent I was with—couldn't stand being so isolated, and we went to a bar so he could get a drink.

While he was ordering, I went to the telephone booth instead of the men's room. Anyway, Gary caught me. He wasn't real happy with me and the agency wasn't happy with either one of us. I tried to call a couple of times, but after Thanksgiving, Gary was determined to keep me in his sight.

"You can imagine how I felt when the agency started making arrests. I wasn't their sole witness anymore, and I could come back to you."

"But you went to a party. Dee told me."

Peter sat forward.

"First, I had to be sure that you'd be safe, that none of the guys were following me." He looked up at her. "The agency closed down the main organization, but there was always the chance that some little guy with a vendetta had gotten away and would come after one of us. I didn't want someone to follow me up here and put you in danger."

"So everything is safe now." Bethany relaxed.

Peter sat back and briefly closed his eyes. He opened them again before he responded with a decisive, "No. There are still some guys out there who have it in for me in a big way, and there are some other things you need to know."

"There's more?" Bethany could not remember Peter ever having spoken so long on one thing at a single sitting. Although often talkative, he was generally more inclined to jump from one topic to another.

"My assignment, as I said, was specific. Most illegal organizations have lawyers who help keep them away from being charged with illegal accounting practices. This one was no exception. I was pretty skeptical about one of the attorneys, and after they interrogated a couple of newly arrested members this week, we got some new evidence."

He sat forward and looked at Bethany squarely. "Bethany, it wasn't a coincidence that I met you in the library that first day. I was assigned to investigate Joseph Panninon, and I knew a friendship with you would provide the perfect opportunity. I wasn't planning on falling in love with you, but that happened, too.

"Sadly, your lawyer is up to his eyeballs in some pretty bad stuff with the organization, but he has covered himself too well to be disciplined or indicted. While I was investigating that, I found out more." He looked tired as he sat back briefly, then leaned forward again.

"Another reason I didn't come straight here was because I was checking on some information I got before I was sent to Minnesota. Bethany," he paused and looked her straight in the eyes, "Panninon is cheating you."

"What do you mean?" Bethany's voice was sharp and intense.

"He's come up with a scheme to take away your inheritance." Peter sat forward, his body completely rigid.

"That's impossible!" She was determined that she would not cry. "I know you mentioned your suspicions of him before, but I can't believe you've found any concrete evidence!"

"Wait. Listen." He held her hand firmly as she turned her face away from him.

"Bethany." He used his free hand to turn her face back toward him. "Bethany, you have to hear this. First, Panninon got enough power over your grandmother's affairs that he could practically write her will himself. Sweetheart, he put in some things that made it so your spouse will have all the control. Your husband will be the real benefactor, not you."

Bethany tried to shake her head. Joseph would not have manipulated Amelia. Peter held her face in his hands so she could not turn away from him again.

His tone was as intense as his stare. "He tried to get you to fall in love with him, didn't he?"

Bethany pulled back from his hold, but she could not ignore his implication.

"You know that it's true, Bethany." His voice softened. "Honey, if that were all, if I thought he would give you the life you deserve, I would not interfere, even if it meant I lost you and you lost your inheritance. But I found out more."

Bethany closed her eyes, wishing fervently that she could drown out the sound of Peter's voice.

"After dating you, Panninon found that, as he put it, he 'didn't want to get stuck with you.' So he figured out another way to get what he wants." He looked at her closely. "Bethany." His hand went to her face again, and he turned so she could not avoid his eyes. "Bethany, even I would never have suspected that he would go so low as to involve your friend Kim in the deal."

Bethany shook her head violently and stood up. Peter rose with her and held her so she couldn't walk away.

"You have to know this," he said, his hands firmly on her shoulders. "It seems that Joseph has fallen in love with our little Kim, and he seems to be manipulating things so that he can cut you completely out of everything."

Bethany pulled away from Peter's hold and sat down on the couch. He sat down beside her and spoke quietly.

"Tell me, Bethany, has Panninon ever shown you the will your grandmother signed? Has he ever told you anything about its terms? Has he given you any information other than about," his gesture indicated the room, "this little house?" He paused to let the thought sink in. "No, he hasn't, has he? And anytime you've tried to question him, he's simply ignored you or avoided answering you, hasn't he?" Peter's tone became quieter, gentler. "Bethany, I can't tell you how hard this has been for me. I spent hours wondering if I should tell you, hoping I wouldn't need to. But I don't think I could live with myself if I let someone I love be duped like this. Honey, I just can't let this happen to you."

Bethany sat motionless on the couch. Peter retrieved a soda from the refrigerator, opened it, and handed it to her. He watched her as she sipped from the can, then set it on the table. He sat down beside her.

"You see, Bethany, he isn't what you think, just as this house isn't what you thought. You do know about this property, don't you?"

Bethany tried to think, willed herself desperately to understand the implication of what he was saying, but she could not.

"He's never told you, has he?" Peter's voice was full of contempt. "Bethany, this house, this little, tiny house and the property it's on, are yours. It belonged to your grandmother. But it's nothing compared to her other holdings right here at Seacrest. This is part of your inheritance." Bethany concentrated on his words. "Amelia Carlisle owned this and an immense estate with an enormous garden and one of the most magnificent mansions ever built on the Maine seaboard. They all belong to you, or they will if you can keep Panninon from taking them from you."

Bethany's mind went quickly back to the garden and then the room she had been in that morning. "What do you mean?"

Peter exhaled before continuing. "I think he may be setting you up so it appears as if you are incapable of managing your grandmother's estate. Bethany, I've been following Panninon and his doings much closer than you realize. I'm aware of his feigned concern over your incoherence when you got hurt at Christmas and your obsession with the story of some woman who used to live here. Things didn't go very smoothly when you were in Boston, did they? Panninon's building up to something, and, Bethany, when he's proved that you're unstable, he'll be named your legal custodian, and voilà! I hope you didn't tell anyone about the messages you got from the corporation I was investigating. He may try to use those to claim that you're delusional—unless we make sure he doesn't steal them. You need to be able to prove that they exist. Why don't you give them to me for safe-keeping?"

"I don't have them anymore. I guess they got thrown away after the tree crashed into the hut. And I didn't tell Joseph about them anyway."

Peter looked upset. "You're sure you don't have them? We could really use those, Bethany. Well, we'll find other evidence. But I'm afraid that Joseph, with or without Kim, may be planning to hurt you. I found some information about some pranks to make you appear deranged or to scare you enough that you do actually become unstable. I understand he has plans to physically harm you and make you incapable of managing a business or property. I had to warn you. Bethany, you've got to get away from here."

Bethany felt totally bewildered. Everything had come too fast. Her quiet, orderly world had collapsed. She was too exhausted to think. "Where would I go?"

There was a sudden look of illumination in Peter's eyes. "Come with me." He paused. Then, with persuasive intensity, he said, "Bethany, come with me! We could do it. We would be safe together, and happy! Bethany, it's the solution to everything!"

Bethany was silent, her thoughts racing. Would his idea provide them both a safety net? Still, everything that he had told her was based on his assumption that Joseph was deceiving her and planning to swindle her out of her inheritance. She found that nearly impossible to believe. Joseph had certainly been acting ill-humored, but trying to cheat her? Perhaps Peter's information was faulty.

She thought back on the words of the last warnings, trying to find any proof of Peter's theory. The warnings had never been specific. The only thing they had demanded was information about Peter, and they had said they'd tell her how to get it to them. But the sender had never followed through, never told her how to give him information—almost as if they knew there would be no information to share!

Why would someone risk giving Peter more evidence against them if they knew there was no information and nothing they could gain by it?

What if it was all a hoax? What if everything had been done for different reasons than she had thought, and by different people?

But if the organization had not sent the warnings, who had? What other reason would anyone have to send them? Was there someone else who wanted to profit from the corporation's problems? How could someone else use her—or Peter—to their advantage by sending threats? What did they want?

Peter's accusations invaded her thoughts. Had Joseph, knowing Peter had evidence against him, sent the threats? Was Joseph simply trying to keep her upset? Was he trying to get her to do something so extreme that she looked incompetent and completely irrational? Or did Joseph think that by threatening her, he could blackmail Peter from disclosing Joseph's questionable practices?

She needed time to think and pray.

Peter noticed her hesitation and released her hand. "Even though I made sure no one would follow me, it's still dangerous for me to be here. If he finds out that I've come and warned you, he'll know we're onto him. I can only imagine what he'll do. I wish I could stay and protect you against him, but with the connections he's set up here at Faunce Cove it's too dangerous. All I can do is warn you, and beg you to come with me."

"Come with you?"

"Oh, Bethany, please. I have always loved you, but even I can't protect you here. Darling, come with me. Marry me and we'll find a way to defeat him."

"Peter," she protested.

"Bethany, just pack some things and come with me now. Have you got some cash? We don't want to use credit cards or anything that he can trace to us. Together, away from here, we'll be fine. We'll fight for your inheritance somewhere far enough away that Joseph cannot hurt you."

She hesitated.

Peter began again. "I can't stay around here. It's risky for me, and it makes it more dangerous for you. I've got a room for tonight on the mainland. If you decide to join me, I'll be there until tomorrow at checkout time." He turned a hotel business card over and wrote a room number on the back before handing the card to her. "I'm not registered under my own name, so you'll have to ask for the room number." He looked at her intently. "Bethany, I came because I'm certain your life is in real danger now, or will be very soon. He may be putting his plan into action now—tonight—or tomorrow. Please come."

With sympathy in his eyes, he looked down at her tired face. "But this is much too fast. How could you possibly believe me?" He considered for a moment, then sat on the edge of the love seat close beside her, his eyes gently begging her.

"Think about what I've said. If you don't believe that Mrs. Carlisle owned this, and that Joseph is lying to you, all I ask you to do is go up the path on the hill—you know the one I mean, don't you? After the rise between the brook and the gazebo, there is a rhododendron. You'll find a less-worn path. Follow it—it won't take you more than a minute or two—and you'll find a rock wall. That's where you'll find the answer to your questions."

He rose, then leaned to kiss her on the cheek.

"Call me, then destroy the card so they can't find us. Come tomorrow."

She watched him through the growing dusk as he climbed into his car.

* * *

Bethany paced the floor, all sense of peace long fled. Though completely fatigued, she was too restless to sit, let alone relax. When she knelt at her bedside, she could barely formulate a coherent prayer.

It could not be true.

Yet, she *had* wondered about the will. So perhaps Peter was right about Joseph's intentions. She wished she could go up the hill to the rock wall and see the evidence Peter had spoken of, but that must wait until there was light.

Kim could not be involved. Not Kim.

If Peter were wrong about Kim—and Bethany felt confident he was—he could also be wrong about Joseph.

There was only one way to find out if Kim had anything to do with this—if Joseph was indeed in love with her. Bethany would ask her! She picked up the telephone. Immediately, she replaced it. Deciding what she would say, she lifted the phone to try again. Exhausted, as she was, she knew if she talked to Kim she would learn the truth.

"Hello?" The voice was very young and definitely not Kim's.

"Hi. Could I speak to Kim, please?"

"She's not here."

"Could you leave a message for her to call me? It's ten o'clock here, Eastern Standard Time, so if she gets in by—"

The voice interrupted, "Oh, that's all right. She left a message for you. She'll be arriving around midnight. She'll just catch a taxi to Mr. Panninon's apartment so he won't need to meet the plane. By the way," the young voice continued, "have they found out anything more about the break-in at Mr. Panninon's office?" There was a slight pause, then a question. "This is Mr. Panninon's secretary, isn't it?"

23

As Bethany started from the hut, it was so dark that she could barely see though the predawn sky that was beginning to glow. It was cold. Thin layers of ice covered the puddles bordering the road. Even the dark brown parka she wore over her sweat suit did not entirely cut out the chill. Heavy clouds rolled from the west, threatening rain as the gusting wind pulled them across the sky. Bethany didn't care. Had she been in a different mood, the incoming storm might have dissuaded her from hiking the hillside, but today she hardly gave notice to the weather.

Rubbing her finger on the business card in her pocket, she knew she must find out if Peter was right. Then she would decide what she needed to do.

She climbed the steep hill, clinging to the tree trunks to pull herself through the slippery mud. Her weak leg, the unstable footing, and the near darkness made the climb very difficult. In the shadows of the pines where dawn had not yet filtered, she could not see enough to avoid the occasional slap of a pine bough against her face. It seemed to take an eternity to reach the aspens, where the leaf buds were still tight, allowing the gray light of the gloomy sunrise to seep through the branches.

Bethany cleaned the mud from her shoes before crossing the granite footbridge, then hurried toward the next rise. She identified the spot that Peter had described, following the scant trail that led to the rock wall. Opening the cast-iron gate slowly, she gazed at the cemetery that lay before her. The front section of the graveyard held modern headstones—polished marble with precisely engraved names. Behind them,

Bethany could see older, thin slate grave markers. She immediately noticed a gravestone marking a plot of thin, patchy grass, and dropped to her knees to touch the crisp lettering.

Her heart pounded as she read the name that stood out vividly against the newly erected marker, *Amelia Courier Carlisle.* Amelia's grave. Bethany knelt and traced her grandmother's name carefully, a knot building in her throat. She wanted to ignore Peter's warning, to disregard everything except her feelings. How she wished to clear her head of the blur of new knowledge Peter had given her.

Reality hit her and she stood quickly. Peter had said she would find her answer here, and she had. This property was not only the property that had once been the joy of Patience Faunce Smythe, but it was also the place Amelia had been buried, and according to Peter, it was part of Bethany's own inheritance from Amelia. Yet Joseph had said . . . No, she corrected herself as she recalled the conversation. *She* had been the one who had assumed that Amelia had been cremated. But Joseph had not corrected her, never mentioned a grave! So many other things suddenly became logical, fibers in the web of lies in which she had not realized she was trapped.

But she would think of that later, later when the danger was past. Now she must get back to the hut and call Peter.

As she neared the brook, she felt the first splashes of rain against her face and paused to zip her parka. The low, rolling clouds promised one of the quick, torrential downpours that often howled through with pelting rain, only to subside into a calmer day. If only she could get to the hut before the downpour began in earnest.

She started across the footbridge without thinking, but immediately wished she had cleaned the mud from her shoes before stepping onto the wet rocks. She slipped on the first slab, but then caught herself and continued. By the fifth slab she realized that it was more than the mud on her shoes or even ice on the rocks that was making her passage so difficult. The rocks were shifting much more noticeably under her weight, and the downpour had turned into a deluge. But there was nothing to do but to keep going.

Bethany had nearly reached the middle of the footbridge when the slab she stepped on rocked and settled into the water at a steep angle. She slid into the freezing stream. She gasped as the cold water hit her, then instinctively screamed as the water covered her eyes and roared into her ears, knowing, even as she bobbed to the surface, that there would be no one to hear or help her. She panicked, arms flailing the water. Then, forcing herself to be calm enough to grasp the sharp edge of the rock, she tried to lift herself. Her fingers were too cold to cling to the wet surface. She couldn't pull up her weight. She thrashed at the creek, trying to keep her face above the freezing water, but she felt herself being pulled down.

Clutching at the rock with one hand, Bethany tried desperately to unzip her parka, now a sodden mass that was weighing her down. The zipper bunched and the fabric ballooned out in the water. She couldn't take the coat off with only one hand, but when she let go of the granite slab with her other hand, she was immediately immersed. She came up gasping for breath as her hair streamed down in front of her face.

Feeling herself being pulled from the rocks by the stream of water, she fought to catch at a ledge each time and kicked her way to the surface. The roar of the water reminded her of its wild course as it tumbled down to the bridge and the ocean. She propelled her body against the flow of the water, fighting with each stroke to move through the current. The stream, though barely the width of the hut, seemed to widen with each stroke she took until she saw a gap in the boulders that formed a steep, granite trough around the once-gentle creek. She vaguely remembered the spot from her exploration of the area and that it opened to a small path. It took a good deal of effort as she fought the water and her fear, but she pulled herself up the gap out of the current.

Finally dragging herself out of the water, she lay gasping on the small path.

She looked at the forest around her. The undergrowth was patchy around the pine trees except where granite outcroppings showed through the layer of dead leaves. Trying to think clearly, she decided to rest for a few minutes, then go back to the hut and call Peter. She was cold and trembling with such intensity that it was difficult to reach into her pocket to feel for the reassuring shape of the business card. Her pocket was empty! Frantically, she felt in the other jacket pocket, then both pockets of her sweatpants. They were all empty.

Bethany looked around her wildly. Seeing nothing in the grass, she looked at the creek and saw a slice of white bobbing at the edge. She needed to reach it before it worked its way back into the current. As she slipped cautiously into the water, her motion disturbed the niche where the card had been sheltered. Each time she moved, the subsequent ripples spread and carried the card farther away. She desperately tried to reach it again but to no avail.

As Bethany saw the paper ripple into the undertow farther downstream, she felt a surge of desperation as the current pulled at her. How could she contact Peter? She fought her way back out of the water and lay down on the bank, exhausted, shivering, and frustrated.

She heard voices.

"I'm sure I heard her."

The male voice was loud, and it had the identifiable slur of intoxication. She listened carefully, trying to calm the fear that chilled her mind as the water had her body.

"It's too early. No stupid lady would come out here at this hour," was the equally garbled reply.

"He said she liked morning walks and comes out every morning. That's why we had to get here so early to shift the rocks. Good thing we did it before we went back for more drinks."

"Well, if she came and you heard her, where is she?"

"Oh, she's here someplace. See that slab? We didn't move it that much. We've just got to find more evidence. He said to make sure she . . ." Bethany couldn't hear the end of the sentence as the voice was carried away by the wind. She lay taut on the ground, grateful that her brown parka nearly blended with the earth.

"Well, how you gonna make sure?"

"I guess we're gonna have to find her. That's what he said if we wanted the money."

Bethany shivered, fighting nausea. She rolled over slowly, carefully so that she could peek through the bushes toward the footbridge. She could see two young men—probably teenagers, maybe late teens—their jackets bright through the foliage. The rain now splattered only occasionally as the wind blew the drizzle from the branches above her.

"He said," one of the voices continued, "that we should shift the rocks around so that she wouldn't be able to tell. I think we've done enough." Again the words were muffled.

"He must be pretty rich."

"Yeah, he's rich all right. Did you see his car?"

Bethany listened carefully, her heart pumping. Were they talking about Joseph's BMW? Had Joseph hired these boys to harm her? He had to know about the grave's location . . . so he'd know she would need to cross the bridge. But how would he know she'd be up in this area? Peter knew, but he didn't know the geography here, and he certainly wasn't rich. She felt very confused.

"No, I didn't see his car. I was too busy showing the girls at the dance those fifty-dollar bills he gave me!"

"Well, the pay's not bad, that's for sure, but it was a rotten night to be out in the cold. Do you suppose he'll pay us more because it's so cold?"

"Well, here's hoping this'll warm us up."

Bethany closed her eyes in dread as the teenagers laughed and tipped beer bottles to their mouths.

"Did you see those senior girls at the dance last night? They couldn't get over my money."

"Well, if you want to get some more of those bills, get up here and help me find her. We need some kind of proof."

"If you heard her and she tipped that rock, it means she's already been here and she fell in since we moved the rocks. Either she's here somewhere or she was swept downstream."

"So, how we gonna tell which?"

Again there was the flash of a raised bottle.

"Well, we'll look around up here, and if we don't find her, we'll follow that path by the creek and see if she's down there. Then we take her . . ." Bethany strained to hear as the wind slurred the words beyond recognition.

Card or not, she had to get away from the water, so she slid down closer to the ground, trying to think through her fear. She couldn't get back to the trail because the men would cut her off. She'd have to get down to the highway, but not on the path because they would find her there.

Lying flat on the soaked foliage, Bethany slowly dragged herself over the dead leaves and pine needles, their crisp points jabbing at her hands as she avoided the exposed edges of granite that poked out of the thin patches of soil and autumn debris between the bushes. She stopped to listen for voices and breaking twigs. Where were they now? She must not let them see or hear her.

Twigs and rocks gouged at her body as she pulled herself slowly forward, occasionally reaching back to upright a plant or roughen the forest floor with debris to hide her tracks. Suddenly a dead branch cracked under the weight of her body. She froze, her eyes closed in fright, waiting until she was sure no one had heard her before moving forward.

When she knew she was far enough away that the trees would completely hide her, Bethany raised to her knees to crawl through the underbrush in the direction of the highway and the ocean. Praying silently, she moved forward carefully, stopping to listen for sounds.

Occasionally, she heard shouting voices or a breaking branch. Nearly panicked, she knew that if she stood up and ran—no matter how instinctive it felt to run or call out for help—they would capture her. Following a course paralleling the stream, Bethany was slightly relieved when she finally reached the edge of the hill. Certain that the men could not see her, she ran between the trees, stopping to listen before running again. Though the thickening foliage hid her from her pursuers, it also blocked her view of the terrain. As she cautiously moved down the mountain, her only guide was the sound of the water and the slight decline. Shivering and out of breath, her heart pounding as adrenaline urged her forward, she stumbled on a root and fell to her knees.

Continuing to crouch, Bethany worked her way into the thick branches of the nearest fir to rest until her heart quit racing. Since she had heard neither voices nor movement for several minutes, she figured the men must have searched the area near the rock bridge and given up. Hopefully, she was out of danger. Now, she thought with relief, she just had to make her way down the mountain to the aqueduct and then to the ocean, where she would follow the shoreline of the cove.

She took a deep breath. The water roared loudly as she cautiously moved a large pine branch in front of her. The branch swung outward easily, too easily. There should have been resistance as the needles scraped at the ground or bucked against scraggly brushes, but there was none. As Bethany moved the limb farther away, the earth evaporated, leaving a sheer drop that fell straight down to a bed of loose rocks and tall pines below. She could not see the waterfall, but she realized that the pounding thunder must be from the water descending the same precipice that blocked her.

Shivering, exhausted, and fearful, Bethany sat on the cold ground clutching her knees beneath her chin. Suddenly she heard the young men's voices shouting back and forth. They were still there, searching for her! Somehow she must get down the granite escarpment.

Bethany cringed when she looked over the edge, noting the narrow ledges that traversed the rock. If only the pines growing at the bottom of the cliff were closer, perhaps she could climb down a tree. But the span between the cliff and the branches was too wide, and only the tops of the trees reached her level on the ridge.

She paused to listen as the voices came closer and the men stopped and looked around. She had no doubt that the men would see her if she went back. With no other alternative, she forced herself to look down the rock again. She must focus on getting down, not on the distance or the nausea that her fear induced. She must concentrate on climbing down, one step at a time. Spotting a narrow outcropping below, she took a shaky breath. Then, holding firmly to the trunk of a small tree near the edge of the precipice, she cautiously lowered her right leg, stretching her toes tentatively to a narrow ridge of stone. She gingerly tested her weight on the rock. It held. She took a breath. She moved her hand to a firmly entrenched root nearer the edge and tightened her grip. Slowly she lowered her other leg over the edge.

For several yards Bethany moved down the face of the cliff, standing on rock ledges where possible, not allowing herself to look farther down than the next step. Finally, she lowered herself onto a wide ledge where she could actually sit. Breathing in deeply, she tried to relax her tingling muscles. Her weak right leg was aching. Though the voices seemed to have retreated, she could still hear them echoing. They were constant reminders that the men would see her if they looked over the edge. She was much too vulnerable.

Peering down at the narrower ledges below her, Bethany barely dared breathe as she clutched the rock face to resume her descent. *Focus,* she commanded herself. Finding a grip for her fingers, she slid her foot off the small ledge to search for another depression that would anchor her weight.

Sliding her hand down the wet surface, she found one handhold, then another. With one foot, she felt a space wide enough to accommodate both feet, and gratefully rested her full weight on the ledge.

Ignoring the shouts and raucous laughter that seemed to be getting closer again, she concentrated on the granite rock face. Praying as she moved, begging for help as she searched for another anchor for her hand, another protrusion to support her feet, she moved slowly, cautiously. She knew she must get off the rock face before they saw her.

Bethany finally arrived at a thin ledge that appeared to run the width of the bluff while angling slowly toward the rocky soil beneath. *Keep focused,* she reminded herself as she worked her way along laboriously, clinging to slender edges of rock with cold, wet fingers—balancing precariously on the slowly tapering ledge.

The voices were louder now, and vulgar. Bethany quietly balanced on the narrow outcropping, uncertain exactly where the men were. If she were quiet, her brown parka might camouflage her. She tipped her head slowly toward the top of the rocks and saw a flash as a bottle flew past her and splattered against a tree. Drops of liquid rained down on the loose stones at the bottom of the abyss. Instinctively she flattened herself against the stone, stifling the cry that rose in her throat.

"Where *is* that woman?" one voice came in a near wail.

"If she ain't up here, she must be down there," came the reply as a second bottle fell onto the needle-covered ground under the pines.

"Well, how do we get down there?"

The voices drifted back and Bethany could not understand them, but she could tell that the men had moved away from the edge of the precipice.

Looking back at the narrow ledge she had been following, she realized that the farther she descended, the more her feet hung over the edge. If she could get down to the bottom—and it wasn't that far away now—and if she could get across the rocks and into the woods without being seen, she could escape. She would have plenty of time while they tried to climb down the face of the cliff. But first she must get down herself.

She moved along the thinning ledge until there was barely a toehold, then no more than slight grooves for her fingers. Bethany could feel her foot slip as she tried to move. Her chilled, nearly numb fingers could no longer hold her weight. She slipped from the ledge, falling to the bottom of the granite outcropping ten feet below.

Lying there crumpled on the broken slabs of stone at the base, Bethany curled into a fetal position. A stinging cut on her cheek dripped blood onto her jacket. The grade of the slope was too steep to stand on, and the layers of broken strata moved under her shifting weight. The wedges of sod she grabbed at in panic gave way as she slid farther down the rocks.

When she reached the thicker vegetation beneath a pine, she stopped sliding. Stunned, she lay still, listening for voices. Had she screamed when she fell? Could the clattering rocks be heard over the tumult of the creek?

Scanning the top of the cliff from behind a tree trunk, Bethany forced herself to relax. She comforted herself once again with the thought that the men pursuing her would also have to traverse the precipice. To her dismay, when the colorful jackets emerged from the foliage above the bluff, one of the men cupped his hands to his mouth and shouted to the other, "There's a path over there!"

24

Bethany waited only long enough for the men to disappear before she forced herself to stand and began working her way toward the ravine. There was no way to cross the highway without being perilously visible. Her only hope was to go under the bridge that arched over the creek, go through the water-filled culvert, and then follow the water to the beach, where she would be exposed. Bethany would need to find Patience's cave.

Her progress was slow. Her movement and prayers became automatic as she clutched at branch after branch, easing herself down to lean on another tree before moving forward. *Let the storm cease. No,* she thought, *let the fear cease. Help me feel calm. Don't let me panic in the water again.* She couldn't panic this time. She would need to wisely use every bit of oxygen she could get into her lungs. She would need to think clearly. If she panicked as she had after sliding from the tipping granite slabs of the bridge . . .

Let the fear cease.

Suddenly she felt confident. She moved on with new energy. She knew what she would do.

Near the bottom of the steep drop, Bethany intercepted the creek and slipped down its bank, holding firmly to an overhanging branch. Fingering her bloody cheek as she said a quick prayer, she then stepped boldly into the swirling water.

The swift current nearly swept her off her feet as she glanced upstream to see if the bright jackets of her pursuers were visible. She saw only the natural greens of the forest and the white froth of rushing water. Bethany closed her eyes and took a deep breath, knowing the oxygen would have to last until she was through the deluge created by the torrential rain, the channel between the treacherous rocks, and then the culvert.

As she submerged, she felt the water close over her head. Numbness erased the pain in her cheek. She pushed against the water confidently, twisting to avoid the rocks and conforming her body to the current that propelled her down through the streambed.

Approaching the culvert, she pulled herself into a ball. Panic nearly engulfed her as the water around her darkened and there was no light, no air. Suddenly claustrophobic, she began to flail at the water.

I will not panic, she thought with determination. Pulling her arms to her side, she forced air from her lungs and concentrated as the water pressure sent her rocketing through the culvert.

Her lungs were aching by the time the darkness began to change. Obsidian turned to murky brown, then greenish yellow, and finally pale yellow. Emerging from the water, Bethany gasped for air, gulping it in again and again. She relaxed as the water slowed, and she bobbed against muddy debris on the bottom of the creek bed.

Glancing furtively around, Bethany crawled in the water along the bank until she found a stretch bordered by tall sea grass. She stripped off her parka and quickly turned it inside out so that its vivid yellow lining showed. Shaking, she rubbed it against her cut cheek. The friction against raw skin brought back the burning. She grimaced as she looked down at the parka, then rubbed her cheek once more until a dark red splotch spread across the coat's lining. She leaned over and carefully placed the parka on the rocks at the side of the stream, making certain that the large bloodstain was visible.

Bethany turned to the beach now, cautiously moving onto the grass to conceal her tracks. She studied the rock formations at the base of the mountain.

It was there.

Yes, there had been a Rock of the Sea God, and she was sure Patience had spent a terror-filled night there.

She ran toward the rock, her breath coming hard, but she could tell before she reached it that it was the right rock. She had calculated correctly on one of her prior walks. Only one outcropping stretched above the highway and also displayed the rugged scar of blasting marks. Beneath the outcropping, one particular boulder caught Bethany's eye. It hugged the mountain, but its coloration differed distinctly from the rock behind it. Undoubtedly, the boulder that now hid the cave had been rolled from its perch on top of the formation when construction crews had blasted through the rocks to make room for the highway. Certain that she had found Patience's cave, she moved toward it, relieved, but too spent to run.

However, she had not counted on the tide—the base of the rocks was covered by water. Scanning the beach unsuccessfully, she realized that in order to find the cave, she had no alternative but to wade into the waist-deep water between the two formations.

Fearfully, Bethany stepped into the cave's dark interior. Unable to see the floor, she was startled when it slanted down sharply and she was suddenly submerged to her shoulders. She shuddered, her mind filled with the terrors of the morning. She must leave this place. Then she noticed that the water felt warm, that it rocked her gently, soothingly. She knew the waves would come, but she would be ready.

The first wave merely pushed her off balance. Then came a series of larger waves in rapid succession. Bethany grasped for edges of rock as she had on the bluff. Only this time the slippery sea growth on the granite denied her handholds. Unseen waves shot pebble-hard pellets of water at her face. Her sweatshirt shifted around her body like a windbreaker in a hurricane. As she tried to wipe her eyes, she bobbed in the water and was caught by another wave and flung backward into the cave wall. She flailed against the water as the sharp rock scraped her back. A new series of waves flung her back again. She was reeling, spinning up and down and around. She lost her balance and wondered how she would survive . . . if she could survive.

Patience had survived.

Another wave rolled over Bethany. She tried to stand through each new wave, but again and again she was lifted and twisted as though she were an autumn leaf falling through the air. All at once, she relaxed as a comfortable feeling coursed through her. The pain still stabbed at her, but it came in soft near-echoes, as if her limbs were someone else's. Her mind was numbing.

The thought jolted her. She must not give up! She could not lose her focus. She must move and she must breathe. As a new wave hit her, she pulled herself into a bobbing ball, then spread her limbs to stand, to find air.

Another set of relentless waves struck the cave. *Please let the sea crest, let the light shine,* she found herself repeating as the water swirled around her, picking her up and throwing her backward once more. The thought came to her as spontaneously as the words had; she must concentrate on the light at the entrance to the cave. Staring through the murky water, she felt the rough rocks in the wall beat at her back. She closed her eyes as she was spun around over and over. How long could she survive the struggle? How would she know it was safe to leave the cave? The water began to rise around her once more. The thought came again, *Let the light shine. Go to the light.*

When the waves calmed, Bethany pushed herself toward the front of the cave. In the wedge of beach she could see between the cave entrance and the boulder guarding it, she caught a glimpse of color, of fading red on bright yellow. Her parka! Had they had found it?

Another series of waves spread over her, but this time her mind was focused. As she regained her balance again, she was determined to see if the parka was still on the rocks.

Tiptoeing to keep her chin out of the water, she clung to the rocks to stabilize herself and moved toward the cave's entrance. She could see one of the boys holding up her parka triumphantly. He pointed to the dark red spot and laughed. Her plan had worked!

Bethany waited several minutes after the boys walked out of her view on the beach, then climbed through the water to the sandy beach. She was free! She was exhausted and numb, but she could go home. She pictured herself in the hut in front of a fireplace full of glowing embers, eating a bowl of tomato soup and a grilled cheese sandwich.

The beach seemed nearly as endless as the ocean spreading beside her. The coarse sand pulled at her feet, weighing her down like ballast. Forcing herself to move, she became aware that she was shaking violently. The light rain had resumed, and she could not escape the sand and the chilling breeze. She knew she must keep moving.

Her bad leg throbbed, and Bethany felt a torturing pressure in her head. Her back felt like she had been flogged. But her pains could no longer distract her thoughts from what Peter had told her.

Why hadn't Joseph ever told her that Amelia had been buried here? It was hard to believe that Joseph would try to cheat her or have her harmed or killed, but what other explanation was there?

Bethany wondered what she should do. Without the business card it would be difficult, but there must be some way she could contact Peter. She could call every hotel, every room, until she found him. Still, she felt uncomfortable about Peter. But why? Was it Dee's call? Was it something in Bethany's conversation with Peter? She had told him she had received some "messages" from the organization, but he had responded with something about threats. How had he known the messages were threats? Did he know more than he had admitted, or was he generalizing from the things others had received? She was too tired to think clearly, too cold. She needed to get to the hut.

It took immense effort to walk, and Bethany closed her eyes to the rain and the monotonous sand. Whom could she trust? Kim? *"She'll take a taxi to Mr. Panninon's apartment."* The memory of that phone call increased the chill she was feeling. Could she trust Peter? If he had been in public at a party, why hadn't he called her first?

She opened her eyes briefly to check her path. When she closed her eyes again, they were there. The eyes. The deep brown, comforting eyes—gentle eyes—eyes that had looked at her with compassion.

She forced herself to open her eyes, remembering the possibility that she had only imagined the man with the gentle eyes. Had there been no eyes, just delusions caused by medications and desire? She knew now that the tunnel was not a delusion—was her memory of the man who helped her also reality? She couldn't say.

There may not have been a man with kind eyes, she reminded herself, but—the thought came with relief—there was Rob. Maybe he would be working in the garden. Could it still be Saturday?

She forced herself to climb the familiar path from the cove up to the hut. Struggling with each step, she pushed herself with promises of warmth and rest, clinging—irrationally, she supposed—to the thought of seeing Rob again.

Bethany had no idea of the time when she gripped the boulder at the top of the path and pulled herself up to edge of the road. She would be safe in the hut until she could get warm and rested enough to go to Rob. But actually getting to him seemed almost impossible at the moment, she was so tired and battered from incessant waves.

She stepped from the rock onto the blacktop. Joseph's car sat empty in the driveway between another car and her Jeep. The drapes in the hut were open, and through the drizzling rain, Bethany could see shadowy movements in the kitchen.

25

Desperation swept over Bethany as she backed behind the boulder. What could she do? She could not go to the hut. Maybe she could leave in her Jeep.

Bethany glanced at the window from behind the boulder. If only she could get to the back of the Jeep without being seen, she could retrieve the small magnetic key box behind the license plate. The Jeep was unlocked. It would be simple to open the door, get in, and drive away.

A shadowy figure moved toward the window. Joseph. Another walked to his side; a face tipped up toward his. He looked down at her and kissed her, then pulled her close as she wrapped an arm around his waist.

Bethany pulled back against the boulder, her hand over her mouth as she tried to hold back the sobs—and her rising fear. Peter had told her the truth.

She could hesitate no longer. She tried to walk calmly to the Jeep, hoping to avoid suspicion and knowing she didn't have the strength to move any faster. She pulled the metallic box from its hiding place and dumped the key into her numb, wet hand. The key slipped from her clumsy grasp to the blacktop. She tried unsuccessfully to pick it up as it raced ahead of her stiff fingers on the hard surface.

She peeked at the window from behind the Jeep. Kim was looking at Joseph, who seemed to be studying the ocean. In the background someone Bethany could not identify walked toward the kitchen.

Huddled behind the Jeep, Bethany tried again to pick up the key. She tucked her hands under her arms, desperately willing them to warm up. She flexed them, then reached again for the key. With it finally in her hand, she stood to move around the Jeep.

Joseph's head turned in her direction. She reached for the handle as she saw Kim look out the window.

Gripping the key solidly in her other hand, she pulled down hard on the Jeep door handle, but it did not move, stuck fast by days of rain. Joseph's calmly spoken words now taunted her: "The door handle sticks when it's been humid."

Too depleted to struggle any longer, Bethany slumped against the cold metal, catching a glimpse of herself in the side mirror. Her face, cold and drained of color, had a blue cast. Her eyes were hollow. A red gash edged by drops of dried crimson lined her cheek. Her wet hair tangled about her face in a confusion of snarls and bits of seaweed.

She did not want to surrender. She was terrified of what awaited her in the hut. But to have to face them—Joseph and Kim—together, looking as she did, added a new dimension of humiliation to her defeat.

Bethany glanced up from the mirror at an approaching car and slumped against the Jeep with relief. It pulled to a stop only feet from her, the blue lights on top flashing. She recognized Police Chief Tom Marshalle's voice as he opened the car door. She recognized his uniform as he climbed from the car.

"Bethany!" his voice was deep and resonant and reassuring. "We've been looking all over for you! Are you all right?" He stared at her with apprehension. "We've got to get you warmed up!" He turned to Scott and Andy, who were climbing from the car. "Grab a blanket. She'll go into shock. Get her into the house"

"Not the hut," Bethany protested feebly. "Please . . ." She forced herself to stand up straight. "I can't go to the hut." But she lacked the strength to explain.

Tom steadied her as Scott pulled a blanket around her shoulders. Tom's eyes followed her gaze to the hut and the couple still visible through the window. His voice sounded sympathetic. "I've seen you with Joseph enough to know it must be hard to face him with another woman and all. Do you need help walking?"

It would be useless to resist. Besides, how could she accuse Joseph when she was shaking too hard to speak? How could she refuse Tom's help when she could barely stand? But she would stand, and she would walk to the hut herself. Joseph would not have the satisfaction of seeing her broken. If he'd planned to use this as an example of her instability—or however Peter had phrased it—he would be disappointed. She was neither shattered nor dead, and she would walk past him and Kim on her own!

"Is Alice . . . ?" She didn't finish.

"Scott will call Alice as soon as we get you in the hut," Tom responded. "Let me help you."

"No, I can walk by myself," she mumbled, taking a tentative step. Tom stood beside her, Scott and Andy behind, ready to help.

She could feel their nearness, felt Scott's hand catch at her elbow to balance her when she nearly stumbled, heard Tom's encouraging words. "We're just about there."

They supported her as she moved up the walkway, then braced her as her knees buckled on the steps.

Bethany's mind filled with a peculiar airiness as she walked through the doorway. The familiar room seemed strangely unreal. Joseph's face held the same mysterious appearance as the room; it looked so familiar, so comfortingly familiar, but at the same time he looked and felt like a stranger—a dangerous, fearsome stranger. Bethany could not force herself to look at Kim.

"She's pretty cold, and I think she's going into shock," she heard Tom say to Joseph as the police chief helped her to the love seat by the fireplace.

Joseph turned toward the fireplace and the man who stood there.

Suddenly, as if in a dream, Bethany saw the man walk toward her. Rob, without sunglasses. What was Rob doing at the hut?

"Dr. Sommers?" Tom looked at Rob as he walked toward them.

Bethany wondered if she were watching a scene from a movie as Rob moved toward her. Rob, the gardener—shaven, his shirt collar unbuttoned under a navy blue, V-neck sweater, his wavy hair trimmed and combed neatly—walked toward her. Why was Rob at the hut? Why wasn't he in his flannel shirt and sunglasses? Why was Tom looking at Rob but calling him Dr. Sommers?

She looked at Rob. His hands looked strong without the gardening gloves she'd always seen him wearing, strong enough to lift her gently, to cut a rubber boot . . . Her world now seemed surreal, confusing. Bethany looked at Rob's face, strangely familiar, even when no longer covered by sunglasses. As she focused on his eyes, she knew they would be the warm, gentle eyes she had dreamed of, the eyes she'd longed for. Yet looking into his eyes now brought only confusion and questions.

Had Joseph accomplished his task? Was she indeed going insane? How could the man with gentle eyes be Rob, and why was Rob a doctor, not a gardener? And why, she jerked her head up at the thought, why was Rob waiting for her in the hut with Joseph? With Joseph *and* Kim? She put her hand over her mouth, remembering Peter's words and her phone call to Kim the night before.

Rob's expression changed from reassurance to concern as he steadied her face in his hands. His eyes became remote and professional as Rob, now Dr. Sommers, looked deep into her left eye then her right eye before glancing quickly at the wound on her cheek.

"Bethany, I'm Robert Sommers, your neighbor." He spoke loud and clear, as though trying to cut through her fatigue and shock. "But I'm also a doctor and I need to take care of you now."

He turned to Kim. "Kim!" His voice was calm but commanding. "Get her out of these wet clothes."

Because the women had moved to the back hall to give her privacy while she changed, Bethany could barely hear the conversation in the front room.

"Dr. Sommers," she heard Tom greet Rob. "Tom Marshalle, police chief. Good to meet you. When Joseph called to say Bethany was missing, then mentioned a neighbor—a doctor—had come to check on her, I was pretty relieved. It can take awhile to get emergency medics up here, and I didn't know if she was hurt. I didn't know anyone lived close around here. Lucky for her you do. She looks like she needs some medical care pretty badly right now."

Dr. Sommers's voice, though somber, reminded her of their conversation in the garden and reassured her. "I got concerned when I found beer cans around the garden where I am staying, and I knew Bethany sometimes goes there."

After Kim removed Bethany's rain-soaked sweats, she helped her into a dry set, then settled her on the love seat and tucked the comforter securely around her. "Joseph, she needs more blankets and something warm to drink."

As she looked up into Dr. Sommers's face, she remembered his eyes, and she remembered that they had disappeared, just as Peter had disappeared. Peter had said . . . She tried to remember but everything was indistinct. She closed her eyes, wanting to shut out the blur.

Strong hands raised her head and held a warm cup to her lips. She began to sip obediently then turned her face away. Questions wildly raced in her mind. What had Peter said? What had Joseph done? Who was holding her drink and what had been put in it? She opened her eyes long enough to see the face above her.

"How's she doing?" Tom knelt beside her, holding the drink.

She heard Scott's voice farther away. "I called and Aunt Alice is on her way. She said Mom called. The state troopers picked up a couple of kids who admitted to vandalizing the bridge. They got a rap sheet faxed in on the guy who hired them, and they're seeing if the kids can identify the picture. Seems he's got a pretty long record, Dad."

Bethany could not understand. Joseph with a record? Scott accusing Joseph as he stood next to him? Dizziness overwhelmed her.

Bethany felt the strong hands gently lower her head. Tom's voice was calm but determined as he rose from beside her. "Thanks, Scott. That will be about the guys we're looking for, so I've got to go, Bethany, but Scott will stay until Alice gets here. Dr. Sommers will take good care of you."

He was gone before Bethany could focus enough to tell him about Joseph's treachery or to ask him why Rob the gardener was there. She forced her eyes to open, frantically struggling to sit up and call him back. But he walked out the door and Joseph replaced him by her side. She turned her head away, unwilling to let him see her fear even though there was no way she could escape him.

Rob looked at her with a strange expression, and his hand went back to her pulse.

"She's stabilizing now but she really needs some privacy and some rest. Why don't you wait out back? I'll call you if she needs anything." His fingers were back on her wrist, and his eyes studied hers. Joseph had stepped up to the living room and was talking to Kim in quiet tones as they stepped through the kitchen and into the back hall. Bethany took a deep breath.

"Drink this," Rob instructed Bethany.

Bethany sipped the hot broth Scott held for her.

Rob fingered her wrist once more. "That's better," he said as he put her hand down gently. "Can you watch her, Scott? I'm going to send Joseph for some supplies. Get her to drink as much as you can. See if she'll take some orange juice, and keep her warm. I'll be right back."

Bethany gulped the juice Scott offered her without hesitation. She felt sensation returning to her hands, and her eyes began to clear, although she was still trembling too much to hold the cup herself.

Rob had joined Joseph and Kim in the backyard. If she were going to escape it would have to be soon.

Scott opened the door at Alice's knock.

It would have to be now.

"Are you all right?" Alice asked as she bent over her.

"Alice, I can't stay here," she whispered. Her speech was unclear, but it was audible. "I have to get away."

Alice looked at her anxiously. "What's wrong?"

"Please take me away from here. Seacrest? Your place?" She struggled to pull herself to a sitting position and looked pleadingly at Alice. "Please!"

Alice sat on the edge of the couch and held her hands tightly. "Scott, what did the doctor say?" She looked up at her nephew.

"He said she had stabilized. He wants Joseph to get some medical supplies."

"But he said she'd stabilized? She can get up?"

"He didn't say she couldn't," Scott replied. "She got all upset when Dad left," he added.

Alice turned back to look at Bethany. "You're sure you don't want to stay here and rest?"

"I . . . can't . . . rest . . . here." It was hard to speak as she turned fearfully toward the back hall door. "Please, Alice. Now."

Alice looked at Scott, then back at Bethany, whose lacerated face was grim with fear. She was near panic.

"Can you carry her to the car?"

He picked her up easily. "Bring the rest of the blankets."

Alice opened the door. Scott quickly moved her toward the car, which Alice had started. Scott tugged the blankets close around Bethany. "Tell them I wanted to take a ride," she mumbled as he shut the door to the sprinkling rain.

Bethany took a deep breath and stared at the front door of the hut. It appeared that no one yet knew she had left. Though her head was clearing, she felt completely drained. She leaned against the headrest but tried to avoid touching her back on the car seat. The numbness was wearing off. Why didn't Alice drive away? They needed to leave!

"You don't look very comfortable. Do you need the seat tilted?"

"No. I just need to get away from here. Quickly. Please, go." She tried not to sound frenzied as her agitation built.

Alice looked doubtful but put the car in gear and did not speak until the hut was out of sight.

"Do you want to tell me what's going on?" Alice asked. "I'm still not sure that I shouldn't turn around and take you back to that doctor in there. Why are you so upset? What happened, anyway?"

"They're trying to hurt me!"

"Start again, Bethany! You're not making sense."

"Peter said Joseph might try to injure me or make me seem insane."

"Who's Peter? Never mind. Just tell me what is happening."

"Peter, a guy I dated at the university, came here last night."

"And?"

"And he said that Joseph has been helping a corporation get away with tax fraud. Then he told me that Joseph is trying to cheat me out of my inheritance by having me declared incompetent and that he is going to have me hurt so that I will either go crazy or look like I am. At first Joseph was going to marry me to get control of my inheritance, but then he decided he was in love with Kim instead, so . . ." She put her hand over her mouth as tears began to trickle down her cheeks.

"And you believed all that?" Alice asked incredulously.

"Not at first. Then Peter pointed out that Joseph had never told me about my grandmother's will, and," she said, shaking her head, still unable to believe what she was saying, "and a lot of other things. He told me he had proof and told me where to find the graveyard where I found my grandmother's grave." Bethany turned to her. "Alice, there is a mansion and a lot of property, and Peter said that they are supposed to be mine. But Joseph never told me about them. On the way back from the graveyard, I heard two guys talking who had been hired to see that I was . . ." The word would not come and the sentence faded. "What else can I believe?" She paused.

"How did you get away?"

"I climbed down the mountain, then hid in the cave under the Rock of the Sea God. I found it! It does exist! I stood shoulder-deep at high tide in the cave while the guys outside laughed about my bloodstained parka."

"Did you tell Tom?"

"I didn't have a chance with Tom, and I would have told Rob but . . ."

"Who's Rob? That doctor in there? I'm confused. How do you know him?"

"I'm sorry, let me back up. Rob is my neighbor. I met him on one of my walks, and he told me he was a part-time gardener who works in the garden that I just found out belonged to my grandmother. I guess he's a doctor too, although he never told me that. Alice, is he in on this too?" She clenched her hands in her lap. "I'm so afraid. But it seems so impossible and unreal. Am I crazy?"

Alice's face was stern above the steering wheel. "No, Bethany, you're not crazy. It sounds like there's a lot people have been keeping from you, and now you don't know who to trust."

Alice pulled into her driveway. "Where do you want to go now? I'm tempted just to keep on driving you to the nearest emergency room or to Dr. Noel—and I would if Dr. Sommers hadn't said that you were all right."

"All I want now is to lie down somewhere safe. They wouldn't try anything here, would they?"

"They have no reason to suspect you know anything—if there is anything to know—and I'll call Tom as soon as you're settled." A teasing gleam came into Alice's eyes. "Your old room is empty."

"Thanks, Alice," Bethany responded gratefully.

Alice reached over as if to hug Bethany, then pulled back. "I don't know where to touch you without hurting you!"

Alice helped Bethany out of the car, then walked with her to the steps.

Ally opened the door and held it for them while Alice supported Bethany.

"Gee, Bethany, are you okay? Uncle Steve asked if I would mind watching the kids. They're in eating breakfast," she explained. "Uncle Steve went down to the station with Daddy to see what kind of information they had gotten on those guys."

"Thanks, Ally." Alice looked at Bethany. "Could you handle some more juice or something to eat?" she asked as she propelled Bethany toward the couch. Then, turning to Ally, she added, "Would you mind checking Bethany's old room, Ally? She's going to be staying."

As Bethany lay on the couch, Alice zipped up her jacket and walked to the door. "Bethany, I'm on my way to the station to let Tom know where you are. Once Joseph and your neighbor discover you've left, they'll no doubt give Tom a call—but I'll let Tom know to keep your location a secret for now for safety's sake."

Bethany nodded, too tired to think and grateful to be lying down. She was hurt, but she was safe. She closed her eyes. Immediately, they flicked open as imaginary waves dashed against her. Soon the waves would go away and she could sleep. She closed her eyes again, relieved to find a peaceful dark.

26

When she heard footsteps on the porch and the door swing open, she was too tired to open her eyes.

"What in the world are you doing here?" Rob's voice was loud and convincingly unhappy. "I leave the room for two minutes so I can send Joseph to pick up prescriptions and when I return, you're gone! What were you thinking?"

The door slammed behind Rob as he walked into the bed-and-breakfast and looked down at Bethany. "Joseph suggested that we split up and that I look for you here while he checks Grace's home—the poor guy's still out there looking for you, sick with worry!" He paused. "Look, I know it was no fun to walk into a room with your old boyfriend and his new girl—under the circumstances I was tempted to inflict bodily harm upon the good counselor myself. But how could you endanger your life just because of a little jealousy?"

Startled, Bethany looked up into his stormy eyes, eyes that no longer looked understanding. She quickly looked down as the tears she'd fought so many times that morning began rolling down her cheeks. Alice walked back into the room, her face filled with surprise. Ally came down the staircase.

Rob turned to Alice. "And Mrs. McClere! You seem to be a responsible woman. How could you let her talk you into this?" He turned back to Bethany. "From what I'm told it's only been a few months since you had a concussion and seizures. And your cheek may need stitches. And what about your lungs? Joseph told me that you had pneumonia, and now, in this cold, you went dashing into the ocean. Then, if Tom hadn't stopped you, you would have gone running off in the middle of a storm in an unreliable Jeep without telling anyone! And now you take off again with Alice even though you're suffering from hypothermia and going into shock! All that to avoid a lovers' quarrel?"

Bethany looked at Alice. Somewhere the strength came to speak evenly. "I think I'll go up to the room now, if Ally can help me."

"Not until I've looked at that cheek," Rob announced.

Overriding the doctor, Alice replied resolutely, "Ally, can you help Bethany, please? Dr. Sommers and I need to talk."

* * *

Bethany had fallen into a light sleep when Alice's soft tap on the door roused her.

"I'm sorry to wake you, but I need to talk to you." She walked over and sat on the side of the bed. "When I went down to the police department and told Tom what you told me, he had a quick check done on Dr. Sommers. Tom just called me back. Dr. Sommers's credentials are excellent and there's no record on him except for a speeding ticket a couple of years ago. Tom said he trusts him completely. But I'm worried about you and so is Dr. Sommers. Some antibiotics now could save you a whole lot of trouble later. Can I send him up?"

Bethany looked up into Alice's eyes. She thought about the laughing Rob she'd known in the garden, the kind-eyed man who had helped her Christmas Eve. Rob wouldn't be involved in anything underhanded, but she felt confused, almost disoriented. Was anyone to be trusted?

"I'll stay right here with you if you are still afraid of him." Alice added.

"That's okay. You don't have to be here." Bethany replied. "But thanks for offering."

* * *

Bethany did not hear Rob's footsteps or the door to her room opening. She was aware of his presence only when he stood beside the bed and said her name softly. She stiffened and would have turned away, but she hurt too much. He pulled a chair over and sat beside the bed.

"Bethany, I'm really sorry for spouting off like that downstairs. I had been worried about you all morning after I found beer cans by the gazebo, and when you came in looking like you did . . . Well, it was obvious that you were in trouble, but you got so upset when Joseph came close that I said you were stabilized so I could get him away from you. I didn't expect Scott to think that meant you didn't need medical attention. When I came back and found that you were gone, I was livid. I had no idea about anything else until Mrs. McClere told me. I should have known you wouldn't be reacting like that without a reason."

He touched her hand gently. "I'm sorry, Bethany."

She began to speak, stopped abruptly, and started again. "I don't know who you are. Are you Rob, a friend and a gardener, or Dr. Sommers, a man who was mysteriously waiting for me in my house with my friends, who, incidentally, were not acting very friendly—waiting for what, I don't know. Who are you, my friend or a doctor or . . . or . . . ?" She couldn't finish.

"I am a doctor who, at Amelia's request, has been doing some gardening as a hobby while I worked on a research project here. I also want to be your friend. Can I be both, your friend and your doctor?"

There was an uncomfortable silence.

"Well, right now you need a doctor." He did not wait for a reply before he reached into his bag. "Let me listen to your lungs, and then you can relax while I take care of your cheek."

The sweatshirt rubbed mercilessly against her back as he raised it, but she didn't allow herself more than a grimace. There was a pause as he looked at her back, then a long silence as he gingerly touched a spot here and there before he began rubbing his stethoscope on his hand to warm it. Still cold, it sent spasms down Bethany's already tense muscles. Finally, he ran his hands slowly over her back, examining her ribs carefully.

"Your lungs are clear, but you've got some incredible lacerations back here." He sounded tired as he straightened and stood. "Why didn't you tell me about your back?" Not waiting for an answer, he popped two pills from their aluminum foil pouches and handed them to her, avoiding her eyes. "These are for the pain."

He watched her wince as she began to move her hand toward her mouth. "Wait." He eased her back onto her pillows then poured a glass of water and slipped his hand behind her head before holding the straw in her mouth. She had never realized how many muscles it took to swallow, but she continued to gulp despite the pain until the pills went down.

* * *

Dr. Sommers—Rob—finished with his examination, and then, to Bethany's surprise, he slid the chair closer to the bed and sat down.

"I know you're tired, but I think we need to talk." Rob looked down at the floor then rubbed his chin before he looked up at Bethany with a boyish grin. "I'm usually not at a lack for words, but, well, this time . . ." He hesitated. "Why don't you relax? This may take awhile."

Bethany rested against the pillows, not knowing what to expect when Rob started talking.

"I understand from Mrs. McClere that you are not quite clear on my status in the current situation—neither is she for that matter. With these new injuries of yours, I'm not sure it's the best time to explain. But, from your reactions, I think we'd better get everything out in the open."

He stood and started pacing the floor.

"I'm a family-practitioner-turned-research-doctor working with a group of scientists—I specialize in botany—trying to answer questions about the process of healing on a cellular level. We want to know if there are certain chemical properties manifest in rapidly regenerating tissues that are not present in deteriorating cellular matter. What combinations of chemicals—vitamins and minerals, or energy sources like acupuncture and magnets—promote the most rapid healing? What kinds of organic compounds derived from various plant tissues provide the greatest curative benefits to people suffering from certain degenerative diseases? That's where I come in. There are two specific plants indigenous to this part of Maine that

I've been studying specifically. So, our group is trying to determine if the same catalysts are equally helpful for everyone. Of course, it gets more technical than that, but that's the basic idea."

Bethany nodded slightly.

"I met Amelia when an oncologist I went to school with asked me if I'd work with Amelia. After a while Amelia and I became very good friends, and she eventually told me a lot about her life—her parents, her daughter, then you. She was particularly concerned that she hadn't shown you enough love and that you lacked self-confidence. To be quite honest, from the little I knew about you I figured you'd had plenty, and I didn't like you much. I thought you were a spoiled rich kid putting an old, dying lady on a pretty distressing guilt trip. But I knew it would upset Amelia if I said anything, so I went along with her.

"She loved Faunce Cove. She had grown up there and raised your mother there. But she was also there when your grandfather died in World War II and when your mother died in Europe. After that she couldn't face living there any longer or even talking about it. She never told you or Joseph about it because it was too painful. But she wanted you to have a chance to live there, at least for a while.

"So, she came up with a plan. For your graduation gift, she would offer you the house you're now in, which has been in the family for years, acting as if she'd bought it recently for you. She wanted to give you time to find yourself while providing you a serious chance to try writing. Of course, that would have followed your trip with her to Europe during the summer. Obviously, that changed when her cancer returned. She developed pneumonia and knew her death was imminent.

"She didn't involve anyone except me in her plan, not even Joseph. At the same time, she made arrangements for a very private burial here—two of her employees who had taken care of the mansion and I were the only ones informed about the ceremony. And she completed other arrangements for the property. All Joseph was to know was that the estate was not to be settled until you had a chance to live up here and write and do what you wanted to do with the hut, which, by the way, like the rest of the Faunce Cove property, had been 'hidden' in her portfolio as an uninteresting property not worth attention and that Amelia never mentioned. Expenditures were to be paid from a preexisting account. Amelia was enthused, to say the least. She could think of nothing else but her plan for you and how it would give you all the self-assurance she hadn't given you."

Rob paused long enough to pour a glass of water from the pitcher Alice had left on the nightstand, offering it to Bethany. When she shook her head, he took a drink himself. Bethany remained silent, her eyes squinting in concentration. "Of course, Amelia and I had become good friends. I think she liked me as much as I admired her. She was a unique combination of energy and self-control. She always had distinctive ideas. Maybe that's why she became so excited about my research. Not many medical doctors are interested in researching the validity of some of the traditional techniques like homeopathy and holistic medicine, so it was hard to get funding for research or a place to set up a lab where I could do the studies. But Amelia loved the idea, and she wanted me to have a place with actual research facilities."

He sat down on the chair opposite Bethany and continued.

"When I worked with Amelia, I was just starting to find other medical specialists interested in the concept, so I had a lot of spare time I could spend with her. Back then her cancer was in remission, and she was living at her place in Rhode Island. When she wasn't thinking about her plans for you, she was working in her flowerbeds in Newport. I had lots of experience with plants of course, due to my botany training, but I hadn't done a lot with flower gardening. Because of her age and health, Amelia was getting too weak to take care of her garden the way she really wanted to. So one thing led to another and she showed me how. I liked working with flowers, and watching her arrange them was as entrancing to me as watching delicate heart surgery!

"When the couple she had hired to take care of the Faunce Cove property decided to retire, Amelia said that my research was too significant for me to be frittering away my time looking for funding for a controversial research program. We both knew that this research could have significant effects on our future health system. Amelia told me to move up to Faunce Cove and live in the servants' quarters at the mansion, where I could set up a laboratory and really accomplish something. She generously made certain I had the equipment and materials I needed.

"I was surprised and hesitant, but she made it seem as if I would be doing her a favor. I loved the area. To be quite honest, her plan had real merits, not the least of which was the location of the plants I had been studying. With computer technology as advanced as it is, there were no real drawbacks at that stage of the study. So I accepted. I moved in, commuting to Boston when necessary."

Rob took another sip of water.

"By that fall, the fall before she died, Amelia's condition had begun to deteriorate somewhat, but she was still doing better than we had expected. She decided to spend the winter in Arizona. Her doctor had recommended the therapeutic effects of the warmer, drier air for her lungs. I flew out to see her regularly. She talked about you continually. She read me your letters and showed me your pictures until I could have drawn your face by heart. She mentioned having you come to see her but decided against it, afraid to disrupt your graduate work. Plans were made to move you in at Faunce Cove after a summer vacation with her."

Rob sat forward on the edge of the chair.

"Bethany, more than once she hinted that she wanted us to meet. That took me by surprise and I didn't know how to respond, especially with my preconception about you as the selfish granddaughter.

"I saw her the weekend before she died. Then I received the phone call from the hospital that she was gone. I flew back to Arizona quickly to take care of the arrangement she prepared for her passing. I remembered that you were expecting Amelia to come for graduation, and even though she'd instructed both Joseph and me that she didn't want you knowing about her condition until after graduation, that all changed when her condition spiraled downward those last few days. It was then that she wrote you that final letter and asked that I deliver it to you with flowers if something should happen unexpectedly.

"After taking care of her burial arrangements from Arizona, I flew to Boston with the letter she'd prepared, and I ordered some flowers. The arrangement didn't look right, so I fixed it her way and took it to your apartment. When your apartment was locked, your landlord said he'd get the flowers to you. He also said you'd learned about Amelia's death that morning and I figured that Joseph must have called you.

"I tried to reach Joseph to ask him if he'd been the one to call you, but he was still in Arizona finalizing legal matters. I decided, almost out of curiosity—although I did think it was pretty tough even for a spoiled rich girl to lose her grandmother on graduation day—to see if I could find you when you came out of the ceremony. I was the one you nearly walked into in your hurry to get away from the bus stop. When you looked up, just for a split second, I saw your eyes."

Rob straightened up and faced Bethany. "I felt helpless." He continued focusing on her. "I knew that I'd been completely mistaken about you. I felt so angry at myself for having judged you. Clearly, you were not spoiled or self-centered. You were a beautiful woman who cared very deeply about her grandmother—and you were in mourning.

"But there was nothing more I could do without breaking my word to Amelia. You see, Amelia had specified that I was to stay completely away from you, not only until you'd finished your book, but also until you'd had enough time alone to discover the beautiful, exceptional young woman that Amelia had already discovered in you long ago. She had also told me she wanted me to stay on at the mansion until I was either finished with my research or you had made other provisions for its maintenance. So I stayed there but kept my distance.

"Then at Christmas while I was madly working on research, you had your accident. Bethany, I'm the one that discovered you, cared for you, and called for help. I didn't worry about breaking my word, because you needed medical care and you were in no shape to remember anything, including me. But I was so worried about you, even after you were admitted to the hospital, that I would come during the nights to check on you and be with you. I had to come at odd hours so as not to cross paths with your other visitors. Being a doctor has its perks—even the all-powerful visiting hours have no hold on you," Joseph said with a gentle smile.

"Then, when you became more coherent, you were transferred to the rehab center, and I came back up to do my research. I had a number of time-sensitive experiments going on so I didn't have an alternative. Then, as soon as I could, since you had found the tunnel and I had gotten more funding, I moved my lab back down to Boston so you wouldn't catch me there."

Rob stopped for a moment, allowing Bethany to process the fact that Rob really was her rescuer. "Look, I know you heard about the snowmobilers who found you. I'm actually the one that mentioned that possibility to a checker in Seacrest's grocery mart just before heading back to Boston that night to check on you—and as I suspected, she was the lady for the job and spread it like wildfire," Rob said with a grin.

"Anyway, after some time had passed, I really wanted to get back to the cove. I had some time at spring break so I came up for a week. That's when I saw you in the garden. I thought I could disguise myself with sunglasses and my beard, but after I'd been with you I started feeling guilty.

"I had admired you since I'd seen you at graduation. I knew a lot about you from Amelia, and the checker at the mart started telling me about the hut and how you'd jumped in to help with Ally. I'd heard about your research on Patience at the service station while I was getting gas. I was impressed."

Rob looked at her closely. "I wanted to get to know you a lot better, but I knew that if I kept on seeing you, I'd really get involved, something I had agreed not to do yet." He paused and took a deep breath. "But I'd already met you, which made it nearly impossible to stay away. I came back up for the weekend to look over the flowers, and came up with an excuse to come by this morning, only to find Joseph and Kim there out of their minds with worry."

He looked at her intently, sensing her pain. He said softly, "Joseph and I have only been trying to do what Amelia wanted us to do, what she thought would be best for you. I hope knowing this will help." His voice faded into silence.

Bethany leaned against the pillows, her body so still that it was hard to tell if she was breathing.

"Are you okay?" Rob asked, looking at her anxiously.

She took a deep breath before she spoke.

"Do you know how many times I've seen Alice hug her kids—not because they'd done something special but just because she loves them? I see that and I remember my childhood." Her words faded as she angrily blotted a tear. "You tell me about Amelia. You tell me about your warm relationship with her, something I, her granddaughter, only dreamed of having. And then you ask me if I'm okay. No, I don't suppose I am." She pulled her arms tightly to her chest, rocking back and forth as if in pain.

Rob reached to her, but she pulled back and straightened.

"My grandmother, the person I tried so hard to please, has involved herself in my social life and my decisions, maneuvering me like a mouse in one of your scientific mazes. She found ways to control me even after she was dead! She had every chance to see that I was intelligent and capable—her friends reported about me, she knew of my grades, my associates—but still, with all that, she never praised or cheered me on or supported me. She couldn't believe in me enough to tell me she was sick or to have someone tell me she had died or where she'd been buried, not enough to let me know about my own family! Knowing about me as she did, she was still unable to trust me to make the slightest decisions about my own life. And you ask me if I'm okay? You tell me all of this, thinking it will help me?" Tears streamed down her cheeks, but she did not notice.

"Bethany," Rob started, "I thought you should know that she loved you, that she was trying to take care of you, and that I acted the way I did because I had made promises to her."

"Loved me? Promised her? I've often wondered why her love for me had to be a love that made *her* comfortable, not a love that helped *me*. And as for promises, why should you be making promises about me? Does your relationship with a woman who has passed away have a higher priority than an honest relationship with me?"

"Bethany, you are tired. I think you should . . ."

"What makes you think you know what I should do? Are you like Amelia? Full of concern for my welfare because you don't think I can handle it myself? Why do you think you know what I need? Look at me! This is what came of her concern for me. Do you think you two, together, did a good job of taking care of me?"

"I didn't know you then. All I knew was what Amelia had told me."

"Have you any idea how condescending that is? You thought you could make better decisions about my life than I could for myself, when all you knew was what a crusty old woman had told you about me?" Bethany rubbed furiously at the tears running down her cheeks. Then she grimaced in pain as she accidentally bumped the bandage.

"Bethany, please listen."

She took a deep breath, then sipped at the water Rob held for her until she could finally speak.

"I'm sorry." Tipping her head back from the cup, Bethany leaned into the pillow and closed her eyes. "I'm tired. Too tired. And I need time to think."

"Bethany?" he began in a soft, warm tone, but stopped when she dipped her head in a quiet no.

Rob breathed deeply. Slowly he arose, slid the chair back to the wall, and walked to the door.

"I think you'll be fine, but you'll need to be checked again. I'll be leaving for Boston the day after tomorrow. I can drop by before I leave, or you can talk to Alice about a local doctor. It's up to you."

As he began opening the door, he hesitated. "You know, I can't help but wonder what it would have been like if we had met under different circumstances. You still in the garden with muddy knees, but me without all the history and promises to Amelia." He pushed the door open. "But I guess we're not strangers, are we?" He closed the door softly behind him.

27

Alice knocked on the door a little later. "Tom is here."

"I must say you are looking a good deal better than you did at the hut," the police chief said with a smile as he walked into the room with Alice.

Bethany wished the painkiller had worked better as Tom shook her hand with a firm grip. The movement made her back throb.

"How are you?" he asked her, not expecting an answer. "I'll make this brief. I just need to confirm a little information." He pulled out a small notebook from his pocket. "Do you know a Peter Stanton or Scranton, maybe even Scranture?" he asked.

"I know Peter Scranton. We dated for a few months, and then he disappeared just before I graduated in June. He came to the hut last night and wanted me to go with him."

"Did you get the guy?" Alice interrupted to ask Tom.

Peter? Bethany tried to sit up, exasperated by the dullness she felt. Why would Tom be after Peter?

She listened to Tom.

"No, we didn't catch him, but we got the boys he sent to the creek, and they identified him from the picture the state troopers faxed in with Stanton's criminal record. His real name does seem to be Stanton, by the way." He looked at Bethany's puzzled expression.

"Let me tell you what we know, Bethany," he started. Alice pointed to a chair, and Tom sat down and unzipped his jacket.

"It seems he's been spending a bit of time in the area lately. I was over at the county seat yesterday afternoon checking on some public records. When I mentioned Faunce Cove, the clerk asked me why all the sudden interest in the area. She explained that a blond young man had been in several times asking questions, copying maps, and looking at everything that pertained to that property. The woman seemed to like to talk, and she kept going on about this guy. It seems he also wanted current burial records and all sorts of disconnected things.

"I didn't think anything about it until the librarian described the same guy doing the same thing. He really seemed persistent.

"Then last night the kids went to their school dance. Ally came home all upset. The principal had announced her invitation from the Maine History Foundation to present the Faunce Cove paper at school yesterday, and a lot of her friends came over to congratulate her. But one kid, a guy she didn't know—and didn't want to, as far as that goes—came up to her with some smart remark about the award and added something to the effect that 'the Faunce diva' wouldn't be feeling quite so perky after tomorrow morning—if she were feeling at all.

"Scott got home in time to hear that, and they got talking about the guy. It seems that some other guy was showing off a couple of large bills, claiming there would be more after he'd taken care of a little detail. He was drunk, Scott said, and when the chaperones escorted him out he walked across the lawn yelling about the cove.

"It was late, but I decided to call Joseph anyway. Oh, by the way, he asked me to give this to you." Tom handed Bethany a folded piece of paper. "He also wanted me to apologize to you since he couldn't be here this morning. Something urgent has come up."

"Something urgent?"

"Let me explain, Bethany," Tom interrupted. "When I tried to call Joseph last night I couldn't get in touch with him initially. It seems that someone broke into his office the day before yesterday, and Joseph had been trying to identify what was missing. His files had been messed up, but he hadn't been able to find anything that had actually been taken. When I finally got him on the phone, he said he thought he knew who it might be, but he needed another hour to make sure. He also asked that I keep on alert for anything strange around here.

"So I drove out to your place early this morning to see if anything was happening. I found the house empty. But I wanted to check out the report from the dance, so I had the boys come up and scout around the mountain. Scott let me know when they found the foot-bridge damaged and a couple of beer bottles on the trail. I'd come to pick up Scott and Andy when we saw you."

"Then Joseph *wasn't* trying to harm Bethany?" Alice questioned.

"As far as I can tell, Joseph knew nothing more about this than what I just told you."

Tom turned to look directly at Bethany. "I understand, Bethany, that Stanton said some things that implicated Joseph in unprofessional activities pertaining to your grandmother's estate—possibly much more. And that's why you were so frightened this morning. Right?"

Bethany nodded.

"I made some calls about his legal dealings, and his reputation seems to be impeccable. We couldn't find any connections to any illegal organization or tax evasion or any kind of investigation. Nothing like that. Now, from what Alice told me about your inheritance, it hasn't been handled in a normal way and I'd be glad to question him about that if you'd like."

Bethany slid farther down into the pillows.

Alice looked at her tired face. "Why don't you give her some time to think about it? I think we should talk downstairs, now," she gently told Tom.

* * *

Bethany gratefully closed her eyes, then grimaced as she twisted to pick up the note from Joseph. It hurt to pull herself up in the bed to read the words he had scrawled and given to Tom. The message was succinct: *Glad you're okay. Need to check on some things. Had a file stolen. May link Stanton to all this. I'll contact you soon. Joseph.*

Joseph knew about Peter? Bethany felt the room spin momentarily, and she took a deep breath, calming herself. She knew she'd *never* brought up Peter, her dating him, or that he'd gone missing to Joseph—ever. She'd always felt telling him about her relationship with Peter would complicate things, especially since she'd fallen for Joseph since then and had decided she cared for him more than Peter. And she'd refrained from telling Joseph about Peter's disappearance because of the warning Peter gave her to tell and trust no one. *Joseph knew about Peter all along? And why would Joseph have a file on Peter in his office?* Questions seemed to mount by the minute, and she realized even more the tangle of lies and secrets that had wrapped around her life these past few months.

Suddenly her thoughts turned to Peter and these new allegations. Could Peter really have sent those two boys after her to harm her—the Peter she'd fallen for so hard? It seemed so long ago. Peter had been almost impish, so full of fun and happy surprises. Her mind reviewed the brief months of their relationship and then stopped abruptly. Although he taught Bethany to relax and giggle, she remembered that not everything was positive with him. She hadn't thought about the other times since Peter left, but now . . .

There were many times after they'd known each other a few weeks when she felt embarrassed and disheartened. Sometimes Peter looked at her with a disgusted frown and scolded her because she laughed too loud or talked too much. But, she convinced herself, he was always right, and she learned to be more refined.

She recalled how his playful kidding got a bit too rough some-times—like the time he tackled her at the local park and pinned her forcefully—unaware or heedless that twigs and even a few sticks were scratching her. She didn't mention it afterward; it felt so good just to be with someone.

Then there was the Saturday they went skiing in New Hampshire. She never really caught onto wedging her skis. "Make a pizza," she heard an instructor tell a group of four-year-olds. She tried but inadvertently got in the way of several advanced skiers. Peter lost his patience. He smiled tolerantly until they were alone, then he scolded her, asking her how she could be so brainless and inept. His expression turned into a scowl, one she'd seen several times before.

Skiing later that day as she passed Peter to get to the lift, she accidentally clipped his skis from the side, causing him to wobble for a second. He angrily yelled, "Bethany, be careful!" Then he reached down and scooped up a handful of snow and pelted her, then reached for more. Locked in her skis, she fell, unable to break free. Peter took a glove full of icy snow and scraped it across her face until her skin was raw.

"Peter!" she remembered trying to scream through the snow when she could finally twist her face out of his grasp. "Stop! That hurts!"

He was concerned as he immediately released her head. "Oh, Bethany, I'm sorry."

"That hurts! It feels like you want to—"

"You thought I was intentionally hurting you?"

"You acted angry!" She found it hard to look up at him.

"I guess I was. Haven't you ever had a guy mad at you before?" He seemed surprised, but then answered his own question, shifting so she could not avoid his eyes. "Apparently you've never been in a real relationship. In a real relationship you've got to expect to see some real feelings. Do you want to know me, the real Peter, enough to put up with a little rough stuff? I don't mean my hurting you—I mean stuff about me that isn't perfect. You know, I'm not perfect, I'm human."

He paused, then relaxed. "But look, I stopped as soon as you spoke up, didn't I? I get tired and bored and mad like everyone else, but you don't really think I could hurt you, do you? I'd never hurt you." His glove was still cold as he held her face, but she didn't mind as he kissed her—she felt like a cold, sore cheek was not a high price to pay for knowing someone really cared about her. When Peter, with his usual boyish grin, came to escort her to dinner that night, he handed her a beautifully wrapped box of specialty fudge and caramels. "I'm sorry," he declared.

Bethany broke from her reverie and released Joseph's note from her fingers. She didn't try to resist the grogginess.

Peter . . . Joseph . . . Rob . . . Their names echoed off into her sleep.

28

Finally breaking through the clouds, the late-morning sun brightened the white lace curtains. After a semi-peaceful night's sleep, Bethany felt more alert. Alice had cracked the window to let in a refreshing breeze.

"We didn't mean to fall in love," Kim began softly as she sat on the edge of Bethany's bed. She looked like she might feel more uncomfortable than Bethany did, which Bethany decided was pretty hard to feel, given the burning in her back.

"I always thought Joseph was good looking and interesting. I also thought he was good for you, but I didn't really get to know him until I drove up to Seacrest with him on Christmas and found out about your accident. He was really upset that we hadn't been there, that someone from the area had found you and had you flown to Boston. He was so tender and concerned. He paced the hospital floor, talked to you, rubbed your fingers, and just sat and watched you and your monitors.

"Your doctors hinted that you needed rest, so I took him shopping. He invited me to lunch and dinner—a real treat after cafeteria food—and we went to a couple of movies. He was very entertaining. We could talk for hours, although that was mostly about you, Bethany."

She looked into Bethany's eyes. "I really tried not to think about him as anything but your boyfriend, even though we found out how closely our tastes matched and how much we had in common."

Kim stood and walked to the window, looking out toward the ocean. As she spoke, she turned back to face Bethany.

"Then you both came to San Francisco."

"Yes," Bethany said, finally participating in the conversation, "that city with steep hills by the bay."

"I guess that's when I realized how much I cared about him. I felt so guilty enjoying those evenings when you rested and I was alone with him." Kim sat back down on the bed and looked intently into Bethany's eyes. "But I saw that your relationship was changing—your feelings toward each other—and that you both were unhappy. When you two were together, Joseph was continually trying to persuade you to do things, demanding that you accept his decisions. You were caught in a losing situation: you couldn't please him and at the same time show him that you were capable. And I could tell that you were becoming colder with him because of his insensitivity.

"After you came back to Boston, I discovered that Joseph had left a tie behind a cushion on the couch. I called for his address. He called to thank me when I sent it, and so on. Then last week we finally admitted that we were both very attracted to each other and that we needed to talk to you. I finally felt free to give into those feelings since you and Joseph weren't really communicating and certainly not dating. But even still, we wanted to tell you up front. We weren't sure how to approach you, so we made arrangements to talk with a counselor before we talked to you."

Her eyes concentrated on Bethany's face with a look of misery. "That was why I flew out without telling you. That is why you talked with a teenage neighbor when you called me. She was there to give Joseph a message if he called about my flight plans."

Her expression became one of pleading. "Oh, Bethany, I am so sorry. I hope you will someday be able to understand. You are a dear friend. I don't want that to change." She leaned over to Bethany and held out an envelope. "Joseph asked me to give you this."

Without speaking, Bethany slid her finger through the loosely gummed seal. Then she pulled out a sheaf of papers. There were a number of formal-looking notices with some names and dates filled in and other blanks underlined and flagged for signatures. On top of it all was a handwritten note signed by Joseph.

I am sorry that I've put you through all this. I should never have doubted you or your experience. You are a lovely woman, and Amelia would be very pleased with what you have done and are becoming.

I guess we didn't have as much in common as we thought. I hope you can forgive me. I don't want to stress you more by talking about our relationship now, but I sincerely hope you feel better soon. I do care about you.

Then a postscript followed.

There is something I feel you are now ready to know—something quite significant that I've been waiting to tell you, per Amelia's request, until you'd had enough time at Faunce Cove to truly find yourself. I believe that time has come.

Amelia told me at one of our first meetings that she would eventually amend the will she had already written, and that when she did she would make certain that the majority of the family wealth would go "to the person or institutions that will best be able to handle it wisely." She was as adamant as I ever saw her when she said, "I will not have the family's inheritance squandered." My congratulations and best wishes as I tell you that Amelia left you everything.

* * *

Ethan Savage was the first to notice Bethany as she slowly descended the stairs that evening.

"Well, look who's here!" he welcomed her as the twins bounced up from a game of dominoes to greet her.

"Bethany's up!" they called excitedly in unison. "Bethany's better!" Jessica declared. Then James added, "Can we have a party to celebrate?"

"I think Bethany would prefer a warm bowl of chicken soup," Alice replied dryly.

Undeterred by her mother's words, Jessica asked, "Do you want to play a game?" She did not wait for Bethany's reply before she opened a closet full of brightly colored boxes.

"Yes, let's play Twister," James called out enthusiastically.

"Oh, I don't think Bethany is quite up to Twister, son." Steve laughed. "Why don't you try Uno?"

"Actually," Bethany said, "I'd love to watch *you* play Twister. I'm more in the mood to be a spectator than a participant tonight."

"I'll spin for you," Ethan offered as the children spread the plastic mat over the floor.

Bethany watched the twins twist, slide, and giggle as they moved from one bright shape to another. Ethan guffawed at their squeals, and Steve encouraged their attempts.

"Me!" Joshua called each time the twins collapsed into a wriggling, tangled mass on the floor. Finally they lay there panting.

"Come on, Daddy. It's your turn, now," James stated.

"Me! Me!" Joshua called excitedly.

Steve moved with ease as he tussled the small boy's hair. "Oh, I'm too big. I won't fit on the plastic."

"Me!" Joshua repeated, grabbing his father's hand.

"Well, Grandpa," Steve said, faking a grimace, "spin that pointer. Come on, Josh."

Bethany couldn't contain her smile any longer as Steve, his long legs bent in awkward positions, moved to Ethan's calls. Joshua stretched from one shape to another, safely encircled in his father's limbs.

Then Ethan called a spin that was nearly out of Joshua's reach.

"Come on, Josh," Steve called. "You can do it!"

"Reach, reach," the twins clamored in a chant.

"You're almost there!" Ethan encouraged.

Alice peeked through the kitchen door to add, "Go, Joshua. You can reach it."

Bethany smiled as Steve secured his balance and steadied his son.

Joshua stretched his short legs onto his toes and finally touched the spot.

Bethany felt a strange sadness and fought back tears as Joshua, exultant in his success, beamed and squealed. Steve pulled him up against his chest and rolled over on the floor with him. Then he lifted the small boy up above him, to the cheers of the family. Steve lowered his son, but Joshua clung to his father with a tight hug.

"I did it, I did it," Joshua called happily. He escaped his father's grasp and ran to Alice, who picked him up with an enthusiastic squeeze.

Bethany stood quickly and walked to the kitchen.

Alice met her at the door. "Go in and eat." She looked at Bethany with a smile, which soon turned to a look of concern. "Are you all right? The kids and their noise have worn you out. I should have stopped them."

"No. It's not that." Bethany could barely voice her thoughts. "You have so much love, so much family, so much . . ."

"And you want it too," Alice finished softly. "You *will* have it, Bethany. You *will* have it, too." Her voice resumed its cheerful heartiness. "But for now, young-lady-who-hasn't-eaten-for-many-many-hours, you need some food." She glanced at the clock.

From the kitchen, Bethany watched the fracas continue as she ate. She usually enjoyed the cheerful noise of the family, but tonight it depressed her. She had shared enough time with the McCleres to feel a part of their closeness. And she had always accepted her peripheral status, confident that she and Joseph would someday have their own family. Now, there would be no home with Joseph or Peter, not even Rob. And, she admitted to herself, she had begun to care about Rob even in their short time together.

In spite of this new dimension to her feelings about Rob, after her reaction to their conversation, he wouldn't be interested in her—that was certain. If he saw her he would probably assume his professional mask and be polite but nothing more. She felt so confused. She wondered if all her relationships with men were doomed.

But it was more than that. She thought of Joshua's giggles as Steve had gently tossed him in the air to celebrate his success at Twister. No one had ever played games with her as a child, no one had smiled and given her a turn, no one had encouraged her attempts or cheered at her successes. Her feelings of envy stemmed not from the lack of an "interested other" or some such title, but from all the other delightful moments her life had lacked. Suddenly she felt a weariness heavier than exhaustion settle over her.

* * *

After receiving the note earlier in the day from Joseph, Bethany was certainly not expecting a phone call from him that night.

"Bethany, I wanted to make certain for myself that you're okay," Joseph began.

Silence met him on the other end. The exhaustion that had overwhelmed her that evening had not dissipated, and her feelings from watching the Twister game were still raw. She felt incapable of responding.

"Are you there, Bethany? There's so much I need to tell you, so much you need to know. I felt I couldn't wait until I could come up there and talk with you in person. I'm sure you have questions that need answering. Bethany, please talk to me."

Resigning herself to a conversation she felt little desire to engage in, Bethany finally replied. "Joseph, an attempt was made on my life yesterday. I discovered that another, in an uncomfortably long line of friends, has deceived me—more than I could ever have imagined. I found Amelia's grave yesterday morning, so near I could have walked to it every day.

"And this evening I watched as a loving family interacted with all the caring and joy and support I never received while I was growing up. A toddler tried to play Twister. I heard his family calling to him, encouraging him, cheering him on until, with his father's help, he succeeded. Then I listened while his family went crazy congratulating him. That toddler received more encouragement to touch a red spot on a Twister board than I ever received on any assignment, any quiz, any project or test I ever attempted during years and years of trying to please Amelia. He got more praise for touching an insignificant circle than I did for report cards covered with A's, or ribbons on science awards, or math tests, or writing awards. I watched a mother hug her child not because of anything special he'd done but just because she's his mother and she loves him.

"It has not been a normal day. In fact, nothing has been normal for a long, long time. Am I okay? My body is basically fine. As for the rest of me? I guess I will have to wait and see."

"Bethany, I could have helped you if you'd told me about the threats you received. If I'd known you were in danger, I would have gotten an investigator to find out what was happening."

"I considered telling you about the threatening letters—I really did, Joseph. But it's much more complicated than that. At first I was silent about it because of Peter's warning concerning the threat it posed to both of us. I wasn't sure whom I could trust. And then after the accident, somehow my mind completely wiped out the memory of that final threat until just recently. And the way you were acting, I also feared you would just say they were coming from my overactive imagination, my fictional world, my inability to live in the present. Just as you did the tunnel."

"I'm sorry, Bethany. I underestimated you. Amelia did too. She had me make arrangements for you two to be together in the summer, but she didn't tell me about the hut until she was critically ill. I should never have promised her I wouldn't tell you about her changing condition until after graduation. I should have known that you would want time with her, that you could have made other arrangements for your thesis. You should have been given the information and the choice. As for the hut, I didn't know any of the history of your family or the cove, just that Amelia said she had recently bought this property so as to provide you a chance to be by yourself to write your novel. You should have had a choice about living there, too."

Bethany could tell from Joseph's voice that he was sincere, but she couldn't hide her bitterness as she spoke. "Yes, Joseph, I should have been given those choices."

"In retrospect, Bethany," Joseph said, "you should have been informed immediately about all the changes in Amelia's health. But you know Amelia, she felt it would be best if you didn't have to worry about her while you finished your thesis and the other last-minute requirements for your degree. And the doctor in Arizona wasn't particularly worried about her at the time. He was fairly certain she would live well beyond the summer. In fact, we all were."

"Oh." It was a flat, dispirited reply.

Joseph continued. "Then, when Amelia's health suddenly worsened, she called me from the hospital in Arizona. She had an entirely new plan in case she didn't survive the pneumonia. You were to have a year in Maine and time to grieve before the remainder of the estate was signed over to you. That would give you time to consider another type of life, maybe even fall in love before anyone knew of your wealth. But even I didn't know about the estate on Faunce Cove, Bethany, and all that you would inherit there. Amelia had so much property, and the information about this was tucked away among other estates in her folder—which I hadn't bother yet to investigate in detail, knowing it would be awhile before we went through it all together."

"Joseph, I'm very tired. Could we finish this some other time?"

"Just one more minute, please, Bethany. There's something else I need to say." He paused and exhaled slowly. "I'm so sorry about what happened to us. My attraction for you was real and that, coupled with your connections to Amelia, drew me to you, especially at first. I apologize for some of the things I said and did. You are a delightful, caring, intelligent, and accomplished woman, Bethany. I would never do anything to purposely hurt you. And I do care about you."

"Thank you." The words were spoken so softly that Joseph wasn't certain they had been uttered.

"Oh, Bethany?"

He paused until he heard her quiet responding, "Yes?"

"Tomorrow I'll send a registered envelope to you with the instructions you'll need so you can access all the information Amelia had about your family. I found out while reading through Amelia's portfolio this morning that all that information is in the mansion."

29

"You're sure you won't see Dr. Sommers?"

Bethany turned to Alice, who stood at the doorway holding a manila envelope. Oak branches hid the driveway so Bethany couldn't see through the window to tell who was in the car she had heard drive up a few minutes before, but the expression on Alice's face confirmed her guess.

"I'm sure," Bethany said as she heard the familiar voice in the car reply teasingly to the children's excited chatter.

"He left a few notes for you to take to a local doctor. He suggested Dr. Noel, and he said to make an appointment this afternoon." She slid the papers onto the nightstand. "Bethany, are you sure this is what you want?"

Bethany didn't reply immediately as she sat down on the bed. The car door slammed and the engine started. Alice turned back to the door before Bethany spoke quietly.

"I guess I'll need to stay here for a while, Alice. Will that be okay with you?"

"Bethany, you know you're always welcome here. Besides that, I wouldn't hear of you leaving now—especially to go back to the hut— while that Scranton fellow could still be in the area. Now, why don't you just lie down and rest. That's what you need."

* * *

Nothing appealed to Bethany. The hut and garden, the mansion and the cemetery were all off limits until Peter could be taken into custody, and she was too stiff and sore to walk around Seacrest. She spent her time sitting in her room until Alice convinced her to ask Tom to bring her computer down from the hut after one of his frequent patrols of the area. It still took her until Wednesday to convince herself to open her files on Patience. Reading her last entries was discouraging—it reminded Bethany of how much her life had changed since she'd been able to immerse herself totally in Patience's life. And yet only five days had passed since her ordeal with Peter's hired men.

Now, Bethany couldn't even concentrate on Patience. Her thoughts made wild swings from Joseph and Kim, to Peter, then Rob, then Amelia's grave and the mansion. Phrases raced through her mind as she reviewed conversations, remembering words she'd heard earlier when she couldn't ponder their meanings—or the feelings they left in her.

And there was so much more. The man with the gentle eyes had turned out to be a doctor and a gardener, and . . . Bethany had prayed for Peter for months while he had been planning something she still didn't understand. Had he planned to kidnap her or just scare her? Why? What had he wanted?

The Peter she thought of now was not the charming man she had known during those fun-filled months of dating. Even though he had those moments of anger, she had never been suspicious of him or his story. That certainly didn't say much for her intuition. At least she was learning. When she thought back now she recognized warning signs she had missed. His impatience, his temper . . .

Bethany pushed her chair away from the computer. She wasn't accomplishing anything trying to write. Since she couldn't stop her brain from trying to process all that had happened, she could at least make a sandwich for lunch while she thought. Names and questions flowed through her mind as she walked down the steps. She realized she still didn't know who had sent the warnings—or why. If the warnings were not from a corporation or Joseph, as Peter had said, who had sent them? Who could it have been—unless it was Peter himself? Bethany found it difficult to believe that Peter could have made up such an elaborate scheme. How had he gotten the information? It definitely wasn't all available in public records.

There was a tap on the door as she walked down the stairs. Even though the noise was not sharp, and she could see the bright gold badge contrasting with the dark blue of Tom Marshalle's uniform, Bethany felt her heart pound.

"Bethany, it's me, Tom. How are you doing?"

Bethany took a deep breath and nodded a noncommittal answer.

"I thought you might like to know some of the latest details about our investigation," Tom said as she opened the door.

"You've talked to Peter?" she asked as she backed away from the opening and sat down on a chair.

"Well, no, but I received more information on him today."

The police chief sat down across from her and pulled out a small notebook. He looked very official as he glanced at the contents.

"We—well, Joseph particularly—are determined to connect the dots on this one. We wanted to find out how Peter got the information about you and your grandmother. So Joseph had his detective run a couple of cross searches. They checked through all your university's personnel and students, then all the employees in Amelia's conglomerates, but they didn't find anything until they checked out medical personnel. Didn't find a Stanton with an employee record at any of the facilities, but did find one doing some court-ordered community service while he was on parole and in a position where he'd probably have had contact with your grandmother, maybe even visited with her. So the detective got ahold of his parole officer and he gave us Stanton's background."

Tom shifted on the chair. "Bethany, this is pretty disturbing information. I'm sorry."

Bethany nodded in acknowledgment.

"Stanton came from an abusive family where his alcoholic father beat his wife, who then took it out on the kid. Stanton took a strong disliking to his mother even though it was his father who was abusive, and when Peter left home at fourteen, he took it out on his girlfriends. He was in and out of juvenile detention on assault and battery charges, although he was usually able to talk his way past the judges."

Tom looked up at Bethany. "By the way, he is a real talker—the parole officer said he could sweet-talk a used-car dealer into giving him a car with driving lessons, an oil change, and a tank full of gas included—all in less than half an hour. The officer said Stanton wasn't lacking in self-confidence, either. Stanton figured he pretty much deserved to own the world, and he kept expecting everyone just to give it to him.

"Anyway, at eighteen, once he started facing the adult justice system, he seemed to smarten up. He kept himself out of jail, if not out of trouble, until a couple of years before he met your grandmother. Then it seems that he started up his old habits—this time with some additions. He attached himself to well-to-do women, then bullied them into paying him to get lost. If they refused, he'd revert to assault and battery. Several wouldn't press charges against him, but when he went back to one all full of remorse and then broke her wrist, she filed. He was examined by a court-appointed psychiatrist who said he showed tendencies toward psychopathic behavior. That doctor put him on medications, but nothing ever came of the psychiatric report. A smart lawyer was able to keep Stanton's old records sealed because he had been underage, and he discredited most of the newer charges. So, Stanton ended up with a hundred hours of community service at the hospital.

"That's where he met Mrs. Carlisle—at the hospital—according to the account of another guy who did community service at the same time. He said that Peter saw a photo she had of you and started asking Amelia about you.

"While he was dating you, he also traveled out of state to get money from a couple of women he'd met previously. Then he made some friends there near your university in Boston. We're not sure if he's been up to anything else since you've moved up here or not.

"Of course, we now have bulletins out on him all over Maine, and we've been keeping a tight watch here at Seacrest since his visit to you." Tom stood and zipped his coat tightly across his chest.

"Oh, about Joseph's file—the one that was stolen. It was on Stanton. The police down there figure it must have been an inside job because whoever got the file—Stanton or an associate—seemed to know exactly where to find it. It seems that your grandmother became more than a little suspicious about him and asked Joseph to look into matters for her. Joseph's detective had a duplicate copy of the file, so I'll get you one, too. You might also want to see the pictures of the minors who vandalized the bridge for a positive identification."

"You mean you are not positive you've got the right kids?"

"Well, I'm positive about the kids because they confessed." He paused but continued when Bethany was silent. "We just need you to identify them for the record, in case they decide not to plead guilty after all. You never know—their defense lawyer might figure out a way to get their confessions thrown out. Then we'd definitely need you to ID them and testify. The crime lab is still going over the threats you received, but they haven't come up with anything yet. I'll let you know if they do," Tom explained as he walked out the front door. Bethany watched him climb into his patrol car.

Bethany stepped back into the room and shut the door, then watched through the window until Tom drove away. She leaned against the door and looked around the large room. She felt like a young child waiting for a ghost to appear.

* * *

Driving the Jeep to her appointment with Dr. Noel early the next morning was definitely unpleasant. The Jeep seemed to shimmy on the smallest cracks in the asphalt, and the bandages made her back hot and irritated.

As Bethany drove, she reviewed what Tom had told her about Peter's criminal record. With his childhood, it was not surprising that he had significant problems. Despite everything, Bethany felt sympathy for Peter—now that she felt safe from him and his teenage accomplices.

Dr. Noel murmured with approval as he took the bandages off the lacerations on Bethany's back. She didn't know if his incessant chatter was an attempt at conversation, or if it was meant to divert her thoughts as he gently examined the painful injuries.

"I hadn't realized that you are Amelia Carlisle's granddaughter. I was sorry to hear about her death." Dr. Noel unwrapped a square of gauze as he talked.

"I knew Amelia when we were teenagers. In fact, I remember her mother, Miranda—Miranda Courier. Her doctor was my mentor long before I headed off to medical school. I went with him to visit Miranda a couple of times. Of course, I was intrigued by the opulent Courier property and its history.

"As I recall, several years before he died in France during World War I, James Courier married Miranda. They were a unique couple. He, full of vim and vigor, about as enthusiastic as anyone you'd ever meet. She, just the opposite. She was quiet and shy—quite beautiful— and I guess you'd say they provided proof for the maxim that opposites attract. People said that when you saw them apart they seemed incomplete—James restless and Miranda completely out of place— but when they were together they fit like a glove."

He paused as he reached for a spool of medical tape.

"Well, Amelia took after James. I think she was two or three years old when he entered the armed services. He could have stayed out of the military, of course, since his businesses were important enough to give him and a dozen other men deferment. But he felt the responsibility, so he joined. That left Miranda to raise Amelia. Miranda loved Amelia dearly, but apparently she was a handful. After they received word that James had died—it almost seemed like influenza killed as many of our boys as the enemy back in 1918—Miranda was pretty despondent. It's not surprising she had trouble controlling Amelia."

He squinted as he concentrated on the memory. "I remember going out there with the doctor one time. While he was talking to Miranda, another woman came in—I think her name was Victoria. She seemed very forceful and precise, and I commented to the doctor that I didn't think I would like having her as a governess. He just laughed and said Victoria was a force to be reckoned with and that she was probably the only force that could contend with Amelia.

"Miranda gradually faded until . . ." He cocked one eye and tilted his head as he thought. "I suppose Amelia was nearly twenty when Miranda died. In those days, everything not easily diagnosed was labeled mental illness. I don't know what kind of diagnosis a doctor would give Miranda now, but from what I recollect, Amelia was quite adept at making snap judgments, and she seemed pretty critical of her mother. She was adamant about mothering: she would lovingly nurture her children when they came, not emotionally distance herself like Miranda had done.

"Your grandmother was quite the woman. She'd come up from the island to participate in weekend dances or to act in theater productions, and she'd set all us boys' hearts astir. She was beyond us—vivacious, enthusiastic, even headstrong. Too much for us local guys to handle. Then she went off to Wellesley or one of those colleges and came back with Jonathan Carlisle in tow. I vaguely remember that she eventually had the one child, but I knew nothing about any grandchildren."

The doctor gently taped more bandages over Bethany's shoulder blade.

"Victoria lived at Seacrest for years, helping Amelia deal with the estate and the business empire she had inherited. When Amelia and Jonathan had their own baby—must have been your mother—Victoria helped with her, too. Jonathan shipped out for the war and died shortly thereafter, right around Normandy, I think."

Bethany could feel the gentle pressure of Dr. Noel's hand as he rubbed another edge of tape with alcohol, then slowly eased the bandage loose.

"Now," he commented as he put down the tape and stood, "no infection going on here, though you've got some pretty bad bruises. I don't think you'll have much scarring on your cheek, and your hair will shadow it. How are you feeling otherwise?"

"I'm stiff and I hurt and I'm tired," she complained, but then continued with a weak grin. "I guess I need to get my mind off myself."

"How's your book coming?"

"I can't concentrate enough to write."

"I'm not surprised, with your nasty fall down the hill and all. How did Joseph take all of that?"

"Actually, Joseph is seeing someone else—my old roommate."

"Sounds like that might sting more than these wounds." He looked down at her over his glasses.

"I guess I was pretty stupid to let myself get into such a mess."

"No. Not stupid at all. Maybe just unlucky. Remember, Bethany, it hasn't even been a year since your grandmother died. We just need to give you time to get through the grieving and back to normal life."

"With all the things that I found out, I'm not sure that is ever going to happen."

"Some of your friends acted irresponsibly. It takes time for those kinds of wounds to heal."

"It's not just my friends, if you want to call them that. It's everyone. I don't know where to start. I spent all my life trying to please Amelia. I wanted to tell her about the gospel and be there when she was baptized. Now that I have the information so I could be baptized in the temple for her, I don't care about it—or I don't want to do it. I'm not sure which. I'm really angry that she ignored me. She wrote a letter saying she cared. I guess that was supposed to make up for her meddling in my life, but it infuriates me. When I think of her avoiding me even though she was lonely, it seems like such a waste."

"I can see that."

"Part of me wants to like her—even love her. Still, at other times, I want to yell at her and tell her how much she underestimated me and how much it hurts." She paused, then looked up with a sheepish grin. "I guess that's still being pretty self-centered, isn't it?"

Dr. Noel smiled. "Trying to justify your feelings may not be the best way to respond to anger, but it is certainly not the worst way either. I'd much rather see you in here complaining than outside throwing rocks at dogs or yelling at old women. It's not necessarily bad to think about your frustrations—that generally gets a person thinking about the things they can change, and that is a step toward improving. Too often, though, people get caught up defending themselves and don't change. Then the real issues never get resolved. Sometimes it requires some hard work and uncomfortable adjustments."

Dr. Noel moved toward the door then stopped. "I was thinking. You and I knew a completely different Amelia. You see her as an unemotional, eccentric old woman who hurt you. I remember her as a talented, vivacious, passionate woman. You should have seen her at play rehearsals!" He paused as if not certain whether to say more.

"And you think I would like the younger version of her better than the older?"

"Maybe, or maybe the *real* Amelia. The person neither one of us knew. The one probably no one here on earth really knew."

"How do I learn who she was?"

"Get to know more about her. Think about her complete life, not just your relationship with her. Pray to understand. You're an intelligent person. If you want to do it enough, you'll find a way."

"Why can't I just forget it all and forgive her? I feel so guilty."

"Any type of change takes time and effort. Remember, we weren't put here on earth to *live* perfectly—we were put here to *learn* how to live perfectly. None of us are the same people we were ten years ago. In fact, we're not the people we will be ten years from now. We make mistakes, learn from them, and change. Then we get on with life. Don't be too hard on yourself or on Amelia. And remember, you are an intelligent, beautiful woman with your life ahead of you. Pray and follow your instincts. The Spirit will guide you.

"As for your friends—it's easy to care about people who never hurt you. When they've caused some pain—taken a poke at your pride—it can be a real challenge to excuse them."

"How do you get over it?"

"Same as with Amelia. Think about them—their entire personality and your complete relationship, not just the things that have hurt you. Pray. When you really want to, you'll find a way.

"Remember, no matter what the problem is, you can find a solution if you pray and trust your feelings.

"But first, try getting out and getting a little exercise to get your mind off all this. A spring day like this is too beautiful to waste worrying."

30

The air had a slight edge of crispness as Bethany walked from Dr. Noel's office to the Jeep thinking about his words. How could she get exercise when she had to stay cooped up, hidden away in case Peter showed up? She wished she knew what was happening with the case. Tom had kept her as informed as he could, but when there was no news, there was no news.

Having followed Alice's suggestion that she get a post office box so she wouldn't have to make a daily mail run to the hut, she slowed as she drove through the center of Seacrest. She passed the police station and then turned by the post office. The postmaster was still sorting the mail, so she stepped back out into the sunshine.

Tom had mentioned bringing her a copy of Peter's file. She might as well pick it up while she waited and save him a trip.

She could see an officer sitting behind the thick glass window as she entered the foyer. He was intent on a voice coming over the intercom, but he swiveled his chair quickly and didn't wait for her to speak when he saw who she was.

"Perfect timing, Ms. Carlisle. Tom has some new information." He turned his head and called, "Tom!" He tipped his head toward Bethany. She could see another officer standing with Tom beside a large map of the area.

Tom beckoned her into the door.

"I was just going to give you a call," Tom said as he pulled out a chair for her by his desk. "We've gotten some new leads on Stanton, and we may have an arrest in the makings." He sat down behind the desk.

"The kids picked up for vandalism at Faunce Cove gave us a good description of the car Stanton was driving. The Walachias Police spotted a deserted car matching the description, and fingerprints on it match Stanton's. A guy matching Stanton's description rented a car late yesterday afternoon from a rental agency. The signature on the lease is pretty hard to read, but the renter said his name was Patrick Staning, and the fingerprints on his clipboard were a perfect match with Stanton's. He rented the most ordinary looking car they had, even though he had to wait for them to change its oil before they'd let him take it.

"Last night we thought he'd head right up to New Brunswick and try to get lost in heavy rush-hour traffic at the border, but there was no record of him crossing into Canada, and the team found a torn section of map scrunched up between the front seats. It was a small piece but large enough to see that he had been looking at the northwestern side of Maine where there's a lot of mountainous space with private roads that require access permits. We got a fax showing a P. Staning ordered a permit for the roads to . . ." He flipped through the paper on his desk, "Millinocket and Clayton Lake on a road that goes to the border with Quebec."

He looked up at Bethany, his expression changing from that of a straightforward officer to a solicitous friend. "Are you all right?"

Bethany felt weak. She was grateful to be safely away from Peter, but realizing the effort he had put into tricking her made her feel sick.

"I'm much better than I might have been by now," she said as she thought of being alone in a car speeding through the isolated mountains with Peter. "I'm fine. Really."

"They haven't actually caught him yet, but the state patrol is watching a car like the one he rented . . . In fact they've had reports of a couple of them." He chuckled and then added, "We're more likely to get identifications on a car than on the face of a guy wearing a cap inside one. It looks as if he is staying on back roads—which actually works to our benefit since people are more aware of a specific person when there aren't a lot of people around. We didn't expect him to use a credit card or leave a money trail. And that part of Maine, like Faunce Cove, doesn't have cell phone service. Tracking him has pretty much been based on luck, but it's been on our side."

"The guy we're talking to right now is from Molunkus. A car cut him off at an intersection. A couple of miles later the driver was on the side of the road changing a tire on the same car. In a few more miles the same car passed him on a hill, and 'bout caused a pileup, so he called with a plate number. The police recognized the description of the car immediately and put a call in to us. Since the driver was changing the tire, our caller got a good look at him and gave us a pretty good description—short to medium height, short blond hair, muscular. He was wearing Levi's and a short-sleeved, blue-striped shirt and cowboy boots with turquoise trim. Does that sound like something he would wear?"

"Tom." An officer from the large room motioned toward the speaker. The machine buzzed and snapped as a new voice began. Tom went into the room to listen. "I'm officer Carter on Route 157. I've got a car that matches the description you faxed. Looks like it could be your man. I'm following at a good distance so as not to alert him. D'you want an arrest?" The speaker clicked as the voice stopped.

Tom spoke into the microphone. "We've got fingerprints to prove he's driving a car of that description and we've got the guy in the same cowboy boots as our man changing that car's tire. We'll start the paperwork and be on our way to get him as soon as we hear you've made the arrest." He looked through the door at Bethany with a broad smile. "I think we're going to be busy for a while."

Bethany smiled back and stood up, taking a deep breath as she felt a lightness fill her. Peter was in custody—or soon would be, and she was safe. Forms and identifications could wait. She was free. She could go to the hut and the garden without fear. She felt a pang of sadness knowing that Peter would be incarcerated, but for the first time in months she did not have to worry about the danger he was in or her own. Relief flooded over her and the sun seemed brighter as she walked back to the post office.

There were so many things to do. She could go to the mansion and the garden—*her* mansion and *her* garden. She could research the tunnel. But first, there was Amelia's family records to explore—*her* family, she thought with a smile.

* * *

Bethany impulsively turned into a nursery on her way out of Seacrest and bought several flats of white violets to plant near the waterfall Rob had shown her. On the way out she saw a small lawn mower. The mansion would have all the lawn equipment it needed, but there was none at the hut. She got the lawn mower and a container of gasoline, along with a weed whacker and clippers.

After she stored the gardening tools in the shed, Bethany went into the hut to change her clothes. There was still enough time before lunch to get some flowers planted. She carried the trays with her through the tunnel into the room she assumed had been the servants' quarters, then through its outside door, which cornered with the tunnel door. She would need to water the tender flowers after she planted them, so, leaving them in the shade by the servants' quarters, she located the gardening shed Rob had shown her, hooked up the end of the hose to the spigot, and rolled the cart with the hose and water wand toward the largest waterfall. The distance surprised her. It took her well over half an hour to collect and connect the hose lengths, lay out the hose to the waterfall, and then return to the shed to turn on the water. She dug into the rich soil, savoring the scent of the damp earth. With the heat of the sun beaming down on the soil and on her, she decided to leave the plants in the shadows by the waterfall until later when the area would be shaded before planting them. After all, she had other things to do—and the family histories were awaiting her.

* * *

The mansion was more enchanting than anything she had imagined when Joseph and Dr. Noel had talked about it. Its sheer size was incredible. Although she had entered through the servants' entrance as Joseph had instructed, her first step inside convinced her that the craftsmanship was superb, and no expense had been spared in its construction.

It was close to noon when she slowly walked through the beautiful structure to the enormous ballroom, holding the directions to the library and the documents she was seeking. The squeak of her rubber-soled sneakers seemed out of place in the majestic room, exaggerating the silence of the walls and the cold, substantial strength of the columns that supported the staircases.

Unmoving air filled the silent room with imagined echoes and sullen shadows. As Bethany thought of Amelia, and wondered about her own mother's childhood, the mansion took on a feeling of foreboding and melancholy.

She tried to concentrate on the structure of the building. The marble staircases, the gracious curves of the balcony and its banisters, the solidly carved doors and inlaid wooden panels—they all harmonized into a beautiful, elegant living area. But one did not live elegantly alone, and the expansive room made her feel insignificant and very lonely.

She moved up the first set of stairs to the balcony that surrounded the ballroom. The room that spread below was empty, yet Bethany could imagine how it must have been—women in full, swaying dresses, and men in tails. She could see Patience's descendants bowing and curtsying, servants slipping in and out with trays of shimmering, tinkling glassware.

But she could not see Amelia. She could not imagine the room filled with slender girls in fringed hems and loops of pearls, bangs cropped in straight lines across their foreheads, doing the Charleston with young men in white suits and loafers. And Glennis. She could not imagine her mother either. There was just so little she knew about these women.

Why hadn't Amelia told her about this place or about Glennis's life? Bethany tried to imagine Glennis. Amelia had never displayed her daughter's picture, never spoken her name.

Bethany turned to the mezzanine where the sun filtered through high, sculptured windows. "Glennis? Mother?" she called out tentatively. "Amelia?"

Not even the air seemed moved by her voice. If she had hoped to find clues about their lives or to awaken her own imagination by saying their names, she'd been mistaken. She quickly walked back down the stairs to the ballroom and into the dining room.

The dining room was as distinctive and beautiful as the ballroom. In the walk-in closet Bethany noted shelf after shelf stocked with china and crystal, tablecloths, and heavy triangular irons. She could picture servants pressing the cloths and smoothing them gently before covering them with gleaming plates, softly clanging silverware, and shimmering crystal goblets.

Bethany looked at the closet. So much preparation, so much energy had been used to fashion these goods and maintain them in their beauty. How many lives had traced their days through these walls, over this culinary ware?

I could never be happy here, Bethany thought.

This mansion was built for comfortable, gracious living, for family. But Bethany did not fit into its world. Its comfort and beauty did not compensate for the loneliness she felt. She had no one. She felt completely vulnerable, completely alone.

"I don't want this," she said. "I only want . . ." She stopped, unable to complete the phrase she had begun. Leaning against the table to look out the windows, she heard a twig rattle as the wind blew it across the patio outside the French doors. "Please, I don't want to be here alone!"

* * *

All she wanted from the mansion was the histories.

Bethany easily found the library, and she opened the safe on the second try. She found the tray Joseph had mentioned, and she slid the lid open. There lay Amelia's pearls, a few other broaches and necklaces Bethany recognized, and a shiny golden locket with the initials *GC* engraved on the back. Glennis Carlisle. Bethany fingered the locket carefully, then secured the golden chain around her neck.

Bethany lifted the family histories out of the safe with reverence. She had longed for this moment from the instant Joseph had told her about them. This was her heritage, her family. She lifted the top envelope, somewhat surprised to read the inscription, "Life Story of Amelia Carlisle." Somehow she had imagined the histories would be of generations further back, but she put it with the other histories, thinking of Dr. Noel's advice. There were dozens of manuscripts beneath Amelia's. Overwhelmed with the number of histories there were to read, she glanced at a second pile of envelopes in the safe. It did make sense that there would be a copy of the life history of the original colonists kept in the mansion, and she was not surprised to see it there. There was a third pile of legal-size envelopes. The top had the words "Re: Attorney Joseph Panninon" typed on the label, then an envelope with Amelia's handwritten "Robert Sommers." Perhaps, Bethany thought, the information might answer questions that had worried her since she had talked to Peter.

31

Sitting down at the large table in the library, Bethany opened the packet entitled "Mrs. Smythe, wife of the captain." Intrigued, she read on.

The handwritten pages, evidently restored—if the term could be applied to the aged paper—by an expert in document preservation, had been placed in archival pockets for protection. Large sections of the edges of the pages were worn completely through or had simply disintegrated. Other pages appeared blank or badly faded, except for an occasional pen stroke. Even on the most legible pages, the ink had dulled to a tan on the yellowed paper. Bethany touched the plastic carefully and read what she could.

The first half dozen pages, those in the worst condition, seemed to be Patience's recollection of her childhood. Bethany could decipher only occasional words—not nearly enough to tell if her version of the child's life was accurate.

She found the next group of pages easier to read, though they left her puzzled until she realized that Patience spoke of their Indian friends, Chief Shabanah and his wife Nasset. Bethany pieced together a summary of the information about the colonial couple's amiable relationship with the Indians who had been guests in the small clapboard house many times. Nasset had told Patience the legend of the Rock of the Sea God.

One day while the men gathered clams, Patience and Nasset had wandered along the shore. Not too far from the cove, near the mouth of the brook, they had come to a large section of boulders with a fissure at the bottom. Patience had been interested in the cave created by the ocean tides and had started to enter it when Nasset grabbed at her hysterically. She would be taken by the Sea God if she went into the cave.

Nasset had told her the story, using as many gestures as words to tell the legend of an Indian boy who disobeyed his parents and convinced his friends to do likewise.

The legend she read was essentially word for word what she had found in Millie's historical records.

So, thought Bethany, that was how Patience found the cave and knew she would be safe within it. She continued to read, although the fading, handwritten letters tired her eyes.

It was also Nasset who attended to the birthing of Patience and Thomas's son.

Samuel was his parents' delight. It mattered little to them that he cried often and loudly, for he was born small and seemed always in need of food. Marveling at his rapid growth, they loved him as a miracle.

Two winters after Samuel was born, a canoe with six Indians from a tribe unknown to Thomas stopped at the cove. Thomas invited them to share his meal in the yard, hoping this gesture would keep the peace as it had with local tribes. Patience stayed in the house, hoping to avoid detection, but Samuel began to cry. She could not still him, and the Indians sitting on the ground with Thomas began to talk to each other in their own tongue, gesturing wildly—arguing, it would seem. Patience felt relieved when she saw them finally step through the shallow water into their canoe. She watched their strong arms bend in simultaneous motion as they rowed from the cove.

That night the Indians returned. By the time Thomas realized their danger, their only option was to flee. Thomas, being the strongest and fastest, took Samuel, while Patience tried to draw the braves' attention.

Instinctively, she went to the one place she hoped the Indians might fear, and she spent the night in the hollow of the Rock of the Sea God.

When the morning came, the Indians were gone, and Thomas's body lay crumpled within sight of the fields he had begun to till, within earshot of the burned mass that had been their home. But

Patience could not find Samuel's body. Long after the cold deepened—bringing with it torrents of snow—she searched for his small shape. But it was not to be found. She left the burned façade of the house intact, hoping that if the Indians returned, they would not investigate it. Patience propped the lumber Thomas had begun to cut for a barn against the fireplace, forming a crude room underneath the charred clapboard. Then she spent her time huddled in the narrow passageway.

Shabanah and Nasset found Patience there in the spring, unable to speak, nearly unable to move. The kind Indian friends took her to their village and cared for her. When she regained her strength, they listened to her story. Shabanah counseled with his braves and sent them to visit other tribes, asking questions, seeking answers.

One night a brave returned, his excitement evident to Patience even though she could not understand his words to Shabanah. The next morning the two Indians left together. Eight nights later, they returned with a wide-eyed but tired Samuel.

From Nasset's mixed words and gestures, Patience gleaned that the squaw of an Indian chief some days north of them had been unable to produce a son for the chief. In her enthusiasm to please him, she promised to pay handsomely for any baby his warriors might bring her. Word passed from one tribe to another until braves from a tribe seeking favor with the chief arrived with Samuel.

While the squaw loved the baby and cared for him, she naturally wanted a native baby. When a squaw within her village died during childbirth, she took that baby boy to raise, too. She had been pleased to trade Samuel to Shabanah for a necklace of shells.

At this point in the story, the writing on the photocopy dimmed as if it had been written with a different batch of ink, possibly finished at some later time. With some passages barely visible, Bethany could read only occasional words to try to piece together the rest of the story.

Apparently, Patience and Samuel stayed with the local Indians for several years. Patience carefully taught Samuel to read and write. His dealings with the Indians taught him a type of mathematics.

The next line made Bethany pause. It seemed that Patience was explaining where she received her own education. *I, myself, had learned to read and write from Hannah. She taught me at night, after the children had gone to sleep, on those nights when Mr. K. did not require her attention.* Wasn't one of Mr. Kraklor's wives named Hannah?

When Samuel was nearly nine years old, an English sea captain called at the village to bargain for some tall timbers to use for ship masts. He was as surprised to find an English woman to serve as an interpreter as she was to be called to act in that capacity. His negotiations with Shabanah, who acted as an emissary between the captain and a number of other Indian tribes in the area, took several days. By the end of that time, he was in love with Patience. Though she respected and trusted the captain, she was still devoted to Thomas. But she agreed to be the captain's wife if he, in turn, would act as a father to Samuel and see to his education and his financial establishment when the time came.

Many years passed before Patience saw the cove again. The captain's ventures had proven very successful, and Samuel, educated well on English soil, shared his stepfather's aptitude not only for the sea but for good fortune as well; the family became very wealthy.

Nonetheless, Patience never forgot or quit longing for the cove. The captain, as she always called him, bought a massive piece of the land surrounding her old home and built her a magnificent mansion near her cove to show his love for her.

The page, half full, ended there.

She stared blankly at the table for several moments before she closed the manuscript.

Curious about the rest of the material beneath Patience's history, Bethany examined more of the documents on the table, finding biographies from several generations of Patience's descendants. She wondered what had happened to the more recent generations. Where had they gone? Bethany opened one of the leather-bound volumes and began reading. It bore the title, *Excerpts from Memoirs: 1675–1712.* Again, the manuscript was handwritten, and though the ink was somewhat dulled, Bethany could tell from a brief glance that the pages were Samuel's account of a portion of his life.

Samuel recollected a number of stories about the woman he always referred to as "Mother." He told how Patience beamed as she showed him her name on the bowls Nasset had shown her how to make. He told how the captain was passionate in his plans for the mansion he built for Patience and his pledge to have the most magnificent staircase she had ever seen. And Samuel explained how, when the staircase was not to the captain's liking, he had painstakingly moved it to the small, rebuilt house where she had survived the first winter—since she refused to let either the house or the staircase be destroyed.

Samuel spoke at great length of his mother's determination as an elderly matron to have a tunnel built to ensure her descendants a means of escape from the mansion in case of Indian attacks. Patience insisted that Samuel and his descendants keep the tunnel a secret unless its use was essential. Accordingly, under her supervision, Samuel had a long tunnel excavated from the servants' quarters past a grove of pines that would hide it from the view of the mansion. At its completion, Patience had walked through it, one hand in the captain's and one in Samuel's. She thanked them profusely, adding that she had a feeling the tunnel would be used by a descendant—used to save their family.

32

When Bethany stepped from the servants' quarters, it was still early afternoon. She had planned to go straight to the hut for a quick lunch, but she had become enveloped in thoughts of the past. Not quite ready to leave this monument—this sanctuary—that had meant so much to a family so long ago, Bethany momentarily paused as she looked at the path that led straight through the pines to the garden and then she turned and followed the cobblestone path toward the front of the mansion. It seemed strange that she had never seen the entrance to her own estate—had not even thought about it.

The mansion sat naturally in the trees as if the surrounding forest had gradually surrendered to its well-groomed foliage. No pronounced demarcation showed where man and nature disputed their claims, but then, Bethany thought, why should it? Patience's mansion with its granite bulwark and white pillars had been there longer than most of the vegetation surrounding it.

As she passed the driveway, Bethany looked back through the deep shade of the evergreens to the entrance of the mansion. A circle of granite steps surrounded a small reflection pool. Low-growing, deep-green shrubs contrasted with the red hues of barberry. Bright sunshine filtered down to almost spotlight the area. Color shimmered through the dusky gloom of the shadows.

Glennis had seen this. Glennis had sat on the steps, dipped her finger in the pool, and snapped a twig from an evergreen—one of these evergreens. Bethany put the folders she held inside the servants' entrance and walked back to the steps.

"Glennis?" she whispered. "Mom?"

She fingered the locket, twisting it to feel the initials traced in the gold. She felt its warmth, saw its glitter reflect the sunshine as she toyed with it. Glennis would have done this, and Amelia would have been there with her.

Bethany felt a sudden sorrow.

Glennis had left and Amelia had been alone, totally alone, in the mansion that had been built for a family.

The feeling came suddenly and the words followed it unknowingly. "Oh, Amelia!"

Bethany turned to the gazebo and the path that led to the cemetery. It took her less than ten minutes before she was kneeling beside Amelia's headstone. Tenderly, she brushed the fallen leaves from the base of the marker. She tipped back on her toes to study the lettering: *Amelia Courier Carlisle.* The back of the stone held additional information: *daughter of James. F. and Miranda W. Courier, wife of Jonathan P. Carlisle.*

Why had Amelia been buried at Faunce Cove? Of all her properties, of all the places she could have been buried or sent her granddaughter to travel or live, why had Amelia chosen Faunce Cove, where she had once been so happy, and then so desperately lonely? Bethany would probably never know exactly what Amelia had wanted her to learn. She certainly could have discovered her own likes and dislikes in any number of other places—but Amelia had set up a complex arrangement to get her here.

Why?

Bethany straightened her head as a thought she had never before considered came to her mind. Amelia had never spoken about her husband or parents, never taken Bethany to a cemetery to visit their graves. Were they also buried here?

Bethany scanned the gravestones around her, noticing that the lettering lacked the absolute crispness of that on Amelia's new stone. A few were dated in the early 1900s, the stones wide and strong with the names clear and precise. As she walked back among the graves, she found thinner tablets of granite clustered within cast-iron fences. The aging of the stones became more apparent not only from the dates but from the greening tinge of algae and moss that had begun to obscure the engraving.

In the center of the cemetery stood a majestic obelisk. Scripted on the base were the words, *Until the day breaks and the shadows flee away.* Names with dates and places were listed on the flat surface. Bethany scanned them quickly, surprised at the number of names. Evidently, the names represented relatives of those buried in the cemetery whose bodies had not been returned for burial. Would Amelia's Jonathan be there?

Bethany glanced down at the list, the name catching her eye. *Captain Jonathan Philip Carlisle, beloved husband of Amelia Courier Carlisle, died June 6, 1944, in defense of his country at Normandy.*

Beneath it was another inscription.

Bethany read it slowly. *Glennis Carlisle Trabenitti, died July 12, 1980, Genoa, Italy. Beloved daughter of Jonathan Philip and his wife, Amelia Courier Carlisle.* There was another notation beneath that of Glennis's death. *S. R. Trabenitti, died July 14, 1980, Genoa, Italy. Husband of Glennis Carlisle.* Her mother and father. Amelia had recognized the marriage of her daughter, even given her husband's name a place with the family in the burial grounds.

Bethany looked around her. In a row next to the obelisk, she found Miranda's stone, and she rested her hand on its firmness.

Amelia's closest family members were buried and memorialized here, but still Bethany wondered why the family had chosen this place. It was beautiful and private, but so far from everything. Why not at Seacrest or one of the large, landscaped cemeteries on the mainland? Why here?

Bethany looked back at the obelisk. Midway up the side of the obelisk, she saw *Lieutenant James F. Courier, died Sept. 10, 1918, near Verdun, France.* Amelia's father.

Bethany turned and walked farther back into the graveyard. Thin slabs of dark gray slate, rounded on the top with carvings of urns or skeletons, replaced the granite tablets. These markers were difficult to read. Chips roughened the edges of several, and someone had bolted iron shafts across split slabs to hold them together. Even the slabs that seemed solid were almost completely covered with lichen and moss.

Bethany didn't think she would find the one marker she really wanted to see, but she rubbed at the plant life anyway, struggling to read the inscriptions. She looked at one of the bolted stones, the middle stone in a row of three, probably the oldest—and the hardest to read—in the cemetery. She stopped cleaning it when she found a deeply indented circle attached to the bottom of the first line.

It was not the *P* she was trying to find.

She moved to the next marker, hoping this would be Patience's grave. The slab was slightly larger than those beside it. A skeletal head and batlike wings topped the main rounded section, while scrolls decorated the sides. Bethany rubbed eagerly at the lichen that made the first words illegible. She had cleared only a small section when she knew with certainty that the marker would read *Captain Richard Smythe, died Nov. 6, 1687, age of 78.*

Since the marker of the captain was still there, Patience should be there too, beside him. Bethany moved to the third stone in the row, finding it similar to the captain's. An edge of the slate chipped as she brushed at a twig caught between the rock and the iron shaft holding the two sections of the broken stone together. Cleaning it gently, Bethany spent several more minutes before she could read the words *Thomas Faunce, died Nov. 1640, killed by Indians.*

Bethany sat back on her heels, stunned as she fought tears. She had not expected to find Thomas. Where was Patience?

In the row behind Captain Smythe, the gravestones proved to be those of Samuel Faunce and his wife, then several children. There were more men who, according to the dates on their stones, would have been grandsons of Samuel. It was easy to follow the lines of the daughters with their differing surnames, even though, as Grace had said, the spelling of the names often varied phonetically, and colloquial letter formations made the names hard to recognize at times. Bethany found a number of Faunce grandchildren and great-grandchildren, but not Patience.

Bethany went back to the captain's stone. Everyone else was there. Why couldn't she find Patience?

And who was the mysterious person who had been allowed to rest between Patience's husbands? It had to be Patience—or the woman whom Bethany had been calling Patience.

Moving back to the stone, Bethany gently—almost reverently—began removing the moss and mold. Even after she had cleaned the stone, she could not read all the letters, so she backed away from it.

The sunlight caught at the irregular surface, casting shadows into the lettered indentations that had, centuries ago, been chiseled into the stone. She studied each form carefully, still unsure of the individual letters as she moved back and forth, cleaning a spot, then pacing back to try to identify the letter. Finally she moved back to gaze at the complete name. There was no doubt. The first name was *Bethanee*. She and the Faunce Cove woman shared the same name!

Had Glennis come to this spot and wondered at the history of Patience—Bethanee—too? Was this where her mother had gotten her name Bethany?

What must Amelia have felt when she realized her runaway daughter had named her baby after the first woman of Faunce Cove, the home she had once held so dear?

Amelia was buried in the same cemetery with Bethanee Faunce! Why?

The answer seemed obvious, but Bethany had to prove it before she admitted it. She started searching through the older granite tablets behind the obelisk, finding a number of Couriers, but not the words she was looking for.

Several rows back into the thinner granite markers, Bethany stopped. The marker was like those around it, but the words impacted her mind like a scripture. *In memory of Abigail Bethany Faunce, wife of Phineas Hazen Courier.* Abigail, a Faunce, had married a Courier and their descendants would have the surname Courier. Amelia had been the descendant of Phineas Hazen Courier and Abigail Bethany Faunce. And she, Bethany, would have descended from the same Courier line.

She was a Faunce, and Patience—Bethanee—was her ancestor.

She looked at the markers around her, comparing names and dates, mentally collecting family members into groupings, then searching through the markers to find the missing links that made her conclusion certain. She, Bethany, daughter of Glennis, granddaughter of Amelia, was a great-great-great-great-granddaughter of Abigail Bethany Faunce Courier, who was also a direct descendant of the original Bethanee Faunce, the woman who had strengthened and fascinated her for so long. Bethany was named after her! These were her relatives! This was her family!

* * *

The violets were barely shaded when Bethany returned to finish planting them. The hose and gardening tools that had been left in the bright spring sun were too hot to touch. Bethany realized it had been several hours since she'd brought them out, and she knew she'd have to be careful not to spray the heated hose water on the delicate baby plants or they would be burned.

She pulled the plants to the edge of the granite rockworks by the waterfall before she looked up, suddenly aware of the shadow that covered her.

"I knew you'd get out here eventually," Peter said cheerfully.

Bethany twisted to look up. Peter stood above her on the grass beside the granite outcropping. The sun behind him shadowed him into a perfect silhouette as he moved away from the thorny rose-bushes and down the steep slope toward her.

"Peter!" She tried to keep the alarm she felt from showing in her voice. Obviously the man near Medway had not been Peter. *How had Peter tricked the police?*

"You didn't think I'd leave you any longer than necessary, did you? I was afraid Joseph and Kim would try to brainwash you again. At least they didn't get you to leave! You don't still believe them, do you?" His voice was casual, almost teasing, but he became more serious when he saw her frozen response. "I can see why you'd want to stay— the mansion and all—but don't worry, we'll be back here once we've got a new lawyer and the escrow is settled."

"Peter . . ." She stepped back another pace. She was shocked that he still thought she believed him. Had he no idea that the boys he hired had been arrested, that Joseph would have warned her about him by now? But how would he know? Still, a reasonable, rational person would suspect that she would find out. Bethany suddenly knew that Peter's sanity was not to be trusted. He was severely unstable to put it mildly—and she was in great danger.

"Didn't you find Amelia's grave? You know that all this property belongs to you—that Joseph was holding out on you." An edge of harshness shadowed his face. "Isn't it time to get away from him and trust me?"

Bethany's heart pounded as he moved toward her.

"Wait, Peter!" she said firmly as she stepped back from him.

"He was lying. I proved that, didn't I?" he queried. His voice became a mixture of anguish and anger. "Do you still prefer to stay here, even though I've shown that you are in danger and I'm taking a big risk to come back for you? Bethany, I love you too much to leave you to face him alone. I'm not leaving without you."

"I'm not in danger. Joseph is back in Boston. He hasn't talked to me since last week." She forced herself to speak calmly.

"Then he must already have the trap set. You can never tell what he's set up to hurt you or make you seem unstable. Bethany," Peter spoke sternly, "we don't have time to kid around. You'll want to pack some clothes, some money, and your papers. Now come!"

He stepped toward her grasping her wrist. Tom had said he had broken a woman's arm. She twisted her hand and pulled out of his reach, trying not to panic.

Bethany knew she must remain calm. She didn't dare make him angry. The week before at the hut, he had given her the choice of going with him or staying. Now, he had made the choice. She knew from Tom's report that he could be dangerous.

"I'm sorry, Peter," she started again, steadying her voice. "You were right about the inheritance. There were some irregularities in the way Joseph handled Amelia's will, and he wasn't completely forthright about the inheritance, but he had some other considerations and when Tom Marshalle, the chief of police, investigated—"

Peter interrupted with disdain. "Yes, he's police chief in a place where that is about equivalent to playing safety guard at a school crossing during summer vacation! You trust him above me?"

Bethany remained silent, trying to think of a response that would calm Peter. *If* he'd ever cared about her like she had cared about him, he would want to know friends were looking out for her.

"And there are other people that are looking out for my safety. Rob, Dr. Sommers, the doctor that took care of Amelia, my grandmother . . ."

Peter's scoff stopped her. "You call her doctor by his first name?" he laughed harshly. "Oh yes, Dr. Sommers. I've known about your Dr. Sommers. You know I heard about your grandmother when I was supervising a group of kids from a halfway house doing community service at the hospital. One of the kids kept asking questions about Mrs. Carlisle, her condition, her money, and her family. When I asked the kid about it he said it was for a Dr. Sommers. Dr. Sommers knew there was a rich patient, but he wasn't her doctor so he was paying this kid to find out about her and to give him the information. Bethany, your Dr. Sommers never met Amelia. He never laid eyes on her, not even once!" Peter spoke emphatically, his expression severe. "He needed information so he, along with Joseph, could con her out of her money."

Peter's eyes burned into hers, and she glanced away quickly as she thought. Peter was angry and wouldn't hesitate to hurt her. She had to find a way to appease him, to gratify his ego and stall for time— enough time to find a way to escape. Looking at Peter, she tried to remember everything she knew about him—the real Peter. She knew so little for certain. Tom had mentioned Peter had a connection with community service. Could Tom have gotten the details confused? That seemed very unlikely, but she needed to know. Now!

Suddenly she thought of the skiing trip in New Hampshire when Peter had rubbed her face with snow. He had shown violent tendencies then. What would he do now? A shudder ran through her.

"Bethany, you've got to get away from Joseph's control. As long as you own the property here, he's going to try to take it away from you. The only solution is for you to come with me, or to sign the property over to someone else until we can get rid of them. Isn't there someone you trust?"

Realizing a reply might give her some time, Bethany thought of answering him, but before she could mention Dr. Noel, Peter interrupted her thinking.

"Bethany, I know this may sound absurd, but I have to suggest it anyway. If you sign your property over to me, they'll leave you alone. I know it would put me in even more danger, but it would save you. It wouldn't take more than a couple of months to find another attorney and I could sign it right back to you at that point." He looked at her solemnly. "Bethany, I'm afraid if you don't, they will destroy you, one way or the other. You have to do this for your own safety."

"I need time, Peter. Maybe it isn't as bad as you think."

"Bethany!" Peter moved angrily toward her. A flat of small plants awaited planting. One caught on his shoe and he viciously kicked it away. "Listen to what I've been telling you! They are trying to take your inheritance away from you any way they can. You have to understand and do something now—this afternoon! I've come to help you, to save you. You've got to know how much danger you are in! I heard about those boys that Joseph hired to hurt you."

If Bethany had ever doubted whether Peter was capable of violence, there was no doubt now. She watched as he moved toward her through the tender plants he had carelessly trampled, grinding them into the soil. Joseph would have stepped around the plants—even if just to keep his shoes clean. Rob would have bent down to restore the plants if he'd damaged them. Rob had learned how to make Amelia's floral arrangements, and she was the only one who could have taught him! Amelia had handwritten his name on an envelope. But Peter said Rob had never met Amelia. Peter was lying. There was no room for questions or doubt this time. Peter was a liar.

Bethany looked up at Peter with a new awareness. His face was no longer handsome and controlled, but ugly and—she had been slow to identify the quality that had begun to cloud his features before, but she knew it now—vindictive.

Suddenly it hit Bethany with great force that the "organization" didn't even exist. Peter had never been in danger—it was all a lie—everything since the day she met him. And it was not a simple, spur-of-the-moment fabrication or a convenient exaggeration. He had invented a complicated, detailed scenario. The organization, the government agency, were all formulated to frighten Bethany. He made up story after story, knowing each new alteration of the facts would pull at her fears and tear at her longings. Then he continued, even here, to lie, telling her tales with just enough realism to make them seem plausible. And he'd sent the letters to scare her. Somehow he knew there was a file on him in Joseph's office, and he'd obtained that information. That meant he also had accessed the information Joseph had on her. Could Peter have sent that first email about Amelia's death? Joseph had not been perfectly honest, but his motives seemed magnanimous compared with Peter's selfish maliciousness.

"Peter." Her voice was as firm and confident as her sudden resolve. "I'm not going to sign any papers, and I'm not going anywhere with you. Not now. Not ever." She took a step backward, feeling the hot hose against the back of her ankle. Quickly she looked down at the hose. "I've got to do what I think is best for myself." She stepped backward again, this time carefully avoiding the heated plastic. "I'm going now."

Peter reeled to face her, a gun protruding from the hand he pulled out of his pocket. "Yes, Bethany. You're right. You are going, but you are going with me!"

Bethany froze. Peter stood with the gun pointed squarely at her.

"Peter, please," Bethany murmured quietly.

"This is all your fault, you know. It still could have worked so easily if you had believed me when I came last week or even today. But you'd rather trust your rich attorney. That's wrong, Bethany, and that makes me mad. I'll just have to use this little enforcer," he motioned to the gun, "to help you do the right thing. You're coming with me and you're going to sign some papers." His cold eyes squinted into a glare.

"Now!"

Bethany felt her stomach knot. She didn't know this strange Peter, but she knew she could not go with him. Nor should she unduly provoke him. He was psychotic.

"No, Peter. I'm not going." She stood firmly, surprised at the steadiness in her own voice as she ignored the way he tilted his head to motion her toward the mansion.

"Oh, you will." He pointed the gun at her face, laughing derisively. Then he sobered and spat out, "Since you're fighting me on this, Bethany, I may as well tell you the real story so that you don't underestimate the trouble you're in . . . or how dangerous I am." He paused letting his words echo through her mind, then continued his explanation with a crazed look in his eyes. "You know, I did meet your dear Amelia, but it wasn't through supervising delinquents. It was while *I* was doing community service at the hospital to keep out of prison."

Bethany's heart pounded, and she glanced around the garden as she listened. The lawns spread for several acres, intermittent hills spreading from the robust stream with its falls and pools. Granite boulders rounded in contrasting mounds above the velvet-like grass, but they were too far from her to give her cover. There was nothing nearby she could hide behind, nowhere to run.

"I did some thinking," Peter continued his tirade about Amelia. "She was rich, and she wasn't in the oncology ward for nothing. She had a picture of you, and I figured the best way to get to her money was through you."

What can I do? Bethany thought desperately *He has a gun!*

"After several months of misery dating you, I figured you owed me for putting up with the two of you. I would have settled for getting married—I could have gotten some of the inheritance or alimony—and it wouldn't have hurt you. You don't know how to use money; you'd have lost it all to someone else anyway. Look at you! You own one of the grandest estates in this part of Maine, and you're living in your little hut, writing your precious novel. You're as wearisome—and as crazy—as your grandmother."

"Amelia was a difficult woman—" Bethany started in sympathetic tones, hoping to change the focus of Peter's anger.

He interrupted her immediately with a sneer. "Amelia wasn't difficult. She was a hypocrite, like you. She said I was smart, until it came to getting me into one of the universities that would have admitted me if she'd just snapped her finger. I would make an excellent employee but, to her way of thinking, just for an entry-level job. I was capable and interesting—but not someone she'd let hang out with her granddaughter. When I mentioned getting to know you, she went absolutely berserk. It was as though you were the descendant of some canonized colonial saints and had inherited their saintliness." The sarcasm in his words was pronounced. "Even though the men you fell for lied to you.

"You were so above all the rest of the girls—too busy or too good to party with them—so Holly decided to get even with you. You remember Holly, right? Pretty Holly who partied with Dee a lot, who used to turn you green when she flirted with me in the library? Unbeknownst to you, she got a job in Joseph's office as his secretary to show you she could get his attention. She figured getting involved with him would really show you up. And after she was there, it was easy to find out about Amelia's condition and your whereabouts. I got a copy of her keys and made friends with some of her coworkers. I could find out anything I wanted to know about you and your whereabouts. How did you like your graduation email?" His mouth formed into a sickening grin.

Bethany moved her foot to keep her balance. It nearly caught on the metallic water wand but Peter didn't notice.

"Holly's job didn't last long, and she was ticked off. I wasn't planning to come up here. I was just going to threaten and scare you through the mail and by hiring locals to help—but Holly was so angry, blaming you for her termination, that we came up to see the place. As soon as I said I was an inspector, they let me in. Then I jammed your lock. Holly and I spent a pleasant evening together sawing spindles. And a short while later, I convinced a couple of kids to loosen your lug nuts and spill oil on the road—for a small fee, of course.

"It wasn't as easy to notch out the tree—especially trying to conceal the cut with spray paint. It may not have made your Christmas, but Holly had a good laugh about your house. I planned to visit you in the hospital but there was always someone around. I was going to convince you that you needed me to take care of you so you'd marry me."

Peter's gun had not wavered. Bethany continued to pray for guidance and protection. *Keep talking, Peter*, she thought. She needed a plan—and time to prepare it. She couldn't get to the Jeep parked at the hut without going through the tunnel since the bridge over the stream had been vandalized. Even if there were some miraculous way that she could get Peter's keys, she had no idea where he'd left his car.

Peter's face twisted into an angry sneer. "I did some research, found out about the mansion and worked out a deal with those kids so that if they caught you and forced you to come, then I'd stop them and make it look like I was a hero rescuing you. There's only one road from Faunce Cove and I could have stopped them anywhere on it. I planned to explain that I was on my way back to your house because I was so worried about you that I couldn't stay away—and to say how lucky it was that I drove by at that moment."

Peter's eyes bore into hers as he explained menacingly, "I know you, Bethany. You would have fallen for it. I mean, look at you now. You own miles of undeveloped land surrounding a waterfront that could become a yachter's haven, a rich man's playground, a vacationer's paradise—and you play housekeeper and gardener!" he sneered.

Bethany watched Peter's expression as she thought. The phones in the mansion had not been reconnected after Rob left. She had not tried the keys to the front door, she had only used the access from the tunnel and the door from the servant's quarters next to the tunnel.

"You'll still sign, and I'll get the money. All the other women have—I just had to find the right button to push. None of the other women wanted it known that they couldn't get a man without their money, or that someone could trick them. Pride, Bethany, pride. And loneliness. You'll sign because you're afraid of me, but you'll stay with me, too, because of your loneliness and your fear of me. I'll set up my own private club with income to run it any way I want, and you will sit behind me and won't say a word. Oh, don't worry, after a while you'll be grateful that I came to take care of you. You'll be like the others—you'll beg me to stay."

She needed time. Time to plan, time to position herself perfectly.

"How did you get here, Peter?" If she could keep him talking . . . "You were sighted near Medway. And why did you get permits to go on private roads in the mountains? Are you planning to take me to Quebec?"

"See, Bethany, I know how to get things done. I ditched my sports car and got a model half the country's driving these days—impossible to identify. And with a few bucks to pay for another anonymous call, I bet I could get our efficient police force out and searching most anywhere. The good citizen that reported the careless driver sporting cowboy boots wasn't even on the road—he's sitting in a nice hotel room just down the way here in Bucks Port. He did such a good job I paid him an extra fifty. It was worth every cent of it to see you standing here now, knowing you're completely under my control."

Bethany had seen this look on Peter's face before, but it had never been so intense. Why hadn't she recognized his malevolence while they were dating? Now he sounded vicious, violent. And she knew he could be brutal.

She couldn't wait. The metallic sprayer lay next to her foot, the hose stretching back toward the spigot. As she grasped its plastic handle, her fingers burned, but she hardly noticed as she switched on the water and leveled the full force of hot liquid at Peter. His eyes flashed in surprise and anger as the force of the hot spray pounded onto his face.

He gasped for breath, his hands and the gun flailing the air wildly as he fought at the pressurized water. She brought the metal wand down on his wrist, and the gun flipped from his hand.

Bethany glanced at his face to see him clearing the water from his eyes. Obviously infuriated, he looked for the gun and quickly saw it near his feet.

As he reached for it, she brought the wand up and steadied the hot stream back on his face, praying there would still be sun-heated water in the long hose. Peter held one hand up, trying to fight off the water as he leaned over to pick up the weapon.

Bethany rushed at him, trying to blind him with the water as she forcefully shoved him. She kicked at the gun as he stepped sideways. Then, still spraying the water into his eyes, she carefully bent down and picked up the gun.

She was not surprised to hear him swear profusely as she backed away from him, lowered the hose, and trained the revolver on him.

"I'm not going with you, Peter, but I do think you should leave now."

"Oh, Bethany, the fun has just begun. I'm not the one who is going." Though the menacing expression on Peter's face frightened her, it was the change in his voice that sent a chill through her spine. His voice sounded controlled, too controlled. "You will," he declared emphatically, "come with me, or," he mimicked her firm intonation, "you won't be able to go at all! Do you really think you could pull the trigger on that thing? Do you think you could hit me if you did? We've got us a little standoff. You won't shoot, so you can't make me leave—and even with that gun you can't safely go, because I'll follow you and I'll end up getting the gun—and getting you." He stepped menacingly toward her.

33

Bethany backed up several steps, trying to keep her hands from shaking as she held the gun. Peter had assumed correctly that she had never fired a gun. Even she doubted she could aim at a person and pull the trigger.

"Or, Bethany, here's an even better idea. We can stay here. There are so many good alternatives." He took a step toward her.

"Stay where you are, Peter. Don't move another step." Her voice sounded surprisingly calm, and she reassured herself she could remain in control.

"Sure, Bethany, I'll stay. *We,*" he emphasized the pronoun, "can stay here at the mansion and take a walk." His voice was mocking, but he stopped walking toward her. "There are a lot of ways a person can have an accident in a place like this. We could walk down by the beach—the ocean, all that water."

Bethany recoiled as she recalled bobbing in the dark, cold water of the creek, but she held the gun steady.

"You liked that, didn't you?" Peter glowered menacingly at her reaction. "Yes, there is the ocean, and those beautiful cliffs." He looked past her. "And there is the whole mansion with stairways to explore." He snickered. "It's cool enough to need a fire tonight, and it's so easy to get burned starting one. And that Jeep—it's like an accident waiting to happen—again." He stepped toward Bethany. Despite her resolve, she stepped backward.

"You're weakening, Bethany. It will happen, you know. You're going to drop your guard and get distracted. Just give me the gun and come with me willingly. You liked having me around while you were working on your degree." He looked at her with a grin. "You're getting tired holding that heavy gun in that position."

Then he tilted his head as if in thought. "Actually, the gun was just to get your attention so you would listen to a little common sense. I'd much rather share your money and property than see you hurt. So let's just forget about the gun. Mind if I sit down?" Peter's voice had calmed. He sounded as if they were sitting together in her apartment waiting to slice a pizza.

Bethany kept the gun on him as he smoothly eased himself to the grass next to the tray of violets now soaked from the sprayer. His self-assurance was intolerable.

"Peter, stop! I'm not playing your games anymore."

Rage again filled his face. And fury.

"Really?" He stood. "Now, here's a new plan," he said, faking a thoughtful tone despite his bitter expression. "Look at these lovely little white flowers." He dug his finger into the tray of violets and pulled one up by its roots, dangling it in front of Bethany before dropping it on the ground. "They need to be planted, don't they?"

He picked up another. "Now, what if you were carrying this box of plants along the edge of the water and you missed a step and fell." He continued to pull out the plants and drop them contemptuously as he spoke. "You hit your head on the rocks and end up face down in the water. But someone comes by and saves you in time and you have just enough brain damage to lose your ability to care for yourself and your property."

Swinging several violets back and forth, he stepped over to the granite embankment by the waterfalls to drop them into the water. "A rare, tragic accident, where you marry the hero who saved you." He stirred his finger through the dirt in the emptied tray until it was muddy. He exhaled loudly, then taunted, "Wouldn't that be romantic?"

He changed his voice abruptly. "Enough waiting, Bethany. You're only ten feet away. I'm coming. Give me the gun!" He started toward her with muddy hands.

"A lot of people would doubt the circumstances of a tragic accident if investigators found a revolver in the stream. How good are you at diving for treasure, Peter?" she asked.

As she flung the revolver toward the water, he lunged at her, his hand catching her arm as she released the gun. The weapon flew into the air off course, missing the stream and falling on the ground a few inches from the waterfalls.

Peter stood between her and the gun.

The outrage on his face turned to a sneer as he, too, saw the gun resting on the rocks. He scrambled toward it, his shoes once again making mush of the loose, wet dirt and the tops of the uprooted violets. Bethany could only watch with dismay as he clambered up the slope, knowing she could never beat him to the gun—or to cover.

He looked at her triumphantly as he reached down to get the weapon. As he picked it up from the rock, he swiveled deliberately, obviously preparing to aim it at her. He seemed surprised as the gun slipped from his mud-slick hands and skidded toward the water. Leaning forward to grab it, he hit it instead, sending it flipping through the air. As he fought for his balance, his arms thrashing, the gun flew end-over-end into the middle of the deep pool at the bottom of the waterfall.

Peter tried desperately to right himself, but his shoes tangled in the grass and he tripped and fell onto the bank and then slid down the slippery embankment into the water. Bethany saw his legs slam against the rocks on the side of the pool before he collapsed into it.

She watched him splash to the surface by the edge of the stream. There was a white splotch across his forehead where he'd apparently hit a rock, but he didn't seem to notice.

Bethany saw him glance toward the middle of the pool and knew he was looking for the gun. From her position on the bank, she could see it shining against the rocks in the crystal clear stream water. Peter looked up at her then grimaced as he tried to stand. Obviously in pain, he pulled himself to the side of the pool and stared at her hatefully. "I am good at diving for treasure, Bethany, especially in clear water. Watch and see!"

Bethany saw him slip under the water. If she could keep him from seeing the gun . . . She looked around in desperation and saw the container of muddy soil beside the pool where Peter had left it. Grabbing it, she threw the contents as hard as she could toward the gun. The mud immediately dirtied the water, blurring the rocks on the bottom of the pool near her, then spreading to the area around the gun.

Peter came up for air through the cloudy water.

"What the—?" He stopped in midsentence, disgusted as he looked at the murky water around him. His forehead was swollen and purple, but it was his stance that drew Bethany's attention. As he tried to put weight on his leg, he grabbed at his ankle and bobbed back into the pool instead.

He came out of the water sputtering. "Bethany, help me. I've hurt my leg. I can't stand. This water is spring runoff. It's like ice."

"I know. I spent some time in this same creek not too far from here last week because of you."

Peter's voice was a whine. "You can't leave me. I can't get out of this water on my leg. I'll get hypothermia."

"Peter, you aimed your gun at me."

"I haven't got a gun now. I need your help."

"But I'm tired, remember? I'll make a mistake." She relaxed her shoulders. "Peter, I don't trust you. You're violent. You're sick."

"You're going to leave me here to drown?"

"Give me your car keys. With your leg injured, you won't be able to drive anyway."

Peter flinched when his foot hit solid ground. He looked at her reproachfully.

"Give me your keys."

"Bethany . . ." Peter seemed to struggle with his submerged pocket, then pulled the keys out. "You know this is unnecessary. I can't walk or drive."

"Then you won't mind trading your keys for my help so you don't freeze."

He hesitated, then raised the keys in his hand. Bethany reached toward him. She stopped suddenly, realizing what she had almost done. "I'm not going to let you grab me. Put your keys on the bank where I can get them. Then, move away or I'll leave."

Peter watched her closely, his eyes narrowed in thought.

She waited, but he didn't move. She turned to go.

"Wait." Peter used precise movements to place the keys on the bank, then backed away as she had directed.

Bethany watched him carefully as she scooped up the keys. She looped around the waterfall and up to the rosebush, glancing back at Peter as she moved. She threw the keys into the depth of the briary patch then turned back and shouted to him. "If you can use your leg, you can swim for your gun and claw for your keys, or you can wait here until Tom or some of his officers show up. I don't have anything you need, so don't follow me."

Bethany looked closely at Peter. Though he appeared to be standing still, the water around him was muddy. Despite his leg injury and the apparent pain he was in, he had been trying to climb the bank and had stirred the water while she had gotten rid of the keys. He looked enraged.

34

Looking around desperately, Bethany started to run up the hill. She had to get away from Peter.

Where should she go? How much had Peter learned about the layout of the garden and the mansion? How much would his injured leg slow him down? Was it even injured, or had that been another ruse?

Instinctively Bethany ran toward the woods, hoping to conceal herself as she made her way back to the mansion. Her leg wasn't yet at full strength, and she ran slower than normal. Expecting Peter to follow her or try to cut her off by intersecting her path from the side, she swung wide toward the forest, arching her way between trees and bushes, hurrying as fast as she could while trying to judge where she was in relation to the mansion. She hoped Peter thought she would hide in the dense foliage, that he would be slowed as he tried to outguess her destination. But if he knew the area better than she . . .

She curved in toward the driveway, trying to remember exactly where the path to the walkways was. Winded and tiring, she wondered if she had ruined her chances of escaping Peter by trying to outwit him.

Where was he? Although it was torture not knowing where Peter was, she was afraid to find out. Had he assumed she was going to the main entrance of the mansion and gone there to wait for her? Where could she go? How could she escape his viciousness? The thought caused Bethany to stumble but she caught herself before she fell. *I've got to find a place where he won't expect me to hide,* she told herself.

Where had Patience—Bethanee—gone to escape the Indians who killed her husband?

A terror-driven Bethanee had escaped to the forest, then to the sea cave. But learning from the horror of that night, she had done more. She had prepared an escape route—the tunnel.

Bethany must get to it—and through it—without Peter catching her first.

Bethany swerved around a tree and was relieved to see the driveway in front of her. Soon she would be at the mansion, then within the tunnel.

How much did Peter know about the mansion? And did he know about the tunnel—the family secret? Questions she had not considered before suddenly frightened her.

She had to get to the entrance before he did!

Now she could see the circular driveway, the edge of the reflection pool, the bushes with tiny flowers that would turn into red berries. She swung past the massive front door she had never opened and followed the narrower path to the entrance of the servants' quarters.

Where was Peter? Did he know she had passed the main entry? Would he stop at the door and try the lock to see if she'd gone into the mansion? Willing herself to look forward, resisting the impulse to peek back, she clutched at her stomach.

She grasped the door handle just as she heard the solid pounding of shoes on the walkway behind her. Peter! She opened the door and stepped into the servants' quarters.

Does Peter know about the tunnel? she asked herself again. It didn't matter, because she had run out of alternatives. She couldn't run any farther.

Doubling over to try to catch her breath, she pushed against the swinging door to the tunnel, feeling it give way to her weight once again. She slid through the door, then leaned back against it in relief as the door moved into place and there was silence.

A very brief silence.

Peter had followed her to the entrance of the servants' quarters. He made no attempt to conceal his presence as he burst into the room, separated from her only by the door to the tunnel that she leaned against. Suddenly there was an absolute hush.

He would be listening for her movement so he could find her. Did he know about the door or the tunnel? Bethany stood motionless, afraid to breathe.

Was Peter on the other side of the door, leaning against it to listen, separated from her only by the resistance of her weight as she held her body stiffly against it?

Why couldn't she hear anything? What was he doing?

Bethany heard his footfall as he stepped away from the door. She heard heavier movement as he walked around in the servants' quarters. Slowly Bethany shifted her weight from the wooden panel.

Had he learned about the tunnel from something he'd seen in Joseph's office or had he heard comments about it as part of her alleged incoherence? But Bethany was almost positive that he could not know about its entrance or where to find it.

Bethany would have time now to make her way down the tunnel. But she must be quiet. She must not alert Peter with sounds from her retreat.

Each step seemed perilous. If one hand disturbed a loose stone on the wall, or one footstep kicked a fallen stone along the floor . . . How much could Peter hear through the door?

Bethany could stand still, waiting and hoping that he would go away, but then, she knew that Peter—this unfamiliar, cruel Peter—would not give up. Her best chance would be to move as far down the tunnel as she could while he was noisily searching. Still, she would not know when he paused or if he had stopped to listen, so she must be perfectly quiet.

As she carefully walked down the tunnel, her ragged breaths seemed to roar in the hushed silence. She would not run, she reminded herself. She would go slowly, and she would not touch the wall or step on a loose rock. She would walk down the tunnel to safety.

Had Patience—no Bethanee, her ancestor, Bethanee!—felt this way as she stealthily crept away from the Indians? Bethany knew Bethanee's heart had pounded too.

Bethany heard Peter shifting furniture in the servants' quarters. Wooden legs squealed as they were dragged across the hardwood flooring.

The end of the tunnel seemed so tiny in the distance. Had the tunnel been this long on Christmas Eve? She had survived then, and she would survive now. Though she longed to run, she must keep walking carefully.

With her eyes adapted to the darkness around her, Bethany could easily identify rocks on the wall, even clumps of moss and the few stones that had fallen to the floor. Methodically, she stepped around them.

Suddenly, she heard Peter. Though she could not understand his words, she recognized his rage as he rampaged through the room, slamming doors and throwing furniture. The noise came from the farthest end of the servants' quarters.

As quickly as it started, the noise stopped. Bethany stopped, motionless. She knew why he had quieted.

Peter had realized that there hadn't been enough time for her to go up the stairs into the mansion or hide in the room before he had gotten into it. He had realized there was another exit from the room.

In a frenzy, Peter pounded on the walls and stomped on the floor, sounding like a spoiled child in a tantrum.

No longer needing to be silent and forgetting the weakness in her leg, Bethany sprinted down the tunnel, aware that she must get out of the tunnel and into the shed and yard before Peter found the door and—even more critical—caught her.

Bethany wondered where she could go once she emerged from the tunnel. If she went to the hut, Peter would break down the back door or throw a log through a window. He would find some way to get to her. But at least she could call 911 first. She heard the door between the tunnel and the servants' quarters splinter. With a growing sense of terror, Bethany realized that Peter was now in the tunnel with her. After running through the woods and nearly the length of the tunnel, she felt exhausted. Willing her feet to move, she placed one calmly in front of the other. Her progress seemed to unfold in slow motion.

Peter, on the other hand, was gaining on her. His reverberating steps, at first hesitant as his eyes adjusted to the darkness, gained speed. Now they echoed in the hollow tunnel, pounding toward her through the dim light in a steady, measured tread. Bethany realized that he'd exaggerated about his leg injury earlier—as she had suspected.

As she neared the end of the tunnel, Bethany thought she could see a small spot of light. Was it the keyhole? It had to be. Peter's footsteps were becoming louder as he moved toward her. Her prayers had become simplistic and insistent: "Help me reach the light. Please, help me reach the light."

Shaking at the sound of the footsteps coming closer, she pulled on the door handle, relieved that she had left it unlocked when she'd carried the trays of white violets through it before lunch. With solid wood on the tunnel side and stone-covered wood on the other, it was heavy and it slowed her as she struggled through it and closed it into its rock-concealed casing in the stone wall.

In the shed, she leaned against the shelf. The door separated her from Peter—a thick, strong door. Now where was the key? *Think!* she told herself. *Remember what you did with it after you opened the door before you picked the trays of plants back up.* It was not on the hook by the door. Had she knocked it off with the cumbersome trays or brushed against it with her shoulder?

She could hear Peter now, the thump of his shoes was steadily growing louder, his nearness unnerving her. Bethany knew he would not give up, and she was too exhausted to run. But if the key had fallen in the shed as she'd gone through the door, she might still have time to find it and get the door locked before Peter got to it.

She grabbed a candle and felt for a match. The candle hit an old, deteriorating bag of fertilizer, puncturing its decayed covering. Particles of the chemicals began filtering toward the floor, but Bethany ignored the dust as she searched the shelf for the matches. Grasping for one, she held it firmly as she struck it against the box and it began to burn. Carefully, she picked up the candle and held the match to the wick.

The sound of Peter's rapid steps revealed that he was only a short distance from the door as the wick flared into a bright flame.

Dropping to the floor, Bethany held her face close to the dusty surface as she looked for a metallic gleam; she saw nothing but dirt. She reached into the corners but there was no key.

Peter's steps were nearly at the door.

A feeling came suddenly to her. A sense, more than a voice, but it was as direct and clear as a command: there was no time to look for the key—she had to get out.

Bethany stood quickly, dropping the candle as she stumbled backward across the shed, her legs nearly too tired to hold her weight. She tried to balance as she twisted to face the outside door, but she had used all her strength. Her elbows and knees jarred painfully against the floor as she fell forward.

Suddenly it was almost as if she were being pulled up as strength surged into her limbs and the thought again filled her to get out now. She stretched toward the shed's exit and grasped the doorframe, pulling herself up and toward the opening. As she lunged out the doorway, she realized the burning candle lay dangerously close to the gasoline can, and that particles of unstable fertilizer floated in the air.

She could hear Peter scream in anger as he raced toward the door. When his steps did not slow, she knew he planned to throw all his weight against the door and bash through the wood. No key could have helped her.

The crash of Peter's body against the inside door sounded like an explosion. It sent tremors up Bethany's spine as she lay on the ground, but he didn't come hurtling from the shed as she'd feared.

His shoulder slammed against the door again.

"Peter, there's a fire. It's going to explode!" She screamed the words through the noise of his body pounding the door. It was still unlocked—would he try the handle?

"Go back, Peter! Go back!" she pleaded, but she knew the plea was more for herself than for Peter.

35

While talking with Alice on the phone, Bethany lay quietly on the love seat, covered by a blanket, as Scott and Andy had insisted. Her ears still rang from the thunderous reverberations caused by the explosion, and her eyes still smarted from the fine pieces of dirt and dust that had gushed out of the shed. Miraculously, she was not injured. Humbled and grateful, she thought about the feelings she'd experienced in the shed before the explosion. Then her thoughts were interrupted by the twangy, muted sound of Alice's voice repeating a question.

"Bethany? Did you hear me? Are you sure you don't want to stay over here tonight?" Alice had called as soon as she'd seen the ambulance coming from Faunce Cove Road, then again several hours later to make sure Bethany was all right. "After being terrorized then nearly knocked unconscious by an explosion, I thought you might want someone older and wiser to talk to than Scott and Andy."

Bethany had thought Scott and Andy were part of a mirage when she saw them rushing toward her through the blur of dust. She was grateful Tom had sent them out to check on her when he realized she'd gone back to the mansion all alone thinking Peter was in custody. They had gently helped her into the hut; then, after making sure she was all right, turned their attention to Peter. She had been aware when the ambulance came and Tom had called to say that Peter had regained consciousness in the hospital and would be arrested as soon as the doctor authorized his move. He would probably be arraigned after the weekend if he'd been released from the hospital. There were several outstanding warrants against him from other states, so it seemed like he'd be out of the way for quite a while.

"I'll be okay here, Alice. I'm feeling fine now. And thank you," Bethany acknowledged.

As she hung up, she smiled and looked around her. The hut was home, and though her experience with Peter had been terrifying, she wanted time alone in the hut, cuddled in her favorite quilt on the love seat by the fireplace. She thought of telling Alice about her discoveries in the cemetery, but she was too tired. She needed a night alone here in Patience's home with her newfound knowledge about her. She smiled as she remembered that the grave she had found was real, not part of the imaginary story she had been writing and the woman was Bethanee, Bethanee Faunce—her ancestor—the woman whose name she'd been given.

Bethany had barely put the phone down after speaking with Alice when Joseph called.

"I got a call from the police department up there saying that the guy who broke into my office had been caught."

"Peter paid me a visit this afternoon, and we had a little explosion. Peter is in the hospital, but he'll be in jail as soon as he's released."

"Are you okay?" Joseph sounded concerned.

"Oh, I may be a little rattled, but it's nothing I can't handle," Bethany responded, trying to sound casual.

"I'm not sure there is anything you can't handle," he answered quickly, a little too flatteringly. Bethany sensed he was searching for words when he hastily continued. "You are a very capable woman." There was an uncomfortable pause. "I hope you don't mind me calling. I didn't mean to interfere—I was concerned."

"No. I'm glad you called. It's good to talk to you." Bethany was surprised at how true the statement was. "How is Kim?"

"Oh, she's fine. She'll be coming back out in a month or so." Joseph paused again, obviously unsure of what to say.

"I went to Amelia's grave yesterday," Bethany said, filling in the silence.

"When I was there, I heard that you had found it. I never knew what she had arranged to have done after I put her body on the plane. I'm glad you've found the grave. I hope it gives you some closure."

"Would you like to come see it? You and Kim?"

"I'd like that. You're sure that would be all right with you?"

"Yes. You know, Joseph, you are like family." She was surprised at the tone of her own voice. She had not spoken to him with such warmth for several months. She added sincerely, "Thanks for calling."

Sitting back on the love seat, Bethany realized it felt good to talk to Joseph. No more questions about their relationship, no more wondering if she were hiding behind an imaginary experience. They shared a friendship. Of course, their conversation had been strained, but that would ease with time.

She smiled. For the past week, she had spent a great deal of time thinking about Joseph and Kim, and about Peter. Now she didn't need to worry about all of that. Resolutely, Bethany got up and scanned the items in the cupboard. She wasn't hungry, but she fixed a cup of cocoa anyway and then gazed out at the ocean. The waves peacefully brushed the shoreline while the pines stood like silent, steadfast sentries. She felt a contented, wholesome quietness settle over her as she sipped the last of the hot cocoa. Then she took a deep breath before she lit a fire. She should go to bed, she thought as she snuggled into the comforter on the love seat, but she didn't want to sleep yet.

She looked down at the table. The last time she had organized the information she had gathered about Patience—Bethanee—was after her trip to Boston. Her notes on Bethanee and Samuel lay in a pile on the table, with the envelopes and folders from the mansion library spread across them. She had wanted to know so much, and it was all here before her.

Shuffling the information into piles, she paused as she read the name *Joseph Panninon* on an envelope that she had avoided earlier in the day. Perhaps now was the time to read it.

Six pages summarized the first five years of Joseph's career, offering a positive endorsement: Joseph Panninon was clearly a qualified, competent attorney.

The next page was a letter addressed to Amelia. Bethany skimmed it, stopping when certain phrases jumped out at her. *As I have reported to you before* . . . So she had not been the only one Amelia had observed. *I have observed Mr. Panninon's professional and ethical conduct on a number of occasions. I want you to know that not only has he been honorable in every capacity in which I have seen him function, but he has been silently benevolent on many occasions. I congratulate you on having an outstanding attorney.*

Bethany folded the papers and placed them back into the envelope. She was satisfied that Amelia had depended completely on Joseph for good reason—but could *she?* Total assurance, she realized, would have to come from within herself, and that would take time. Their conversation had been a start.

She picked up the folder for Rob Sommers and put it with the material she'd read about Joseph. At least she didn't have to deal with her feelings about Rob right now. She doubted that she'd ever see him again anyway.

Restlessly, she picked up Amelia's envelope and removed the papers.

* * *

Bethany woke to the bright light of sunshine glowing through the living room. Tossing off the comforter, she didn't need to look at the clock to know it was almost noon. Today she'd make a trek to the garden to check on the plants. She'd take a trip back to the nursery to replace the unsalvageable ones if necessary, go grocery shopping, and then thoroughly clean the hut. She wanted everything ready so that on Monday she could concentrate on writing, using the new information she had secured from the mansion.

She still had questions about Amelia. The history Amelia had written was full of facts and events, but lacked emotions. Bethany had been fascinated by her accomplishments and even some of her escapades. She had felt a new admiration for her grandmother but also sadness for the woman who, even in her writing, seemed to find her successes a hollow substitute for an unnamed desire. Amelia never mentioned her own wealth or accomplishment—the figures discussed in boardroom meetings and, later, fund-raisers. Perhaps, Bethany considered, that was the most marked indicator that Amelia felt her life was lacking: she did not seem pleased with any of her successes, only determined to achieve more.

As Bethany started to place Amelia's history into its folder, it stuck. Bethany reached in and found a small envelope with her mother's name written on it. She pulled it out and glanced at the handwriting, unmistakably Amelia's but in a more delicately curved, intricately detailed hand. Each slant and oval seemed perfectly aligned as though the words themselves were a work of art. Bethany slid a finger across her mother's name before she slipped her fingernail under the seal.

Then she pulled a single sheet of paper from inside. It was a diagram of the mansion. She looked at the map and laughed knowing that she owned a house and didn't know how to find her way around in it. It belonged to her, but she had no idea how many rooms it held—or how many secrets.

On the map, one of the mansion's rooms was heavily outlined . . . and there was a key taped to the bottom of the map. Bethany took the locket from her neck and added the key to the chain. Then she studied the map.

She drove to the mansion, unable to enter the tunnel after the explosion or cross the bridge due to the vandalism. After entering the front door and crossing the entryway, she climbed the staircase, fingering the key. With the map, Bethany found the room easily and unlocked the door.

The room was exquisite. The large canopied bed was dwarfed by the rest of the room and its matching furnishings. It was the desk next to the door, though, that caught Bethany's attention. An envelope addressed to Glennis in Amelia's handwriting was conspicuously propped against the lamp. Bethany pushed back tears as she realized it had been there for years. She sat down, accidentally kicking the wastebasket beneath the desk and tipping it on its side. She ignored it, anxious to look at the envelope. She picked it up and opened it to remove the single sheet of stationery it held. Unfolding the paper, Bethany found a handwritten letter, the language formal and unemotional. Amelia wrote that she had tried to be a good parent, that she hoped someday Glennis would realize how much she loved her.

Bethany reread the letter, her disappointment palpable. Had Amelia ever expressed her emotions in anything but flat, dispassionate grammar? Bethany stood up. Then, remembering the wastebasket she had knocked over, she reached down to pick up its contents. Several sheets of stationery with Amelia's embossed design had fallen across the floor.

Bethany picked up the top sheet. It looked like an unfinished copy of the letter she had just read until she studied it closely. Several verbs had been changed and adjectives crossed out leaving the corrected near-duplicate a blander version of the discarded letter.

She looked farther down into the wastebasket. Each letter was altered slightly from the previous. There were crumpled tissues layered among several pages where the neatly written wording was splotched with smeared ink. Here, at last, Bethany thought, was a sign of Amelia's emotions. Her own throat knotted as she thought of the woman who had cried as she had sat in an empty house writing letters to her daughter.

Bethany delved into the basket to find the bottom letter, assuming it would be the first Amelia had written. It was completely different from the succinct, precisely worded, carefully crafted letter on the desk. Rather than a few short paragraphs, it covered several pages, each laden with emotional explanations—the vulnerability and loneliness of the author evident in every paragraph. The letter was a plea for love as Amelia tried to explain the relationship she had shared with her daughter.

> *I had lost everything but you—my father and husband to wars in Europe, my mother to her own memories of the man she loved—and I made a pledge that I would not lose you, that I would give you everything that your father could have given you. I would raise you with all the love and attention that my own mother—the woman I refused to call my mother because of the neglect I felt at her hand—could have given me had she not given in to grief. I believed that love and attention would build a bond between us so that you would never leave me. Victoria, my mother's nurse and my governess—who became somewhat of a substitute parent to me—told me I was spoiling you. She said that I needed to give you less and to*

require you to be responsible for more, that I needed to be a mother who taught and constrained your passionate demands, not a chummy playmate who pampered you with every possible luxury. I refused to listen, saying I would never stand for a relationship like the one I'd had with my mother once I'd tasted the delightful companionship and the loyalty I shared with you.

You are beautiful and lovely, but I should have listened to Victoria. If I had the chance to raise you again, I would follow her advice. I should have rewarded your soberness rather than your vanity. Victoria often said that a child should be seen and not heard, but you were all that I saw or heard. Can one love too much or show that love in too many ways? Did I let my love overrule my common sense? If I were to have another chance, I would be wiser, so much wiser, and I would do precisely as Victoria told me.

Bethany sat at the desk, her head down. Amelia had cared, and Amelia had tried! Perhaps it was up to her, Bethany, to prove whether Amelia had failed or succeeded.

Spending over an hour comparing the progression of the letters, Bethany easily connected their development—and Amelia's emotionally distant state—with the way she had treated Bethany. For the first time, Bethany realized that behind everything else, Amelia had a deep need to be loved, but an even deeper need to avoid emotional vulnerability and any further rejection or loss.

After gathering the letters together, making sure she kept them in order, Bethany searched the bottom of the wastebasket for anything she might have overlooked. She found a piece of paper wadded into a ball. Spreading it out carefully, she read the words: *Landed safely in London. Stop. Plan to stay here for several months then on to Paris. Stop. Will contact you regularly. Stop. Please understand. Stop. Love. Stop. Glennis.*

She sat back down at the desk to think, then walked slowly over the luxurious carpet, cautiously touching the articles in the room.

Finally she picked up the letters and quietly left, locking the door behind her.

Bethany walked slowly out to the garden. Searching through the tool shed, she found a set of clippers.

She ignored the scene around her—the buds on the azaleas beginning to spread, the bleeding hearts swaying like pendants in the breeze, the dainty, pale blue forget-me-nots that spread like a cloudy mist around their stems. Instead, she carefully cut the tallest, most majestic flowers from a stand of magenta tulips. Then she added a shoot of bright basket-of-gold to wind between the rich shades of purple. Nearly as an afterthought, she clipped some lavender tulips and some daintily ruffled white iris for the obelisk.

After walking up the path to the small cemetery, Bethany first decorated the obelisk. Then she walked to the bundle of purple tulips she had placed near Amelia's headstone. When she finished arranging them, she stood back. "Amelia, I didn't know. I didn't think you could love, but you did. You loved too deeply, and your losses hurt too much."

Late afternoon sunshine cast long shadows, brightening the color of the new spring grass and the budding leaves on the trees. Bethany stepped away from Amelia's grave, aware of the other gravestones that stretched around her. This was the family cemetery, and all these people were her relatives, many her direct ancestors.

This was the reason Amelia had wanted her here! Amelia wanted her here to learn about and gather strength from her ancestors, to understand her full inheritance and to be a part of their family. Had Amelia feared that Bethany would undervalue or even disregard her inheritance if she, Amelia, had tried to force it on her after all the years of impersonal interaction? How little Amelia had really known about her! How great the cost of her ignorance had been to them both.

Walking back to Amelia's grave, Bethany knelt on the grass beside it. "Amelia," she began, "you judged me. You thought I would not accept and love you. How could you have thought that I wouldn't understand? I would never have left you alone. I wouldn't have judged you." The thought came to her gently but firmly that she *had* judged her grandmother. She had judged her, and she had nearly thrown away the chance to do Amelia's temple work and be a part of her own eternal family. Their family. Bethanee and Thomas's family.

Bethany looked around her in excited bewilderment. She had discovered her ancestors' graves on the day Peter had shown up with the gun. With all that commotion, the full impact of the finding had not struck her. She had a family—and she could seal them all so they would be an eternal family!

36

Bethany waited impatiently for Grace to answer.

"I'm so glad you phoned." Grace's voice was enthusiastic. "I was sitting here in the middle of an article on one of my family lines that I've barely put down in a week. I didn't see you on Sunday and I've meant to call to see how you're doing, but you know how I am about family history. How are you? Is Joseph still giving you a bad time about Patience?"

Bethany realized that her whole life had changed, and Grace knew nothing about it. It had been last Saturday when she had first seen Amelia's grave and the sea cave.

"Actually, Joseph and I . . . well, Joseph is seeing someone else."

"Oh, Bethany, I'm sorry. Are you all right?"

"I actually am. Well, maybe I miss having someone call me, but . . ." She tried to sound flippant.

"I know a guy. Would you like to meet him?"

Bethany cut her off quickly. "I'm not ready to try a blind date."

"He's a member of the Church and good looking. He moved out of the ward before you moved in. I thought about mentioning him before, but there was Joseph."

"No blind dates."

"He'll be visiting tomorrow. I can introduce you at church."

"I'm not sure I'm ready to meet any new men for a while."

"Never mind then. Sometimes it's good to have a break," Grace acquiesced.

Bethany glanced at the clock. It was much too late to try to tell Grace about the mansion or the cemetery if they were going to get to church on time. "I found some more things about the Faunce family that I want to check out in the Family History Center. Is there any chance I could get in after Relief Society to see how much temple work has been done on the line?"

"Sure. You can check on the Church website now, but I'd be glad to help you in the library. On lines that far back in New England, generally the temple work has been done by another convert in the family for the older generations, and you can connect in pretty easily."

Feeling disappointed, Bethany hung up the phone. It would be nice to have relatives in the Church, but ever since she realized that Bethanee Faunce was her ancestor, she had thrilled at the thought of doing Bethanee's temple work. Still, there were certainly a lot of Courier and Faunce graves, along with other relatives, to keep her busy checking and submitting names for several months.

And she still had her book to finish.

She followed the process Grace had described for the Church website, nearly giving up several times as she fidgeted with the numbers that would allow her to sign in. But the form Grace had described finally appeared. Tapping Glennis's name in, Bethany did not expect to find a person with matching information in the Church's database, and she didn't. She typed in Amelia's name, and again there was no match. Bethany felt certain there would be a match when she typed in Bethanee Faunce but still found nothing. She tried Bethanee Pers, Bethanee Pierce, even Bethanee Smythe. She tried spelling Bethanee several different ways. She found a few matches for Bethany Smith but none in Plymouth or Seacrest, and no one born before 1712. Trying to locate Thomas Faunce, Bethany found no matches for him, for Richard Smythe, or even for Samuel.

The temple work had not been done! Bethany thought of the graves she had studied that morning. She would be sealed to her mother, Glennis, and her father, S. R. Trabenitti, and then have Glennis sealed to Amelia and Jonathan. Bethany would have the ordinances completed for each generation of her family all the way back to and including Bethanee and Thomas Faunce and their son Samuel! She could not describe the elation she felt as tingles went up and down her arms. She would be responsible for reuniting and sealing her family for eternity!

It was Amelia that Bethany dreamed about that night—Amelia crying at a desk, stationery strewn around her. Bethany stepped through the door, her arms loaded with brilliant flowers. The blossoms were suddenly transported into a glowing marble vase, which Amelia, with a radiant smile, took from her.

* * *

Bethany slid from her seat in the Relief Society room as the closing prayer ended. She had found it difficult to concentrate on the lesson with the sun shining through the window beside her and a squirming baby pulling at her purse strap. She had hoped to sit by Grace so she could tell her about her Internet search and find out how to enter the names into Temple Ready, but Grace had come in late and sat in the back row. It took a few minutes for the sister beside her to scoop up the toys and settle the baby in her infant seat. Then Bethany made her way past her, smiling at the other women on the way toward the door. Before she could get to the middle of the room, she saw Grace walk out.

"You're looking better." Dr. Noel stopped her as she started down the hall. "Any more tenderness in your back? What about headaches after that explosion?"

Bethany reassured him as quickly as she could and looked toward the foyer. She could not see Grace in any of the groups slowly making their way down the hall, so she turned the opposite way.

"Hi there." The brightly patterned print of Sister Clark's skirt reminded Bethany of the tulips she'd placed on Amelia's grave. "How are things going up at Seacrest?"

Bethany didn't want to be rude to her visiting teacher, but she wanted to find Grace as soon as possible.

"Oh, I'm doing fine. Have you seen Grace Winton?"

"I think she just went around the corner." Sister Clark turned to walk with Bethany. "A good friend is visiting, and I think they were going to meet by the library."

They stepped to the edge of the hall so a cluster of Sunbeams could pass. Then they turned the corner. Bethany could see only the back of the head of the tall man in a dark suit that Grace was facing. Noticing Bethany coming down the hall, Grace immediately called out.

"Oh, here is the woman who just found information on her ancestors."

The man beside her turned toward Bethany.

"Bethany Carlisle, this is Rob Sommers. He's the friend who took me to dinner when I was with you in Boston."

Rob's eyes showed the same surprise that she felt. She had never seen him in a well-fitted suit and tie, his dark hair combed neatly. She had never seen him standing relaxed, talking to friends who appeared to be as enamored with him as fans with a baseball idol. His hand automatically moved forward to shake hers as she felt a blush spread to her cheeks.

"Yes, he's the doctor we went to see when we visited you in the rehab center," Sister Clark inserted enthusiastically. "He was going to visit last Saturday, but he got caught up in an emergency and couldn't make it, so he came back up today."

Grace glanced back and forth between the two. "Have you two met before?" she asked suspiciously.

Rob stood motionless, his eyes suddenly unreadable.

"I may have met someone who looks like you," she said hesitantly, remembering how he had wished they were strangers without a preexisting history the last time she had seen him at McCleres'. "Your eyes look very familiar, but," she said as she turned to Grace, "I don't think I know him. We must be strangers."

Grace looked at her intently, a squint wrinkling the corners of her eyes as she turned to Sister Clark.

"Blanche," she said as she took Sister Clark's arm and began to turn her. "We're going to be late for choir practice. We'd better get going."

Sister Clark looked puzzled as Grace drew her toward the chapel. "I thought you were going to the Family History Library," she protested in a loud whisper as the two moved down the hall.

"Strangers?" Rob asked questioningly before his forehead smoothed and a mischievous gleam came into his eyes. "Strangers."

A smile flitted across Bethany's eyes. "I'm sorry. I don't think I caught your name. Did Sister Winston say Rod?"

"No. Rob. Robert Sommers . . ."

Bethany looked up at him with a questioning, puzzled expression that she edged with the touch of a smile. "What? What did you say your name was, and your occupation?"

"My name is Robert T. Sommers," he responded in a mockingly serious tone. "Dr. Robert Thomas Sommers, since you'll want a totally honest answer from a stranger. My occupation?" There was a mischievous grin when he continued. "I've actually changed my occupation recently. I had kind of been house-sitting and gardening part time for a wonderfully eccentric, terribly unique elderly lady. But I muffed that—got too involved with a young relative and got kicked off the job, so to speak. So I decided to get more involved in the medical research I'd been doing." He looked at her as if daring her to respond as glibly. "And what about you? What do you do?" He looked at her with a half-questioning grin.

"Well . . . honestly . . ." She toyed with the word as she looked up at him. "I finished my master's degree about a year ago, then started working on a historical novel while an attorney processed my inheritance."

"An inheritance! How interesting."

"It includes a garden. A lovely garden. And a creek."

"It sounds a lot like the garden I worked in. I've wondered how a garden like that would look in full bloom." He looked at her questioningly.

She took a deep breath.

"I suppose you could come see it if it's not too far out of your way."

"I'm sure I could make the time—if it were convenient for you to show it to me." He looked at her with a smile. "So you inherited a garden."

"It turns out that my grandmother willed me a large estate that has been in my family since her ancestors settled in the area. Apparently, they were the first colonizers in Seacrest. I just found a cemetery with row after row of the graves of my family. I can get the names ready to have the temple work done almost immediately."

Bethany suddenly stopped and looked at him questioningly. "Are you just visiting with Grace, or are you a member of the Church? I haven't seen you in this ward before."

"Well I do live in Boston," he replied with a teasing gleam in his eye. "And as for the latter question . . . a teacher who got me to train a hamster—I must tell you that story sometime—was a member of the Church, and she introduced me to the president of the Young Men. I was baptized my senior year in high school and worked until I was nineteen and could go on a mission. I go to the Boston temple every chance I get."

* * *

Rob looked around in amazement. Flowers spread in layers and overlays of luminous color, drawing Bethany's eyes from one area to another as she stood next to him.

"I didn't imagine it could be this vibrant. Can you imagine what it will be like later on? Look at all those buds." He looked around. "You know, one day when Amelia and I were working in her garden in Newport in the spring, she looked at the garden and said, 'Isn't it beautiful?' I wondered what she meant because everything was just in bud and green. She looked at me and laughed, as if she knew something I didn't. Then she said, 'Look, Robert, look at all the buds. Look at all the promises. It's the prelude. It's the dawn. This is just a glimmer of things to come.'"

He followed Bethany past the rhododendron, touching a heavy head still tightly drawn into a green cone. They walked silently along the path toward the rock wall with its cast-iron entrance.

Bethany raised her hand to the gate and paused. "I miss her," she said quietly. "I wish I could hold her hand and comfort her. I think she needed to be loved even more than I did. We were both so alone."

Rob opened the gate and walked through behind her. She could feel his arm against her shoulder as she looked at the grave markers. The sternness of the ridged stones was softened by the spring-green grass softly waving around them.

Bethany looked around at the gravestones. "But I'm not alone now, am I?" She turned around to face him, her blue eyes smiling.

Rob looked down at her. "No, you're not alone." His eyes were soft as he looked into hers. "There are wonderful promises here," he said, "promises she never considered."

Rob reached down and took her hand, but he was still looking into her eyes.

THE END

ABOUT THE AUTHOR

photo: Smith Photographers

Marlene Harris Austin is Idaho-born, Montana-raised, and Utah-educated with a bachelor's in elementary education from Brigham Young University. Despite all her ties to the West, one hot, humid day she stepped from a near-claustrophobic, travel-cluttered car onto the crowded streets of Cambridge, Massachusetts. It was the land of her New England forefathers, but she knew no one there, and at the time had no job or apartment—only the conviction that she had been led to Massachusetts to do genealogy and to write. The next day she met Tony Austin, whom she married two years later in the Ogden Temple. They have made their home and raised their family in Westford, Massachusetts, and now divide their time between there and Peterborough, New Hampshire.

Marlene is passionate about family history and spends much of her time during the spring and fall visiting old burial grounds, trying to read inscriptions to identify her ancestors and their descendants. She is captivated by the history of colonial New Englanders and is intrigued by the area's aged houses and rock fences. She also enjoys her flower gardens in the summer and writing in the winter. But her greatest joy of all, family, isn't seasonal—it's year round.

Marlene is working on her next novel, fine-tuning the plot and characters as she roams New England and its cemeteries to gather ideas. If you would like to contact her with fascinating tidbits you've discovered, or for any other reason, she would enjoy hearing from you via email at info@covenant-lds.com or by snail mail to Covenant Communications, Inc., P.O. Box 416, American Fork, Utah 84003.